RESURRECTION:

HOME BEFORE DARK

A Novel

by

Merle Temple

Southern Literature Publishing
www.southernliteraturepublishing.com

Resurrection: Home Before Dark

ISBN: 979-8-218-22025-9

Printed in the United States of America

Unless otherwise noted, Scripture references are taken from the Holy Bible, New International version, International Bible Society. Used by permission.

Where noted, Scripture references are taken from the Holy Bible, King James version, kingjamesbibleonline.org. Used by permission. All rights reserved.

Characters appearing in this work are fictitious, unless otherwise noted. Any resemblance to real persons, living or deceased, is purely coincidental.

Southern Literature Publishing
southernliteraturepublishing.com

www.merletemple.com

FOREWORD

After almost thirty years as a psychologist in the criminal justice system, I can recall only a handful who truly regretted the mistakes they made…only a few chose not to only work to heal themselves but then to reach out to as many others as possible and encourage them to make positive changes in their lives. Merle Temple was one of those people.

When I first met Merle, he was…at the lowest point of his life, but rather than wallow in his own misery, he made the decision to improve his life…and the lives of as many others as he could.

It seemed like such a simple thing to bring men together to view a movie with a positive and uplifting message, yet it became so much more. Each week the numbers grew and in a very negative place, hope and inspiration were blooming.

He has continued to spread the message of hope and redemption… a beacon of light and hope in this crazy world in which we live.

Dr. Tammara Bryan, Psychologist
Former Regional Drug Abuse Prevention Program Coordinator
Edgefield Federal Prison, Edgefield, South Carolina

Reviews and Comments

"I was in the Edgefield prison visiting room when Susan Temple came to see him just before she died. She looked into my eyes, squeezed my hand, and said, 'Take care of my Merle.'"—Rev. Kyle Simmons, Charleston, SC

"He sat in a federal prison for over 5 years...but that time was spent spreading the love of Jesus to others—anyone who would listen. Those who did left gangs and started following a true leader."—*Jackson Clarion-Ledger*

"Reading his books was a blessing to me as well as many federal prisoners with whom the books were shared, men who share his experiences of the harshness and cruelty of prison, as well as his knowledge of the Source of help, injustice in our society, man's inhumanity to man, and the redeeming Grace of God. He...crafts words that paint pictures of dark places. I felt as if I was back there with him during many of the scenes of Michael's suffering." —Gary White, Montgomery Federal Prison Inmate

"Some speakers the saints endure, some they enjoy. They enjoyed Merle."—Rev. Toy Arnett, Faith Assembly, Miramar Beach, FL

"I walked into the bookstore with a heavy burden...the Light of Christ I saw in him opened the door... We talked and my burden never held me captive again."—Apostle Maxine Evans Gray, Jackson, MS

"I've never seen the Light so bright around anyone as when he spoke to students at the Academies of West Memphis."—Pastor Michael Knowles

"I met Merle through cancer. It was like being reunited with an old friend I never knew I had. Through his books, I met Christ." —Jimmy Dozier

"A story like we had never heard. Greeted by a thunderous standing ovation."—Bo Thomson, Moselle Memorial Baptist Church

"Whispers Jesus louder than most shout Him, a writer I trust because he dips his pen in the blood of Jesus."—Rev. Danny Bell, Hernando, MS

"When he came to Eutaw, we all knew he was a vessel for God. There was such peace and joy in the ancient First Christian church that day."—Linda Gillum, Eutaw, Alabama, Arts Club

"There are familiar names of secular authors. Christendom has its own...Merle Temple."—Ritchie Latham, Christian Talk That Rocks

"His words affected my students, who were enamored with Deputy, bridging a divide between a Southern officer of the law from decades ago and young people of color in Cleveland today."—Professor Rhonda Fabrizi, Cuyahoga College, OH

"When you can hold the heart and minds of 18-year-olds for over an hour, you have a great, passionate storyteller, and that storyteller is Merle Temple."—Dr. Samir Husni, Ole Miss School of Journalism

"When I left for the Holy Land, I took his books for Andrew White, the 'Vicar of Baghdad,' and they were placed in the library for Christ Church in Jerusalem."—Dawn Arnett, missionary

"Our fourth-graders were studying writing when Merle came to speak. They hung on his every word."—Al Gardner, Destin Elementary

"I'm young and black; he's older and white, but the world doesn't understand that we are spiritual twins. When he rode with me, we praised and prayed."—Sgt. Marius McKinnon, Lee County S.O.

"An infectious personality. He could sell books like few could, but he was really offering Christ to the lost. While we rang up sales, he prayed and cried with customers."—Chris McCormick, LifeWay Bookstore, Tupelo, MS

"Seduction, betrayal, a fall from grace, imprisonment, redemption. He says, 'All I want is to show people my redeemed life that they might meet my Redeemer.'"—Sylvia Cooper, *Augusta Chronicle*, GA

"Every saint has a past, every sinner a future."—Pat Sabiston, The Write Place, Panama City

"A man at once intimately familiar with the world's worst facets, yet not at home in even its best offerings."—Errol Castens, *Daily Journal*

"The way you go back and forth with Scripture in your stories…in the end all the glory to God. I passed your books on to friends in the chapel, one moved off of death row. I've listed others who need to hear your story. I am trying to find purpose in pain as you wrote. Please pray for my son who was a child when his mother killed herself the day I was sentenced to natural life. I want nothing but to live in poverty, solely dependent on God. You are a blessing. God bless you."—Inmate, Menard, IL

"Everyone in our dorm enjoys your books. You know what we are going through. I look forward to the day I am out of here, and we can meet face-to-face. Until then, we will hold each other up in prayer."—Inmate, Wrightsville, GA

"Mr. T. Bet it's been a long time since you've been called that. My family heard you in Destin and spoke highly of you, your attitude, and your story. I'm reading your books and think we should have met. You knew the mobsters I knew. They're all dead now. I think I understand how you and I stayed alive. The Lord watched over us. We were the pick of the litter. Ghost."—Inmate, Milton, FL

"He saved my job and likely my life twice."—Judge Randy Clark

"I think one day his books will be considered Southern classics." —Butterfly's Booknerdia Book Blog

"A generation of a certain age, even today, at the mention of his name will recall a good story or two about him and those times." —John Howell, Publisher, *The Panolian*

"He spoke to my class at Saltillo. His life experiences and stories really hit me hard and made the decision for me."—Ashton Ellis

"A master at delivering spiritual messages within secular bindings."—K.B. Schaller, *Indian Life Newspaper*

"A journey of wandering, omens, tragedies, friendships and a homecoming."—Fully Booked, England

To my Lord and Savior, Jesus Christ

"In the beginning was the Word, and the Word was with God, and the Word was God...In Him was life, and that life was the light of all mankind. The light shines in the darkness, and the darkness has not overcome it."—*From the Prologue to the Gospel of John*

"Come...let me tell you what He has done for me."—*Psalm 66:16*

"He reached down from on high and took hold of me; he drew me out of deep waters. He rescued me from...my foes."—*Psalm 18:16-19*

"I've been held by the Savior...I'm no stranger to prison. I've worn shackles and chains... But I've been freed and forgiven. I've been washed in the blood."—*"All my Hope is in Jesus," David W. Crowder, Edwin Marin Cash*

"O Ploughman of the sinner's soul. Oh, Jesus, drive the coulter deep. To plough my living man from sleep."—*"Everlasting Mercy," John Masefield*

"Thou has taught me to say..."—*"It is Well With My Soul," Horatio Spafford, Philip Bliss*

"This hill, though high...the way of life lies here. Come, pluck up heart; let's neither faint nor fear."—Pilgrim's Progress, *John Bunyan*

"Tis enough to know that Christ knows all, and I shall be with Him."—*Richard Baxter, theologian*

PREFACE

"In the land of the blind, the one-eyed man is a
hallucinating idiot…*for he sees what no one else does:*
things that, to everyone else, are not there."
—Marshall McLuhan

"Once upon a time, the world was sweeter than we
knew…but once upon a time never comes again."
—"Once Upon a Time," Strouse/Adams

"You wandered down a lane, far away, leaving me a song
that will not die. Love is now the stardust of yesterday."
—"Stardust," Hoagy Carmichael

From a journal kept by Susan Parker:

When they called him a lone wolf, I bought a sweatshirt for Michael that depicted a lone wolf howling on a mountaintop beneath a mysterious mournful moon. If you looked at it long enough, the clouds seemed to drift past the moon, and the wolf would turn to look at you with melancholy eyes because no one had answered his cry. It seemed perfect for him.

I had always known he marched to his own drummer, one day a soaring Sousa march for a charge up a hill, the next, a mournful dirge when depression overtook him as he bore the death of innocence like a lost child. It was always a cadence only he could hear. He was an iconoclastic square peg that didn't fit well in any of the round holes and entanglements of the collective conformity of an artificial world, always an outsider looking in, unsure if he was welcome or wanted to be, playing solitaire, only pausing to tilt at windmills and sing the tune in *Man of La Mancha*.

His romantic view of an America of yesteryear was where he lived in his mind, where his jukebox played only the golden oldies, where he walked on the hot coals of bedrock values that burned him but never turned him. It drove him to try to fix everything he viewed as broken and rescue women he believed were Tess Trueheart tied to the railroad tracks with the big train bearing down on them.

He was an "in the nick of time" kind of guy who secretly said things like "unhand her, you fiend" and looked for the prizes in the bottom of Cracker Jack boxes while some tried to find their treasure in the bottom of the bottle or the prick of the needle. His emotions were warehoused and crowded, and I knew they would one day spill out for better or worse.

When he was called a lone wolf Michael took it as a compliment, not a warning or threat. He knew he made them nervous, though neither he nor they were quite sure why. He was stranded on the rocky shoals between the fallen world and what he wanted it to be. When some saw progress at any price, he saw the decay, the fresh coat of paint covering the blood of innocents, the smiling death masks of counterfeit players.

The guys at the tiptop liked him. He reminded them of their younger selves, before all the little compromises snowballed and nibbled away their core. They also needed someone who would stand his ground and protect their assets and that fine, clear line between right and wrong that so many tried to erase in the name of "getting theirs while the getting was good."

He stumbled in the end from self-inflicted wounds, a story of hypnotic siren calls, ships wrecked on rocky shoals, Greek tragedies, knife sales on the Ides of March, and the tale of a man who one day understood that the world he wanted to save was not far removed from the one that crucified the Savior of the world.

After his world crumbled, I found him staring at an image of a man ascending to heaven while a beautiful temptress, a Jezebel, held to him tightly, tempting him to stay in and of the world. He stared at it for hours until I urged him to come to bed. He looked at me and said, "I just wanted to see who wins."

For better or worse, for richer or poorer, in sickness or health, and for all of his constancy and complexity, I told him I loved him one night at the 78 Drive-in in Tupelo and love him still until death separates us. It was why I saw him in the shadows at our last meeting but with the growing Light of Christ coming to redirect him to the actual battlefield, to tell him Who won in the image he had stared at for hours.

He was beginning to understand as "self" yielded to "surrender," as he realized God could use him, that He could use all of it in a one-eyed man's life. Pearl's little boy, who had once played the role of pastor in a play when his Methodist church visited the Parker Grove Baptist Church, was becoming the new man the Lord was building.

I knew that last night, though I would not live to go with him, Michael would rescue many in prison. He would write and speak, finally find peace and an anchor for his idealism, not in the transient world he never understood, but in the transcendent, Someone and Something to believe in at the foot of the blood-stained Cross, where death became life for him, where the plow of God began to till the soil of his life to bear fruit for the Gospel.

We played word games that night and I recited the old nursery rhyme, "Tinker, Tailor. Soldier, Sailor. Rich Man, Poor Man. Beggar Man, Thief."

In our last embrace, he looked deeply into my eyes and said, "Love, Loss. Words, Wounds. Sinner, Savior. Survivor, Servant. Redemption, Resurrection."

As I left for the last time I said, "I will watch for you in God's furrow."

He waved to me and said, "See you…here, there, and in the air, on the better side of goodbye."

"If you must die, sweetheart, Die knowing your life was the best part of mine."—"You," Keaton Leslie Henson

PROLOGUE

"Stories deal with our moral struggles, our uncertainties, our dreams, our blunders, our contradictions, our endless quest for understanding. Good stories do not resolve the mysteries of the human spirit but rather describe and expand on those mysteries."—Tim O'Brien

"Somewhere in the world, there is a defeat for everyone. Some are destroyed by defeat, and some made small and mean by victory. Greatness lives in one who triumphs equally over defeat and victory."—John Steinbeck

"We played the pipe for you, but you did not dance."
—Matthew 11:17

Federal Magistrate Judge Alex Martin sat at his desk in downtown Atlanta, signing orders, perusing the day's docket, and reading anonymous online attorney comments that claimed he had worn out and discarded the Constitution and was operating his court on his own bylaws.

His case load was heavy, and he had left his home in the suburbs without shaving. His jawline bore the shadow of stubble of a heavy beard, and his hairline had raced backwards. His linen suit was rumpled, but he reckoned his robe would cover that in court.

The knocking at his door jolted him from his grooming blues. He looked up to see Paul Berry, his former partner when Martin was an Assistant U.S. Attorney.

"Alex, I was in the building and thought you might like to know that Michael Parker is being released from Talladega Prison Camp today," Berry said.

"What!" Martin exclaimed as he looked at Berry with a wide-eyed look of incredulity mixed with slack-jawed astonishment—or something akin to fresh notification that someone had killed his dog.

"How did he get out so soon?" Martin asked, remembering the day he asked the federal judge for twelve to fourteen years for a nonviolent, first-time offender. He casually canceled the non-renewable days of Michael Parker's life like the federal deity he fancied himself to be, though the average sentence for nonviolent, first-time, white-collar offenders was twenty-three to twenty-seven months.

He asked for 144 to 172 months, enough time to make him ineligible for a prison camp and confine him in a high-security prison, enough time to finish off Parker for not playing ball, embarrassing the government, and forcing Martin to change his entire script and paint Parker as the mastermind in his prosecution.

"He was accepted into the drug program due to his addiction to Xanax, left over from the governor's campaign. He looked like death warmed over when we saw him in the Atlanta Detention Center detox unit in 2006, where they made him go cold turkey off the pills. We told him we were there to finish some paperwork. Of course, we just went to jerk his chain. The FBI agent enjoyed it, but it was a painful sight to see. Parker completed the drug program in prison, and they knocked time off his sentence.

"My friend there said he did prison ministry at three facilities and was well thought of by most Federal Bureau of Prisons staffers, including the Edgefield, S.C. head psychologist. She partnered with him to reach the lost for Christ. I'm told the ministry he started at Edgefield, Prisoners of the Lord, is still going strong. Some in the BOP think it is the most successful inmate-led prison ministry in the history of the BOP. He also got married at the Millington, Tennessee, prison camp after Susan Parker died and was a pastor of sorts to the inmates there and at other institutions," Berry said.

"Prisoners of the Lord? Pastor? Humph! He was just a prisoner of the government, a convict like the rest, no matter what they call themselves. Come now, Paul. They don't know him like we do, do they?" Martin asked, rolling his eyes.

"Never mind. I got my appointment in 2006, the year Parker entered prison, despite him wanting to play the hero, and now the local federal judges have renewed my magistrate appointment. I may never be a federal district judge, but I'll be up for Chief Magistrate when the current judge retires, and Parker will never be the same after prison. None of them are. You have to break 'em, Paul, leave 'em nothing more than shuffling little old men afraid of the outside world and those who run it," Martin said with an amused sneer.

"I've never told anyone this, but that day in court at sentencing when he was so humble, thanking the judge and all, looking so pitiful, I walked over to him and shook my finger in his face..." Martin trailed off.

"I remember you lost your temper with the judge at the bail hearing after he granted Parker's request for a second bail to go home before prison to arrange care for his wife. When he granted Parker's request, we thought the judge was going to smack you with contempt when you argued with him," Berry said.

"You thought I was wrong? What are you trying to say?" Martin asked, mouth agape.

"I walked past the room where Parker was confined while the judge deliberated. The guard had left, and I peered in at Parker. He was face down on the table; arms spread across it. He was prostrate before the Lord, and the way he spoke was unlike anything I had ever heard, like something out of the Bible. Not exactly begging but crying out to God, like he was linked to some other place, a place outside of our jurisdiction. The room had taken on a strange light, and I backed away as the intruder I was. Then when the judge shocked everyone, against all odds and precedents, and granted his petition...well, I just don't know," Berry said.

"No, no, those words with the judge are all forgotten and expunged from the court record so it can't impede my career. I've never told anyone this. When he returned to Atlanta for sentencing,

I wanted to strike Parker across the face, slap that Boy Scout look off his face, and crush him under my heel. I know he hated me as I hated him. He had to. I wanted him to, but he just looked at me with that wounded look, like I was some injured animal he had found on the roadside, like he pitied me," Martin said, grinding his teeth.

"And that man with him, the professor from Ole Miss, Timothy Charles. He wanted to rise from his chair to rebuke me and defend Parker. I could see it in his face. A professor of Criminal Justice, all he had done in his storied career for the law, but here he was…so protective of Parker, driving all the way to Atlanta from Oxford, knowing his presence would not change the outcome, only comfort Parker. Parker fooled a lot of people, but not me. I saw him for who he was," Martin said.

"I remember Professor Charles," Berry said. "He was the professor for Parker's undergraduate and graduate degrees and later his director at the Mississippi Bureau of Narcotics. Parker was his captain over the north half of the state. When Parker left the MBN, Charles protected him from the governor's people, who wanted to punish him for opposing them. Charles arranged for Parker to receive the University of Mississippi Distinguished Alumni Award for his life's work. They were looking for his address for the invitation to the ceremony when they discovered we had indicted Parker. Local agents said everyone in Mississippi was stunned and couldn't believe it. In his letter to the judge, Charles said the assistant professor who searched for Parker's address came to him with the news and said, 'This can't be. He's the most honest man I know.'"

"Unbelievable! Well, he crossed the wrong man when he messed with me," Martin said.

"Word is that he has written a book and is a fair writer. The *Atlanta Journal-Constitution* contacted the Bureau of Prisons at Talladega for a story, and the warden told them Parker just wants to serve Jesus when he is released. The journalist wrote about his prison ministry, Prisoners of the Lord," Berry said.

"He has forfeited any audience with the world. I saw that article. He was just playing for sympathy, a jailhouse conversion. No one will believe a word he says in his book or books, either, but just in case, don't honor any request to reduce his probation period. The U.S. Attorney's office has to sign off on it, so if it comes to your desk…conveniently lose it. Slow him down, limit his travel, and run out the clock on him. He's not a young man. Better yet, let U.S. Probation know you won't even entertain anything less than the full three years of probation," he said as he stood to don his robe in front of a gold leaf likeness of Lady Justice on his desk. The blind lady holding the scales of justice was an award from the local Bar Association for impartial prosecutors and jurists.

"Did you know the *Augusta Chronicle* asked him if he forgave everyone involved in the case? He said he had forgiven as Christ forgave him and prayed for all who made mistakes as he did. They asked him if that included you, and he said especially you," Berry said.

"Some of us have to do our jobs and punish the guilty, even if others won't. The law is the law. There's no room for sentimentality or mercy. We erased him, and the world was better off without him. God will reward those who punish the lawbreakers," he said, straightening his tie.

He headed to the courtroom but paused at the door and half-turned, checking his image in the long mirror and the sudden lack of luster in his star-spangled eyes. Though he pressed at his wrinkled pants and brushed his sparse hair, it was not a good look for an imperial magistrate who had softened and sagged with the years. He was disgusted with what he saw and looked away quickly, hoping to leave the puffy image he loathed trapped in the mirror, alongside the frumpiness no amount of good tailoring could conceal.

He looked down at his shoes, which needed a shine. He remembered the night he pressed Parker to "remember" more things to pin on Mary Ruth Robinson. Parker kept saying "that didn't happen" or "I don't remember that," all the while staring at Martin's creased, cracked, and thin-soled loafers.

Martin remembered snapping at Parker, "Why are you staring at my shoes?"

He could still see Parker looking up at him and saying, "An old sheriff once told me shoes reveal more about a person than fingerprints or DNA."

"What?" Martin roared at Berry, who was staring out the window.

"The U.S. Attorney released that statement we wrote for him, accusing Parker of greed," Berry said.

"Yeah, so what?" Martin asked.

"Parker was guilty of many things, but we never alleged he profited from Robinson's conspiracy or received a buffalo nickel. To my knowledge, he didn't. You know we were going to use him as our star witness until he told Robinson he planned to tell the truth on the stand, and she turned him in for violating the no-contact agreement. It was only then that we had to paint him as the Big Bad Wolf and her as Little Red Riding Hood," Berry said.

"What's wrong with you? Did you come here to impair my judgment before I ascend to the bench? You concurred in all of it," Martin said.

The esteemed magistrate, his mouth permanently turned down at the corners from sucking on the bitter lemons of life, looked up at his bookcase and the three wise monkeys, who swore off any association with evil and looked down at him like deacons of doom. He turned toward Berry with a sickly mendicant smile.

"They won't believe him...will they?"

> *"And must I now begin to doubt—who never doubted*
> *all these years? My heart is stone, and still it trembles.*
> *The world I have known is lost in the shadows."*
> —Les Misérables, *Victor Hugo*

***

Hundreds of women in the women's prison camp near Orlando were clotted in and around the government dorms. The camp's most famous resident, former Georgia Education Superintendent Mary Ruth Robinson, sat in her room, humming a tune with no name and watching a dove that had come to rest on the ledge of her small window.

She alternately cleaned the CPAP machine she slept under, read fantastical books of escapism, and thought about the year or so more of confinement that lay before her and how the years had not been kind to a woman once known for her physical beauty.

The cheap little mirror from the commissary clipped on her locker reminded her that time might seem to crawl but it was marching on. The facelift she had before prison had begun to go slack where it had been drawn tight. The eyes that once sparkled were weathered and dulled by the deprivations and humiliations of prison and were entrances to some dark recesses where flames once burned. The cloudiness in her eyes was not cataracts as some suspected but the gray ashes of fires of old and dry bones better left interred.

She took her time and scrubbed the tub of her CPAP. The power always failed when she was at the Tallahassee prison, leaving her without her unit at night. She once was always in a pinch for time, speeches and meetings, trips to Washington, so much to do. Then she found herself in prison with all the time in the world, time enough to think and rethink…everything.

She looked outside her cube at her community and social club. Two elderly women were playing chess. Mary Ruth had once been a formidable chess player. A woman across the way was using an old toothpick to extract a glob of cheap government meat from between her incisors. Another smoked a "roll your own" soggy, contraband cigarette. Others often smoked the kind with the pungent odor late at night and dreamed of flying right over fences and razor wire and flaming out in the sun.

The dorm was a dark place this time of day, full of shadows, calendars with days marked through, time trickling through the hourglass like molasses, and pinups of Chippendale dancers. There were gambling games, but they were rigged, and the stakes were too high. Some of her fellow inmates huddled in corners, talking low so no one could hear the secrets of lives lived in rejection and the times before all of it when their laughs were fresh and genuine and not forced.

Older and educated, Mary Ruth had gained status among the inmates and was a source of kindness and advice to them, the local "Dear Abby" in shared bleakness, often shoring up frail courage for some with strength and humility born of captivity, occasionally confiding in a few how all of her troubles were because of one man, a familiar tale grown stale in prisons for women. She adopted the wounded ones, much as she had her beloved basset hounds. The demons that once plagued her had moved on to greener pastures, though horror novels and succubus tales still were favorite reads, and she had a gentleman caller who came to visit now and then, a widower who thought her beautiful and a mail-order bride-to-be.

Mary Ruth had seen her share of trouble, but this was the first time life had truly tested her, day after day, night after night. Still, sometimes she imagined herself as a gypsy queen, the femme fatale on the cover of romance books, or her favorite obsession, Guinevere of the King Arthur tales.

It was her code name when she held high office, and she often sent her trusted aide, Michael Parker, cryptic messages signed "Guinevere." She was obsessed with the stories, an alternate reality where she retreated before prison and during the long days of confinement, a way to stare down loneliness, to transfigure failure.

A sudden cool breeze caused Mary Ruth to look up from her Arthurian book toward the open door and the figure hovering at the entrance to her unit. The breeze ruffled her book's pages and carried a most foul odor.

Adrianna West, the new unit manager transferred from the Millington, Tennessee, camp, stared at her, clutching a paper with her stubby, thick-fingered paws, looking like the cat who ate the canary. Torturing inmates had always been her favorite pastime.

"Well, hello, Mrs. Robinson, I've got something for you to read, fresh off the BOP intranet." She handed it to Mary Ruth.

"Your old associate, Michael Parker, is getting out earlier than you," West said.

West waited, tapping her foot in anticipation, but got no response.

"Not only that. Parker got married before I left the camp, though we did all we could to foul it up," West said, playing her trump card.

West waited again but still got no response, no sign of emotion.

"I dealt with him at Millington Camp, you know. He was always throwing up the name of J-J-Jesus to me, always in his room praying or trying to save other inmates. He helped men there who kept suing me. Parker and his buddy, Andrew Alexander, turned the Memphis U.S. Attorney against me with all those lawsuits. They both could write, and I knew it was them, conspiring against me. They just kept on until my husband left me and ran off with my daughter, and I was transferred here," West said, wildly stabbing at her ghosts with her finger.

Mary Ruth nodded and picked up her book. She thought of days when Michael defended her and kept her going in the governor's campaign, even in her addiction to pain pills, though he advised her not to run. She thought he could have been Lancelot and told him so. He was gallant and loyal, too loyal at times and naïve, a weakness. She thought heroes are just never as strong as the men in her books.

As West milled around, waiting impatiently for her to digest the news, Mary Ruth turned the final pages of her book and read of Lancelot's death as a monk hermit, where the hermits told him he had forsaken God, and she read of Guinivere's last days as a widowed nun.

She realized or admitted for the first time that she had been wrong all along. Michael had never been Lancelot, inspired by earthly love. He was Lancelot's gentle son, Galahad, inspired by heavenly love, the selfless, chivalrous knight seeking the Holy Grail and the vision of God. In her books, Galahad found and mended the sword of David and saw the Grail, the cup of Christ.

She considered that all Michael ever wanted was communion with Christ to complete his incompleteness. He was mistaken if he had imagined a reservoir of warmth in her. It was not there for him or anyone else, but his quest was not temporal. Michael and Galahad did not have the sword, Excalibur, but they found the Sword of the Spirit, the Word of God.

Understanding and remorse fell over her like thunder and lightning, like shards of broken truth, and her frail hands with the blue veins twisted the spine of the book until it cracked.

Mary Ruth squarely faced West with her chin up and said precisely, almost apologetically, "Good for him."

As West stomped off, Mary Ruth imagined Michael waiting to enter the room of the Holy Grail. She imagined him turning to look back at her, but she knew he never would. He may have stumbled, but he would always try to do the right thing in the end. While she was tipping, he was tithing, and she had second thoughts about heroes, those flawed but not weak, gentle but strong.

Mary Ruth thought of "So help me, God" and crossing her fingers behind her back. She thought of the truth she testified to that never happened, while he was near death in the Atlanta dungeon because the absolute truth was inconvenient and situational that day, the blurred line between fact and fantasy, the sharper line between damnation and innocence, and angels offering one last chance to flee Sodom and Gomorrah before the rain of sulfur and their admonition to never look back. She once considered her trusted lieutenant almost an appendix, but courts were battlefield triages to determine who received appendectomies.

She sat with her chin on her hands for a long time, tears leaking from her eyes. She closed her book on the Knights of the

Round Table, gave up on romance novels and fairy tales, and picked up her Bible.

The former ballerina, once dubbed Cinderella, finally discovered that the glass slipper never really fit her, and you can't dance at the ball barefooted.

She looked up as the faithful dove at her window flew away, leaving her a freshly plucked olive leaf, a sign of new life, restoration, and baptism.

> *"Something inside her broke and healed at the same time."*—The Guinevere Deception, *Kiersten White*

CHAPTER ONE

"I will stay in prison till the moss grows over my eyelids rather than disobey God."—John Bunyan

"Hardships often prepare ordinary people for an extraordinary destiny."—C.S. Lewis

"For even in the likeness of the suffering, there remains an unlikeness in the sufferers…it is in that same affliction the wicked detest God and blaspheme, while the good pray and praise. So material a difference it does make, not what ills are suffered, but what kind of man suffers them. For, stirred up with the same movement, mud exhales a horrible stench, and ointment emits a fragrant odor."
—St. Augustine

Michael Parker, former cop, corporate manager, political operative, aspiring Homeric hero with an Achilles heel, and inmate turned evangelist, was pale, peaked, and thin as a rake the day his wife, Judy, came to take him home from the prison camp in Talladega, Alabama.

Venus had just made its final transit of the 21st century between the Earth and the sun, appearing as a tiny shadow or disc crossing the face of the sun, and here he was, another shadow about to make his terrestrial journey.

The dappled light from his tiny window caressed him in the odd geometry of his prison cell and cast his shadow on the worn floor of the alcove that had been his home. The retreating night, mixed with the light of morning and prison disharmony, exposed every crack in the stark architecture and the broken hearts within.

He sat on his bunk for the last time, clutching all his meager worldly possessions and an unexpected, poignant letter from

Tammy Sue Jenkins, a young woman from a former life who still addressed him as Captain.

Almost unbearable, bittersweet emotions swirled within him and came to tug at his heart and beg, "Take us with you when you leave." Someone whistled a mournful spiritual somewhere in the muted darkness of predawn. Michael's wet eyes glistened, seeping water constrained by emotional dams during years of isolation in a world of gray morality, where it was necessary to maintain an iron grip on dignity and sanity.

Deliverance was at hand, but his mind was overwhelmed, and his heart was numb. He felt weak and strong, a thousand years old and a newborn child in the grasp of tentative joy mixed with melancholy.

Michael opened his Bible and read Ephesians 2:4-5. "But because of His great love for us, God who is rich in mercy, made us alive with Christ even when we were dead in transgressions. It is by grace you have been saved."

He knelt before his bunk, with his elbows resting on his bed and his hands clasped, and he said a prayer for the verse he'd read.

"My Father in heaven. When You raised up Christ, You raised me up from my dead state. Thank You for bringing me from death to life. Forgive me when I stumble. Stay with me, use me, and light the path You have set before me. In the name of my Lord and Savior, Jesus Christ, I pray. Amen."

Then, as he had done for nearly six years, he turned to his retreat, the endless library of songs in his mind, secular and sacred, and sang a line from an old song. He was not a good singer, but inmates would often stop to listen as the words and pain bled out of him like his Sunday night sermons in the chapel.

"Slow down. Slow down. There's no hurry because my life isn't mine anymore," he whisper-sang through abducted vocal cords.

He laid his homemade cross on his bunk and pinned his treasured copy of the Valley of Vision to his pillow for the next pilgrim who would rest there. "Lord, High and Holy, Meek and

Lowly…Thou hast brought me to the valley of vision. Let me find Thy Light in my darkness, Thy life in my death, Thy joy in my sorrow, Thy grace in my sin, Thy riches in my poverty, Thy glory in my valley. Amen."

Michael heard his name on the staticky intercom, which invited him to report to the visiting room to sign out and climb the hill to the discharge parking lot. As he left the dorm for the last time, he saw hands wave goodbye to him above the concrete cubicle walls. "See you outside or up there, man of God," one said.

He passed through the shifting shadows and into the light. He walked slowly past the gray government facades, though he wanted to sprint up the tilted slope of a world out of joint. The wind rustled the leaves of trees on the hillside, a beggar cat mewed behind the chow hall dumpsters, steam escaped the kitchen vent, and he could feel the warmth of morning caress his face and smell the fresh fragrance of freedom.

A gathering of crows cawed above the man inmates had dubbed "Bird Man." The birds seemed to be passing judgment on his truancy from life. Folklore dubbed them a murder of crows in old tales because they supposedly gathered to decide the capital fate of another crow.

Michael also heard the barking of the camp dog named Banjo. Inmates joked that when Banjo and other stray mutts got into a howl fest, it was "dueling banjos," like in the movie. Laughter was demanded no matter how tired the jokes until it sometimes came to fisticuffs, a matter of comedic honor.

The disputes were mostly fraternal or mock sparring to relieve the pressure and tension of close confinement in a polyglot universe. All the comedians were seeking their own "Deliverance," but they needed new material, and many of them suffered from the effects of the wonder drugs they once tried, only to wonder what they had done when they woke up behind bars.

He doubted he would ever be in another place where so many dialects, idioms, diction, accents, slanguage, and cadence merged under one roof. There was a dangerous and volatile murkiness between figurative and literal meaning at times. Their words were often fragmented and broken, but it was okay because they were broken, too, and tears were a language of shared suffering. Not all shed blood, but they did shed tears.

It was jarring at first, but after a while, he no longer longed for *Star Trek*'s universal translator and became fluent in prison speak, moving seamlessly from one camp to the next, speaking the one word they all knew: Jesus.

When times were tense and tempers short, mercurial men forgot their fear of hell in the heat of white-hot anger and looked for someone to burn. Fortunately, the sparks of would-be fires flew upward when tempers flared, or men lit illegal cigarettes, for which they would likely try to delay the Second Coming for a last puff of the black-market tobacco.

Michael always hesitated before he crossed group boundaries or entered rooms and cubes to say, "Hello. It's just me and Jesus." Sometimes inmates would say, "Jesus is welcome, but we're not so sure about you." Laughter would follow, tension subsiding, seeping out like air escaping from a balloon near bursting, and Michael rode in on the coattails of the Lord, Who enabled him to drown out angry voices without raising his.

Just as a booming voice on the loudspeaker announced that "Elvis has left the building," Michael faced her on the hilltop, backlit by the rising sun, which cast an elongated shadow over their reunion. His hands were clammy, his tongue tangled, and his heart pounded to an allegro rhythm.

Judy opened the car door and said, "Hey, mister, I've been traveling alone too long. I'm so tired of traveling by myself. Want to ride with me? I know the way home."

The sunlight made her brown hair sparkle, and her hazel eyes kissed his and framed a golden smile for him, and her pupils were open wide like her heart to receive her husband.

She squeezed his hands, and he realized that she would not only be a part of his life but all of his life forever more. He had so much to tell and no one to tell it to until she came to bring him home.

"Got any room at your Bed and Breakfast?" he asked as he sat next to her. It was then he first noticed that if he looked into her eyes too long, her irises changed from hazel to green and back again, and a pink flush crawled up her neck as she gnawed on her lower lip. It was a rare visual admission of vulnerability by a strong woman, and he felt privileged to see it and silently vowed to never abuse his access.

She walked across the stage with him in 1966 at their high school graduation. He was best man at her wedding in 1970, and after the death of their spouses, she came to the prison camp in Millington to see her classmate and best man, her friend's widower, to find comfort in their mutual loss, and they were married there in 2010.

He turned to her after the pastor's "I pronounce you" and said, "Look at us, Judy. Who would've believed it?"

Michael told her she was not getting any prize with her tired, shambling husband, but he had ceased telling her for she would not listen. He had choked down too much rotten food, dined on rancid lonesome stew, and received too many years of inadequate medical care. The object of constant abuse from those who hated him because of his age, faith, and race, he had spent too many days living on the thin ledge of danger, surrounded by enemies, but he knew he had made his own bed and had to lie in it.

Subtraction of years from life expectancy on actuarial tables accompanies such environments like free crackers at the takeout line, like penalties that never end. There had been too many blind alleys and dead-end streets, too many nights talking to himself until he began to talk only to God. The bough had broken many times, but Christ cradled him.

He eased into the passenger side of her car, wondering if it was a dream and someone would arrest him for being joyous in the first degree. Would they set the hounds on him like Cool Hand Luke, tell him he wasn't housebroken, and that they were locking the door and throwing away the key due to a "failure to communicate"? He had guarded his emotions for years because he was at the mercy of a world that had no mercy.

He turned to Judy and said, "Someday, I'd like to go to a Southern restaurant where they serve breakfast all day, a place like Waffle House where they call you honey, sugar, and baby. I haven't had real food in a long time, and no one has called me honey, sugar, or baby for nearly six years, and for that last part, I thank the Lord."

Judy laughed at that and thought his humor and resilience was still intact.

She said, "Well, honey, sugar, baby, I'll serve you breakfast three times a day if you like, and I have no ends to my terms of endearment. You can even flirt with me if you'd like!"

Michael thought he never wanted to fall in love again, but here he was. He couldn't help it. He looked at her with a crooked Elvis smile and a bruised tenderness and said, "I'm a bit rusty, but I think I can remember how. One more thing I forgot to ask. Do you squeeze the toothpaste tube from the bottom or the top?"

As they drove toward Mississippi, there was a partial lunar eclipse with the earth casting an umbra shadow across the moon. The sky and scape reminded him of the pulp art for Edgar Rice Burroughs' John Carter of Mars series he read as a child and Burroughs' inner earth Pellucidar series he reread during his "inner earth" incarceration.

It was a strange sky, and the mocking mile markers passed by too fast, like blurred flashcards in a test of what time is it, where are you, and how did it all go wrong? Things were slower in the old world of black and white, a snail's pace of a long, slow death, but it was a predictable torture. There was too much startling color, too much randomness, and too many monsters, even for Burroughs, and the slightest whisper was too loud.

Michael saw a house in a field near the interstate. He recognized it as an old Sears and Roebuck home someone had restored. In the first half of the 20th century, kits were ordered from the Sears catalog to build a home, and they shipped about 75,000 of them.

Everything needed arrived by train car; the door was sealed with red plastic like the old seals on official letters. Framing lumber, cedar shakes, doors and doorknobs, and blueprints came. They promised buyers that the average person with rudimentary skills could build the house within three months. Best of all, they said, "You don't need a carpenter." As the house faded from view, Michael thought that he had once tried to build a home and a life but found it was all in vain without the Carpenter.

Michael softly sang, "If I were a carpenter or an inmate, and you were a lady, would you still love me?"

Judy smiled and said, "I'd answer you, yes I would."

He no longer wanted to neaten up the world, just prepare for the next. He longed to step out of the shadows of lonesome town and see it all along the roadway, every nuance of freedom, though it was jarring to his senses…the green of the pines, the groves of cedar trees begging for Christmas lights, the weathered picket fences that made him wonder if he was inside or outside the fence line, old country barns that leaned westward, pointing the way for pilgrims back to Eden, ladybug kamikazes on the windshield, garish billboards advertising the best buffets, the tempo and rhythm of the traffic, the cracked irregularities in the pavement, a crowd gathered round a small pond in a pasture for a baptism, birds sitting on a ragged scarecrow that had lost his hat and his scare in a cornfield, and the down-on-their-luck hitchhikers thumbing rides on the fast highway home.

He was almost relieved to see people using their thumbs to get rides after Judy told him that people had started texting with thumbs only while he had been away. Thumbs up or down in the coliseum, shelling butter beans and peas, opening cans, and hitchhiking, but thumbs as typing digits?

Judy throttled her Murano to a soft purr in heavy traffic near the Leeds exit, where construction workers in slow motion held signs that read "slow." Michael saw one inventive nomad on the side of the road. He had long hair, a beard, and what looked like an imitation crown of thorns on his head. He held a sign that said, *I've just come from Jerusalem, where things are going bad. Give me a ride to heaven, I need to talk to my Father.*

Michael turned his head to look at him as they passed by, and the man smiled, mouthed the word "peace," and flipped his sign to the other side, which read, *It is finished.*

Suddenly chilled and shivering, Michael shoved his hands in his pockets and curled up against the passenger side window, and a deep sleep consumed him as years of weariness and wariness suddenly arrived. The divide between the bright light and the deep darkness framed his life, the life of one pilgrim plucked out of the fire by the hand of God.

His day of transition had been a long time coming…like the never-ending trains with a thousand boxcars he had counted from the prison yard. Over time, he could see the changes from a distance. The conductors no longer waved at America, and all the freight cars hid their faces beneath railroad yard graffiti.

Michael finally ceased his count of the cars like the days of his confinement, only to find one day that someone had done away with the caboose like a forgotten IOU while he Rip Van Winkled. He mourned the death of the caboose, cut loose like he had been, a relic from a bygone era kicked to the curb. Like the song, he and the trains had the "disappearing railroad blues."

He had sung all the hymns, psalms, and dirges he knew, prayed all the prayers a thousand times, cried too easily, and bled from the heart too frequently. Almost six years were gone like a knock on the door, like yesterday and the day before, like dry leaves blown by a relentless tumbleweed wind.

Time didn't have to hurry because all the broken clocks had stood still, but the dungeon became his church, and many inmates, once unrepentant and fresh out of alibis, had become prisoners of the Lord in the prison that became a womb, a place of second birth. They had donned the robes of parishioners and wept as they confessed, prayed, and wrote their wills on bended knees.

The inmates saw him walking the compound day and night, Bible in one hand, bird book in the other. He heard their prayers late at night when men told God that they were so far down in life, they just had to get high with the silver pricks that needled their souls, but when they sobered up, their house of cards had collapsed. The deck was stacked, and they had played their hole card and bet it all on the clicks and snaps of the devil's Russian Roulette.

Michael had become their confessor, their bargain-basement pastor, the substitute who had to do until they found a real one, the familiar monk figure walking through the prison yard come rain or shine, looking up for birds and the Almighty and whisper-singing "I'll Fly Away." He bent beneath the weight of his flock's sins and sorrows, always grinding in second gear as he picked up his cross to follow Christ up that steep hill as a victor, not a victim.

As he dreamed and twitched on the passenger seat, Michael was swallowed up, like Jonah in the belly of the whale, by the shadows and light of a vivid dreamscape rich with rushing scenes of beauty and vignettes of horror from a Forrest Gump life. People were kneeling at a giant altar, prayer warriors were praying fierce prayers, and he sensed the prayers were for him.

Then he heard the door clang shut behind him, and he knew that the old man was interred where he could not visit him until it was time, buried in a sepulcher where lonely ghosts cried ghost tears. He could no longer rub the phantom pain and second-degree burns from years of standing too close to those who wore five-and-dime-store halos, those who could quote the Word but spoke fluent demon and were bound for the lake of fire.

As he dozed in and out, the world rushed at Michael. The colors were too bright, the sounds too loud and harsh. There was no melody in the noise, and he could hear Lazarus and a million, million voices begging for a drink of water while crying a billion, billion tears. He first thought that the old world had been washed clean, but he saw that it was only a fresh coat of paint, some cheap makeup to cover the bare and bitter wormwood of darkness.

Steam rose from a parched land after a hard rain, and no one seemed to know his name, but they pointed fingers and shouted, "Walk on. Don't look back. You might see something God wants you to forget," but Michael had learned that we don't get to choose the place of our martyrdom, that Christ had not come to get us out of trouble but to get into trouble with us.

Just before Parker Grove, a heavenly choir was softly singing. An angel leaned over the balcony of heaven and whispered in his mind's ear, "Fear not, Michael Parker. God will make your enemies your footstool."

Michael awakened with his hands over his ears to squelch the accusing voices, the wagging fingers, and the script of the former chapters of his life that Christ was partitioning. He remembered the days he thought he was barely living but also the nights he thought he was surely dying, sleeping with his Bible open and his finger on John 3:16. It was the only passport a castaway would ever need to cross the reef in case Michael didn't make it until morning to row his boat ashore. Hallelujah.

He removed his hands from his ears and listened as the disappearing sounds of yesterday receded into life's rearview mirror. He opened his squinted eyes and looked at his image in the mirror, as if he were Robinson Crusoe home from the sea to say, "I was a prisoner, locked up with the eternal bars and bolts...looking out to sea in hopes of seeing a ship...looking until I was almost blind, lose it and sit down and weep like a child. I was removed from the wickedness of the world. I had nothing to covet. The hand of Providence spread my table in the wilderness. Wait on the Lord, wait, I say, on the Lord."

He turned to Judy and asked, "Do you hear that, Judy?"

"What? I don't hear anything but the drone of the car," she said.

"I was dreaming that I was shipwrecked on God. I kept hearing a man named Fredrick Buechner saying, 'Listen to your life. The place God calls you to is the place where your deep gladness and the world's deep hunger meet.'"

It was his first testimony from the summit of his years as the car hurdled toward Lantern Waste to the lamplight whose Light never ends.

"The quiet angels sing... Love, love, love has come for you."—*"Love Has Come For You," S. Martin, E. Brickell*

CHAPTER TWO

"After the darkness, I hope for light."
—Latin translation, Job 17:12

"All we have to decide is what to do with the time
that is given us."—J.R.R. Tolkien

*"Recalled to life."—*A Tale of Two Cities, *Charles Dickens*

As Judy drove past familiar but altered landmarks in Parker Grove and across dividing lines, Michael saw that someone had been erasing all that was while he was on layaway until the time payments were complete, before he was moved to the lost and found department and claimed by Christ.

Across the shushing, rolling surf of time, Michael could almost touch all of his yesterdays as waves of nostalgia tugged at his heart, squeezed the water from his leaking eyes, and made it hard to swallow the lump in his throat or ease the pain in his innards. But the joy of Christ swept him along the shoreline of life toward eternity—all the sights, sounds, and smells of a time when it was raining grace and mercy, when angels wept for him as he was suspended between heaven and hell and battered like a piñata by blind men who didn't know Christ.

He could taste the salty tears, hear the needles bounce on the 78 rpm records, and catch the creak of the handle on the rusty old well pump. He could still savor the sandwiches Susan made for the picnic by the pond, feel the Mississippi mud between his toes, smell the cornbread on the stove, and hug memory in her Sunday dress, as if Pearl had just stepped out on the back porch for a minute to watch a sunset set the horizon on fire, all choreographed to the warm and mellow clarinet of Pete Fountain playing "Just a Closer Walk With Thee."

It was all so close, then was now and now was then, Daddy plowing the hard ground, Mama praying for the soaking rain. Michael felt as if he could turn around and step into yesterday, like going into another room where lost loves and precious remembrances were tickling his ears, rubbing shoulders with him, embracing him and stroking his cheeks, and begging him to pull up a chair, to sit and stay a while on the front porch in the summer breeze before it all faded away, before they had to leave and sleep again with the ancients.

Judy was silent as she drove him through Parker Grove in search of Michael's home, the womb of his childhood, a graveled road back then when Michael thought you must be rich if you lived on a paved road and didn't have iron-on patches on your jeans. It was when porches were where you grew up listening to bobwhites in the hollows and the loud silence of adults in rocking chairs, menfolk smoking, womenfolk shelling peas, and someone reading the local paper aloud to nods and grunts by all until the sun's light yielded to evening's curtain.

When he was a boy roaming the wildwoods of Parker Grove, Michael Parker built a cabin of sorts deep in the forests and cut the thick grapevines that ran high into the upper terraces of the leafy canopy that blotted out the sun and a world where he felt like a stranger. Like his hero, Johnny Weissmuller, in the old Tarzan movies, he could swing from one vine to another as his dogs ran beneath him, barking.

One day, young "Tarzan" found the rusty steel trap of a poacher. The trap was sprung, but there was no animal in the jaws of the snare, only a leg. It looked as if a red fox had chewed part of its leg off to escape the jaws of death. Michael removed the foot, and as a chickadee came down to watch and mourn, dug a hole and buried the paw in a solemn ceremony.

Filled with anger, he beat the trap against a giant oak tree repeatedly until the metal broke into unusable pieces. Exhausted, the gravedigger and pallbearer slid down the tree trunk, sat by the grave, and wept at the thought of the chances of a three-legged fox surviving in the wild.

Years after he found the trap and the severed leg, long after he had graduated from grapevines to girls, he was walking home from his father's watermelon patch bordering the deep woods that ran down to the fertile bottom land when he saw a flash of color emerge from the forest. A bright-red fox, fur glistening in the sun, nose lifted to catch Michael's scent on the breeze, stood motionless and looked at him. The fox was beautiful, had a regal bearing, and it only had…three legs. It gazed at him for a long time as if they knew each other. Then two small pups emerged from the thicket and stood near their mother.

She shooed them back to safety, paused to look back one last time at Michael, and then disappeared into the dense timberland.

The fox had learned how to be whole again though she was broken. She had been left for dead, but like Michael, she had been healed and resurrected.

She was gone. Hungry logger blades had felled the wet spring-smell of the woods, and the cedar grove on the hillside by the lake, where he once harvested prime Christmas trees, was also missing from the landscapes of memory. The little gravesite he had made neath the giant oak for Katie the cat had been plowed under by "progress." He wondered where all the wild things had gone and if anyone cared about them.

The weeping willows no longer wept or swayed when heavy with caterpillar catkins, but their residuals lingered, and when he bent low to the ground, he could see the seedlings of a new world…life, stubborn life, rising again.

The old house had been torn down. It lasted longer than it should have. Daffodils and yellow bells were still blooming. The leaves on an ancient oak nodded as a breeze passed by, ruffling the feathers of a bluebird watching Michael from its perch on an old fencepost. An old tractor tire was in the yard, the boards of the smokehouse where meats once hung peeked from beneath honeysuckle vines, and a cracked butter churn hid under a green holly bush heavy with pale spring blooms. Evidence that good people once passed this way, but their rhythm and voices had drowned beneath a flood of too many todays and tomorrows that overwhelmed their yesterdays.

He could almost smell the kerosene from Pearl's old coal oil lamp, hear the buzz of the hummingbirds feeding on the buttercups, and feel the laughter coming from the kitchen, but even after a hundred years of his family walking this earth, it was no longer home, no place for interlopers to intrude or look for lost loved ones. He was already beginning to feel funereal, but the old homeplace was a touchstone, a musty-dusty-rusty jumping-off place to begin his search.

Things looked different, and he was someone else, a stranger. He wondered when he had ceased to be the child of this grove, but he had made a new map crafted from Scripture and psalms of ascent for wayward pilgrims leaving Bunyan's City of Destruction, seeking to serve, searching for the Palace Beautiful, Christ's church for the respite of pilgrims on their way to Mount Zion.

He thought he had overstayed his welcome and wondered if he could drown in shallow water. The salty water stood in his eyes like a stagnant pond left behind after a sudden storm. Still, he felt the warmth of Judy's hand on his, the whisper of trembling comfort on her lips. He could already hear the porter ringing the bell and his brethren saying, "Come in, thou blessed of the Lord."

CHAPTER THREE

"I can hear gospel songs…on Sunday morn, Saturday
nights around the radio. You can't go back again."
—*"Tupelo's Too Far," Kate Campbell*

"One does not simply walk into Mordor…evil there does
not sleep. The very air you breathe is a poisonous fume."
—The Fellowship of the Ring, *J.R.R. Tolkien*

"Christ will hold me fast."—*"He Will Hold Me Fast,"*
Ada Habershon

They left Parker Grove to visit the ancient graveyard in Tupelo where Susan rested in a field of stone. There was only time for Michael to kneel by the gravesite, softly touch the roseate headstone, and trace the letters of her name and his chiseled into the marble.

Their names were framed by two hummingbirds, silent sentinels in a hovering vigil above the words *At Peace in the Valley.* Just a moment to remember the nights after she was gone when she came to him in prison dreams, nights he pleaded, "Please stay. Don't go," nights he tossed and turned and woke to find her gone, until one day she came no more. She had left for the one place he could not follow then, but the circle was unbroken.

The first fat drops of water began to disturb Susan's ground as the heavens grumbled and growled at Judy and Michael with peals of thunder and flashes of lightning with running fingers. The wind howled, huffed and puffed, and the sun hid its face and ran its race behind a veil of darkness blowing in from the west.

Then the faucets of the heavens opened on their scramble to make it to the halfway house. The wipers were fighting a losing battle with the whipping sheets of rain when they arrived at a sort of crusty, rusty ghetto for members of the fraternity of the formerly incarcerated, men and women looking to begin again in a place of transition, a place for those on the skids.

The building looked like an island in the flood, a scummy riparian hotel situated on a hostile river with a million empty beer cans floating and bobbing like aluminum corks in the churning, boiling brown water and an armada of moccasins from nearby Town Creek slithering in squiggly lines.

The street was home to convenient package stores with dope under the counter, the shells of abandoned lounges, and collapsing motels once rented by the hour for low-rent rendezvouses. There were no trees, no bushes, and nothing green except the faded paint on nearby warehouses, where the homeless took shelter under the eaves.

Tacky, ugly, and dangerous seemed to be the theme of the area, and up the street, a logjam was forming in the soapy, rushing current. Trash and medical waste washed down the hill from the hospital. Urban blight not to be confused with urbanity.

It suddenly struck him as more alternate universe than an island. It had no structure, no credit cards, payroll deductions, insurance policies, retirement benefits, savings accounts, none of the old Green Stamps he and Susan collected, no time clocks, newspapers, mortgages, deodorants, checklists, time payments, political parties, lending libraries, television, actresses, chambers of commerce, pageants, and no sermons or Bible studies, just an artificial universe held together by duct tape and baling wire, spit and tar, greed and grime, and sin and self.

The storm had blown in from the west. A dirty gray rain came down in punishing torrents whipped by a wild wind, the kind of rain that once made old Noah build a giant Ark, but the water couldn't clean the mean streets on this side of Tupelo.

The wind took the rain and used it as a weapon to thrash the ancient building that housed "Halfway Home," a government-subcontracted house run by mercenaries and pirates on the corner of Industrial and Greene Streets. Michael peered through the monsoon that pummeled Judy's car and saw that the street sign had been altered to show the halfway house on the corner of Satan and Temptation.

A solitary man, maybe homeless, possibly a street preacher, or an angel in disguise, stood in the downpour holding a sign that said, *You are entering enemy territory. To God Be the Glory.* Over him, a neon light sputtered and flashed, a beacon light blinking what appeared to be Morse code, a survival guide from the heavenlies.

The storm thrashed about like a beast in its death throes, but it could not blow down the nondescript World War 2 structure. The building's flat roof and tar patches had pools of standing water, puddling black rain that ran off the eaves to leak inside a structure that time and urban development forgot.

There was nothing outwardly to suggest that there was any sign of life within or without the building, except for the man in the driving rain holding his sign, shaking his head and mouthing the word "Repent" and the giant, wet rats scurrying from a hole in the pavement near the front door to escape the river flooding their dens. The rats resembled creatures from a 1950s dystopian movie about mutant animals after an atomic war, so large that even starving stray cats wouldn't attempt to take them, lest predators be turned into prey.

When Judy gave him a bittersweet, tearful kiss of goodbye and pulled away, Michael dashed toward the foggy glass doors, splashing through deep puddle pools as thunder boomed, lightning flashed around him, and the raindrops seemed to ripen into something like hail. He stood just inside the steamy front doors, swaddled in uncertainty, shaking himself like a wet dog. He wiped the glass and peered out at the deluge, watching her disappearing taillights in the gloom as separation choked his full throat.

The gutters in the streets overflowed, and the drains gushed bubbling, foaming muddy water into byways that could hold no more of the flood. Though the building's roof had been gobbed and gobbed again, even tarred and feathered it seemed, the rain still seeped inside. While looking for the director's office, he almost stumbled where the bucket brigade had placed pails in strategic places to catch the liquid invading the building.

Both the building and the roads had seen better days, forgotten or afterthoughts, like the men inside the halfway house for men and women who exited the dungeons of the Federal Bureau of Prisons to be dropped off at this final step down before freedom.

Others who had left prison before Michael had warned him of the halfway stations, where they landed. Many said they felt safer in prison than in the houses where security was scarce, illicit sex between men and women was rampant, and often dangerous and mentally ill men chased residents with baseball bats.

So, here he was to see if this home was any better, and he already had the feeling he was both waiting while someone was watching in a house of horrors. He noticed the door to the women's quarters crack open ever so slightly and saw curious female eyes along the opening peering out at him, appraising and giggling.

One girl, he would guess Mexican, with big, brown eyes and dressed in shabby clothes, was pushed out by the others, followed by a cloud of bargain perfume. She gawked at him for a moment with melting eyes and said, "Hi, I'm Maria. You new here?"

"Yeah, I feel like I just swam all the way from Talladega, Alabama," he said with a smile and a sudden shiver from wet clothes.

By her English and phrasing, he guessed her to be a border town girl, a poor girl with babies to feed, offered quick, easy money to mule some drugs across the Rio Grande, and then things went sour. A closer look behind heavy makeup revealed the lines around a young face, the wear and tear of prison, abuse, and bad diet. The earthy, hot-blooded beauty he guessed she once was had been worn away by the harsh winds of misfortune. Her lower lip sagged away from her teeth and gums, giving her lips a pouty look gone bad. She was heavy and not subtle but likely a victim and harmless.

She would probably say she was not a good girl, but not a bad señorita either, a fellow traveler who wrestled with faults and flaws, knowing who and how we are but who we should be and could be. As she talked, moving from English to Spanish and back again, he caught fleeting glimpses of someone's little girl long ago, a child who peered out from behind the frosted glass of yesteryear and chances washed away in the muddy Rio Grande.

As she talked, he smelled the pungent smell of marijuana mixed with the dankness and mold of the building, stale beer, and the ammonia smell of urine that had seen one too many infections. Ashtrays in the hallway were overflowing, and open garbage cans were full of paper bags housing empty liquor bottles.

Michael's friends had written to tell him that the halfway houses they went to after their release were far more dangerous than prison. Cheap drugs and cheaper women were everywhere, things for men to fight over, and some facilities doubled as housing for the homeless and the mentally ill. The former inmates told him to protect himself and warned that corruption in these "pay to stay" transition centers was rampant, maybe even worse than the Bureau of Prisons.

Just as she discovered to her delight that his name was Michael…Michael and Marie, the ancient intercom with the squeaky speakers suddenly screeched. A metallic voice akin to those on worn-out burger takeout boxes said, "Mr. Michael Parker, report to the director's office."

"A pleasure to meet you, Maria. Thanks for the welcome," he said as she scurried back into girls' world, where the rapturous giggling of many young women began, followed by, "He's nice. "Who is he?" "He seems pretty old." "Maybe a sugar daddy."

Michael knocked on the frame around the entrance to the director's office. Her office had no door, only a sign that said *My door is always open*. The head of the privately owned facility, which contracted with the Federal Bureau of Prisons, peered at him over half-rimmed glasses perched precariously on the end of a button nose. She was a tiny black woman, skin like coffee with cream, with what Michael sensed was a deep pool of anger residing just beneath the surface. The darkness around her was a suffocating cloud, eclipsing the natural and manmade light in the room. It made Michael want to recoil, to back up a step.

"Welcome to paradise, Mr. Parker. I'm Juanita Jones. That's Director Jones to you. You're the oldest man we have here, but you'll be required to work just like the rest. I've read your file and your internet exploits. You're nobody here, nothing special anymore. You and your medals and trophies are less than nothing. You'll need to find a job, probably something menial and hard for a man with soft hands who has lived off the sweat of people of color. You will give the center our cut if you ever to get passes to visit your wife. Married in prison, weren't you? That's interesting, women marrying inmates and old ones like you at that. She must've been desperate. You probably won't need as many passes as these young bucks here. Old men just don't have the desires, the urges these little gangsters do. Isn't that true?"

All of her babbling lecture and questions were rote, incoherent, rhetorical, and designed to provoke him, but Michael just rolled with her flow, smiled, and listened as she rambled on and pored through a thick file that bore his name.

"I have this file on you, Mr. Parker. See, it has your number on it, 56447-019. Kinda like those numbers they stamped on people in the concentration camps, numbers that can't be erased. They didn't deserve it. But you…you deserved it every bit of it, didn't you, Mr. Parker?" she accused and taunted as she drummed a rapid cadence on the desk with a pencil with teeth marks on the wood.

"More than you know, Mrs. Jones. I got off easy," Michael interjected with a confessional smile and nod. The more she demeaned him, the stronger he grew. She was barreling through an imitation of life with her brakes on while he already had one foot planted in eternity.

"Uh-huh. I see that you got religion in prison. Are you just another jailhouse conversion, Mr. Parker, or you some born-again holy man out to save the world? Maybe you gonna become one of them TV preachers and cheat old ladies out of their money? Never mind. It says you started ministries at three prisons, Christian movie nights. They say you had lots of dumb followers. You plan on trying to force that mess on the people here?"

"If you permit, Mrs. Jones, and the Lord so directs me to try, certainly not to force, just to offer a free gift of life to the lost…to people who decide to follow Who I follow, not me," Michael said.

"You ain't going to be no trouble for me, are you, Mr. Parker?" she asked as she looked up from her files spread across a desktop stained by coffee and other old sources and fluids of questionable origins that Michael didn't want to think about.

"Gosh, I sure hope not," Michael said with his best boyish smile that seemed to irritate her as much as it did when he said Jesus to the demon-possessed Mrs. West at the Millington Prison Camp. Mrs. Jones mounted another assault.

"You not only the oldest man here. You the only white man. Do you have problems with black people, Mr. Parker?" she asked, dropping her smudged glasses on her desk with a dramatic flair worthy of the worst actor award at the local dinner theater.

"Mrs. Jones, I would have never survived five-and-a-half years in prison if that were the case. Bad news comes in all kinds of different packages and disguises. God lets me see only the once-born and the twice-born, not skin color," Michael said, witnessing to a drowning woman whose twisted gargoyle scowl would make a train take a dirt road.

"You so humble, so quick with the answers, aren't you? Your eyes, something about them. You look like I amuse you, that you think you're better than me," she snapped.

"No, I am no better than you or anyone else. I am the chief sinner who met a great Savior," he answered, his smiling eyes never leaving hers, which caused her to look down.

"You find yourself a job, Mr. Parker. Give me my money, make me look good, and maybe you and your new wife can hold hands or whatever it is that you do when geriatrics are alone. I can give you overnight passes, maybe a weekend, or I can keep you here for the full six months until you go under the supervision of Federal Probation agents.

"Don't give me any trouble. Just go along and get along. They told me that you were suspected of bypassing good order in the Bureau of Prisons, getting things done that no inmate should have been doing or able to do, even going against the government chaplains when it suited you, just a convict who didn't know his place," she said.

"Some chaplains were good men, Mrs. Jones. Some were only guards with crosses around their necks, putting question marks after God's Word. They weren't men of God but wolves in the midst of the flock, but that was then, and this is now. I'm just a pilgrim passing through and ready to go home to my wife and the ministry God has given me," he said.

She reared back like a woman who had saved her last load of buckshot in her shotgun and fired. "This is not your first wife, is it, Mr. Parker? That poor woman who died waiting for you, how would she feel about your new wife?" the cruel little woman sneered as she nodded up and down rapidly, a gotcha volley.

"They were best friends. She loved Judy and was maid of honor in her first wedding," Michael said through gritted teeth. His hands had become clenched fists, and he dropped them to his side and silently prayed, "My Father Who art in Heaven and here with me now."

"See Jimmy the orderly, the dummy out there eavesdropping on us. He'll find a bunk. It's just one big room here, no secrets. Don't ruffle feathers, Mr. Parker, or it could be hard on you, dangerous," she said, leaning across the desk to punctuate the warning with a wagging index finger.

"Do you have an attorney, someone who's going to stick his nose in my business and come nosing around here?" she asked.

"Yes, ma'am, there is Someone who will always come to my defense, but He comes and goes as He wills. He heals the lepers and cleanses the temple. He doesn't file suits, but He does issue judgments," Michael said as he smiled and pointed up.

With that and the sudden presence of the Holy Spirit, a sudden shudder began at her ankles, worked its way up to her face, clacked her teeth, and rolled her eyes back up into her head. At that moment, she reminded him again of Adrianna West, the terror of the Millington Camp.

She recovered and shook her head. "Well, there ain't no angels here, only devils, Mr. Parker. I hope you enjoy your time here at our hotel from hell. Dismissed!" she snapped.

Michael stopped suddenly as he walked into the large room lined with bunk beds. The devil is here, he thought. I can smell him. Someone left a door open, and he just slipped in.

As the door closed behind him, he could see Mrs. Jones jabbering away to someone in her office, but no was there but her and her demons. She was a woman who barked loudly but trembled at her guilt and the deafening ticking of the Master's clock when there was no visible accuser. Running faster and faster, the director could not outrun her own shadow, the accusing voice within her, and the judgment of God. She was a tired, leaden-muscled worldly commuter trying to catch a train that had already left the station.

CHAPTER FOUR

"Glory follows afflictions, not as the day follows the night but as the spring follows the winter; for the winter prepares the earth for the spring, so do afflictions sanctified prepare the soul for glory."—Richard Sibbes

"Time to leave something behind."—"To Leave Something Behind," Sean Rowe

"A time to be reaping, a time to be sowing, a time just for planting, a time for plowing."—"The Green Leaves of Summer," Dimitri Tiomkin

"Follow me. This is your bunk right here, pops," Jimmy said, pointing to a lofty bed in the nosebleed section of bunk beds that hugged the walls of an open room bordered by a dirty floor. Michael saw a pair of red dice and holes burned into what once was shag carpet of indeterminate color. The butts of smoked joints littered the floor.

Jimmy was tall and painfully thin with a pinched waist and a voice like fingernails on a chalkboard. Michael guessed his age at somewhere between forty-five and fifty-five. He had a long neck, like a man who had once been in traction too long or like the inmate at Millington Camp who had hung himself when no one would heed his pleas for help.

"I'm not your pop, Jimmy. My name is Michael," Michael said. He had grown tired of that overused phrase by young gangsters in prison for everyone with gray hair.

"Okay, old school," Jimmy said, putting his hands up, palms out in mock surrender while using another tired cliché.

"We just thought we'd put you up top so you'll be closer to heaven if you were to croak in your sleep," he said, laughing so hard that he gasped for breath and fell onto the lower bunk bed.

"You coming out of federal prison, huh? What'd they get you for?" he asked, wheezing like a man with a bad heart who had smoked one too many cigarettes.

"Terminal stupidity, regrets by the trainload parked on fields of broken glass. Promises someone wrote in disappearing ink. The world makes and breaks promises by the hour. I got sidetracked, diverted to the novelty shop, but I found my way back to the antique shop where nothing important ever changes," Michael said.

Jimmy coughed and hacked like Michael's precious Katie the cat once did when she had a furball.

"Yeah, man. I hear you, but I didn't get much time, not like you. I don't think I coulda done that stretch. Someone like you getting all that time, you musta made some bigshots mad. They threw the book at you," Jimmy said.

"Yeah, they locked me up and threw away the key. They threw the book at me, but a higher Authority threw another Book at me," Michael said.

"Huh? Oh, okay, I get you," Jimmy said, coughing again.

"Sorry for the wheezing. Sometimes I can't breathe too good. Someone punched me in the throat when I was young, and it messed up my voice and breathing. My father was gone, and we couldn't afford a good doctor," he said.

"Uh, I read your file while I was cleaning the director's office. We heard you was coming. Bad news travels fast. Snitches everywhere. They say you was a troublemaker in prison, maybe before prison, too, but a straight shooter. People didn't have to see which of your two faces was talking cause you only had one. That's what they say, anyway," he said.

"They say you didn't look right through people like they weren't even there. I can see you looking at me now like I'm somebody. Hope you don't mind me nosing around in your file," Jimmy said.

"No, I have no secrets. Where is everybody?" Michael asked.

"They out working, most of 'em anyway," Jimmy said.

"Why are you here in heartbreak hotel, Jimmy?" Michael asked.

"Me? Well, I just put some sedatives in my wife's coffee each morning. I wasn't trying to kill her or nothing, just slow her down and keep her out of the clubs. Her home asleep was better than nothing. At least she was near me and our boys, not them crack dealers. So, I'm just doing my time here, instead of in the big house, and I'll go home soon. She told me she wasn't mad at me and asked the judge not to be too hard on me," he said.

"That's good. Better just give her straight Folgers from now on," Michael said with a grin.

They both laughed. Jimmy wheezed, coughed some more, looked all around, and put his finger to his lip in shushing motion.

"I heard stories about you from my daddy when I was a kid. He said he met you when you was a deputy sheriff here in Lee County, a pain in the rear wannabe hero Boy Scout, he said. After he died, I heard you was the head narc when I was dealing as a kid. They said you used to travel all the time in a Winnebago from town-to-town, no home, a ghost that never slept. People swore they saw you in different towns at the same time, that pictures made of you came out blank. Other dealers told me you could catch a whisper in a whirlwind. Was all that true? Anyway, it scared me, and I quit dealing, but I was never mean like my daddy," Jimmy asked.

"Well, I may have acted heroically at times, but that didn't make me a hero, just a knight in rusty armor, clanking along, without God's full armor…maybe more heel than hero at times, a sinner in need of a Savior. I was clueless. I thought I knew everything but didn't know anything, Jimmy. I didn't even suspect anything," Michael said with a chuckle.

"People said a lot of things, then and later. Some true, most not. Don't ever take the bait, Jimmy, and start believing your own press. Doesn't matter now, but I'm glad you gave up dealing drugs," Michael said.

"They also said you told the governor back then to shove it. They say now you don't fear men because you fear God so much," Jimmy said, just bursting with admiration.

"All that was a long time ago, Jimmy. They say if you dig deep enough, you can find good in anyone, but with that governor, I'd have to say you'd probably need a backhoe," Michael said with a smile.

"A backhoe! That's a good one! You don't have to worry about me saying nothing to nobody," Jimmy said in a conspiratorial whisper so low you had to strain to hear it.

"Say nothing about what?" a guttural voice bellowed from behind them. The smell of putrid breath filled the room, like a zombie and soul stealer who'd never brushed his teeth, something that had died last week and was late for its own funeral.

CHAPTER FIVE

"God, won't somebody tell me, answer if you can...
just what is the soul of a man?"—"The Soul of a Man,"
Blind Willie Johnson

"There will come a time I will look in your eye.
You will pray to the God you've always denied."
—"Dust Bowl Dance," Mumford and Sons

"That I'm scared of heights, and here young Jimmy has put me on the top bunk where the fall would kill me if I rolled over in my sleep," Michael answered without looking back at the speaker, reverting to the days of yesteryear, the fast-on-his-feet undercover agent he once was.

Michael turned to see a young black male with dilated pupils, thick shoulders, and gleaming gold in his front teeth. He sucked on a gnawed toothpick in the corner of his mouth and had white powder near his nose. He had what appeared to be the outline of an illegal cell phone in his pocket and the bulge of a small-caliber pistol hooked under his belt and beneath his shirt.

His eyes were small compared to the size of his head, giving him a beady-eyed look, and his arms and scarred hands hung down near his knees. He wore the gangster look like a suit tailor-made for him since the day he was abandoned by his father who was abandoned by *his* father, a life buried under the rubble of generational curses.

The man dunked a big piece of chicken in a cup of hot sauce, mixed with what smelled like bourbon, as he sized up Michael, casually dripping the concoction on the tattered yellow-green carpet. He was the metaphorical poster child for this building. Nothing matched, and everything needed a coat of paint. The old structure was likely full of mold and asbestos, a flytrap to catch flies for the Lord of the Flies. The casting director in this play of horrors had typecast him in the recurring role of "Born to die young."

"Yeah, well, you just mind your own business whatever bunk you in. Hear no evil, see no evil, speak to no one of any evil, even in your prayers, your hotline to heaven. Know where I'm coming from? Dig my slanguage?" he said, slurring his crusty and profane words.

"I hear you loud and clear," Michael said, looking at Jimmy, who was shaking.

"You best forget everything here until we leave or you leave. It'd be a shame if the boys had to take an old fossil like you to the sewage pond down the road on Eason Boulevard. We call it the Dead Sea cause that's where the bodies of troublemakers are dumped. We might throw a bouquet on you before you sink and stink, but dead noses smell no roses.

"This is our territory. The police come but not back here. They scared or like the short skirts of the girls we furnish. I don't think Jesus would come here, either. The devil, though, he comes. We save a bunk and an altar for him," the man said, staring blankly at Michael and weaving to and fro. The darkness enveloping the man was suffocating, but he was not the darkness, just the aftermath of close encounters with evil.

"If you need a little pain relief, just let me know. I got a special on tequila right now. We are throwing in the worm and a woman at no extra charge. I double as the house undertaker, pimp, and doctor. Most call me Delight, but you can call me Eli for short, cause I'm the high priest of bad," he cackled maniacally, smiling like a possum that had just happened upon a dead mule, as he began to focus and eye the cross around Michael's neck.

"That's just how I roll, holy roller. Just think of me as the thorn in your side, the rock in your shoe," he said, stirring his drink with a large knife and then wiping it on Michael's slecve to test him.

Michael looked at his sleeve and at Eli, who was so oily that he looked like he was auditioning for the greased pig contest at the old Tupelo fair. Michael remembered his friends' warnings about the danger hidden along the midways of banal dens such as this.

"I got a spine of steel wrapped in barbed wire. That's why lightning strikes me. I'm bad from shin to chin," Eli said with swagger and stagger.

"I'll keep that in mind," Michael said, returning his stare, and just for a moment, Eli looked away from Michael's eyes, but that angle only accentuated the deadness, the nothingness there, and confirmed that no one was home in the earthly tent that had smoked every leaf and snorted every line.

When Eli wandered off, Michael looked at Jimmy and said, "Well, he just slobbered a bib full, didn't he? Some people just brighten up the room when they leave."

Jimmy stopped shaking and had to excuse himself for a visit to the men's room. When he returned, he told Michael that Eli and his crew were only temporary residents of the halfway house. They had violated their probation just before their time was up, and the Bureau of Prisons would not take them back for such a short term.

Jimmy said, "They're not people you want to mess with. There's no one here to help you, and you are an old man now, an old white man at that. You're not the man my daddy told me about that did all those things. The old you might as well be in the cold, cold ground. The director and her staff are afraid of Eli and his gang or paid by them. Mrs. Jones ain't rocking no boat or risking a trip to the dead sea. Eli is dealing out of this house and running girls, too. He's wild and crazy. Don't push him. Sometimes in life, there are some rings you just got to kiss. You just gotta bite your tongue and learn to like the taste of blood."

"So people keep telling me, but I must have missed that seminar. Jimmy, you said that your father told you about me. Who was your daddy?" Michael asked, changing the subject.

"My name is James 'Jimmy' Streeter, Jr.," he said, puffing out his chest and straightening his posture in what passed for pride or preparation to defend his father's honor.

"You're the Pusher's son?" Michael asked, his jaw dropping at the bridge to another time, another life.

"You remember him?" Jimmy asked excitedly.

"Yeah, I do," Michael said, remembering the brutal photos of his father's body from the parish police files near New Orleans, his outstretched hand, and stories of his dramatic conversion and rejection of a life of brutality.

"Do you know how he died? They just said they found his body near New Orleans and wouldn't tell us much else except that there wasn't much left to bury. They said my great-aunt, GAL, took care of the arrangements, and we heard it was quite a celebration, a big party on Bourbon Street," Jimmy said with a catch in his voice.

"Funny the things you remember. My father used to tell me that shooting stars were just angels flicking their cigarettes over the balconies of heaven before the Big Boss Man caught them. He and my mama had a bad history, and she blamed me.

"I remember once when he hit her right in the face with his fist. She took one step back, shook herself, and said, 'I hope that ain't all you got.' Then she hit him and lived to talk about it. Daddy said you couldn't beat her when she was sober, but you had to when she was drunk.

"He had lots of women, but I was his only son. He came to see me the night he left. Somebody, some monster out of Memphis, was chasing him, he said. I had never seen him scared before of anything, but he was scared that night," Jimmy said.

"Did he say the monster was ghostly pale?" Michael asked.

"Yeah, that was it, ghostly white, he said, so I'd know to run if I saw him. How'd you know?" Jimmy asked.

"Long story," Michael said.

"Daddy told me that my mama was the barb in his wire and the spark in his fire when times were better between them. He told me that night that I wouldn't see him anymore, but he wouldn't tell me where he was going. He was afraid the monster would torture me to find out. Then he said, 'Don't be like me, and don't marry a woman like your mama. She's the reason you're ugly.' Then he left me with her.

"Mama said I was a bad seed, his seed. I used to get up each morning and apologize for being his son, just to get it out of the way. When I was dealing and using, I was over the line. Rivals were after me. I was guzzling snakebites and injecting high-velocity speed, seeing things in the shadows, trying to convince myself I wasn't who she said I was, and wishing I had six fingers, cause that middle one was always getting me into trouble.

"I'd come to the front porch and the back one, too, but I guess she had given up all she could yield. Mama locked me out of the house when I was on the run, hungry and tired. She wouldn't let me come home or unchain the door when I pounded on it, begging for shelter and some food. 'I ain't him, Mama!' I cried, but she started praying to God to take 'this demon from my door,'" Jimmy said as he twisted his head right and left, left and right.

The tears were tracking down his face, and he was gasping for air.

"My health wasn't good. The days were short, and my own mama was praying me into hell, but she really left me before she birthed me. I just quit fighting. I just curled up in the fertile position on her doorstep, woke up in my own vomit, and ain't never been back.

"I been so low I was sitting on a dime and swinging my shoeless feet. There are days when I think God is watching me but others when I wonder if I even exist. I smell the scent of death like cheap perfume. Is there hope for a homeless mutt like me, mister?" he asked, his voice deepening as he looked at the floor.

"The fertile position?" Michael asked to bring him out of his despair.

"You know, like babies," Jimmy said.

"I know this, Jimmy. Your father proved that it is never too late, that we serve a God of second chances. People who were not saved heard that story and surrendered to Christ because of him. They figured if God could wash him clean, there might be hope for them, too. The rest of it was between him and the Lord, just as it is between you and Christ now. Sometimes we ride horses that have been dead for years and find out one day that it's time to dismount. You're not an orphan, Jimmy. You have a wife and children and a heavenly Father who loves you," Michael said.

At that moment, men began to return to their bunks, just as Jimmy wiped away the hot tears that burned furrows into his cheeks. The men ran the gamut: tall and gangly, muscular and stocky, and jittery and evasive, none maintaining eye contact, except for one young pup who everyone called Judas the snitch. Jimmy said he stayed one step ahead of death and disaster by squealing on everyone about everything, true or not.

Jimmy wiped his eyes, shook Michael's hand, and said, "Thank you, sir. Sleep with one eye open here, Mr. Michael, and keep your wallet on a chain. These boys only know their father below, and the staff never comes back here to brave the flames or breathe the fumes in these satanic mills. I heard so much about the devil that I look under my bed every night to see if he's hiding there. Mr. Michael, if all we got is friends like these, who needs enemas."

Michael smiled and thanked him.

In the distance, Michael heard the pant and sigh of a train at the nearby railroad crossing on Eason and the rumble of a diesel truck likely bringing paper and barrels of ink to the *Daily Journal* on Green Street, maybe to print headlines about more bodies found in the sewage pond down by Town Creek, the pond locals called the dead sea.

The air-conditioning unit suddenly shuddered and died with a final shushing hiss. With the passing of the storm, the thick Mississippi heat and humidity smothered the corner of "Satan and Temptation Streets" like a soggy wet blanket. The weight of the air seemed to seep into the marrow of Michael's bones, while the ghost of the Burlington and Santa Fe brakeman carried his lantern through the darkness of night flagging down slow trains to nowhere and old Greyhound buses trying to beat the warning lights and cross his rails.

CHAPTER SIX

"Behold, I send you forth as sheep in the midst of wolves:
be ye therefore wise as serpents, and harmless as doves."
—Matthew 10:16

"Woman shined the apple, and the man had to take a bite.
Well, they woke up naked with a big headache, done in by a
slippery snake. It's been that way since the git go."
—"Git Go," Bill Joe Shaver

The first night was mostly uneventful. Michael tried the showers and found them to be little more than a rusty trickle. He looked out a high window on the slanted roof over the shower area and saw the shimmering moonlight filtering through the passing clouds. He thought that it was the same moon over Okaloosa Island, but he didn't think about it too long.

Some men slipped out of the female quarters, others rolled dice in the far corner of the room, and a card game that began at midnight went on into the wee hours. Michael heard Eli making drug deals on his illegal phone and, at one point, putting up his girls as collateral in his poker games, but there was no sign of a staffer.

Michael noticed at one point in a game of five-card stud, Eli just turned all of his cards face up, and though he had nothing, the members of his gang kept their cards face down, threw up their hands, pursed their lips, and said, "You got us again, Delight."

No feet were put down, and no challenge was offered, though all were armed and, from what Jimmy said, not shy about using them. A big lean guy named Darrius, who seemed so close to rebellion and to bursting at the seams, stewed like a pot over an open fire and kept mentioning his mother and God frequently as he stomped around the room, patting the pistol in his back pocket. His rage was eventually absorbed into the ether of lost souls.

The moon was full, and this carnal room and carnival midway was dripping with mood and atmosphere in a shaky and shacky waystation. It was a reminder to Michael to always drink upstream from a feral herd like these motherless wild ones, never corner something or someone meaner than you, plow around the stump if you can, and remember that silence is sometimes the best answer.

Michael always had trouble with that last one, so he rolled over, put in his earbuds, and listened to *Songs in the Night* out of Chicago's Moody Church and radio preachers talking about the men who cast lots for the clothes of Jesus.

He dreamed he was on the phone with Mrs. Clarece Collins, the wife of MBN Director John Edward Collins. She had called him in Augusta one night, long after the MBN days and long before prison, and told him she had terminal cancer. She said she just wanted to talk to him because he "had always been so faithful and loyal" to her and Mr. Collins. She told Michael that people were worried for her because she had not been able to cry since she got the news.

"Isn't that silly?" she asked with a laugh that deteriorated into a muffled snuffling. Then she began to cry, then to weep and sob as the dam broke and a river of emotion flowed down into her valley of death.

It was before the Lord had subdued Michael, and he listened and was kind to her, but he did not have the words of comfort that the Comforter would later plant in his heart. He thought the words but didn't know how to release them in the name of Christ, though she had chosen him to share her grief and fear and felt safe to cry with him. It was the last time they talked before her death.

He awakened in this strange new environment with the bitter taste of failure and regret on his lips and a feeling that sometime in the night he had heard the roar of a high-combustion engine, squealing tires, passing screams of wailing sirens that got louder and louder and then faded away from no-man's land. There were angry voices, too, some female, all outside the front door of this hybrid reformatory and breeding ground for crime.

Morning light filled the room, and everyone was gone but Michael, Jimmy, who came in to clean, and Eli, who was dead drunk and snoring like a freight train. His .32 caliber pistol had fallen out of his pocket, and Michael saw that the safety was off on a hair trigger, and all of his pockets were full of cash, bills that were wet, soiled, and crumpled.

Michael looked at the cash like a fastidious raccoon with OCD. Even if he had wanted to, there was not enough Purell in the world for Michael to have touched that germ-ridden and devil-stained currency. Eli seemed exempt from all of the house rules, and no one took away his deadly toys or shipped him to a secure facility like a county jail.

"Better get to the kitchen before it's all gone. If you hurry, you might meet Willie, the big night manager you never see. Never trust him. He's not a bad man, but he is a weak dude who sees nothing but tells the director everything about the powder keg they are sitting on. Keeping the beds full is what matters to them, keeping those federal checks coming, but any threat he might make to anyone is nothing more than a kiss from a mosquito. He is always shadowboxing and losing," Jimmy said quietly.

Jimmy moved to whisper conspiratorially in his ear and said, "I'm going up in a bit to feed my birds some leftovers."

"Birds, here? I used to feed birds. Where are they?" Michael asked.

"They're on the roof, and I go up through a secret ladder in the utility room. They are homing pigeons, and I tie notes to my babies, and they take them to my wife and kids at our trailer near Corinth when I can't see them. They send them back with notes, too," he said.

"Jimmy, you're like Noah sending out doves to look for land and life after the flood. You never cease to amaze me," Michael said.

Jimmy looked pleased but then frowned and asked, "He's the guy with the big boat, right?"

***

Michael went to breakfast, such as it was. The garbage cans were overflowing, and he could hear the old refrigerator clinking and struggling to keep cold stuff lukewarm. Maria and a few other residents were milling about. The air unit was still out, and someone had hooked up a small oscillating fan that only stirred the heat, dust, and smell of old food. It hummed along its plodding path in a sweeping rhythm and labored left and right, trying in vain to dry the sweat on the diners, who fanned themselves like summer congregations under the tents of old country revivals.

Some were matronly, slightly mustached, and hadn't been in the sunlight for a long time. Reentry would be hard for them with family and friends gone since Jimmy Carter was in the White House. Other women with uncertain, listless eyes spoke to him just as the fan blew their breath in his direction. It reminded him of blind dates as a teenager when kissing a girl often required holding your breath.

A big guy with a beefy face, the color of mahogany, was grabbing some freebies before he left for home after his shift.

He looked up at Michael with a broad smile and said, "Ah, Mr. Parker, isn't it? Welcome aboard! I'm Willie Jones. Let me know if I can help you with any problems on the night shift!" His jocularity fell short and seemed contrived, wooden, and clumsy, like some prison guards and other government bureaucrats Michael had met who said they were just there to help.

As he walked away, Maria said Willie manned the all-night shift up front and conveniently disappeared when the gangs made their late-night runs. She began to paint a picture of a sprawling soap opera of life in the halfway house, a rancid stew of whispered intrigue, betrayals, and the guests in this "tourist trap" who had already taken up where they left off before prison.

She said when Willie disappeared, she and other women went outside to smoke, play music, dance, and sometimes walk to the nearest convenience store to buy ice cream. She said the director ate pills like candy, maybe speed. Maria said there were cameras that the home office could monitor, but they were disabled when the real action started, and the live feed and the backup tapes started snowing just as the curtain went up on this nocturnal cardboard stage.

Maria told him she had saved some Pop Tarts for him if he was hungry. She brought his grape Pop Tarts, almost soured milk, and imitation orange juice to his table to sit with him, along with a hunk of cheddar cheese that looked as if it had crawled onto the plate by itself. He ate by faith, not by sight.

She began to tell him her story, women's facilities where she'd been confined, the good and bad of each experience. Maria said that she would go to bed on the long prison nights with a razor she had stolen and kept close to her to fight off unwanted advances of guards and the bull dykes who tried to overpower her until one night she marked a woman with her blade that left a scar that let others know that her bunk was not a place to tarry.

By accident or design, her knees bumped his under the narrow table and lingered too long. She told Michael that she would spread her long, dark tresses across her pillow and bosom and dream of someone, a knight and hero, maybe the archangel Michael, who would come to rescue her. She smiled shyly after her story, and her eyes floated on a sea of fireflies, flowers, and fiddles. She smelled soapy and sweet and heaven was still in her eyes, dreaming of a better life to come, standing in the shadow of her real Savior, and occupying a space she had created between heaven and hell to wait for Him or His emissary. Hope and prayer were the wine of a dreamer on cold winter nights when she built snow castles in her personal hell.

"What are you going to do today?" Maria asked.

"Well, I have an old friend who might give me a temporary job, anything to get me home sooner. I think I'll ask for a pass, grab the taxi, or get Judy to take me there," he said.

"That's your wife who dropped you off?" she asked.

"Yes," Michael said.

"Are you happy? Do you love her?" she asked shyly.

"Yes, I do. She makes my sun come up every day. I'm ready to go home and get about the business of my Heavenly Father," he said.

"All I want is someone to tell me they love me, even if they don't mean it. That's not too much to ask, is it?" Maria asked with a laugh that was a cross between a giggle and a sob, as her hands twisted and knotted and clawed at her gnawed nails.

"No, it's not," he said.

She shrugged and said, "I think they're investigating you. They don't like you very much. You might want to be very careful while you're here."

He thanked her, and as he turned to leave, she began to hum an old tune, whisper-singing a lament from long ago by Blind Willie Johnson, a song that Michael knew.

"What's that, Maria, and where did someone as young as you pick that up?" Michael asked.

"An old black woman I did time with used to sing it all the time, and it stuck like flypaper to my mind and just wormed its way into my heart, I guess," she said.

"Well, I like it, and you sing it with feeling and reverence," he said.

As he walked away, he heard her singing it louder and with genuine sorrow, just as it had been written, just as she had learned it and lived it.

Won't somebody tell me, answer if you can
Won't somebody tell me, tell me what is the soul of a man?
I reads the Bible often, I tries to read it right
As far as I could understand, a man is more than his mind.
When Christ taught in the temple, the people all stood amazed
Was teaching the lawyers and the doctors
How to raise a man from the grave
Won't somebody tell me, answer if you can
Won't somebody tell me, tell me what is the soul of a man?

When Michael looked back, she was crying, and her carefully applied makeup had stained her face and lashes in the blackness of mascara and the mixed hues of powdered magic that no longer concealed but revealed.

CHAPTER SEVEN

*"Now we wake up with our memory and fix our gazes on
that which was; whispering sweetness, which once coursed
through us, sits silently beside us…"*—Uncollected Poems,
Rainer Maria Rilke

*"Some 2,000 years ago, God planted a tree east of
Eden for the healing of the nations."*—Canon Theologian
of the Bible Belt

Michael signed out for permission to seek temporary
employment and decided to catch a taxi. The rain had stopped, and
the waters had receded as if Moses had walked through the area
with his staff. The gutters were full of trash turned to paste, and a
scum line from the flood marked the high-water mark on the
center's entrance. Michael paused and thought of the metaphors,
scum and scandal.

Some of Eli's troops leaned against the front of the building,
barefooted in the sludge that looked like a cross between peanut
butter and melted fudge. Some were nodding, and some were hung
over, but they were skilled agents servicing customers driving up
in rides with lighted wheel spokes and rap booming from the
speakers. Some came in expensive cars, the rear windows bearing
Ole Miss and Mississippi State emblems.

They were all there for the quick exchange of drugs for cash,
but the hirelings had a thinly chained volatility as subtle as a
clenched fist. They bobbed their heads in recognition at Michael,
and some almost showed flashes of toothless smiles until a swarm
of horsefly-sized mosquitoes, likely scooped up in a swamp and
deposited by the tornadic storm, swarmed the drug traffickers as
they swatted wildly and ran for cover inside.

Michael squinted into the bright lemon sun and rubbed his dry
eyes with the knuckles of his hands. He listened as the sun's hot

fist sizzled the pavement, making the fresh roof tar spit and split. He took a deep breath of freedom or this facsimile thereof, thought of bright days when the sun danced like diamonds on the Gulf in places like Okaloosa Island, Cedar Key, and the pass at Destin. He was ready to find a quick path home to get far away from a place where he could not only sense but taste the danger.

The local taxi of sorts reminded him of the one in *Escape From New York*, and the old lady driver was full of stories and eager to talk. She wore a bad lopsided wig and looked like wrinkled dark chocolate. She had a scar at the corner of her mouth that looked like a botched surgery after an accident or an attack. Michael thought it was likely an old prison incident, followed by surgery by BOP "doctors" who got their degrees from third-world diploma mills.

He liked Shirley immediately, except for her high-pitched voice. It sounded like a nesting eagle squawking at her mate for bringing her and the kids a small perch when they needed a big bass to feed a growing family. Shirley was overweight and said she was a type two diabetic. She was a church lady who loved to talk about her good works, her sugar problem, and the sweetness of the Lord, which didn't bother her sugar levels at all. Michael didn't mind that, but that voice.

"Where you going, honey, and how long did Godzilla give you?" she asked.

They both laughed. He found her laugh much more pleasing than her regular voice.

"I have three hours to go to the Allied Collection Agency. My friend owns it and a park near it, I'm told," he said.

Shirley said, "Well, honey, if you got any extra money, we got time to drive by the dairy bar and get you a chocolate milkshake to make sure you are strong when you see him. I bet you ain't had one of them in a long time. Am I right?"

Suddenly Michael didn't mind the pitch of her voice at all. In fact, he thought she must be an angel who had just screamed at the devil until she strained her vocal cords. He could already taste the milkshake.

"I've heard that there are actually some folks who don't like chocolate shakes, Shirley. I don't trust them, probably terrorists, serial killers, or foreign saboteurs, maybe agents of the devil. We'd better go on down to the dairy bar and make sure some of those folks are not there, contemplating mischief," he said.

After he had consumed not one but two chocolate shakes and also bought her one, they drove out near the airport where he used to land when he flew home from Washington when he was in the FBI. It was near the collection agency center where a large tree was entangled by what he used to call a strangle vine.

A flock of ring-billed gulls circled over the top of the building like a band of angels on a Maranatha morning. When he got out of the taxi, the voices of agitated bill collectors spilled out of the main call center where dozens collected bad debts for creditors. Loud and stern, rising and falling, these preachers of debt salvation offered one last "or else" chance to their flock of tardy tithers.

A lady showed him to the office of the owner, Don Franks. Time had left its mark on both men. Don's hair was mostly gone except for white tufts sitting over each ear, and there were more lines around his eyes and brow than Michael remembered. He wore a white knit shirt against a golden golf tan, and light leaking in through the shutters on his window bestowed a sort of halo effect around his forehead.

Don lifted a slow hand of greeting, and they shook hands. There was an understandable awkwardness and distance at first, a narrowing of the time between then and now. There was a brief recalculation of water under and over the bridge of life, a futile search for the men they once were and the protocol for this strange reunion of prodigals.

"It's been a long time, Don," Michael said as he sat down a bit too heavily in the big chair across from him, sinking into the first real chair Michael had sat in since they locked him away.

"A lifetime, Michael," he said, leaning back in his chair, then forward and back again, as the chair cushion sighed and shushed.

"Who would've thought we'd meet again under these circumstances?" Michael offered.

Old times and tall tales were tossed around, and both agreed that this moment was a long, circuitous route to a reunion of friends who were likely never to meet again. When Michael left Greenwood and collections for Bell in North Mississippi, Dan's office was in a different location then and much smaller. He had done well and owned a park that introduced school children to animals they would likely never see without his animal refuge.

The reminiscing had a thin edge of denial, of not knowing where to go, what bridges between then and now needed to be crossed, and how to cross them. In the middle of it all, an awkward silence intruded now and then. Both bore scars and memories of failures.

Michael's failures were rooted in the "who wins" image he once stared at for hours, a hypnotic fatal attraction to what he perceived to be a damsel in distress. Unmasked, it was but a pale Lilith, a snarling thing some try to call love. Treachery, coarseness, Pandora's box, rationalizations, and complications followed. Then came the "thumbs down" people in the coliseum who demand to be amused by your life, those who die without knowing that gargoyles guard the grotesqueries of life.

As they talked, they revealed permanent scars, the real struggle to try and move on, a feeling of losing something very special but finding something they had never known. For a while, Michael saw through his eyes and, in turn, was able to view his own journey in a new light, a new dimension in the reflection of Don's little, and not so little, ups and downs. Old doors were opened that had been bolted shut for a long time, and the sunshine poured in.

"I've written a book about my time in drug enforcement, and people who've read it seem to like it. I will try to sell it to someone, maybe go to Hollywood. Who knows?" Michael chuckled.

"People who knew me a long time think I could probably play the godfather. Thinking about those days would curl my hair if I had any left," Don said with the first easy smile to soften his countenance.

It was then that Michael saw the eyes of the old Don, the one he knew officially but not personally, who was a part of the garden of his life planted long ago and about to bloom this day, just as God planned.

"So, your book is about crime then, the days in the Bureau of Narcotics?" Dan asked.

"Yes and no. It's that, growing up in Mississippi, Bell, politics and more but really about one man's journey to God," Michael said.

Don leaned forward, elbows on his desk, hands clasped, and suddenly the distance between them narrowed, melted by a sudden warmth and twisting of his heart as his testimony came rushing to shore on a sea of tears, on a roar of pain, regret, and redemption.

"Life has many mud puddles, Michael, and I've stepped in more than a few, but the path is still straight, and the gate is still narrow, isn't it?" he asked, an emotional hiccup punctuating his testimony.

"Our lives have been a series of second chances, Don, and where we are going, there is no darkness but God's Light, the Lamp of Christ, and no more crosses to bear," Michael answered.

They both had found Christ, and the tears flowed from both sides of his massive desk in a celebration and sharing of just how close they had come to being lost forever, rescued before the big door slammed on second chances.

As they talked, the past seemed to drift far out to sea, things lost and thrown away. Michael could see it all leave and hear the sound of the surf just as he did when he put the big shell to his ear as a child in Florida. He could see the outline of the hills of tomorrow, the future. This place of reunion was a waystation Michael knew he was destined to visit.

"I appreciate you seeing me, Don," Michael said, reaching across the desk to shake his hand.

"So, you need a job for a while?" Don asked.

"Yes, I hate to ask, but if I'm to get home to Judy anytime soon, that's the rules down at Halfway Home, or 'Halfway to Hell,' as we call it," Michael said.

Don laughed and said, "I think we can use you to work some new clients for us. You know a lot of people.

"What's your plan after you get out of there?" Don asked.

"To tell people about Him. To show them my redeemed life that they might want to meet my Redeemer," Michael said.

After they had some fresh tea, the house wine of the South, they parted with a handshake that evolved into an awkward man hug, and when Michael looked back, he saw his friend wiping his eyes and blowing his nose.

Way back in yesteryear, Michael thought they both knew something was wrong with the script of life, that life was more than just waiting for death. The world where they lived was broken, and there were people or angels in adjoining rooms whispering secrets, but the prodigals couldn't quite get it. They didn't know how to fix it until they walked down parallel potholed paths and met Christ.

As Michael stepped outside, his clanking taxi with the squealing fan belt pulled up. His driver smiled a crooked smile that tickled her right ear as he gave Shirley a thumbs-up.

He saw an old man the color of cinnamon with a head full of silver hair at the base of the giant tree, hacking away at the strangle vine that would one day choke the ancient tree and kill it. The sun reflected off his shears, giving his garden tools what seemed more of an electrical charge than a reflective glow.

"Glad to see you are trying to save that big old tree. Are you winning or the vine?" Michael asked with a grin.

The old man looked up, squinted in the bright sun, and said, "These vines just grow and grow like the sin that gets all tangled up in your roots and branches, and before you know it, the tree of your life is lost, and you've been cut down and tossed in the furnace. Every whack at it I take, I just pretend it's the devil himself I'm rebuking and beating back."

Just then, a mournful heron passed over them with a deep, rich basso profundo croak that sounded like…Amen!

Someone said no matter how many times you visit the past, there's nothing new to see, but Michael knew they were wrong. The past can't be reversed, but relationships can be redeemed, and it can be a fertile field for an evangelist and a place of communion, a place for the Lord to show you things you just couldn't grasp then.

The halfway house had the smell of death, what some called the death stink that wouldn't wash off, but here, at the foot of the old tree that strained toward heaven and in Don's eyes, Michael saw the promise of life and resurrection.

CHAPTER EIGHT

"Rain slowly slides down the glass as if the night is crying."—*"Trace," Patricia Cornwell*

"If I speak in the tongue of men or of angels, but do not have charity, I am only a sounding brass or clanging cymbal."—*1 Corinthians 13:1*

When Shirley dropped Michael off at the halfway house, she adjusted her dentures, smiled, and said, "Son, you've had a big day. You saw an old friend, got a job, and had some good milkshakes. I think the hand of God is on you, but you are pasty pale, as white as buttermilk. I'm gonna get you a coupon for a free session at the local tanning bed parlor."

"Thanks, Shirley. Prison will do that to you. That might be a good title for my book. I could call it *A Ghostly Shade of Pale*," Michael said as he slammed the taxi door.

"You skinny, too. We got to fatten you up. By the way, if there's tire skid marks on the lot at Walmart, you can match them to my taxi's tires. There's no need to call *CSI* or *Criminal Minds*. Competition for fares is stiff down there, and I have to do a little wheelie or two now and then to beat the other taxis," she said as she smiled wryly and began to drive away.

Michael watched her leave, shook his head, and smiled. She was genuine, no pretense, a rare treasure in these times.

Now that he had the required job, Michael was anxious to paddle around this logjam he found himself in and get on with life and his ministry. The protestor/street preacher he had seen when he first arrived at the halfway house was back. This time he held a sign that said *Souls for sale here.* He nodded at Michael as he passed and said, "The Lord is with you, Michael Parker. Let your trumpet sound."

Michael stopped and turned to look back at him, but he was gone. Only his placard remained, leaned against the building as if to keep it from collapsing or to topple it like Samson.

The air was off again when he stopped by the director's office. It was always the same. You wait to be invited into a place where only horrible things will happen and run the gauntlet in a room where the residuals of other victims still linger in the stale hot air like spirits trapped between the hereafter and the nasty now-and-now.

Juanita Jones looked up at him, mouth open, her pink tongue lolling like a panting dog in the Southern summer heat. Her lips were chapped and bleeding. She narrowed her dull, lightless eyes and wrinkled her nose like he was a skunk that had just moved his entire family under her front porch, tails all raised to spray on her parade. He saw what he had thought was just garden-variety meanness but now reeked of madness, and he smelled what he guessed was the odor of liquid courage framing her slurred words.

"Whhat?" she asked, slurring her words.

"I got the job and will start tomorrow," Michael said.

"It's just so easy for you, isn't it?" she snarled, daggers in her eyes.

"I just go where the Lord sends me," Michael said, ignoring her baited barb.

"Well, He's not in charge here. I am, and He never answers me when I ask is there anybody up there. Make sure you pay me on time every day you are paid, and maybe we'll see about some weekend passes after you've been here a few months," she snapped, swatting at something near her face that was not there.

"A few months?" he asked.

"Maybe, maybe not. I have many considerations. My bed count brings in more money from the federal government. Every night you sleep on my cot, you put money in my pocket. So, it's a socko-boffo, better-than-even-money bet that I take my cut of your wages and also keep you here in my little government-funded anthill as long as I can. I ain't going back to working the graveyard shift at the Chickasaw jail. You do understand economics, don't you, college boy?" she said.

Michael looked at her and was reminded why Noah, except for his family, only let animals on the Ark, not humans or facsimiles. She had no center, no core, and no truth.

He walked toward the common area, his hope of going home to Judy deflated.

Jimmy called to him from his bunk.

"Hey, man. No luck on the job?" he asked.

"No, I got the job, but I don't have favor with the director, it seems," he said.

"That's her. Hell on heels, we call her. She don't like you too much, and she's scared of the thugs in here right now. She gonna coddle them like she was their fairy godmother until they're gone. If you're gonna stay here for the six months, you best be careful. You don't know them like I do. If you interfere with them, you will be stepping on the devil's toes. The fact that you're a Christian, a man of God, won't keep a knife from slipping into your throat if they decide to put one there. You are the only one who's been nice to me, and I don't want to see you hurt."

"I appreciate the concern, but a great spiritual war is raging, and neutrality is not possible. I'm late to the front now, and I can hear the blare of the bugles and the roar of the congregation of saints. So, I can't be stuck here in this potato-sack race, tethered to this thorn tree," Michael said.

After calling Judy with the news, he settled in with an old book by John D. MacDonald. He dozed in and out, lulled by the rhythm of a drizzling rain on the roof, the shushing sounds of waters in the tin gutters, and the rumble of distant thunder. He had wanted to stay awake to drink in this circus of the damned under Juanita's big top, replete with clowns, knife throwers, truth jugglers, and fire breathers.

Michael was startled awake when he heard what sounded like whimpering coming from the bathroom/shower area. The main room was empty, except for Jimmy, when Michael sat up on his bed, looked around, and stood up.

"Where you going?" Jimmy asked.

"To the bathroom," Michael said.

"No, don't go in there yet, Mike," Jimmy said frantically.

When Michael entered the men's bathroom, he was surprised to see a girl, a shade darker than amber and no more than fifteen, sitting on a commode. She was holding an empty mason jar and wearing a t-shirt that said *Los Angeles, City of Angels*.

She didn't look up when he walked up to her. She was hunched over and sobbing. Her eyes were puffy and shadowed with weariness, and there were bruises on her neck. She was disheveled. Her blouse had been torn, and her skirt was soiled. She wore a tiny cross of sorts around her neck, possibly a hoodoo charm made from rosebuds dipped in honey, a decoration maybe or a faith healer's imitation made in China, a fortune teller's last-ditch potion, a tincture of hope, a "holy" horseshoe or talisman that up to now hadn't worked for her.

She had all the signs of a lost lamb trying to figure out how she got in this rut and on this merry-go-round, a gypsy pup chasing its tail, a sinner looking for a place to turn herself in, someone to hear her confession and her pledge of "I swear I ain't gonna do this no more."

He could almost see the vulture of death perched above her, hear the rustle of the wings, the creaking of the lid on her coffin. Somewhere outside, a hound straight out of *The Hound of the Baskervilles* howled sorrowful lamentations, and an owl asked, "Who, who?"

She was someone who had been turned away by those who declared there was no more room in their inns. She had worn out her welcome, only the lion's den remained when the bad tricks wore thin, and the choirs were already gathering to sing over her bones. Her life was hanging by a thread attached to a rusty nail.

"Honey, are you all right?" Michael asked.

She looked up at him with blank pools of brown and said, "Mister, I can't anymore."

"What's your name, honey?" he asked.

"Candace," she said meekly.

"Candace?" he asked.

"My mama said it was something from the Bible, a queen," she said proudly.

"She was right, Candace. The Apostle Phillip met one of her eunuchs and converted him to Christianity," Michael said.

He knew it also meant pure and innocent, but she had long ago lost her innocence. It had departed many times, but it could be resurrected.

Michael squeezed tears out of his eyes and words out of his heart as he took her hand and prayed a petition of mercy over a drowning soul, a lost lamb going down for the third and last time.

Through her gasping sobs, he learned she was a runaway, taken in and trafficked by Eli. He gave her to his boys as payment for services rendered in his drug cartel. They were supposed to pay her a nominal amount, but each one told her that the next one would pay, and no one ever did.

So, she just sat there with her empty jar they were supposed to fill, her jar of last chances. She was living out of her old rattletrap car and had planned to use the money to go on the run, to get as far away from Boss Eli and her old self as she could before they missed her, maybe go home to Mama.

"It was my last chance," she said.

The light was bright and garish in the room, and she tried to cover herself and her sin, but no darkness could hide her shame.

"Candace, do you know who Jesus is?" Michael asked.

She nodded and said, "I know, Mister, but He wouldn't want to know me."

"He knows everything about you and loves you and me still," Michael said, swallowing hard.

She began to cry again.

"Do you repent of your sins, Candace? Do you accept Christ as your Lord and Savior?" Michael asked.

"Yes, yes, I do," she said.

Michael breathed deeply and sighed at sorrow.

"Candace, just freshen up and let me borrow your jar. I'll be back in a minute," Michael said.

When Michael walked out into the main room, Jimmy was still alone. He looked at Michael and said, "There ain't any heroes anymore, Mike. You too old now to be messing with killers. She is trash. Why risk your life for her? Look at what they did to Jesus when He made trouble."

"Jimmy, it's because of what they did to Him and what He did for me. The shadow of the cross rises up to meet me," Michael said as he walked outside.

No one was at the front desk. The gang was all outside except for Eli. The rain had stopped, and they were sitting on the hoods of their cars and grew quiet when he walked out the front door. They had the look of the creatures under the rotten tree trunks and rocks that Michael turned over in the deep woods of Parker Grove. When the light hit them, they hurried and scurried for cover. Those creatures and these had photophobia, a fear of the light.

The thought crossed his mind that he might be preparing to sing Psalms to dead horses, but he could feel that Darrius was almost ready to make his move against Eli, to assert his authority over the men who had grown tired of Boss Eli, as he had, but were afraid to make a move against him. He just needed a nudge.

Michael walked over to him, and his intense eyes were dangerous, boiling cauldrons of inky blackness. The others were mindlessly dangerous, but he was cheek to jowl with darkness, a walking crime scene, crouching and waiting until men let their guard down.

"Man, this is a mess. The girl's family is about to get involved. Feds will be here by sunup, and everyone will be charged, separated, and shipped to some facility in the Bureau of Prisons. Maybe it was all a big misunderstanding or a joke about the payment that got out of hand. Maybe you thought one of you would pick up the tab, but something went wrong, and someone dropped the ball. I don't know, but you need to do the right thing and pay her what you contracted for, or things are gonna go south in a hurry," Michael said.

"I figure Eli won't be too happy about all of this attention if she talks to someone. So, I'm going to pass this big old jar around and let's see how full we can make it. I'll start with my own donation," Michael said.

He put in all he had and passed the jar to Darrius, the leader in waiting, who looked at the jar, then at Michael. "I think your halo has gotten too tight, Grandpa, and just cut off the blood flow to your brain to come out here like this, but you do make sense. She's not worth the trouble it could cause, and Eli should never have set it up this way and put us all in danger. So, I'm putting in my money. It's time. Some changes got to be made around here. Some respect is due," he said.

"Y'all hear me?" Darrius snarled.

One by one they stepped up with contributions. Some were a little light until Darrius glared at them. Soon, the big jar was overflowing with green.

"Will this do, old man?" Darrius asked, handing the jar to Michael.

"I think it'll do just fine. I'll take care of it," Michael answered.

Just as Michael took the jar and turned to go back in, he saw Judas slip into the night around the corner of the building. Gone to tattle to Eli.

Candace had washed her face and put on a fresh top and pants, courtesy of Jimmy. There was a hint of soap and a breath of cheap perfume in the stale air that the noisy old air conditioner was slowly stirring, and she was gulping down some cold tea, also courtesy of Jimmy. Her eyes went wide when Candace saw the jar. She was scared, but she walked outside with him to find that everyone had left, and the only sound was the buzzing of a neon on the fritz.

"Candace, you take that money and give up this life because it's no life at all. You got a church? Find one if you don't. Get on down there and get baptized. Let the Lord wash your sins away.

"I've prayed for you. It is on you. These guys won't bother you anymore because their father can't cross the blood line Christ gave to us when He poured His soul in the sin offering," Michael said.

She opened her car door, looked back at him and asked, "Who are you? Are you an angel?"

"No, just a sinner saved by grace, but the Lamb knows where you are. He has settled your debts and mine out of court," Michael said.

He smiled and said, "God never leaves a cleansed, surrendered vessel unused. He has plans for you."

She started to say He couldn't use someone like her, but Michael held up his right hand in an "I solemnly swear" pose, smiled, and said, "These things come to me straight from headquarters under sealed orders. Honest!"

She returned his smile and gave Michael a long, watery, tender-eyed stare. She opened her car door and sat in her car a full minute with her hands and head on her steering wheel as she wept once more.

The lingering clouds from the storm parted, and Michael watched her taillights begin to fade into the starry night. Her little car sputtered, coughed, clanked, and belched black oil by the quart. It had seventy horsepower, and half of them were dead.

On her bumper was a faded sticker: *Honk if you love Jesus.* The last thing Michael heard was music from an ancient cassette player in her car. It was Mahalia Jackson singing, "Lord, don't move that mountain, give me the strength to climb."

Suddenly, the whole place seemed deserted. If the women were in their unit, they were very quiet. The whole place had the air of a mortuary or maybe a tomb where the stone had been rolled away for one lost lamb, maybe also the lull before a different kind of storm.

CHAPTER NINE

"I trembled when he laid me out. 'You won't feel a thing,'
he said, 'when you go down. Nothing gonna wake you
now.' If you ever walk this way, come and find me, lying in
the bed I made."—"Flowers," Hadestown

"Troublesome waters much blacker than night are
hiding from view of the harbor's bright lights…
I cried to my Savior, 'Have mercy on me.'"—
"Troublesome Waters," Johnny Cash

"When you feel alone on your journey, He will see you
through."—"He Will See You Through," Dirk Powell

Michael sat on his bed and read from a tiny, tattered Bible Jimmy left there. It was open to Revelation 12:11. "They overcame him by the blood of the Lamb and the word of their testimony. They loved their lives unto the death."

He looked around to find Jimmy, but he was gone. He finally fell asleep, an uneasy surrender, no sentinels posted. Dreams consumed Michael; dreams drenched with vagabond vistas on a narcotic night.

Politicians and soul gamblers he had known from Atlanta to Washington reached for him with bony fingers from fiery, eternal prisons and asked him for forgiveness, a drop of water, and a key to the oven door. They promised they never meant any of it. Honest.

"No hard feelings. Nothing personal, you know? Every life has its ups and downs, don't they? Tell Jesus that we're sorry," they said as they banged their tin cups against the molten doors to their cells and tried in vain to wet their cracked lips and summon up spit to swallow.

He saw traps set for the gullible, baited with tasty temptations, and some pulpits were writing a blank check to government tyranny and calling it Romans 13. The slippery snakes-in-the-grass offered up the sour fruit of a social gospel and asked, "Did God really say?"

And the echo chamber heard them and said Amen to the trendy devolution, which was more than the run-of-the-mill moral corruption and meanness of fallen men. It was a compounded demonism that preached hobnobbing with Sodom and getting chummy with Gomorrah to show them the light, but they weren't turning on the lights, just getting the sheep used to the dark.

The prophet out front and the hitchhiker were warning against thinking all churches were faithful, that some churches he would encounter were "Ichabod Memorial Churches," full of wolves in sheep's clothing tiptoeing through the tithers. The glory had long since departed sanctuaries full of morning glories who bloomed once a week on Sunday around eleven and then lived for the world's theological bordellos, not Beulah Land.

Michael saw a narrow path before him, a narrow gate in the distance with intense light seeping through the seal, and a hand that kept him from turning to the right or the left where the carcasses lay, lost to the vanities for sale in Bunyan's Vanity Fair. The America he was returning to was a shaken bottle, and the fizz was threatening to pop the cork, the giant temporal plug that constrained man's excesses until Christ returned to right all wrongs.

Michael could see the straw men preaching and leeching to the masses, but there were straws in the coming tornado that he could not see. He saw that all the wires got crossed while he was in the monastery, and the rules and the old template no longer applied, if they ever did. The train had jumped the track, and hard times were coming, places to defend. Abraham was asking Isaac if this was the hill he wanted to die on, and angels warned of getting used to the darkness of the world, the slow dimming of the light.

Then he saw the new city with a river running through it, and the tree of life stretched across the water with fruits to heal the nations.

As the dreams began to fade and Michael tossed and turned on the narrow, metal bed, he was asked, "Do you hate evil, Michael?"

A familiar putrid smell invaded his sleep, the breath of something not quite dead but a creature that would gag a buzzard, limping toward the grave.

When he opened his eyes, the curtain of darkness was impenetrable. He raised his hand to his eyes and wiggled his fingers, but he couldn't see them, something akin to the atheist's hopeless horror of the moment when darkness falls upon their door.

The smell persisted, and as his eyes adjusted to the gloom, he could see the outline of a face almost as black as the night with one prominent gold tooth against meth-eroded enamel. Then cold steel brushed Michael's forehead, and he heard the unmistakable click of a revolver being cocked.

"Wake up, old man. Prepare to die and meet that Jesus you're always talking about. I've met some prickly men in my life, Pop, but you are a giant cactus, always sticking your nose where it don't belong. I don't understand your brand of crazy, but I respect your total commitment to this Man you talk to like He's real or something," said a mocking face with jaundiced eyes.

"Old man, I knew you were gonna be a problem. This girl was not your business. It means nothing to me, to the men who pay for her, nothing to her, and should be nothing to you. This interference is messy, and my business can't be messy. She's just the sacrificial animal, our offering to a meaningless spasm," Eli said.

As he talked, Michael noticed that he had lost the tooth next to the gold one, and his tongue kept finding the angry hole, giving him a kind of lisp. He held his yellowed eyes wide open like the villain tying the damsel to the railroad tracks in the old serials Michael favored as an impressionable child, the look of a silent-movie fiend. He was covered in ugly scars, legacies of a life of violence, and like a cheap watch, he was wound too tightly, the spring almost sprung.

"You just sprayed acid in my eyes and misted my world. Love is only something that Jesus and Hallmark peddle, a trap for suckers. You ain't that pure. I can see the hate in your eyes right now. You'd like to kill me, wouldn't you, Christian, and then water my grave just like you do to make your roses grow?" Eli boasted.

"No, after I left prison, I swore I'd never stand in long lines again. Besides, it's going take more water than I've got to put out the fire where you're going. Unless you change course, you won't live to see thirty," Michael said.

"Yeah? What would you know about it, old man?" Eli asked, a slight left-right, right-left tremor in his gun hand.

"I know I could have killed you the other morning when you were stone-cold drunk, and your pistol had fallen out of your pocket with the safety off. I could have shot you dead right then, wiped it clean, and told the front office that it was an accident. Could that have happened to you a year ago, six months ago? You're on the downhill pitch of that slippery slope. If I didn't do the deed, Darrius would have. He's impatient, just looking for an excuse, and Judas would have egged him on, selling you out. That's why they call him Judas," Michael said.

"You better stop, old man," Eli said.

"No matter who killed you, Mrs. Jones would have filled your bunk the same day and got out her brooms to sweep it all under your bed with your brains to keep the money flowing. The cops and the coroner would have come, and the autopsy would have shown enough drugs in your body to kill a moose. Maybe the coroner would have looked at your hollow face and jaundiced liver and wondered how you ever lived this long, but probably not."

"Stop!" Eli said, holding his hands over his ears.

"He'd just push your eyelid up, see the death stare, and just toe-tag you for the meat wagon. The district attorney would have taken one look at your rap sheet, said case closed, and maybe given me a medal. In your stupor, you still might've heard the 'bang' when the spinning bullet and gases left the barrel and maybe felt that explosion inside your head from the cavity and shock waves and then nothing but hell forevermore, no one back here to mourn you. Only your victims would come by your barren pauper's grave to curse you and soil the dirt around you, the cheap casket leaking your enemy's revenge," Michael said.

With that, Eli began to shake violently. A fog seemed to settle around him. His nostrils flared and ran, and his eyes leaked. He wiped at both with the backs of his hands, and his mouth was pinched tight with his bloodless lips sucked in, giving him a plucked-chicken look. He withered before Michael, teetered back and forth on his heels and toes, pitched forward on his knees, and lowered the gun to the floor. For a moment, Michael thought Eli was going to turn it on himself, but he dropped it and uttered his first prayer: "Oh God, I don't want to die."

"It's all closing in on you, Eli. The door is closing, but He stands and knocks. You were empty but you don't have to be anymore. It's late. It's later than it's ever been," Michael said.

Jimmy was trembling in the corner and holding something behind his back, and Judas ran out the front door.

Michael bent down and picked up Eli's gun. He was unresponsive and began to crawl toward his bunk. He had crashed and burned. The wiring short-circuited, some bolts broke loose, and welding pushed to the limit suddenly failed. The light had been turned on for Eli to see what had crept up on him, and he realized the beast in the dark was the bill collector, and it was payday.

Jimmy came over and couldn't stop shaking. He showed Michael what he had behind his back—a gun.

"I thought you was dead, and I just couldn't start my new life by witnessing your death and doing nothing, you know?" he said.

"You're a good man, Jimmy. The rest will be here soon. Get rid of both guns," Michael said.

Just as Eli reached his bed, the whole crew returned, led by Darrius, Boss Eli's one-time understudy, his main man, now his successor. For a moment, Michael felt like Daniel in the lion's den or a Christian entertaining in the Roman Colosseum at feline mealtime.

Darrius ignored Eli and strutted like a deadly peacock for his serfs. The king is dead; long live the king. All kissed his ring and hung on his every word, while Judas was already plotting his next betrayal.

Darrius nodded at Michael, then bit his lower lip until it bled and said to his troops, "Let's get the dice and break out the bottles."

Soon, the drunken revelry began and continued until the wee hours.

If this had been God's first mission field since prison, Michael thought the Timekeeper had also greased the gears and mainspring of his clock. Time was short, the days were few, and it was time to force the issue.

Michael prayed, "Bury me under an altar, just not this one, Lord. Amen."

Michael walked up front to find Willie at his post, miraculously reappearing after the evening's events. He was sitting in front of a big box fan that barely disturbed the hot foul air, reading a comic book, and eating Cheetos that turned his fingers orange. Maria said he had once been a boxer, more aptly a punching bag, and his nose looked like it had been broken so many times that it might fall off from a hard sneeze.

"Willie, no one can sleep here. Someone is going to die here in Death Valley. Can't you do something?" Michael asked.

"No, man. I'm sorry," Will said, looking down, avoiding eye contact.

Michael stood at the front door and looked out at the parking spot reserved for the director's electric-blue Cadillac.

"Well, come tomorrow morning, I will contact the Federal Bureau of Prisons and ask to go back to finish my time there. As bad as it was, my odds of making it to full discharge were better there. The odds offered by Vegas slot machines are better than this dingy casino where the rats gnaw at the roulette wheels," Michael spat.

Michael sighed deeply and said, "Cue the sad trombone."

As Michael turned to walk back into the melee, shiny bugs of prehistoric proportions popped at the glass of the front door to the swamp of nothingness within, and the bug-eyed, slack-jawed night manager sagged against his chair and then grabbed his phone with sweaty palms, swallowed hard, and hit the only electric-blue number on speed dial.

CHAPTER TEN

"Even the darkest night will end and the sun will rise."
—Les Misérables, *Victor Hugo*

"The secret of the LORD is with those who fear Him, And
He will show them His covenant."—Psalm 25:14

"If the cards are stacked against you,
reshuffle the deck."—John D. MacDonald

Michael woke after a fitful sleep to find the crew sleeping off another wild night. A snoring contest was in full flower. The neighbor's rooster had barely done his first cock-a-doodle-do and was tuning up for his second when Juanita Jones burst through the door into the living quarters, the first time Michael had ever seen her there.

"Get your stuff together. I want you out of here now!" she shrieked at Michael.

Her eyes were bloodshot, and she wasn't coiffed and dressed for success in the shell game they ran. She had on pinkish overalls and tennis shoes. She looked as hard as a twenty-minute egg, and if she smiled, her clenched face looked like it might shatter.

"Pardon?" Michael asked.

"You heard me. Just pack your stuff and sign the papers on the way out. I've already called your wife to come and get you. You ain't my problem anymore," she said as she paced to and fro in the room like a caged tiger, kicking garbage cans and swearing like a drunken sailor.

Some of the men who were not comatose began to stir, and Darrius opened one eye at Michael and began to laugh uproariously and clap his hands.

Jimmy stirred, and she turned on him.

"You, too, Mr. Streeter. Y'all seem chummy, so it's time for you to take your birds and get out. Yeah, I know about your birds on the roof. Some of them left surprises on my new Cadillac and may have ruined my paint job," she seethed, wagging her finger at him and blaspheming God.

And just like that, she stormed out of the room, and the whirlwind was gone.

Michael looked at Jimmy and said, "If I had only known that I had the secret code to going home, I could have played that card a long time ago. She just has no sense of humor," he said as he felt the tension of many years flee like demon pigs rushing to the abyss.

Jimmy bore a silly smile of disbelief at what he had seen and his good fortune. Darrius slapped his knees and cackled. He saw Michael look at Eli's bunk. "He's all right, man. Nobody's gonna hurt him until he goes home, but he is done. He has been divested of all of his holdings."

Michael could smell the air of a crushing, the tearing down of the old man. All that defined him was gone, nothing now but an empty vessel to be filled, a bulldog reduced to a puppy that can no longer bark. It is when God does His best work with those who can learn to bark the loudest for Christ.

Michael walked over and left Jimmy's Bible by Eli's bed, and as he turned to leave, Darrius sat on his bed, cupping his hands around the flame of a match as he lit a joint. Darrius took a deep toke and called to him with a look of amusement, then confusion, "Hey, old man. Just who are you anyway?"

"Just a sinner saved by grace, going home to drink sweet tea out of old pickle jars, Southern tea sweeter than a first kiss," Michael said.

"No, I think you're one of them bleeding hearts. I can see the stain on your shirt," Darrius said with a smirk.

"That speck? Nah, it's just a paper cut. I don't need to rush to the ICU when I can consult the Great Physician," Michael said as he waved his hand.

"I heard stories about who they said you was when you was my age, but look at you now. You ain't the man you used to be," Darrius said.

"I never was," Michael said.

As Michael signed out, the door to the women's quarters opened, and Maria stuck her head out and smiled, a tiny tear resting in the corner of her right eye.

"I'm happy for you," she said.

"I hope you can go home soon, Maria, and get far, far away from these folks," Michael said.

"That bad guy you saw me with meant nothing," Maria said.

"What guy?" Michael said and hugged her goodbye.

When Michael stepped outside, a sudden whoosh came from the roof as Jimmy's doves rushed to beat him home. A big, sudden wind seemed to lift them up toward heaven.

The zephyr was a welcome relief from the Southern heat and many restless nights. Michael looked up, breathed it in and said, "Thank you, Lord."

He raised his arms in the breeze and felt that if he flapped hard enough, he too could fly away like the doves. He closed his eyes and began to softly sing his prison refrain, "Some glad morning, I'll fly away."

Jimmy appeared with his backpack and stood next to Michael, saying nothing.

Finally, he looked at Michael and said, "Meeting you has changed my life. Who woulda thought it when my father was who he was, and you were the law?" Jimmy said.

Michael smiled and said, "The Lord moves in mysterious ways."

"Uh, there's something I didn't tell you," Jimmy said sheepishly.

"What's that, Jimmy?" Michael asked.

"Back when I was dealing dope, I ran with a bad crowd. Some were connected to crooked cops. They told me there was a girl back then that got hurt real bad. They said she was snitching to you. Two guys beat her up and left her for dead in a car trunk, but she lived. Somebody, the cops or the local hoods, thought she might talk to you. The guys that did it disappeared right after that. The word was that they chopped them up and dropped those boys in a well somewhere. They said they had them in a trunk for a while just like she was with socks stuffed in their mouths. They called them dead owls because right up until the end, their eyes were big, and they made gagging, hooting sounds begging for their lives.

"If she was something to you, I just thought you might like to know they paid for what they did. That was another sign that I should quit dealing after I heard that. I was already allergic to that kind of life and was always breaking out in handcuffs, and I sure didn't want to wind up in no well," he said, looking down into an imaginary pit.

Michael heard the roar of an overhead airplane motor and the hiss of a big rig's air brakes on Gloster. The years melted away, and the past reached out and squeezed Michael's heart as the images of the young girl so savagely beaten came roaring back.

The milk truck driver who found Tammy Sue Jenkins told Michael that vultures were already drawing death circles over her in the air as she crawled up the road. The heat had dried the blood and the sweat on her like a second skin. The scent of death was overwhelming in the unstirring air. He said all the milk on his truck soured that day, and he quit his job.

Michael looked up at the blue of the firmaments, took a deep breath, and held tightly to his joy as yesteryear flooded his memories, echoes of virtue, pain, sorrow, laughter, and tears, all interdependent and unable to stand alone.

"Thanks for telling me that, Jimmy. It means a lot to me. She meant a lot to me," Michael said, looking far away for a moment, all the way to the seventies and the hospital where he first saw her battered face. Hearing Jimmy's news was as if a big period, or at least a comma, had replaced a question mark on an incomplete sentence, and a bandage had been ripped off an old wound for healing.

"You're welcome. I also been meaning to ask you about a puzzlement of mine. You sure do have a lot of trouble come your way to be a man of God. I don't know much because God was just a curse word round our house, and for a long time, I thought she was proof He didn't exist, but I thought y'all were supposed to be blessed and on easy street or something," Jimmy said.

"Jesus said the world hated Him and would hate us, too. I know it sometimes seems like God sharpens his axe on the devil's grindstone, but as long as we think we can save ourselves, He won't intervene. He says your will be done, and sometimes, Jimmy, the Lifeguard must knock out the drowning man to get him to shore.

"It's the same with our country now. Hard times are coming, but we won't repent. The folks in Washington think they have all the answers but don't even know the questions. They think they can handle what's coming, but they can't. We must experience what holy desperation really means, like Jehoshaphat did," Michael said.

Michael knew he was probably losing Jimmy. He paused and looked at Juanita Jones' electric-blue Cadillac, now so covered in white bird droppings that it looked polka-dotted or the victim of a rogue abstract painter who used her hood as his canvas.

"There's a war coming, Jimmy, and maybe a few evangelist authors, fresh home from the front, can speak the truth to a deaf nation. These won't be the usual temptations but attacks from unseen powers and spiritual agents from the very castle of evil. It is going to catch us unaware and off guard.

"Grandmother Pearl used to tell me, it's dark and getting darker. While some are out recruiting for the army of the Lord, many in the regular army are either already AWOL or so infected with a cheap imitation of the real thing that they've been inoculated against the true gospel. It's like they've been given a bad vaccine that only protects them from the medicine they desperately need. There is no evidence of the gospel in their lives.

"The emptiness in them moves from church to church, transferring corpses from one mortician to another, unless they find a church that preaches the Good News of Jesus Christ. I hope you find a good Bible-believing, spirit-filled church for you and your family," Michael said.

Jimmy scratched his head and said, "I don't know about all that, but as for Christianity, I could take it or leave it."

"Don't say that, Jimmy. If you do, you'll always leave it. Think about what your father found before it was too late. The smell of smoke was on him, and his house was on fire, but he fell to his knees and crawled to the foot of the Cross before the flames overcame him, before it was too late," Michael said.

Jimmy nodded and said, "I will, Michael. I will be seeing things better as soon as I have my Cadillac surgery."

"Cadillac surgery?" Michael asked.

"They said I was kinda young for it, but I got these Cadillacs in my eyes," Jimmy said.

"I think they meant cataracts, Jimmy, but even if it's Chevrolets, I hope you see 20/20 physically and spiritually," Michael said.

"But today, right now, I'm going home. It's like when you're waiting for rain after a long dry spell; then the showers come with that feeling that all things are possible, that I could even buy a pink Cadillac, move to Memphis, and drive through the gates of Graceland like family," Michael said, grinning.

Just then, he heard the crunch of tires on loose gravel in the lot, and Judy's silver Nissan pulled up. He saw her big smile, the strong line of her throat, the perfect head of brown hair, the smooth framing of her face by cheeks flushed with joy, and he could almost smell the slight hint of her perfume that reminded him of Confederate jasmine.

Michael looked at Jimmy and said, "On the other hand, the pink Caddy can wait. A silver-gray Murano will do just fine, and my chariot awaits."

"You be careful, Mr. Michael. I think there's a lot of people still taking potshots at you," Jimmy said.

"That's okay, Jimmy. The Lord is with me. I'm out of range now, and they are out of bullets," Michael said.

"Man, I bet you used to be cool," Jimmy said.

And with that, Michael laughed as he piled into her car with his meager possessions and asked her again, "Got any room at your Bed and Breakfast?"

She smiled and said, "I just have an opening if you don't mind bunking with the proprietor."

"She doesn't snore, does she?" he asked.

"Like a freight train," she said.

"Good," Michael said, "I love trains."

CHAPTER ELEVEN

"My feet are itching to get back home. I'm coming home, this time I'm going to stay."—"Goin' Home," Joy Byers

"My heart is anywhere you are, anywhere you are is home…"—"Home Is Where the Heart Is," Sherman Edwards/Hal David

"I'm a soldier in the army of the Lord."—Lyle Lovett

When they arrived home, a breeze was blowing around the side of the brick house, and the boughs of giant pine trees swayed above the pitched roof and waved at the new arrival. Scattered beams of sunlight made the green pine needles twinkle like Christmas sparklers. A chattering kingfisher flew over the house on the way to the lake, and the white clouds were so dense and puffy that Michael felt he could walk on them and jump from cloud to cloud on a stairway to heaven.

It was suburbia, Southern style, almost country but close to the city, just clinging to the precipice of urbanity by its fingernails, refusing to be defined. Somehow there was a faintness of yesteryear here, remembrances of past homes and hearths with Susan that squeezed his heart.

He knew this could be a fine home, a place they could make their home, following the tried-and-true pattern of their past lives, building on trust and resting on love. He could already see the landscaping additions to make it a sanctuary for birds and blooms, a garden spot to walk with the Creator amongst His creation.

This could be a place to heal, write, and lick old wounds until they fully healed and the rotten things fell away. This plot of ground could be a place for Susan's apprentice gardener to get his hands in the soil under the sauna-like heat of the Mississippi summer sun and begin that unique restorative therapy that only gardeners understand.

Here he could have long, private showers without men on the other side of plastic curtains cursing and bellowing "she did me wrong songs" like moose in heat…long hot showers to wash the pain away and cleanse the wounds of lingering infections.

Judy watched with vivid eyes as Michael surveyed it all and said, "If you don't like it, we can move to the country where it's quiet and private, where there're lots of birds."

"No, honey. It's like the line from *Field of Dreams*, 'Build it, and they will come.' Some flowers, some bushes, plenty of birdbaths, something always in bloom and in the process of beginning again, and right here on this rise, a cross with a light for those at night who get lost in the dark," he said.

He could feel the urge to get on with it, the press of the starter's block against his feet, as he looked up and listened for the Referee's starter pistol.

They walked through the house and to the desk that was to be his. She had hung a framed encouragement next to his desk that read *Your story matters. Share it with the world.* He looked at the gift for a long time, the words written over the image of an old-fashioned typewriter.

There was a shuttered window in front of his desk. He sat in the plush desk chair, sighed at its softness, and opened the shutters. He never got near the coveted window bed in the monastery, but here he was with his own private windows. He opened the shutters, closed them, and opened and closed them again and again until he had to blink away the tears.

When he opened his eyes, a flock of honking Canada geese winged by in a V formation, headed to the community lake, and a giant orange butterfly bobbed on the breeze like a cork in a pond as it drifted past his window…his window.

Yes, this will do nicely, he thought.

Judy told him that the Federal Probation Officer had been by to inspect the home to make sure it was a place of "rehabilitation" and free of drugs, weapons, and temptations.

"I tried to make it as perfect as possible. People told me to hang some of your clothes in the closet and fold some for the drawers, and I borrowed some from family since you didn't have any to spare. They told me to make it look like home, a place a man will stay and not just pass through.

"He was nice, but my dog barked at him constantly while he was here, and I finally had to put her up. He asked if there were guns in the house, and I said no. He said I could never have a gun to defend the house because you live here. I told him that I didn't like guns anyway," she said and smiled.

"Any suspicion that there was a gun here while you are on probation would prompt a search, and if any were found, probation would be revoked and new charges added for a felon in possession of a gun," Judy said and paused as her throat tightened.

"He said that even after probation, if we had a gun and shot an intruder, you would go back to prison, no exceptions for nonviolent, first-time offenders. He also said no knives bigger than a bread knife were allowed while on probation. He said there would be periodic inspections without any notice, and any violation could cause your probation to be revoked," she said with a sudden catch of fear in her voice.

Michael sat and listened and thought again about what he already knew. Neither he nor Judy could ever have a firearm to defend their home. Judy was vulnerable because of his mistakes, and politicians in both parties used convictions as a back-door avenue to make possession of guns illegal for Americans with convictions.

It was always understood that it would one day be this way because government draws its skirts tightly around itself and puts ideology aside because power exists to maintain power. You were either in or out, and the price of admission was your soul. Even the tough-on-crime boys in Congress, who picked the pockets of those they claimed to care about, voted to deny Second Amendment rights to millions of people while claiming NRA endorsements and deaconships back home, until one day all the copies of the Constitution had been misplaced east of Eden, then banned, and finally made illegal, along with the Bible.

They sat up on the front pews of their churches and talked about forgiveness, about people satisfying their debt to society and seeing their past washed away by the grace of paternal government. They made a false comparison to the debts paid by Jesus on the Cross, but they didn't mean a word of the forgiveness they preached. They denied the right to defend homes and the fundamental right to vote in many states, a debt they marked outstanding and compounding until the grave.

These were the same men families once watched at wakes and funerals, lest they stole the coins from dead men's eyes. They were the venal voyeurs who demanded amusement, clowns who juggled lives, dropped some now and then, and said, "Oops, my bad." They were the ones who showed you what men are capable of in the here and now and in the beginning when Cain's impulse sins were out of control.

Michael once heard the story about a man who underwent brain surgery. The doctors removed his brain, but the body got up and left the hospital. They didn't find it/him for three years until he was located in Washington, D.C., working as a brainless government expert advising heartless congressmen on ways to sucker the masses.

After a day of laughter and planning, a long walk to put some color in his chalky pallor, and a belly full of delicacies designed to put some weight on his gaunt frame, Michael awoke late in the night and had to get his bearings to see if peace was real, or fight or flight was still necessary.

He could see the flickering white light from the TV in the den. Judy was watching a *Forensic Files* episode, and he walked to the den and plopped down beside her.

"Can't sleep?" he asked.

"Dozing," she said, putting her hand over a yawn.

"Yes, too much happening, too many little things worry me that aren't worth worrying about, just housekeeping details, I guess, and wondering if this is what you thought it would be, if you're happy, and if you'll ever be really happy," she said.

They sat there for a bit, bathed in the white light of the television.

"When I was in prison, watching TV was not like this. Here there is no profanity, no people just walking up to change the channel in the middle of your movie and daring you to object.

"The only time it was different was one night when a movie with Denzel Washington was on, *The Book of Eli*. The inmates were quiet and respectful because it was Denzel. I don't think they had any idea that he was defending the Bible in a post-apocalyptic world. They just saw Denzel and lots of action. They didn't realize he was blind before the war and regained his sight after finding the Bible and hearing from God that he was to find a safe place for the Word. I watched them watching him in the movie and thought, only God can do this. Then Denzel said, 'The Lord is my Shepherd. I shall not want.'

"I was given swimming lessons on dry land, sink or swim, or have faith and walk on water in that wretched boot camp. I found myself at the bottom of a well with no ladder to climb out, no shovel to dig tunnels, and only time to labor in the mines of regret, bouncing into the walls of confinement with no place to escape self, memory, remorse, and self-loathing.

"Something happens, something undoes you, and you are changed; your life is changed, as well as the lives of everyone close to you, friends and enemies. The tiger of treachery is unleashed on all sides. Plaudits turn to jeers, and innocence is gone forever, and there isn't an eraser big enough to make it all go away. All that remained until you came along was an indigestible heaviness," Michael said as he squeezed her hand.

"Denzel prayed a prayer at the end of the movie. I saw the movie many times and memorized it:

"'Dear Lord, thank you for giving me the strength and the conviction to complete the task you entrusted to me. Thank you for guiding me straight and true through the many obstacles in my path. And for keeping me resolute when all around seemed lost. Thank you for your protection and your many signs along the way. Thank you for any good that I may have done. I'm so sorry about the bad. Thank you for the friends I made. Please watch over them as you watched over me. Thank you for finally allowing me to rest. I'm so very tired, but I go now to my rest at peace. Knowing that I have done right with my time on this earth. I fought the good fight; I finished the race, I kept the faith.'

"That's all I want to do, Judy. Time is short to serve the Lord, and there is no one I'd rather finish the race with than you," he said, laying his hand on hers as she laid her head on his shoulder. They fell asleep that way until they were startled awake when some woman on *Forensic Files* wailed in court after she was convicted of poisoning her husband with arsenic and antifreeze.

Michael stretched, yawned, and said, "Let me know if I ever get on your nerves. Maybe I should check the pantry and the garage." They laughed again, and laughter turned into howls.

Then Michael said, "Well, I suppose enough antifreeze might save on the cost of embalming."

Then, through giggles and hoots, Judy uttered her signature line when she was tickled: "You ain't right!"

When they were about to turn the light off in the bedroom, he switched on a song he used to quietly sing to Judy when she visited him in prison. He sang along, and this time, he danced for Judy as she watched, laughed, and then cried.

"I walked into this empty church. I had nowhere else to go when the sweetest voice I ever heard whispered to my soul. I don't need to be forgiven for loving you so much. It's written in the Scriptures. It's written there in blood. I even heard the angels declare it from above. There ain't no cure, there ain't no cure for love."

She held out her arms to him, and as he turned out the lights he heard the whine of a passing jet, the distant rumble of a large truck on the interstate, and then God rotated the stars in the heavenlies, and the silence of night fell across their world. They fell asleep in each other's arms, talking about chasing shooting stars, catching lightning bugs to light jelly jars, swimming in Town Creek, and spoon-scaling perches for Southern fried suppers.

His indigestible heaviness melted away in their murmurs and coos, and Michael thought a woman like Judy would never be found on the marked-down, bargain counter of life. She was a woman to cherish as the precious minutes of life ticked by too loudly and too fast.

CHAPTER TWELVE

"Grace changes us, and change is painful."
—*Flannery O'Connor*

"There is a certain kind of man who knows how not to be stampeded. He is not valued in any generation, for he consistently is a pain in the neck, but after he is dead and deep, the praise starts to trickle in."—Skin and Blood, *Douglas Wilson*

The moonlight was gone from his window, and a stubborn grayness adorned the morning. The early fog gave their nest a private feel, and the thunder from the storm opened a mood door for the writer. Words flowed like the rain that threatened to streak the window by his desk forever. He would've put on his slicker and walked in the rain if he wasn't writing.

In prison, storms drove everyone inside all at once, breathing the same humid, germ-filled air, claustrophobia to the max, smelling like moldy, damp clothes or old wet dogs fresh from a close encounter with a skunk. So, Michael became a rain walker with no umbrellas allowed because they could be used as weapons.

Prison officials at Edgefield watched him from behind their metal curtains in the big prison tower up on the hill, a room sealable in case of a riot. The warden thought him an unbroken resident, a man too free to be in prison, as Michael walked, arms raised toward the heavens, singing like Gene Kelly, "Just singing in the rain, just singing in the rain."

An inmate who worked in the warden's office was taking out the trash and heard the warden and his assistant talking about Michael.

The grizzled old warden asked, "Who is that?"

"Parker, who else?" his assistant replied.

"Does he not hear the booming thunder and see the crackling flashes of lightning all around him?" the warden asked.

"Parker tells officers that he feels the caress of God amidst the storms and waits for God to speak to him from the storm as He did to Job. Do you want me to order him inside?" the assistant asked.

"No, leave him be. I've known a few like him. No matter what life throws at them, they will always find a reason to believe. Just roust his cubicle, shake it down good, disorder his order," the warden said as he closed the blinds.

"We won't find anything," the assistant said.

"I know. We just need to remind Parker that he is not free, no matter his faith. Keep him on a short leash," the warden said.

***

Michael thought of storms he'd walked in, and storms he had weathered. He decided the sky looked as if it would rain all day, but it stopped just as he left in the new car he purchased from Jimmy Streeter, who had found work as a salesman at the Nissan dealer and membership in a local church.

Michael walked past other salesmen at the dealer as they put the rush on him. He waved them off and said he wanted a test drive with their newest salesman. It was Jimmy's first sale, and he was beaming.

They stopped at Baskin-Robbins for a treat and then drove down to the halfway house, which looked abandoned, so silent and still. They stopped and stared at the lifeless structure until the chocolate ice cream and waffle cones were gone. Michael told Jimmy that with his commission, he should be able to afford some prime Folgers for his wife, some feed for his birds, and a generous contribution for the offering plate at his church.

Michael drove his new Murano with his new driver's license to have his first meeting with his Probation Officer, something new to him but in the same file drawer as a visit to the dentist for a painful extraction or to the proctologist who kept saying, "Relax." Michael hoped the mood of the federal officials didn't match what most people would think of as a gloomy day.

The building, just across the street from Calvary Baptist Church, was in deep shade when he arrived, and a clump of daffodils was in the throes of a late-blooming cycle. Michael looked for a moment at the intersection, which seemed a sort of Bermuda Triangle of his life. Just across the street was the former headquarters of the Mississippi Bureau of Narcotics and the parking spot where the Holy Spirit had warned him to go back for the bulletproof vest the day of the ambush in 1976. Further up the street was the old duplex where he had the final encounter with Fredrick.

Now he was at the U.S. Probation office, across the street from the big stately church, so much a part of Tupelo's history. It was almost overwhelming, too coincidental, too full-circle to be chance.

The décor of the government office was standard fare, meaning minimalist with dull, plastic plants and a lifeless receptionist with cropped brown hair who looked at him as an annoyance, a nonentity. Only two pictures adorned the walls, one of Barack Obama next to his appointee as head of the agency.

It was as silent as a mortuary and so cold that you could hang meat on hooks. They didn't skimp on air-conditioning. Three other men and one woman were in the waiting area. From the looks of them and their tattoos, grooming, and demeanor, it was likely a safe bet that they did not know Christ. The one with the acne craters under his scraggly beard had the browned skin of a construction worker mixed with a tint of green beneath, and he wore thick glasses with lens that looked highly polished. All seemed fidgety and nervous, and the skinny girl with rotten teeth and pupils like dinner plates had a nasty rash on her face and arms. She picked at her skin and had chewed her fingernails back to her elbows.

Drug tests were likely when they saw their government keeper. Michael looked at these lost lambs, remembered the flowers outside, and thought it might be a daffodil and infidel kind of day.

The lady behind the sliding glass slapped a clipboard on the counter and mumbled something about forms to fill out while he waited. He took her government pen, and she asked him to return it with his records. She encouraged him not to write outside the lines, to fill in the dots precisely so the new government computer could efficiently scan his life. Michael smiled. He had been under the thumb of the government for too long and, before that, corporate autocrats. He had always been across someone's line or writing in forbidden margins.

He finished, requested The Salvation Army as his place to fulfill his required community service, and she took it without comment. One crooked eye tooth and the listless saffron eyes of a bureaucrat gave her the look of a lopsided vampire, but she reminded him of the change girls he had seen in their cages in Las Vegas. They made sure you never ran out of coins to feed the one-arm bandits and oil the machinery of make-believe, but they never really looked at you.

Michael said cheerfully, "You're welcome!"

It startled her, and she smiled before she caught herself.

Steven Ballard, the young officer who had visited Judy, stuck his head out the door and said, "Mr. Parker?"

Ballard looked like one of the Mouseketeers, maybe Bucky. Young, prim and proper, and clean-cut, much like Michael looked forty years ago. Young Mr. Ballard was Mickey Mouse Club wholesome and could be a grandson Michael never knew he had.

He followed Ballard down the long hallway. Michael had never been there but felt he could have drawn it from memory. It looked like so many government offices he had seen, the modern version of the orderly openings of the cliff-dwelling Puebloans of the Southwest. There were offices and closets. Michael had the urge to try the doors and look in the cabinets like he did with Susan when they were looking at homes in their many moves. He had been checking the closets of his mind for almost six years, cleaning, flushing, sanitizing, and evicting squatters and parasites who ran from the Light.

When they finally perched in his office, Michael had a good feeling about him. He did not have the bearing of standard government issue.

"Settled in yet?" he asked.

"Pretty much, still detoxing from my former life and routines. Loud sounds and bright colors don't jolt me quite so much now, the drivers no longer seem bent on fender-bending me. Putting on some weight. I told Judy that the average person couldn't understand how important good food is until you no longer have it. Milkshakes and the potato salad my uncle used to make with his BBQ plates at the TKE drugstore fountain are fully appreciated delicacies now," Michael said wistfully.

"What do you plan to do now?" Ballard asked.

Michael noticed that the young man was studying him but not in an obvious way, the kind of studying that did not raise your guard but lowered it.

"Try to publish and sell my book and see if people think I can write. Maybe friends and family will take pity on me and buy a few copies," Michael said with a shrug and smile.

"You should relax here in Tupelo and not worry that people might be whispering about you behind your back. Hardly anyone from these parts reads the paper from Atlanta except me," Ballard said.

"I hope so, at least a brief reprieve, some space for me to get the book printed and hit the local Rotary, church, and school circuit to tell them my story and His story of redemption. After that, it won't matter so much because I hope to tell the whole story, warts and all," Michael said.

"Is there anyone you have any lingering problems with? Anyone that you bear a grudge against?" Ballard asked.

"No, not really. Revenge requires two graves. Anger and revenge are the ugly stepchildren of desperation, and I am no longer a desperate man. There are some people I wouldn't care to see again and some who probably should be flagged for hitting below the belt, unnecessary roughness, and unsportsmanlike conduct. They probably won't make my Christmas card list, but there's no one I would waste precious time on unless it were to witness to them. Some need that in the worst way. They don't know Who I know.

"The Lord showed me early on that if I wanted to serve Him, I couldn't be dragging that junk around with me in my trunk. So, I nailed it to the Cross and left it there. I snuck back a time or two and took it down, but I finally left it where I first saw the Light and asked for a new life, where mercy and grace poured out on me from His wounded side.

"It was like being set free from the biggest prison imaginable. Negative thoughts, anger, and 'poor me pity parties' were long gone, and people I might have thought had done me wrong were no longer standing between me and Jesus Christ. No one but the Lord had any hold on me," Michael said as Ballard watched the light come over Michael.

"May I ask a question?" Michael asked.

"Sure," the earnest young officer answered.

"From what you said, you are pretty familiar with all that happened in Atlanta?" Michael asked.

"Yes, not voyeuristic, just interesting, and given this was where you grew up, I thought I might see you again in an official capacity if it pleased the Lord," Ballard said.

Michael liked him more and more with each passing minute.

"For what it's worth, I felt like David, down in the stream looking for smooth stones for my sling. Sure, some thought I could be a pain, that I said intemperate things now and then. I wouldn't drive in the middle of the road, straddling that yellow line of surrender, and I wouldn't go along and get along or even hop along, but how was I to know that 'uncircumcised Philistine' would offend Goliath so much," Michael said.

They both laughed until Michael's face grew grim.

"Next thing I know, the local king wants to lock me up, and the U.S. Attorney thought it would be a swell idea. I thought I was defending truth from the high ground of ancient oaks and the roots of righteousness, but when my idealism came unraveled, I realized I had just been standing on soapboxes, giving hollow 'stump' speeches," he said, his toes tapping like a nervous tap dancer under the table.

Michael paused and started again.

"Sometimes you can get clubbed so hard by life that your compass no longer registers to true north. Life's fist to the gray matter knocks the light right out of you, snuffs out the candle, and leaves you in the dark, but in my case, it woke me from a long sleep, like a cicada buried and waiting to make some holy noise.

"I was blind like John Newton. She was efficient and clever, a piquant black cat crossing my path, Delilah sharpening her shears. Her acting was terrible, but her halo was blinding, and the convincing con job seeped into my mind, only to find that, like soap opera actresses, she only cried glycerin tears. There was always something there—moving, watching, and changing behind her eyes.

"Words don't always reveal the heart, but it's the space between the words, and in her spaces, you could hide a herd of elephants. I didn't see it at first, and when I did, it was too late, or maybe just in time. The shades had been drawn in those sour hours before Amazing Grace. I lost something precious back there but tasted costly grace. I suppose the locker-room historians still talk about it when new news and gossip are in short supply.

"Unlike the kings I offended, the King had an assignment I never saw coming. I became all ears and began to listen to that still small voice. I began to look upward, not inward. Like children, who first master black and white, I moved on to a palette of color, shades, and nuances. I sometimes feel like the Starship Enterprise, caught in His tractor beam. My life is His. I have the illusion of driving, but He is steering my starship.

"Call it atonement or penance, but I am ready to share what I learned, to speak of a better way, to throw lifelines to drowning swimmers who know I've been in the same pond, people like that girl waiting outside to see you, the girl with the rash, sores on her ankles, and the dirty hair. I've been on a long, low-heat boil, and simmering is not something I do well. I had enough of that in prison," Michael said, taking a breath and wiping away the beads of sweat on his upper lip.

"There was a time when everything I held dear was consigned to a theater set, far, far away. I could see it from a distance but was trapped in nothingness, waiting for what I did not know. Call it insanity, illusion, the Xanax; I don't know. I just know that the door was left unguarded, unprotected, and undetected, and darkness jumped into my life. I didn't see it coming. I should have, but I was already incarcerated in this corrupted flesh. The weight of it all split the mountain like the mass of the sun. Mount Parker split in two, but the Holy Spirit groaned for me deeply in words that cannot be uttered, and Christ pulled me from beneath the rubble.

"'I'm sorry' wouldn't cover my sins. It seemed it might require something akin to David's loss of his infant son, but when I crawled to the foot of the Cross, I told Him I had ruined this life, asked for another, and I found forgiveness. It has been a rocky road and hard ground to transverse, but I hope, like David, that I may still be a man after God's own heart. I was a drowning man who began to follow the Man Who walks on water," he said.

A long interval of silence passed without interruption, and Michael thought perhaps he had said too much, revealed more than he meant to, but Ballard was a good listener, and it was just more cleansing, one more testimony of many to come.

"Thanks for listening," Michael said.

"Thanks for sharing," Steven Ballard said.

As the meeting ended, Ballard said, "One more thing."

Michael turned to look at him.

"You wouldn't know anything about gang activity at the halfway house, would you?" Ballard asked with a hint of a wry smile.

"Well, I think people coming home should not have to ask to leave a halfway house and return to prison. Seems something might be amiss, termites maybe or a stench from something that crawled up under the director's office and died," Michael said.

"Some exterminators are looking into that now. Some shepherds just won't give up looking for smooth stones and giants to topple, I guess," he said with a sly grin.

"There were a lot of fallen angels and demons in Georgia, legions, I think, and some folks that howled at the moon and were so bent toward sin, they were ready to topple over, there and in Mississippi, too. These days, I'm just seeking the will of God and trying to stay in His lane the best I can, trying to stay as far away from my old self as I can and encourage young warriors to don the full armor and discern the difference between angel eyes and assassin eyes," Michael said.

"Oh, you asked about grudges?" Michael asked.

"Yes," Ballard said, pausing as he got up.

"In the interest of full transparency, since that's an 'in' phrase today, I must confess that I occasionally burst out into song for no apparent reason," Michael said.

"I'll bite. What's the song?" Ballard asked.

"Thank God and Greyhound She's Gone!" Michael deadpanned.

They both laughed at honesty and irony until it hurt, and it felt good to see pain retreat before the joy of the Lord.

As Michael walked through the waiting area, he stopped and looked again at the lost lambs slumped in their chairs, rubbing their arms, emptiness etched into their faces.

"He's not so bad. Meet him halfway. Jesus loves you. God bless you," Michael said.

The motley assembly stirred from their apathy, straightened in their chairs, stopped smacking worn-out gum, and looked at Michael as if he was a distant memory of a pastor who had warned them about straying or a parent they had failed or who had failed them.

For a moment, they found the ladies and gentlemen they once were and could be again. They managed surprised smiles and a mumbled, "Yessir. And, uh, God bless you, too." That last part almost strangled their tongues because it was so long neglected, too many old memories attached, and still too raw or too precious for them to utter easily.

The girl behind the glass stared at Michael as he left and leaned back in a swivel chair that creaked like a dry board.

Just as Officer Ballard stepped into her room, she said, "Well, he's different."

Ballard said, "You have no idea."

Michael walked outside. A shower had come and gone while he was inside for what could have been minutes or hours. There were puddles of water on the rain-wet sidewalk, and the air smelled almost as clean as the air he once breathed aboard the *Sea Princess* in Glacier Bay.

He looked at the big church next door and thought it might provide the structure and formality he sought. It seemed meant to be. There was so much history and pieces of his life colliding at this intersection. For a moment, as his pulse thundered in his ears, he didn't know if now was then or then was now. It was all side-by-side and overlapping, and the players were brushing shoulders and whistling right past each other.

Like the satellites in the heavenlies that can zero in on a plot of earth such as this and count the hairs on your head, he felt God was watching him right at that moment, counting his tears and weighing his heart with His perfect and just measures that would lengthen Michael's second life God had given him.

As Michael looked up at the blue sky, a dove cooed and rocked back and forth on a utility wire, teetering against the breeze that fanned Michael's face and whooshed down North Church Street.

Michael tried to remember old lyrics that nibbled at the edges of memory, "like a bird on a wire, like a drunk in a midnight choir... If I, if I have been untrue, I hope you know it was never to you."

At that moment, an eastbound Greyhound bus passed him, the black diesel smoke boiling out around the taillights, the motor playing a familiar rhythm.

Then the dove flew up and up until he could no longer see it, and the traffic light turned green for go.

CHAPTER THIRTEEN

"So send I you to bear rebuke, to suffer scorn and scoffing.
So send I you to toil for Me alone. So send I you to bind the
bruised and the broken, over wandering souls to work, to
weep, to wake. So send I you to die to dear desire, self-will
resign, to labor long and love where men revile you. So
send I you to lose your life in Mine."—*"So Send I You,"*
Clarkson/Peterson

"Go now my little Book, to every place. Where my first
Pilgrim has but shewn his Face: Call at their door."
—Pilgrim's Progress, *"The Second Part," John Bunyan*

The transient light of false dawn, sunlight reflecting off dust particles in the inner solar system, had beaten twilight to Michael's window before he realized that the man in the moon had already called it a night and retired to light the dark ends of streets just over the horizon.

Watching the faint glow seep through the shutters gave Michael the feeling that God was watching him again. Michael liked to think of Him out with His lantern on the wings of the wind, stepping off the clouds, not distant and impersonal, but the Nightwatchman walking His beat in the cool of the morning. Pondering the ways and paths of man, the bruised reeds and smoldering wicks, He marches through the wilderness, making darkness into dawn with His everlasting light, without end or beginning.

When the beams of His upper chambers, the full brightness of morning, arrived like a searchlight from heaven looking for lost lambs and the odd fallen sparrow, Michael squinted into the sudden radiance and stood up to yawn, to stretch away stiffness, bow, and bend his knees in prayer before God's silken presence.

He had been up all night polishing the manuscript, editing, and sweeping out the chaff. He wanted it to be more than a triumphant paean to yesteryear or some encyclical letter on a fallen world.

The story outline and the memories that made the story had been nailed to the walls of his mind for years as he rearranged the framed images and poetic words in his private gallery. Now it was time to take down the sticky notes and see if one of Michelangelo's angels was in the marble waiting to be set free. The manuscript would never be ready for the perfectionist to let it go or set it free, but it was close enough for someone to read, to say, "What a masterpiece!" or "Who wrote this drivel?"

When Michael was at Talladega, he met an inmate named John Banks, tall and thin with silver hair and a beard to match and a long stride Michael had seen in farmers who had stepped over too many cotton rows.

Banks and Michael had little in common. John was an old hippie and a Buddhist who loved Barack Obama and was always getting into near-fights because he talked too much. He was also a socialist, and inmates are generally not fond of socialists or communists.

One inmate chiropractor was adjusting John up on the hill when John's tongue got all tangled up in Marxism. There was almost a different type of adjustment made to John before others intervened and offered him a chance to get off the hill while he still could. Even so, John limped for a while due to that unfortunate case of runaway mouth disease.

He also smuggled drugs in from Mexico via small planes. He said he was trying to go straight but wanted one last big score for his wife and small child in Guadalupe. He said everything was fine until his plane was surrounded by Border Patrol and DEA agents waiting for him when he landed at a small remote airfield.

It was the same old story. Agents either tracked John coming in or someone squealed on him, likely to make a deal while to divert attention from their own larger shipments. There was no honor among smugglers. It also could have been John's partaking of his wares during the flight, which he was known to do.

John read an early draft of *A Ghostly Shade of Pale* and was intrigued.

"You might have something here. My cousin is big in Hollywood now at the TV show *Criminal Minds*. He was a profiler at the FBI, took Horace Greeley's advice, and went west after the attack on the Twin Towers. He was a first responder and got cancer from the dust. He helped them set up *Criminal Minds* and approves everything aired for authenticity.

"I think he might like this. You two would get along pretty well, I think. His name is Jim Clemente. Tell him I sent you, and if you make anything off it, please remember my family and me," he said.

He said, "Rosa is my wife, my first legal wife. I always thought marriage was a wonderful institution, but who wants to live in an institution?"

Michael smiled and reminded him, "Look around us."

So, Michael read up on Clemente and emailed the draft to Jim Clemente to see what he had to say. As John said, Clemente helped the people at *Criminal Minds* set up the show while he was recovering from a bone marrow transplant, so the move from New York City to Los Angeles to be a writer and subject matter expert followed.

When Jim Clemente awakened in Los Angeles later that morning to find the email and attachment from Michael in his inbox, he groaned. Not another one, he thought. So many aspiring authors and screenwriters sent samples to him, hoping to make it big in Hollywood, and most were pretty bad.

Clemente answered Michael and said he would take a look at the book. It was, after all, a referral from his cousin.

With the book sent, Michael set out to buy some clothes that weren't prison green, to register to vote, to find someone to build the cross he wanted for his developing gardens, and to see a dentist to repair nearly six years of neglect. He also began looking for a publisher, having no idea how to do that.

So much to do, so little time. Michel felt like one of those contestants on TV who get a makeover. He was bursting with excitement, happy the seams were not showing from alterations made to his life as he flapped about like the cardinal outside that kept seeing its reflection in the window, thinking it was a rival.

***

He and Judy also decided to attend Calvary Baptist. Michael thought the Lord had something there for him. It was his first service since prison, where a combustible mix of Baptists, Pentecostals, Methodists, Adventists, Nazarenes, and occasional disgruntled Catholics and Mormons made up his congregation.

Michael thought there was something about a Sunday morning. You sit on a wooden bench, waiting for the announcement, "turn in your hymnals now to four hundred and sixty-one, number four-six-one." The organist played so loudly that Michael wondered if the angels were leaning over heaven's rails to see what all the fuss was about.

He was pretty sure there would be no prosperity or social gospels, which weren't the gospel at all, preached at Calvary. Michael had met with the pastor, who didn't think the gospel needed any adjectives. Some spoke of the evolution of the Word, but that was devilution.

On a Sunday morning, guilt can sneak up on you, stab you in the heart, and confront you with sins and regrets, accusing you of trying to be a saint on Sunday morning after living like the devil on Saturday night. It is kinda like someone opens the door where all that had been hiding and says, "Sic him, boys."

Michael wondered if all the perfect people around him could see his rap sheet, the ledger posted for all to see. He looked around and studied the faces of the congregants who had death grips on their hymnals, singing out of key but looking for the Keeper of the keys, and he suspected they were too busy with their own struggles to worry about the new guy in the fourth pew on the right.

Working in tandem with guilt were memories of happier days before sin overtook him. These were times he had forfeited but longed for. He could see his family eating fried chicken, turning the crank for homemade ice cream, and cousins returning from the pond with their cane poles and their fresh catch, dogs barking at their heels as a stringer of poor bass gasped for breath and wiggled and flopped for a last chance at freedom.

Michael remembered those days and began to understand how it all worked together to shape his life within the grand mystery of sin, suffering, and redemption and how it still offered him a chance to resolve honor and shame, "in it, and of it" actions and consequences, and escape hatches for prodigals who once sang "guilty for the rest of my life."

All of his ghosts seemed to have sidled up to his pew, plopped down beside him, and commenced to wash his dirty laundry in a place where God had sworn the saints to secrecy. Here in this house of worship, he thought of his finer moments and times when he fell a little short by a mile. He could hear Mama singing along with the car radio in their old Ford, "Ain't a-gonna need this house no longer, ain't a-gonna need this house no more."

During services at Calvary Baptist, Pastor Paul Warren often quoted seemingly obscure theologians from Christian antiquity to some but familiar to a former inmate with lots of time on his hands and books to read.

This Sunday, he quoted Soren Kierkegaard in his sermon as he glanced at Michael. "The greatest hazard of all, losing one's self, can occur very quietly in the world, as if it were nothing at all. No other loss can occur so quietly; any other loss—an arm, a leg, five dollars, a wife, etc.—is sure to be noticed."

The pastor paused and quoted the theologian again, "Life can only be understood backwards; but it must be lived forwards. God creates out of nothing. Wonderful, you say. Yes, to be sure, but He does what is still more wonderful: He makes saints out of sinners."

He looked down from his pulpit at Michael, and Michael smiled and nodded, and across the church, he saw Steven Ballard, his probation officer, and he, too, was smiling and nodding.

He thought this message might have been meant for him, and as he looked at the pastor and his probation officer he told Judy, "These guys plow pretty close to the corn."

As Michael and Judy filed out the door, Pastor Paul said, "I know you've read Kierkegaard, that you found him through Malcolm Muggeridge. I doubt most of the congregation know either of them, and it sure didn't inspire any aisle-walking or hanky-blowing, but from our talks, I knew you would and that these words would resonate with you."

"Pastor, those words made me want to crawl down the aisle and thank Him again for loving me," Michael said.

Michael had been stranded on a deserted island like Tom Hanks in the movie *Castaway*, a pilgrim in an unholy land, but a complementary crossroads for that pilgrim in forced monasticism, a rendezvous point, a place on an ancient map of his life written before he was knitted together in his mother's womb. It was a better-late-than-never reunion with his Creator, who already knew everything that was, is, or will be, things Michael once thought he could control before he was a bruised reed made whole.

As he walked to the car with Judy, he was tending a flock of revelations when he suddenly thought of Lazarus and the resurrection of all that was good, beautiful, and pure, the entirety of what it once meant to be a Christian.

He looked at her and smiled. Every now and then these days, Michael would catch himself smiling for no reason at all.

CHAPTER FOURTEEN

"Suddenly a weird garble of nonsensical, voice-like sounds broke in."—The Short-Wave Mystery, *Franklin W. Dixon*

"A gentle breeze blows…o'er Lullaby Bay. It fills the sails of boats waiting to sail your troubles away."
—"Hushaby Mountain," Richard Sherman

"The deadliest commitment of all is to be committed only to one's self. Some realize this after they are in the nursing home."—John D. MacDonald

Michael used to stay up at night when he visited Okaloosa Island, staring into the inky black of night, watching for the lights of the tankers, tugboats, and giant yachts traveling under cover of darkness, and the bobbing beacons and buoys pointing mariners to safe water channels.

He once tuned his radio dial on the squealing short-wave band until it yielded its mysteries. The cryptic bursts of Morse code and hushed voice clips from the boats had the feel of broadcasts from other planets or messages from the depths of a bottomless sea, the Coast Guard chasing smugglers, or passages from one of the Hardy Boys books he read as a boy, books like *The Short-Wave Mystery*.

He once dreamed of being a private eye, working out of his office on the island. He considered returning there after prison and hanging out his shingle—Michael Parker, Extremely Private Investigations. He could see the sign with the big pelican eye on the weathered wood board that creaked and sighed with the salty breezes.

Damsels in distress and people who had been wronged with nowhere else to turn would show up at his office, characters that John D. MacDonald and Mickey Spillane would have recognized.

It was part of his vivid imagination and his longing to transcend the transient, to be somewhere other than where he was, where the quicksand of the mundane didn't swallow up dreams, where the Lilliputians weren't always trying to tie Gulliver down, where the good music was still playing in his heart and above his head, where innocence still bloomed like perennial flowers, a place of peace close to God. Michael was certain that God must live on Okaloosa Island or at least visit there often.

Sometimes, his dreams all seemed like the acts of a long play, a book bursting to be read or written, or maybe a movie he'd seen, but he couldn't remember if it had a happy ending, if any hope was revealed in the rolling credits before…The End.

For all he knew now, all these years later, the channels off the coast could be impassable, and ship and shore might've divorced. The short-wave band could have been silenced, the sun diamonds might no longer dance and sparkle on blue waters, and the bright-orange sun might just hang in the sky near dusk, no longer melting into the blue-black of the deep off Okaloosa, but he didn't think so.

Some places in creation stand on tiptoes waiting for deliverance, groaning but enduring until the glory, no matter how hard man tries to turn treasure into trash, no matter how much forbidden fruit he consumes.

Michael's loud desk phone rang and jarred him from his musings and remembrances. He lifted off the chair, looking all around him, thinking for a moment he was back in prison or the halfway house where he always was on guard.

Michael stretched and muffled a yawn as he reached for the phone with the "wake the dead" ringer.

"Michael, this is Tim. Did I wake you?" asked the familiar, steady voice of Dr. Tim Charles, professor, friend, and former MBN Director.

"Hey, Tim. No, I was dozing, I guess, and thought for a moment that I was back in boot camp and had missed the last call for the chow hall," Michael said with a chuckle.

When Michael first met Tim in class at Ole Miss, he hadn't known what to make of him. He wore spurs on his boots to that first class, and his students could hear him jangling down the hall like Eastwood.

He was unorthodox in his methods, and unlike the other starched and pressed professors Michael encountered, the Word informed his worldview and his view of his students, not ink-blot tests and ACT scores. His word was his bond, embedded within a marriage of humor, mildness, and authority. Michael should have known that they would become close friends.

Tim shepherded Michael right through his Bachelor's degree and internship with the Lee County Sheriff's Department and eventually through his Master's degree.

When the governor finally succeeded in hounding Director Collins out of the MBN's top spot, the governor tagged Tim as director of the Mississippi Bureau of Narcotics, hoping Tim's credentials would stem the criticism from the firing of the MBN's respected director and founder.

At the first management meeting Tim held, Michael looked at the other captains seated around the conference table. They looked like ministers who had just come from dusting their pulpits or students with shiny apples for a new teacher. Word had gotten around that Tim was a Christian, and his father was once the state's highest-ranking Baptist.

Butter wouldn't melt in their mouths as they marched into the room in solemn lockstep, like centipedes wearing holy flip-flops. Their piety was deep-fried as they spoke of church, Sunday school, reading their Bibles, and the retreats they'd led.

Michael looked at them in disbelief and listened as each man polished his halo, each one upping his compadres. Finally, Tim asked Michael if he had something to offer.

Michael looked at them and said, "They look like the same people, but they don't sound like the same people." If looks could have killed, Michael would have died that day, but it struck Tim as the kind of hilarious honesty he had come to expect from his former student, and he slapped the table and laughed until his sides hurt.

That infectious laughter from yesteryear was still ringing in Michael's memory when Tim said, "Michael, I wanted to let you know that I have cancer."

It was the dreaded word that took Clay and Mama, the thing that took the life of the Edgefield inmate who was denied treatment, until they bore him out on a stretcher when he grabbed Michael's hand and said, "Pray for me, Michael. They've killed me."

"I'm going to begin treatment and have a bone marrow transplant," Tim said in a measured tone.

Michael's heart thundered like a runaway train, his mouth went cottony dry, and he was quiet for a pregnant moment. Sometimes silence born of bad news can be deafening. The sky falls, the earth's rotation stalls for just a click, the Gulf waters pause their lapping at the shore of the beloved island, and you cannot swallow the boulder in your throat.

"What can I do, Tim?" Michael asked.

"Just say a prayer for the family and me. I'm always ready when He calls. Maybe this is just a wake-up call, a 'to be continued' communique," he said with a muted imitation of his famous chuckle.

"I pray so, Tim," Michael said.

"Hope your landing has been as soft as I promised, as we wanted it to be, Michael. Just in case you might be interested in returning to the university, I asked the Dean of the Education Department if we could work you into the leadership track of their PhD program with your Master's degree, experience in education reform, and your record of leadership in public and private sector management," he said.

"Thanks, but just take care of you and your family. Don't worry about that; not sure that's where the Lord is leading me now anyway," Michael said.

"Well, that might be best. The university is not the place you remember. With your record, the dean just flat refused to admit you to the doctoral program or even to entertain the idea of redemption and grace. She thought it a disgrace that we gave you the Distinguished Alumni Award," Tim said solemnly.

He paused, and Michael could almost see him stroking his beard as he had so many times as professor and director when he was pensive or searching for just the right words.

With a pained wrinkle in his voice, Tim said, "But I told her, you don't know who he was and what he did before…"

Michael closed his eyes and hung his head. Tim's generosity and friendship were overwhelming. He could hear the resignation in his friend's voice, and once more, Michael felt the sting of remorse for friends he had failed and silently vowed to never be that wrong again.

"She was unmoved. Count yourself lucky, Michael," Tim said, clearing his throat.

"I do, Tim, and nothing they could give me could compete with what Christ has given me, and another degree means nothing next to your health," Michael said.

Michael also knew if they had accepted him, the price would have been too much, a promise to "let you back into our world, only if you promise to be good this time and not cause any more problems on crusades that offend our financial benefactors."

It hadn't been that long since a team of activists, who'd read too much Marx and not enough Mark, was touring America and holding debates at universities on homosexuality. No one would agree to debate them at Ole Miss for fear of retaliation, but Tim said he would represent the university, against the advice of his peers who said, "The university will get you, Tim."

After the debate, the visitors said it was the best give-and-take they'd had in an academic setting and the most respectful discussion they'd had anywhere, but when they left the campus, Dean Foster, who seethed and steamed like a boiling kettle from his seat at the debate, called Tim in.

The dean was a knotty little man with a squeaky voice that sounded like helium escaping from a pinched balloon when he got agitated. His rimless glasses and severe hairstyle gave him a marked resemblance to Himmler when he turned a certain way, but he was overwhelmingly a clerkish Goebbels, especially when he made his imperious gestures.

Foster was indignant when he met with Tim.

"We heard your arguments and your citation of stories in the Bible, and we don't want your kind at Ole Miss. I'll expect your retirement papers by the end of the day," the dean snorted, arms flailing, tiny baby fists pounding his desk.

Tim said he waited until the little man wore himself out, like a welterweight boxer flailing away at a heavyweight.

Tim told him, "I don't see how I could retire at my present salary. You've been withholding my pay raises for years because you don't like my politics. Now if you were to phase in the raises you withheld, I might be inclined to retire." He was tenured and knew they couldn't force him out, no matter how much the little man strutted and snorted.

Tim recounted the whole ordeal to Michael with triumphant sorrow. "For a while there in his office, the hot glare of the sun through the window reflected off his glasses, and I couldn't see his eyes. At that moment, he looked like the future, a future that jettisons truth and all the things that depend on it, a future full of automatons and ciphers hurling chunks of ancient citadels and stubs of crosses as expendable armaments in their culture wars.

"He was just another guy who'd been talking with the serpent in the Garden, all about the oppressed and oppressors with God cast as the Oppressor. What could it hurt? Just a little dialogue with darkness," Tim said.

Tim paused that day, flashed that mischievous grin, and said, "Dealing with these folks who hate people like us is just mind over matter, Michael. I don't mind, and they don't matter."

Tim got the raises but stayed on to inspire countless other students who looked up to him, as Michael had and did.

When they said their goodbyes on the phone call, Michael sat at his desk and remembered all that Tim had done in his life. He had been the youngest state crime lab director and testified in civil rights cases, though the Klan left threatening notes on his windshield at church and rattlesnakes in his mailbox.

His unpopular belief in the "mad bomber of the KKK," Tommy Tarrants, took a confused young man from prison to Tim's home, a seminary PhD, and the directorship of the C.S. Lewis Foundation in Washington, D.C.

Tim was an expert on terrorism and trained Christian missionaries how to avoid being taken hostage in foreign lands. When some were taken hostage, Tim Charles went to negotiate their release.

When Michael left the MBN, it was Tim who protected him from the long reach of his enemies in the governor's office, and it was Tim who came to Atlanta to stand with Michael when he was sentenced to prison, to hold him up when his legs were wobbly and his voice but a hoarse whisper.

Judy came to Michael's side. She had been quietly listening, and her eyes were big and wet, and the ceiling fan was blowing her hair. She held his hand as he told her the news, the sterile facts of it, the false certainty that it would all be okay, the breaking of the dam, and the flood of scalding tears that reddened his face.

"You know, it wasn't supposed to be this way. I just got home. There was supposed to be a pause, a grace period, a time for living," he said, resting his wet face on her wrist.

Michael finally unclenched his teeth, relaxed his fists into hands of prayerful petition, a repetitive pleading for his friend and mentor, a groaning petitioner returned to the ruins of a wrecked world to comfort those who had comforted him.

He was suddenly homesick for heaven and the glory to come, homesick for Okaloosa where there were no crooked streets, where he might find in the short-wave messages what he and America had lost along the way: clarity on a waystation between the here and the hereafter, where all of creation gives testimony to its Creator and longs for better days.

CHAPTER FIFTEEN

"Write from the heart; a book without a pulse is like a person without a spirit."—Linda Radke, President of Five Star Publications

"Gossip, as usual, was one-third right and two-thirds wrong."—Chronicles of Avonlea, *L.M. Montgomery*

"I came home with good intentions…"—*"Stranger in My Own Home Town," Percy Mayfield*

Judy had been busy fattening up Michael, whose Halloween skeletal bones looked sharp enough to pierce his pallid skin. He ate everything in sight, and milkshakes were a staple with each meal. He had gained twenty-five pounds almost overnight, and his doctor scolded him about a possible heart attack.

Michael cut back on the calories and began to shop his book, and the rejections from agents poured in. Most said that they couldn't sell *A Ghostly Shade of Pale*, that the drug wars were dated, a hackneyed story that had been told and retold.

Some huffed that the time for such sentimental books had long since passed, thankfully interred in dusty archives where they were not accessible by today's enlightened readers, who demand less of a clear line between right and wrong. A few climbed up on their soapbox to lecture a man just home from prison about books chronicling a time of "white privilege."

"More sin, less moralizing, less literature, and more gutter language. More Satan, less God," they said.

One consumptive publishing house, bearing all the signs of decay and Faustian deals, asked him if he could add neon to his writing and returned samples of his writing all dressed up with four-letter words and language for modern-day sewers, back alleys, and residents of Sodom and Gomorrah. They had scrubbed God from his pages and told him they were the experts.

Michael replied to their letter:

"We have plenty of descriptors to paint our word pictures without resorting to the use of profanity, which has nothing to do with good writing. Words we write today are like epitaphs on our tombstones. Perhaps others choose to be remembered for expletives and four-letter words, but I do not. I am writing to honor God, to produce a book I wouldn't be ashamed for my mother or my English teacher to read if they were still living. P.S. There is only one Expert I listen to. He says go; I go. He says do; I do."

Michael found a listing for a small publishing house. Their titles were sparse, and the expanse of their digital footprint seemed a mile wide but an inch deep. Nevertheless, he was unfamiliar with self-publishing options, so he attached his draft to his email and asked an unknown publisher if they might take a look at an unknown author.

Venturing out into the world felt strange. Michael had been invisible for years, disposable and dispensable, just dropped in a government box, slotted into what felt more like a coffin than a bed, a waiting bunk in a shuttered world. No one could call him or see him from the nearest road. Idealism was shattered, and his mind scrambled, frayed around the edges. The cherished places and people were lost, and Susan had gone home.

The country changed while he was invisible and had lost its spiritual moorings. People who had not been in forced isolation couldn't see it or hear it yet, but it bowled Michael over. There was no sense of urgency, no one rousing the populace. The *Titanic* was listing, and the lifeboats were empty, but he was learning to look people in the eye until they no longer saw him but Christ, so he could tell them things they didn't want to hear. He could feel an awareness of him by the world, the come-hither eye-battings of Satan's seductresses.

He received a call from Carl Hunt, an older man at Edgefield when Michael was there. He was a tough old buzzard with a pencil-thin mustache. He was once a fearsome sight when he guarded his acres of weed and his moonshine stills in the hollows and mountains of Tennessee.

He wore that tall, gangster fedora hat with the brim pulled down to his brows, high-pocket trousers, and a string tie to go with his long trench coat in the cooler months to hide his sawed-off shotgun. He always had a .38 Smith & Wesson with him, and the stories of him pistol-whipping trespassers were legendary. True or not, they were enough to scare away weak-kneed rivals.

Michael saw him cane-whip some inside at Edgefield who were much younger, and Michael warned them, "Don't cross him."

"We don't want to hurt the old man, but that cane hurts," the new breed of gangster whined.

Michael laughed and said, "Just leave him alone and let him watch his shows in the TV room. He may be old, but he's tough as nails, and at his age, a life sentence or execution for killing you in your sleep is not much of a deterrent."

Mr. Hunt was an aficionado of real country and mountain music. He knew the singers and pickers and shared endless stories and folklore with Michael. After Susan died, he told Michael about Vern Gosdin, and one day, while they were listening to the radio, Michael heard Gosdin sing, "You don't know about sadness till you've faced life alone. You don't know about lonely till it's chiseled in stone."

Michael cried a bucket of tears that night for the woman who loved his rightness even when he was sometimes wrong.

Mr. Hunt slept with one eye open, and when Michael went to wake him for a meal once, he spun around on his bed and hit Michael square in the mouth, loosening his front teeth. Mr. Hunt felt terrible about it, but it was just the way of someone who had walked on the wild side of life and fended off assaults for too many years in some brutal prisons.

Michael always picked up some ice cream for him on commissary day since Mr. Hunt's funds were spent, his money poke bone dry, and Michael read letters to him from his friends because his eyes weren't so good. One family in North Tennessee began to write Michael after asking who this man was who read their letters to Carl and answered their inquiries.

Without fail, Michael went to his room to pray with him every night before lights out. Mr. Hunt said he couldn't sleep if Michael didn't pray with him. As tough as Mr. Hunt was, the old outlaw cried the day Michael left for the Millington Camp. He wouldn't look up as Michael passed his room. He just sat on his bunk, sobbing. Michael had a pang of guilt for leaving him there.

Mr. Hunt called to tell Michael he was now home, living with his granddaughter in the mountains of Tennessee, overlooking the hollows where he once plied his illegal trade. Mr. Hunt said he was trying to serve the Lord and make amends, to speak to younger versions of his old self.

"Michael, can you feel it?" he asked.

"Yessir! It's smothering," Michael said.

Mr. Hunt said, "A man came to see me. 'We'll give you everything if you come back to us,' he said. I said, 'I have everything.' The man got angry then. He clenched his fists and said, 'Then we'll take everything you have.' I told him, 'I don't have anything.'

"His black eyes flashed at me, and he said, 'The Carpenter will never take you back. You are ours.'" Mr. Hunt's voice quivered, and he gasped for air.

"He was a demon, Michael. I know it. My friends said he wasn't, that I was just looking in the mirror and saw myself, but I know...I know. You be the watchman now. Man your post, Michael," he said.

With its unquiet eyes, this wizened age was the enemy, but how do you explain the inexplicable to people? Michael wondered.

CHAPTER SIXTEEN

"Sometimes I feel like a motherless child, a long, long way from home."—"Sometimes I Feel Like a Motherless Child," Isaac Holt, Eldee Young, Ramsey E. Lewis, Jr.

"Just a little boy standing in the rain. And the grass is gone, the boy disappears. The rain keeps falling like helpless tears."—"What Have They Done to the Rain," Malvina Reynolds

Despite all he had seen in the rough-and-tumble world of politics, Michael wanted to vote again and couldn't imagine not voting. Some states restricted the right to vote for felons, disenfranchising those they assumed might not vote the right way, linking it to a false claim of being tough on crime.

Securing his right to vote was not just something he sought for himself. He was a shepherd who had left his flock behind in prison but had not forgotten them. Michael wanted to challenge the idea that it was permissible to punish people beyond the sentences they had served, to tether them to mistakes they tried to leave behind, to act as their warden in open-air prisons.

He researched Mississippi law and learned the statute was for state convictions in Mississippi. His offense was federal, not state, and not in the state of Mississippi. Michael thought the law was clear on disqualification being a state conviction, and so did the Secretary of State, who issued guidance for local jurisdictions.

Michael assumed local jurisdictions would be unaware of the guidance or care about such nuances and distinctions. After all, an inmate is an inmate is an inmate. So, he asked the Secretary of State's office for a signed copy of the opinion in case he encountered resistance.

As he suspected, the supervisory clerk told Michael he could not vote after he registered. Michael thought he enjoyed it a bit too much and didn't say he was sorry. Michael produced the written guidance from the Secretary of State and informed the clerk he was wrong. The clerk retreated and said he didn't know.

Michael thought it unusual they would routinely research federal convictions in other states for each new voter registrant. He suspected they may have heard of his return to Tupelo and decided to protect the sanctity of the ballot from the last of the Boy Scouts. He also suspected these guardians of the law likely sat on the front pew every Sunday with furrowed brows, dipping their spoons into every sermon to see if they needed more salt.

Michael said, "I know you're just doing your job, following the law as it was given to you, but how many people who've paid their debt to society have come here to start over, to rejoin the community, to be good citizens, to seek forgiveness, only to have you resurrect the past and slam the door on the future? Their lives matter. Please stay current on the law. Disenfranchising people and barring them from the ballot box should not be a casual, clerical thing. If all men are created equal, 'except for' overturns that ideal, and all of it comes unraveled."

***

With his new car and voter ID secured, Michael drove to Nettleton to see friends. Making the rounds, he dropped by the home of his third-grade teacher, Nan Rogers. Nan was widowed and lived in a stately old house from yesteryear just across the street from the old Nettleton Medical Clinic.

Old oaks surrounded the house, the kind people had tied yellow ribbons around when local boys went missing in action, with carefully tended flower beds, what people once called a victory garden of vegetables. The house was quiet and so big that it could swallow up one resident, but there were too many memories there for Nan to leave.

As he knocked on the front door, he thought of her when she was his third-grade teacher. He was nine and full of curiosity that killed the cat. Special decorations made of crepe-paper flowers were on the bulletin boards, and visitors were coming by to inspect the classrooms. Nan told the class not to touch or disturb them as they filed out for lunch, but Michael's hand moved involuntarily to the pretty paper roses. In the poverty of the 1950s, he had not seen anything so perfectly perfect that almost promised a fragrance.

Nan called him into her room later when the other students were at recess. She told him that she had to paddle him. Those were the rules. The gentle, hesitant whacks of the paddle didn't hurt. What hurt were the tears that streamed down Nan's face. He had made his teacher cry.

Almost twenty years later, when Michael was the MBN supervisor, he spoke to a local church. Nan was there. After the speech, she apologized for paddling him when he was nine and said she had regretted that every day of her life.

"In those days, they taught us that if we said something, we must enforce it with the paddle, but you were such a sweet little boy," Nan told him.

He told her it was okay and was so sorry he had made her cry. Then he saw the tears that night and realized he had made his teacher cry again.

Michael heard movement inside the house, and Nan opened the door. Older, loneliness etched in her face, the squint lines of a gardener around her eyes, but still one of the sweetest women God ever made, a teacher you wanted to protect, to make proud.

"Michael, my goodness. What are you doing here? Come in this house," she said, her eyes lighting up as she hugged her little boy.

They talked for a long time, and she showed him around the house with its high beams, off-white walls, and Hunter ceiling fans. She spoke of how big and empty it was after her husband, Jim, had passed, and his picture was prominent in the foyer. Michael could tell she was still mourning, the same gentle, tender-hearted woman who had cried when she disciplined him so long ago. Time had not dimmed who she was, and that was a bridge to yesteryear, like the music from the '40s and '50s playing on her phonograph.

After they wore out conversation and drank every drop of fresh iced tea from her clinking pitcher, Nan grew grim and serious. He could tell there was something she wanted to ask, something bursting to get out, a burden she needed to lay down.

"Michael, I was at a class reunion of sorts recently, and there were people there who knew you," she said, wringing her weathered hands.

Here it comes, here it comes, Michael thought.

"Michael, one of the former students told us all that you had been in prison. I told him that couldn't be true, not Michael, that there must be some mistake. Not you. I told them you were probably just working undercover like you did at the narcotics bureau, but he said it was true. His wife is friends with Judy," she said.

Michael guessed who it was and could see his moon face and stubby fingers. He wasn't a bad person, but his compulsion to gossip, to tell "secrets" to gain status, sometimes overwhelmed his normal aversion to destroying anything.

"It's not true, is it, Michael?" she asked.

A white-hot spear of guilt and shame pierced Michael to his core, trickles of sweat tracked down his back, and he saw the memories and innocence he had come to rekindle suddenly shattered, and with them, the place he came to rest for a while. It was vital for her and his witness that he show Christ in his tortured face and not indulge his own pain or anger, to meet this moment as he would have to meet others to come.

Despite the assurances of the probation officer that no one in Mississippi knew, Michael had been certain it would all come out. Gossipmongers love to feel big by making others small, airing the dirty laundry of others, and pointing to the stains. He just wanted it on God's timetable as the novels were published, so he could tell it all in books, interviews, speeches, and testimonies in churches like the one he and Nan once attended. He didn't seek kid gloves or feather dusters; he just didn't want the lost to turn against him until they could hear his gospel message of grace and redemption.

Michael looked into her sad basset eyes begging for an explanation, for the truth she wanted to hear. He could almost hear the rattle of the pages as her mind furiously turned the pages looking for an excuse, a missing page of life's script that would make it make sense.

"No, it's true, Nan," he said in a voice not quite his own. He wanted to be the child and receive comfort, but he had to be the adult and comfort her.

Her mouth sagged, her eyes teared, and disbelief was written in her countenance and the blow to her heart. One tear overflowed and burned her cheek before she wiped it away, her searching, pleading eyes never leaving his. It was something she could not process, something that was impossible, a cruel joke, a mistake, a bad dream.

Michael took her hand and said, "Let me tell you about God's purpose in pain."

They talked for a long while, and it was a test. If Michael could find the words God had given him, if he could pass this test with a teacher he loved without running away, overwhelmed by shame, he could face those who would not be so kind, those who would want to destroy him and silence his story, God's story. At times he thought he smelled smoke and imagined the devil sitting in the corner, blowing smoke rings in his face.

The talk was intense, full of sorrow, then forgiveness, and finally joy. He began to notice the scratches on the album playing on her vintage record player. Then, as their talk and tears wore down, the last album ended and was stuck in a steady "cushoo, cushoo," like the ebb tide carrying the hurt out to sea, the flow rushing back to shore with a shush and pop. The tonearm rested on the dead wax between the recording and the label, but Michael could feel the calming waters of Okaloosa around his feet.

Sometimes, worn needles get down to the bottom of the grooves in the record where there is no music, a fine line between annoying white noise and soothing alpha waves. For a bit, Michael and Nan had been at the bottom of the grooves where the hymns were hard to hear, but by the time they finished, she was clutching his paws in her weathered hands and asking how she could help.

For a moment, he was back at the edge, wading around in the shallows of what-ifs, whys, and wreckage, hesitant to drop his pail into the well of his soul, knowing what's in the well will come up in the bucket, the reruns of his life and all the deleted scenes that did not fit, to see it all and not turn away.

There was no reason good enough for anyone to hurt Nan, but I guess I started that ball rolling, didn't I? What was that really all about anyway, a death wish, weariness, unworthiness, something to prove, dragons to slay, or just a little time stolen from responsibility, a timeout from the weight of the world for a compulsive cleaner-arranger who wanted to neaten up the planet? Or was it just sin as old as the Garden?

Loved ones and faithful pets depended on me, confident I could fix any bad thing and emerge from the briar patch without a scratch, but one day the Energizer Bunny's battery lost its charge and slumped over just when the enemy had encamped all around, people who had driven their tent pegs deep into the soil of a corrupted world. They brought so much artificial illumination but not the Light that sees and knows when the odd sparrow falls.

They all said I was a round peg in a round hole. Just keep my nose clean, my pants pressed, and my hair combed, and I was set for life—the pension, stock, gold watch, and country club—until they reserved a room for me at the Shady Rest Nursing Home and then a final resting place with cold granite as my pillow.

But it wasn't enough. It was never enough. That distant drummer Susan referred to kept playing louder and louder. Something greater, a calling, an unknown itch to scratch, a world to save, until I realized the world already had a Savior, and his name wasn't Michael.

They hugged goodbye, and as the light of day dimmed, Michael saw her headed for her flower bed with her trowel and heard the rattle of her ancient wheelbarrow. He smelled the fragrance of her gardenias as a cardinal tried his best to drown out a chirping tree frog and a mosquito's whining search for blood near his ear. They say they can smell the protein in blood over a hundred yards away. He smiled and thought, *There's power in the blood.*

When Michael left the "Prison Chronicles" behind, he aimed for a new life without having to apologize for and constantly explain the former life, but you always take yourself with you wherever you go, and some will insist that you show them the splinters in your paws and the ragged edges of old wounds. They want you to sing sorrow from your diaphragm while you want to sing joy from your heart. But not Nan.

As he emerged from his cocoon, Michael was beginning to suspect that all of it—Tim, the Dean of Education, voting, and Nan—were all part of the journey. The metamorphosis, the changing of a person from the old to the new by natural or supernatural means, was accelerating.

Layers of the old were flaking off; roles he had played at home, in Atlanta, and prison were peeling off of the statue of a fool. No more role-playing, not half this and a quarter of that accretion until the core identity was revealed or rediscovered. He knew that the path ahead was a minefield, and there would be much more to come before he found the Michael Parker God was resurrecting.

No identity or past roles fit right now. Like bad suits, they were all too tight or too loose, made for someone else. These were the growing pains of a born-again man, grayer and physically weaker but spiritually stronger than ever.

As he inspected the new man in the mirror, the face looked back at him, different and uncertain, outside its comfort zone, but not fully formed, a work still in progress by the Sculptor.

Then, apart from it all for a moment, he saw himself as God sees him.

Michael whispered to the confused image in the mirror, "It's going to be all right," though he wasn't quite sure what that meant.

As he drove away, he thought perhaps sunspots made the gossipers spread their foul condiment on the dishes they served. The news said sunspots and solar flares were active, affecting the grid and radio transmissions, maybe making a frangible earth a tad off-kilter, loosening the careless, reckless tongues that pierce like swords.

Despite the cool spots on the sun, dusk was rosy-colored like fires burning on the horizon, like the decorations he had touched so long ago, and he could feel the faint warmth of the retiring sun through his open window.

Michael drove toward the scarlet sky behind the tree line and said out loud, "Red sky at night, sailor's or shepherd's delight."

Jesus told His disciples they knew fair weather was coming when the evening sky was red. They could read the signs in the sky, but like many today, could not discern the signs of the times.

He turned on his radio, and an old man was praying a blues song. "Jesus, won't You come by here. Jesus, won't You come by here. Now is a needed time. Come even if You can't stay long."

CHAPTER SEVENTEEN

"Consecrate me now to Thy service. Draw me nearer, nearer, blessed Lord, to Thy precious bleeding side. Let my soul look up with a steadfast hope, my will be lost in Thine."—"Draw Me Nearer," Fanny Crosby

"God walks the dark hills to guide my footsteps. God walks the dark hills to show me the way."— "God Walks the Dark Hills," Audra Czarnikow

"If buttercups buzzed after the bee. If boats were on land, churches on sea, if ponies rode men and grass ate the cows, and cats should be chased into holes by the mouse, if mamas sold their babies to gypsies for half a crown; if summer were spring and the other way around." —"The World Turned Upside Down," John Renfro Davis

Sometimes when Michael woke up or was about some tasks, he had to stop and remind himself what day it was, where he was, that this, the here and now, not yesterday or tomorrow, was real. At times it took several seconds or minutes to accept the present as real and the other as a seduction or diversion from the task before him.

Occasionally he would feel a rush of a current of guilt, a flash flood of recrimination as if the Dutch boy had removed his finger from the dike, allowing the sharp thing to stab him beneath his spiritual armor. For what? Past sins, living when Susan died, living the good life when friends were still in prison, or the scarlet letter he imagined on his forehead that made him want to confess to crimes he had not committed? He wasn't sure, maybe all of it or just his old adversary, the one he answered with, "It is written."

Under the glare of an unmellow yellow sun, Michael dug holes for flowers and began his transformation of their yard to build a wall of green to shut out the noise, lights, and prying eyes of a lost world. Only birds, blooms, and the bounty from God would be allowed.

A robin came up to peer longingly at the red worms wiggling in the disturbed soil of Michael's new worm factory, dashing forward to gobble worms exposed by Michael's shovel, then backing up to await the next excavation, the proverbial early bird.

One of Michael's favorite Bible verses was Matthew 6:26, "Consider the birds of the air, for they neither reap nor sow nor gather into barns; yet your heavenly Father feeds them. Are you not of more value than they?" Michael considered it an admonition to watch birds, to listen to the voice and testimony of nature to our Creator.

Such pauses took him back to Parker Grove when he listened to the whistling, trilling flutes, melodies, and symphonies of the forests he roamed, days when he felt the groan that longed for the glory, for what could have been, something better, Someone to come, though he didn't yet understand Who or why.

When he was in the pits of hell in the Atlanta jail, the first verses read by a struggling man inmates would later dub "Bird Man" were Psalm 91:3 and Psalm 124:7. Michael used them in prayers he fashioned from Scripture. "He will deliver you from the snare of the fowler." "We have escaped like a bird from the fowler's snare."

As Michael raked, dug, and mined for meaning, a swallowtail butterfly with its spatulate tail floated on the shuddering breeze, rustling the pampas fronds. A nuthatch squeaked at him from the trunk of a giant pine tree, and a rabbit hopped up to see if any usable nesting material was left over from the gardener's labor.

He leaned on his shovel, mopped his brow, and thought of church services he had attended or watched on television and the internal strife and widening fissures he saw. He listened closely to the words of young preachers whose theology confused Biblical justice with "social justice" as they preached an empty hyphenated gospel that was like Grape-Nuts, neither grapes nor nuts.

When he voiced his concerns to one of them, the toffee-nosed pastor said, "You're just out of prison, aren't you? I've been to the best seminary in the country. Do you think you understand the gospel? Do you think you're some sort of prison prophet?"

Michael could smell the sugar in the Kool-Aid; someone in a cage who didn't know Christ had opened the door.

Michael smiled and said, "No, as Amos said, I'm neither a prophet nor a son of a prophet, but I have eyes to see the moral decay around us. I also know you can't trade the transcendent for the transient. Do I understand the enormity of God and the gospel? No, I'm too puny, and despite your degrees, I suspect you are, too.

"I don't understand electricity either, but I don't just sit in the dark until I do. I go to the Light. I know where churches used to be. When they get right, they'll be where I am because I'm where they used to be. That was when they were still fishers of men before some of them handed over the ship to the mutineers and began to baptize pagans to pad their rolls. Church is a lifeboat, not a showboat.

"I thought I had to hurry and catch up when I came home, but now I think the shoe may be on the other foot. I know Jesus could never make peace with the world, and affirming sin leads to denying the gospel, as sure as fall follows summer.

"Some sermons I hear seemed focused more on material poverty than salvation, words drafted by sociologists and philosophers rather than theologians. Some wag fingers at the congregation about making peace with the world instead of pointing to the Cross. They don't talk much about repentance and forgiveness and seem to suggest it is God who should repent and seek man's forgiveness. I'm just a gardener, but I know you must keep your garden weeded lest it choke out the good stuff. Some folks today act as if they graduated from cemeteries, not seminaries," he said with a winsome smile.

"Well, we just had a meeting of one hundred pastors who agreed we need to make the gospel relevant to today's issues," the pastor huffed as Michael saw empty pews in churches, graves within congregations, reflecting the common grave of a lost world.

"I'm not sure one hundred blind men can see better than one. God doesn't change. If He spoke today, He'd repeat Himself," Michael said.

The young pastor said, "I guess you're one of those old folks who used to say the world is going to hell in a handbasket."

"No," Michael said, "the handbasket got saved. I'm one of those old men who used to say they're going to heaven in a wheelbarrow.

"Pastor, pagans have demanded and gained access to the church. Once inside, they dismantled the foundations stone-by-stone, convincing some that God had locked the church members in prisons, and that they, the pagans, were their liberators. It's the same old story of the serpent casting God as the oppressor and Adam and Eve as the oppressed.

"I'm baffled as to why so many are unwilling or afraid to speak against heresy and defend the faith, but I've been outside the bubble. So many seem to prefer to be united in error than divided by truth. They follow wolves in sheep's clothing who speak Christian words but define them by the world's dictionary and concordance. They try to remake Christ as just a great man and moralist to be admired but not worshipped and talk about heaven coming down when it is the world rushing in.

"I don't know much, but I think such preaching is an ancient poison in a new bottle, a systemic means to marginalize Christ and strip Him of His deity before those who needed Him most, while the flocks are grayed to make the black sheep and wolves among them feel better. I think it has metastasized in too many churches.

"I hope you and your fellow newly minted preachers can shut the church doors to this prevailing wind. There are consequences to watering down the gospel, and we are drowning in a sea of consequences. Nothing is sacred or real, and everything is fluid. Reality is being rewritten by those who've rejected Him and are trying to replace Him or re-create Him in their own image," Michael said.

Michael shook himself from his melancholy, turned to his gardening tasks at hand, and turned up his tiny radio and caught the end of an old sermon by Adrian Rogers.

"Praise God. It is getting gloriously dark. We're living in strange times. They sadden me, but they do not shake me," Adrian said.

He said this is a time of urgency to share Christ with the lost. He cited Luke 21:28. "And when these things come to pass, then look up, and lift your heads; for your redemption draweth nigh."

Michael squinted as he looked up at the white clouds pasted to the blue sky like cotton ornaments. Amidst the songbirds singing their vespers, he could almost hear the heartbeat of the universe, the pulsing drumbeat of life, an answer to the groaning for glory, the inhaling and exhaling of God Almighty. He was suddenly homesick for heaven.

He had heard the sounds before, just before and after the ambush in 1976 when the sniper rounds ripped through his friend's second-chance vest when life hung by a Divine thread. He heard it the night he was kidnapped by the drug dealers in 1972, when the weight of the air above him was heavy but comforting like the palm of a hand holding him or a warm blanket.

Oddly enough, he sensed it in 1966 when he sat on a curb outside Washington, D.C., and counseled a brokenhearted girl. She had one brown eye and one green, a rare condition called heterochromia. He remembered she talked through her nose, wore a yellow pencil behind her right ear, and her shoulders were slumped. Bent beneath her sorrows, she kept looking up at the stars and seemed to be waiting for something or Someone. Just before she rose to leave, she squeezed Michael's hand and thanked him for "sitting with us."

Michael asked, "Us?"

She said, with the ghost of a lisp and a slight whistle through her front teeth, "The Lord and me."

Though he thought he was counseling her, she was miles ahead of Michael that night when the shadow of the Almighty passed over a boy sitting on a curb, giving away kindness.

There were things he still did not understand. He thought of guilt and the things that can shrink you, forgiveness and Susan, and things that make you feel ten feet tall. He remembered her last note in prison. "Be good until we meet again." He was happily haunted by a dream of her after she died, a young girl, no longer in pain, running toward heaven, to the open arms of Christ.

Michael looked up from the tilled earth and saw the silhouette of Judy watching him from the window and thought, *Just when you think you've lost everything, God gives you something precious to protect.*

He wasn't sure God had favorites, but he thought He had intimates. Michael wanted more than anything, more than life itself, to be an intimate of God, to dwell in the house of the Lord forever.

A sudden storm blew up, and he could smell the earthy dampness behind a big rain curtain. The rumble of thunder and the crackle of lightning had a soothing and secretive sound. The wind bent the trees and banged the door shut to the heavens, but not before he felt the pulse of the Almighty and saw the visible promise of the rainbow. He involuntarily raised his hands, crying out to God, straining toward heaven in a foretaste of glory divine.

Everything was moving too fast, but too slow. Michael could see every crack and pebble on the road home; prison was gone as if it never happened. It was like walking out of the dark into the light and pausing to squint and reset your eyes.

He had prepared himself for reentry but not to see the apple gnawed bare. The imitation living water served was not from the ancient well, but the flotsam and jetsam of the gospel still circulated amidst the wreckage.

As he sprinted up the hill ahead of the downpour, Judy called to him from the deck, "Phone, honey. It's your probation officer."

Rain-soaked and out of breath, Michael picked up the phone and recognized the voice of his probation officer, Steven Ballard.

"Michael, The Salvation Army called and asked if you could start today and help serve lunch to the residents and locals," he said.

"Sure, just out working in the garden, but I'll get cleaned up and head that way," Michael said.

"I told them about your Christian movie nights in prison. They said tonight is church night, and all are required to attend. They said you could show a movie tonight if you'd like and speak to the residents," Ballard said.

"I have just the movie," Michael said.

"Michael, I thought you might like to know that the Bureau of Prisons has revoked the contract of the facility you were in," Ballard said.

Michael paused for a long time and said, "Is that so?"

"Yes, the place is empty now. All the staff is gone, and the residents were transferred to other halfway houses or back to prison," the young probation officer said.

"Well, I told them that serving those stale cornflakes would do them in. That must've been it," Michael quipped.

Ballard suppressed a chuckle and said, "I can't say any more, just thought you'd like to know."

Michael said, "Mr. Ballard, if I were still working in the garden, that news would've made me wet my plants."

He heard Ballard snicker again as he hung up.

Michael stood by the window for a moment, thumbs tucked in the pockets of his jeans as the rainwater ran down the panes. He thought of the residents at Halfway Home and the inmates he had known at three prison camps. They weren't cardboard characters in an imitation of life but flesh-and-blood stragglers, ships passing in the days of weal and woe where the dark waters were deep, the angry sea was rolling, and dolphins with sentient eyes leapt above the turbulent waves, awaiting the coming of their Creator.

He wondered if the "same old evangelicals," often the "same old heretics," thought about the end of this world, if they knew that excuses cannot be washed by the blood of Christ. He wondered if they remembered Zion, could tell time in the twilight and get home before dark when there was still light for their sundials, or if they were just too busy negotiating a ceasefire with the world and clutching a pristine white flag of surrender.

Michael thought about green pastures, still waters, and lighting lamps.

CHAPTER EIGHTEEN

"Down a dangerous road, I have come...my dreams and plans all scattered in the wind. I have come in search of Jesus, hoping He will understand. If I give my soul to Jesus, will He stop my hands from shaking?" — *"If I Give My Soul," Billy Joe Shaver*

"What good am I if I know and don't do? If I see and don't say, if I look right through you. If I turn a deaf ear to the thundering sky. What good am I while you softly weep and I hear in my head what you say in your sleep and I freeze...like the rest who don't try?"
— *"What Good Am I," Bob Dylan*

A sun, like a giant egg yolk, sizzled against a restless sky as Michael drove to The Salvation Army, and he saw the street sign for Carnation Street, where Tammy Sue Jenkins was found after her beating. She had written Michael just before he left prison, and Jimmy's revelation on what happened to her assailants was still fresh on Michael's mind.

On impulse, he turned down the street and cruised down the narrow lane. It had changed but retained the old feeling of seclusion in stretches that time, progress, and the tides of history had neglected.

He peered through the fog of time and strained to remember where she was found. He pulled over where the bushes and vines had overtaken the area, and an illegal trash dump showed bedsprings, tires, and an old couch. Small saplings bent beneath his car as he edged closer. Beyond the dumping ground, Michael could see debris, what appeared to be rusty brown metal entangled and choked by honeysuckle and Virginia creeper vines, resting under scrub trees with knotted trunks.

The car where she was left for dead had been dusted for prints and combed for forensics by local police, or so they claimed. They told Michael they found nothing usable, no leads, no snitches offering information, nothing. The blood and the prints were all hers. Then vandals burned the car, they said.

The perpetrators had just vanished, so said local detectives and wiretap specialists who told Michael they knew she was working for him. It was after that when Michael discovered the skinned wires on the telephone protector at his house, a sign someone may have intercepted calls or perhaps waited in the bushes at Michael's back door on Lumpkin Street when Tammie Sue slipped in to bring information and sample Susan's hot chocolate chip cookies just out of the oven.

He could almost hear the sounds of her sandals clacking on the kitchen tile, and he could see her face before it was broken, but the detectives had become faceless.

As he sat at the site he could taste the residuals of death cheated, sweated fear, the metallic smell of clotted blood, and images of her empurpled face when he was called to the hospital. It was eerily still, with no sound of birds or insects at what had been her intended gravesite.

They had left her rings on swollen fingers, likely planning to come back and cut her fingers off. The maps showed this place was in the city limits of Tupelo, but it became another country where evil had erased all boundaries.

The images came roaring at him like a runaway train, filling the dry beds of memory with brim-to-brim horror. The sun had baked her in this oven. Baked and beaten, this was her gateway to death, only a half-step away, but she would not die this way.

Her life had been hard, and she had fallen in with a fast crowd that led her to this place. She told Michael once about her childhood and a little red wagon she had. In the white glare of the hospital room, she told him that they had broken her little cart, and she could no longer pull it because her bruised arms had become like empty sleeves in her dress. She hissed through broken jaws and a mouth wired shut and told him of her visions before regaining full consciousness in the car trunk, and in those visions, Jesus looked down at her from the Cross, and in His eyes was life.

She left for the Air Force, wrote him for a while and sent pictures, then nothing until her letter arrived at Talladega Prison Camp, telling him of a redeemed life as a mother, grandmother, and servant of Christ.

As he roved the backyards of memory and the brackish rivers of yesterday, Michael wasn't sure if he was drawn to revisit these events because he felt he should have somehow prevented them, or maybe it was just in the DNA of the fixer, the errant knight riding to the rescue.

Maybe it was because he distrusted the present or just longed for the familiar, to go back and understand, to make sense of his life, to find missing links or answers left there for him. Or was it to gain closure, to make things right in a world darkly polished by sin? Today he could smell the residuals of yesterday and hear the sobbing, thrashing, vomiting, kicking, and the almost terminal last breaths, when essential essentials had been lost to a young girl Michael thought would never be the same again.

It was in these moments of searching when heaven seemed to come down, and the present became only two-dimensional without depth or substance. Answers hidden in the shoals of his life were washing up on his shorelines like messages in bottles, moving past the third dimension of height, width, and depth into the fourth dimension of time and beyond.

A blue jay flew out of the bushes covering the relic of a horrible crime and accused Michael of violating holy ground. As he sat in the car pondering it all, a restless wind churned up a dust devil and began to pelt his windshield with grit as he opened a letter Judy gave him as he left home.

It was his first letter, a well-traveled envelope with numerous postmarks all over the front and back, mostly from towns in western states.

Dear Michael,

This is your old buddy, Corleone, from the Atlanta jail. I am living the good life, a pillar of the community, or so they say, in an undisclosed location. I asked my control agent if he could find out what had happened to you since I last saw you in the Atlanta Corrections and Detention Center.

I heard your princess died, and I am sorry about that, man. When I called her to tell her that you could no longer respond to me from your cell, that they would kill you if she didn't make a fuss, I knew she was something special and loved you like crazy.

When the boys in the cellblock near us planned the jailbreak with Brian Nichols, the guy who killed Judge Barnes and the others in the Atlanta courthouse, I had to move fast when they asked me if I was going with them. I would have never seen daylight again if I hadn't snitched on them, but I didn't do it to get out of jail.

Listening to you praying day and night and those talks we had late at night through the slots in our doors, something about the things you said made me want to live, to know Who it was that freed you from your enemies, Someone who could forgive me for my foul deeds.

It changed my life. I laid down that heavy load I was dragging around, all of my soul confusion, doubt, and what I once thought was a necessary capability for sudden horror. I can't say much that would identify where I am, but I am no longer alone, even when I'm by myself.

I think of you and our talks about Christ. I think of how it all began with Nichols assaulting a girl because she dated a preacher, how the devil got him on the hard road to hell. I think of that girl, Ashley Smith, who he kidnapped after the murders in court, and how she showed him the love of Christ, read to him from a Christian book, and got him to surrender.

Jesus just kept popping up in my life every way I turned.

You got me talking like a street-corner preacher, but I never met anybody like you. I hope to see you again one day in that place where there is no pain, where I am not black, and you are not white, where we are both young again for a million, million years.

Your friend, the former gangster,

Corleone

Michael slumped in his seat. Beads of sweat formed on his upper lip; his hands had a slight tremor that rattled the paper, and something turned over in his stomach like he might get sick. He stared at the letter through watery eyes and read the words again and again, a note from Tyrone Jones, nicknamed Corleone because some thought he was the godfather.

Coincidence or more pieces of the Divine puzzle? It made his head throb in time with the whooshing of his racing heart. He prayed out loud, and in the stillness of the moment, his voice had a strange resonance. Even the sunlight shining in his face suddenly seemed as frail and feeble as he did, but out on the horizon, incoherence was becoming coherence.

When things are broken, Someone must pick up the pieces like bread crumbs along the trail from the womb to the tomb. The pieces of Michael's life were all falling into place, and in the fragments was the image in Tammy's dreams of a Man on a cross staring down at him.

CHAPTER NINETEEN

*"God, stay with me, let no word cross my lip that is not
Your word, no thoughts enter my mind that are not Your
thoughts, no deed ever be done or entertained by me that is
not Your deed."—Malcom Muggeridge*

*"You are the light of the world. A town built on a hill
cannot be hidden."—Matthew 5:14*

As Michael drove to The Salvation Army headquarters, he
sang their ancient song: "I was lying in the gutter, all covered with
beer. I feared the end was near when along came The Salvation
Army and saved me from the hearse. Let's all sing the second
verse. Hallelujah! Hallelujah! Put a nickel on the drum, save a
drunken bum. Hallelujah! Hallelujah! Put a nickel on the drum,
and you'll be saved."

Bum was not a word used today, but the sentiment of service
was there and attached to Michael's mood as he fished in his
pockets for nickels.

The sky had taken on a yellow hue, making a dull glint on his
side mirror. The courtyard had gravel-like paving with pebbles that
popped and crunched under his tires, like the sounds of the Nestle
Crunch bars he loved as a child. There was no sign of life, fauna or
flora in the compound. The main buildings looked abandoned and
were mortuary quiet, but he knew they served many residents at
the site—the homeless from camps around town, and some down-
on-their-luck elders looking for a free meal.

The main door across from the small apartments opened, and a
small, stern, uniformed lady with heavy glasses eyed him and
asked in a *Dragnet* economy of words, "You Parker?"

"That's me," Michael said, with the full blush of joy from
Corleone's letter still shining on his face.

"I'm Major Howard. I'll keep your time cards for U.S. Probation. See Suzie, and she'll show you what she needs. Can you cook?" she asked.

"Nothing to brag about, known to mess up boiling water, but I can wash dishes, serve meals, and tidy up things pretty good," he said.

"That'll work. Did you bring your movie? Tonight's church night and all residents are required to attend. Be there about seven to set up, speak, or whatever you used to do in your prison program," she said.

"Thanks, I'll be there," Michael said.

She turned to go but looked back at him and said, "I'm sure I don't have to tell you this, coming from prison and a police background, but we help a lot of sad people here. We also encounter some that are not restrained by the things that restrain most people. Some are unpredictable because of brain damage from alcoholism and drug abuse, or they were set free from mental wards by judges or politicians who didn't care what happened next. Others are just primitive and volatile and wrestle quietly with their demons, but all our misfits need the Lord. We have lonely beds here filled with lonely people. Keep that in mind, preacher," she said.

"I understand. My heart was burned in the third degree, but the Wounded Surgeon healed my wounds and grafted a new life onto the charred places," Michael said.

Major Howard stared at him for a long moment and then nodded before she left.

As he walked toward the kitchen, Michael noticed the ancient linoleum looked as if it had been cleaned and buffed a million times, and he caught the toxic smell of a harsh disinfectant mixed with bug spray. In a testament to the latter's effectiveness, Michael saw a roach on its back, feet up in the air, a breadcrumb behind its head like a tombstone.

Suzie, a small woman the color of dark putty, wore an apron bearing the stains of every vegetable and juice found in the South.

A small, plastic radio sat on the shelf behind her, playing gospel music. The radio gave the songs a tinny, metallic sound, but it reminded Michael of the prized transistor radio he had as a teenager in Parker Grove.

She looked up while holding a big knife in her hand and asked, "You Mr. Parker?"

Michael smiled, pointed to her "machete" and said, "Yes, but whatever it was, I didn't do it."

She laughed and said, "I'm Suzie, and you are just in time. Some of the volunteers didn't show up, and before you know it, folks will be lined up here like distant cousins at the will reading of a rich uncle with no close kin."

They both laughed and she pointed him to his very own apron.

Michael began to open giant cans of vegetables donated by groceries, mix bowls of Kool-Aid, and lay out loaves of bread and crackers to go with the stew and flannelly meat Suzie was preparing.

As the people filed in, Michael served platefuls of good, hot meals and greeted them with the love of his Savior. He saw the wounds in their eyes from the bottles, the needles, the unspeakable abuse, the hard times, and the effort required just to lift their eyes and look him in his. Some had hooded eyes, half-closed to hide shame, to guard their souls and not allow anyone to get at their tenuously mended places and fragile fracture lines.

People were grateful and humble. One or two seemed painfully embarrassed, shy, or extra hungry, and had pudgy-legged kids in tow, so Michael slipped them a little extra, maybe a second cookie or three. The spirit of this place was already wedging its way into Michael's heart. He knew his trials were preparation for places like this and the dark corners to come in his ministry.

The knowing was one more victory over the bleakness that had wanted to swallow him, one more touch of the elusive unknown he chased on the long road home. When he felt the darkness prick him now, he thought it was angry and no longer seemed so confident. At times, amidst the noise mingled with the crowd talk, his heart would swell to near bursting with love, and he thought he heard Someone calling his name.

When the meals were finished, the garbage removed, and the tables scrubbed clean for the next serving, Michael thanked Suzie, who was covered in flour, for allowing him to help.

"You're different, Mr. Parker. I bet you'll be steady until the cows come home," she said while grimacing from the dill pickle she was eating.

"Speaking of cows, we ran through enough milk for two or three noon meals. Wonder how that happened?" she asked.

Michael grinned sheepishly and said, "Well, you were busy in the kitchen, and all these kids with swollen bellies and eyes like saucers came up for extra cookies, and you know, it just isn't right to have cookies without milk, and the milk would probably just sour quickly anyway."

"You won't do, Mr. Parker. I'll have to call our suppliers and see if they can run a truck by here in the morning," she said with a pretend frown.

"Just take it out of my pay, Suzie. Why, just before the crowd left, I heard a woman leading several children in prayer, and they recited the Twenty-Third Psalm back to her, saying, 'He leadeth me beside the distilled waters.' A little more milk, a few more cookies, and they'll get it right," he said with a big grin he once thought he'd lost in prison.

Suzie put her hands on her hips, tilted her flour-dusted head to one side, and said, "I'll see you tomorrow, Michael. I can't wait. I think."

Michael put away some chairs, laid out some paper plates for tomorrow, and set off in search of the chapel and the equipment he would need to show his movie to this congregation.

Night fell suddenly, and a sudden wind rattled a loose shutter as the parched and pallid people filed into the little church. They looked thirsty for something, too long in the desert of despair, and the paleness had nothing to do with race. It was in the faces of the black, white, and brown, a washed-out, bleached-out look around the eyes, the pallor of the skin, and that gait or shuffle of too many blows to the soul.

Some of the women with marbled eyes dimmed by pain had several children in tow. Many of the kids recognized Michael as the cookie man and smiled a conspiratorial smile at him, knowing he gave them extra, but they'd never tell. Some of the unattached men looked at the women with glances that were too casual. A few were already half asleep, but when Major Howard entered the room, they sat up ramrod straight, almost saluting.

"Good evening. It's good to see you. Mr. Parker has gone to a lot of trouble to bring you some words and a movie about our Lord and Savior, Jesus Christ. Pay attention, don't go to sleep, and sign the roll when you leave," she said, part missionary, part crusty drill sergeant dishing out tough love.

"I won't keep you long and get right to the movie. We've all traveled a rocky road to get here tonight. As a broken servant of the Lord, it is a privilege to bring you a movie you have probably not seen, about ninety minutes in the dark of the room to find the Light.

"As Joshua (Jesus) says in the movie, 'Sometimes you have to tear something down to build it back up.' He tore down the old man in me to build the new, and I'm a work in progress. We all are. The Carpenter from Galilee waits to begin our renovation. Our eyes always on the Cross, no turning back, no turning back. God bless you," Michael said.

Some people said, "Amen," and just as the lights went down, Michael saw someone slip into the shadows of the back row.

Michael knew some were bored and there only because the Army required attendance for them to receive assistance, but in the dark, he heard people begin to cry, just as he had at Edgefield at the Christian movie nights.

After the movie, the people lined up to shake Michael's hand. Some did it out of duty, but there were tears in the eyes of some, a genuine gratitude for the gift to them and their children. Some held his hand tightly for a long moment.

The haunted, sallow faces filed by, and Michael made a point to look them all in the eye, smile, and thank them for coming, even if their attendance was compelled. He told each person that Jesus loved them.

One little knee-high waif with blonde hair, who Michael had given an extra cupcake and Twinkie at lunch, came up to him, jerked on the hem of his jacket until he looked down, and said, "Thank you." The tiny ragamuffin dug into her pocket, extended her small, fragile hand, and gave him all she had…two pennies and a tiny ball of lint.

"Pennies from heaven," Michael said. "Thank you for your pennies and your pretty lint. You sure you don't need them?"

"No, I love my cupcakes, and I love you," she said.

"Jesus loves you, and I do, too," Michael said as a balm from Christ was laid over his wounded heart.

As Michael tidied up and put everything back in its place, he noticed that the late arrival in the shadows of the back row was still there, hunched over, head down.

"I didn't put you to sleep, did I?" Michael asked.

The man stood up and stepped into the light.

It was Eli, thinner and with clear eyes, but it was him!

"No, old man. You woke me up at the halfway house. That 'talking to' you gave me sobered me up. I passed out and fell into a dream that was not a dream. I met Satan by the edge of this cliff where millions of people were jumping into the bottomless void.

"I heard fallen angels shouting, 'Apollyon, Abaddon, the destroyer, the ruler of the abyss!'

"He told me it was my time, just close my eyes and jump. Then he was trying to push and drag me to the edge, and the hot ground was giving way beneath my feet, burning my feet. He was laughing at me, saying it was the end of the line, a one-way ticket.

"I woke up screaming and could still feel his hot hand on my back pushing me. Darrius asked me what I was wailing about and said no one was around but me and him. I told him that him, me, and the devil made three.

"They sent me to the hospital, then a place to dry out. They said I cried out for my mama. They said I kept crying for Jesus. I blacked out or blocked out the pain for a while and sweated buckets, man. I didn't eat for a long time. Withdrawal is hard. What was harder was when I began to remember the evil things I did. Selling to kids, girls tricking on street corners for crack. Thank God, I didn't remember everything, but I remembered you. By the time I got out of the ward, my probation violation time was up.

"The gang was gone, and I heard Darrius was killed, given a hot shot by Judas, who told him it was some good stuff. A contract was out for Judas, and he hung himself. That would've been me. I wanted a new start. I'm just staying here until I can get on my feet and learn how to live like a man. I've got a job delivering supplies for a parts store. It ain't much, but it's a stepping stone to sobriety," he said.

"Man, I am glad to see you again. I wondered what happened to you," Michael said.

"I was trying so hard to find something to make me feel alive, not knowing I was already dead. I was on the gallows, my neck in the noose, but your words hit me harder than if you had took a baseball bat to my head. My hand wanted to kill you so bad, my trigger finger burned and itched, but I couldn't do it. Even in the face of death, you risked your life for someone like me," he said.

"Eli, if the devil can talk angels into leaving heaven, he can talk us right into hell. We got to forget the things that are behind, close that gate to the world, and get back to the gait of the Man from Galilee. I risked my life because He gave His life for you and me. He walks on the waters of my dreams and shows me who we were, who we are, and who we can be," Michael said.

"Yeah, I'm starting to see now. I've been reading that little Bible you left behind. I don't know much, but I want to know more," Eli said as he took a tentative step toward Michael and offered his hand.

The handshake turned into a hug, and somewhere Michael thought a chorus of angels must have been singing, "Hallelujah, Hallelujah!"

As Corleone said in his letter, Jesus just keeps turning up everywhere.

CHAPTER TWENTY

"When I close my eyes, so I would not see, my Lord did trouble me. When I let things stand that should not be, my Lord did trouble me. With a word or a sign...Did stir me, for to make me human, to make me whole."
—*"Did Trouble Me," Frank Chance*

"Should we continue to look upwards? Is the light we can see in the sky one of those which will presently be extinguished? The ideal is terrifying to behold...brilliant but threatened on all sides by the dark forces that surround it: nevertheless, no more in danger than a star in the jaws of a cloud."—*Victor Hugo*

As Michael drove home from his long day, the streets were deserted, the traffic lights were all a Christmas green, and the road seemed to be leaping at him. The pavement made a humming whine beneath his car's wheels, a nighthawk screeched past his high beams, and giant, shiny bugs decorated his windshield.

The feeling, the roller-coaster rush of the day, was hypnotic, pinch-yourself, dizzying moments. He powered down his windows to smell the fragrant Magnolia breeze that circled his car as moonlight and streetlight danced on the hood of his Nissan. He was still flying high above all the terrestrial distractions, firmly planted in the palm of God's hand. It was good to be home.

He was excited to tell Judy all about it, but it was late. She was asleep, so he checked his private messages on Facebook. There was a note from Frankie Schumpert, the inmate he knew from his time at Millington Camp.

Michael, I need to talk. I'm so alone, man, in so much pain. I can't go on. I can't find God. I remember your words in our Sunday night services at Millington, but I think He has left me for my many sins. I can't take it. I am going to kill myself tonight at midnight, plus one. Today's my birthday. I don't want to die on my birthday. Talk to me if you get this message. I am loading my gun, and the bullets are telling me to 'do it.' I need you, preacher.

Frankie

Frankie was once affiliated with the Giordano Mafia family in St. Louis. His last name was courtesy of his mother's marriage to a non-Italian. She was the sister of the one-time ruling family. Frankie had minor jobs for the family, one earning him the nickname "Headlights." Before votes to unionize at some factories, he was dispatched by the Badolato "Hill Crew" to bust headlights for those who might vote against the mob-affiliated union, a warning of harsher penalties for failure to vote correctly. He also twisted a few arms for those behind on payments to loan sharks and protection grifts.

Frankie became an ally to Michael at Millington against the corrupt officials there and those who thought they might hurt the Christian interloper. He was an ardent supporter and faithful attendee at Michael's sermons and the Christian movie nights Michael brought from Edgefield, and it was rumored he paid visits to some who planned to hurt Michael to let them know he would be very unhappy if harm were to befall his friend.

Frankie was gruff and sullen when Michael first met him, someone not to be trifled with, but over time he mellowed. Michael always thought he was a wisecracker crying inside, his bark much worse than his bite. Michael became a father figure to him. Frankie was searching for something, for Someone. He just didn't know it until their paths crossed.

Michael once told him, "Frankie, it's what we learn after we think we know it all that counts. We don't have to run to every fight we get an invitation to, and we don't have to stop what we're doing to throw stones at every dog that barks at us."

Frankie looked at him a long time that day and said, "You have a way of making common sense sound profound."

So, Michael replied to Frankie's cry for help and asked him if he was all right.

"Michael, I'm in so much pain from a motorcycle wreck. I can't bear it anymore. I can't find God. I cried out to Him, but He wasn't there. He's left me because of the things I did in the past and has turned His back on me. I need you, Michael. Tell me what to do," Frankie said.

"Frankie, the Lord has not left you. He's right there with you," Michael said.

"I don't know, man. The pain is too much, and I can't take it. I just called to say goodbye," Frankie said. He sniffled, and his voice quivered like a kid holding a loaded gun and not liking his options.

"Have you seen a doctor?" Michael asked.

"Yeah, they just gave me some weak pain pills and told me they couldn't give me anything stronger because I might get addicted," Frankie said, laughing at the irony.

"Something else mixing with this pain causing you to despair?" Michael asked.

"Yeah, ghosts from the old life. It's too much. The ghosts are after me, and they're gaining on me, Michael," Frankie said.

"The past is in hot pursuit of us, Frankie. I have been wrestling with it, too, but the Lord is revealing things to me, making sense of it all. After Susan died, I wanted to die. There were days when I could no longer see her face or remember the sound of her voice. I panicked and sunk into the deepest, darkest place. I begged God to take me. I didn't want to live, but He was silent.

"Then one day when I was lying in my bunk, defeated and curled into a fetal position, I had my radio earbuds in to drown out the noise of prison, of the world without her. There was nothing but static, but I didn't care. Suddenly the static broke, and a clear-channel broadcast almost ruptured my eardrums. A voice I had never heard before and never heard again said, 'You there! You there! Yes, I'm talking to you. It's not noble what you're doing, lying there wallowing in your pity party. Now you get up from there and get about your Father's business.' Then it was gone," Michael said.

He heard Frankie begin to cry, and what sounded like a heavy gun dropped on a table.

"I got up, Frankie, and got about His business and fulfilled the faith Susan had in me when she told everyone to watch how God would use me. It was still hard, but He used me. I asked Him to send me anywhere but to please just go with me. I lived next door to sorrow and blues, but I learned to love my troubled neighbors and tell them He loved them, too. Susan came to me in my dreams again, young and beautiful. She held my hand and sang hymns and lullabies to me. She once told me that she would love me forever, and as the curtain was drawn, I asked her how it was there in the Land of Forever," Michael whispered in a raspy, faraway voice.

Frankie was sobbing, saying over and over, "Oh man, I'm sorry. I'm sorry, Lord. Please come down and go with me when I lay down and when I get up. I didn't mean it, any of it."

After a bit, after Frankie had cried it out of him, he honked his nose, sighed deeply, and said, "Thank you, man. You still know the right things to say. I'll be okay. Sorry to lay my worries on you."

"It's always better to receive the troubles of a friend than the kiss of an enemy. I'm always here if you need to talk. Love you, buddy," Michael said

"Love you, too, brother," Frankie said.

When Michael came to bed, Judy stirred and murmured, "Where you been?" she asked.

"In the valleys, on the mountaintops, outside looking in, inside doing inventory, living and reliving, peering into the whirlwind with the Ancient of Days, finding pieces of my life," he whispered as he squeezed her tight.

"Hmmm?" she murmured.

"Tell you tomorrow," he said, as sleep rolled up on him and he floated down into the warmth of a bed of peace.

Two emails pinged his inbox, when the sun rose to rest on his face the next morning. The first was from Hollywood.

You are not only a great writer but a great writer of American literature. That is what your book is, a big crime

story written as literature, written to all the senses. Come
to Hollywood, I want to represent you.

Jim Clemente

Michael's jaw dropped as he sat back in his chair, a day
dreamed of that came true. His mind began to reorder and adjust to
timelines of parallel lives brushing up against each other and
suddenly intersecting, six degrees of separation completed by
random acquaintances, people met in prison of all places.

The second email was from Southern Stories, the small
publisher he had sent the manuscript.

We would like to meet with you to discuss publishing
your book in a hardback edition with an immediate release.

Janis Warren

Michael didn't know the ins and outs of publishing. He was a
novice, an apprentice evangelist who just wanted a book to
promote across America, a calling card, a means of telling his story
and God's story and promises kept. Southern Stories might not
have been the best option, but after all his letters of rejection, he
could hear the clock ticking and was eager to move ahead with the
first installment of his story.

Michael answered the emails and then reached over and
picked up the old seashell from Florida, the imported conch shell
his parents bought for him as a child at one of the old gift shops in
old Ft. Walton Beach.

Through the years, the large pointed shell, once home to a sea
snail called a gastropod, had served as a doorstop for his mama, an
ashtray for his father, and a paperweight for Pearl. When he
became an adult, he had salvaged it from the shelf of an old
bookcase, cleaned it up, and took it with him through the many
moves of his wandering life.

He put it to his ear. The ocean was still there, trapped within
the curved conch warehouse. The roar of the surf, along with his
dreams and ups and downs, burrowed into his ear and heart.
Killjoys told him the sounds were just vibrating air trapped inside
the shell, creating what only sounded like waves and surf, but
Michael wasn't falling for that.

It was many things to him—the will-o-the-wisp, Somewhere Over the Rainbow, memories of shelling for Susan at Okaloosa, her joy at the sand dollars he found, sand castles and rosy dawns, and a boy trying desperately to be a man.

It was his Rosebud.

CHAPTER TWENTY-ONE

*"Sometimes the course of our lives depends on what we do
or don't in a few seconds, a heartbeat, when we either seize
the opportunity, or just miss it. Miss the moment, and you
never get a chance again."*—Aidan Chambers

*"God sometimes takes us into troubled waters,
not to drown us, but to cleanse us."*—Criminal Minds,
Season 12, Episode 08

When Jim Clemente called, he was somewhere on "The 5" or "The 15," the designation used by millions of drivers in Southern California for their roadways and sprawling networks of freeways. In Los Angeles, all the lanes could be jammed up to an eight-miles-per-hour crawl or wide-open, rocket-fast raceways with cars topping hills and screeching to tire-squealing halts in sudden, massive traffic jams.

Fighting the swerving, fishtailing cars, drivers approached another mass of humanity at full stop, managing to stop a foot behind the bumper of the vehicle in front of them. Then, heart pounding, adrenals on fire, motors racing, they waited to start the madness again.

Michael heard the hiss of the highway in the background, the blaring of horns, and Jim's muffled obscene barbs aimed at some errant driver.

"Hello, Michael. Sorry about that, crazy out here sometimes," Jim Clemente said in his slightly nasal, transplanted New York accent.

"Hey, Jim. I'm glad to hear you liked my book," Michael said.

"Yeah, man. You wouldn't believe how many awful submissions we get. Yours is a gritty book," Clemente said.

Michael had read Jim's extensive bio. A former prosecutor and an FBI supervisory agent and profiler, he worked the

Whitewater case involving Hillary Clinton and was the supervisory agent on the investigation of Vince Foster's apparent suicide.

Clemente was also sent to Guantanamo Bay to investigate charges of torture of Muslim detainees there. As bad as some of the prisoners were, true waterboarding and a sense of drowning can elicit confessions to make it stop, often useless and false information.

It would have been easy to rubberstamp the intelligence agencies' activities, but Clemente called it like he saw it. His recommendations were especially poignant since he was a first responder to the attack on the Twin Towers and, like so many, he came down with cancer. He left transplant isolation to talk about a new show called *Criminal Minds*. Clemente retired and left for Hollywood to be a consultant and writer for the show.

Michael knew that Clemente had a heart for abused or abducted children and had saved a little boy whose time was running out. He carried the boy's picture in his wallet to remind his new friends in Hollywood that the show wasn't just a crime drama but also a platform to warn of predators amongst us and how to protect children from them.

Michael decided that he could find common ground with this man. After a long discussion of how they would pitch his book for a movie or TV series and the structure of the contract with X-G Productions, Michael felt he was dealing with the last honest people in Hollywood.

"We won't ask you to give us all your money, mortgage your house, sell your pets, and promise to make you famous. We don't operate that way. If we sell your book for a movie or series, we will all get well then, and you will be technical advisor," Jim said.

"Technical advisor? I like that. I'll be the old guy in the back who keeps saying, 'Excuse me, I would've never said or done that,'" Michael joked.

Jim laughed and said, "We gotta get you out here. We'll schedule dates for a trip to Hollywood for you to meet and greet and introduce yourself to the players in Hollywood.

"When you come out here, don't worry about your past. Your prison time will be a badge of honor in Hollywood. Don't run from it; use it."

While Michael waited on the contract, he met with the publisher, who expressed interest in his book, and several young people who worked in the office. She had a shock of premature silver hair, a bushy mass of gray over watery blue eyes.

She and her team were from a different world and generation than his, and as they talked, he felt as though they were speaking across parallel spheres. Michael felt elderly and dinosauric with the publisher's sheltered young associates. He worried about their lack of a distribution framework and thought he was not quite what they expected and vice-versa. He suddenly longed for the universal translator he once needed in prison.

He sensed an affinity with Clemente, rooted in law enforcement and the dark side of life that both had survived. Michael did not feel that bond with the eager bibliophiles but an awkward divide.

Though he thought their salvation was birthed under far different circumstances than his, they agreed to work with him to prepare the book for a hardback edition and an official launch of the book at Reed's Gum Tree Bookstore in Tupelo.

They may have been partial to modern hymns, the 7-11 compositions with seven words repeated eleven times, while he sang "Rock of Ages," but the odyssey had begun.

CHAPTER TWENTY-TWO

"Sir, we wish to see Jesus."—John 12:21

*"There are crossroads in your life…we never know when
something we say or do will turn a person's life around."*
—Amazing Grace, *Lesley Crewe*

"Fell for his language as a fan of Southern fiction."
—Gila Green, *Author, Israel*

As Michael and Judy prepared for the book launch, Judy was diagnosed with early-stage cancer, and surgery was scheduled.

Judy told Michael, "We have the signing and the trip to Hollywood coming up. You didn't sign up for this."

"I believe our vows said 'for better or worse, in sickness or health,'" he said. So they agreed to ride out the storm on the old T and O, Trust and Obey.

Gila Green, an author in Israel, who read an early draft of Michael's book, told him her Psalms group was praying for Judy and offered to take a Christian prayer written by Michael to the Wailing Wall. When the crowd diminished, Gila took the letter to the Wailing Wall at midnight, and sent photos of her holding Michael's prayer against the wall…kindness 6,600 miles from Tupelo.

Michael left the hospital one morning around 2 a.m. It was like a ghost town; not a creature was stirring, not even a mouse. He walked the long halls and passed nurses' stations without seeing anyone. When he took the elevator, it stopped on the third floor, and a young woman on the late crew asked if she could hitch a ride.

Michael knew immediately that he was supposed to meet her and asked her if she was in a good church.

She stammered, stuttered, looked at the floor of the elevator, and said that wasn't for her.

Michael asked, "What Christian has hurt you?" She looked stunned and pools of water began to fill her oval eyes.

"How did you know that!" she gasped.

"I just know. Don't let old hurts separate you from the Great Physician Who heals our hurts. Let me tell you about Christ and how He changed my life," Michael said.

When they reached the bottom floor, she asked if she could walk with him to the parking deck.

She had many questions as they wound through the maze of the hospital's tomb-like corridors, and when they reached the deck, she thanked him. He gave her a card in case she needed to talk.

She asked when she could get his book, and as they parted, she said, "No one has ever talked to me the way you have."

Michael walked to his car thinking of connections, intersections, and the purpose of existence as God tightened his hold on Michael's soul.

He stared at the vast universe above the garage's top deck and prayed Augustine's prayer: "Late have I loved you, beauty so old and new: late have I loved you. I am set on fire to attain the peace which is yours."

***

As Judy recuperated, Michael interviewed on American Family Radio's "Focal Point" with his friend Bryan Fischer, whom he discovered on the dial of his prison radio. He told Bryan and his audience that the books were coming.

Michael continued his work at The Salvation Army as chief dishwasher and cookie dispenser and visited other shelters like Broken Lives, Restoration Ranch, and God's House of Hope to share his testimony.

The men at Broken Lives, who had lost everything while living for the world, laid hands on Michael and prayed over him when he left his sick bed to speak to them. Michael thought the sound of fifty men praying aloud for him, groaning with such urgency through weeping petitions, was a moment he would never forget.

Some shared their before and after meth pictures, watched the Christian movies he donated, and made pictures with him. They told him to come back, that he brought them hope.

A man named Adam, whom others in the shelter looked up to, clasped Michael's hand and said, "When I was a kid, I was always falling out of bed. I slept too close to the edge, too near to where I got in. Then when I became an addict, I kept falling off the wagon because I was still resting too close to temptation, too close to where I lay down on the bed of sobriety.

"I didn't know the stranger in the mirror who looked like me, so I thought of committing suicide as self-defense, but I couldn't do it. My mother had glued a little plastic Jesus to the dash of my car, and every time I put the pistol to my head, I thought He was staring at me. I wanted to rip it off my dash, but I couldn't. I was so low down I could swing my feet over a dime.

"I swore there was no heaven and prayed there was no hell. I resented God for creating me without my permission, then I didn't believe in Him, and then I resented Him because I had no God to resent. The smell of sin is still on me, like stink on a polecat, and sometimes I can still smell death, but today, when you spoke, I caught the aroma of Christ. I don't want to be that old man no more. Please pray for me, Mr. Michael."

Adam began to cry, and Michael rested his hands on his shaking shoulders and prayed, "Dear Lord, Adam is ready. Guide him to the foot of the cross to wring out his pain from his past sins. Move him away from the edge of the bed of temptation, and let him find rest and peace in You. In Christ's name, Amen.

"Adam, the devil never lacks apples for Eve or Adam. There's only one thing worse than going to hell and that's taking others with you. Christ can use you right here to be a shepherd for these men who look up to you but are on the broad path that has only one exit—destruction. As a servant of Christ, that responsibility and commitment to others will make you stronger, but you must have a life to back up your words," Michael said as he looked at the men who were watching them and crying.

"I'm as common as cornbread. You really think He can use me?" Adam asked.

"If you surrender it all to Him, I know you can. I did, and I'm living proof He can use anyone. When I got to the bottom of self, He was there waiting on me. We live in a world of tooth and claw, and you have some holes in your faith right now, but God fills all available spaces," Michael said as they embraced.

***

Scoffers at the Restoration Ranch smirked when Michael arrived, looked him over, and mockingly asked, "Are...you...our speaker?"

Michael smiled and said, "I'm afraid so."

The man mocked him again and said, "I bet you believe that a whale swallowed Jonah, don't you?"

Michael smiled and said, "Yes, and if the Bible said Jonah swallowed the whale, I'd believe that, too."

After baring his soul in his testimony to the men at the ranch and inviting them to come with him to the foot of the Cross, the naysayers followed him to his car afterward to apologize.

One resident said, "You looked meek and mild when I first saw you. I didn't think you were much, but I was wrong."

His giant partner with a glass eye and prominent tattoos on his arms grinned a toothless smile, courtesy of meth, and said, "Yeah, man, we could listen to you talk all day long. It was enough to bring a tear to my glass eye."

"Y'all remember how it was when there was a warrant out for you, and the police were looking for you?" Michael asked.

They grinned and nodded, and Michael said, "The Lord is looking for you right now, and the best thing you can do is to self-surrender and turn yourselves in to Him. He is a merciful God."

When he left Restoration Ranch, the itinerant evangelist could not erase the stories of sorrows and horrors written into the faces at the shelters and those who came to his Salvation Army Christian movie nights.

The threadbare white clothes some wore had faded to the color of dirty cotton, and the looks on their forlorn faces burrowed into his heart. The slat-thin pale bodies, spindly legs and arms, gnawed lips, and wasted lives tugged at him. He had to fight the instinct to take on their burdens, which he could not bear. He had to resist the urge to "fix" them, to bring home the broken birds and three-legged foxes.

Some had given away every precious thing they had to find someone who might love them, to survive, and to escape childhood trauma and abuse, only to be lost to alcoholism, drugs, malnutrition, and anemia. Defeat was stamped on the brittleness of those who had fallen so many times that it was hard to keep getting up again. Their resilience had worn thin, but the shelters offered a last chance to those just marking time until the end.

The sunshine almost seemed too much for them when they stepped outside. Many lived in the darkness beneath the bridges around town, and they asked him if their prayers reached higher than the bottom of their overpasses that covered too much dirty water and too much sorrow in the soil of their lives.

Some were wedged between shame and shyness and were unaccustomed to gentleness. Some made eye contact, called him Michael, and began to take down the high fences they had erected around their vulnerability. In prison, Michael learned that Jesus and a little kindness seasoned with salt and light can pierce the thickest walls.

His time in the shelters was all instruction, preparing him to find the rhythm of pain, as he had in prison, to minister to those who had hit rock bottom and found that rock bottom had a basement. These castaways of bedrooms and barrooms longed for someone to really look at them, to see them, and say, "Hello, in there."

He never saw Eli again, but he was seen passing out gospel tracts at some of the homeless encampments. Someone who had known him before he met Christ could not believe he was the same man. And he wasn't.

Michael was the baby bird standing on the edge of the nest, flapping his wings, wanting to fly. His head was near bursting. His mind was expanding, trying to absorb everything flying at him as he separated the wheat from the chaff. He was learning not to confuse spiritual growth with Satan's attempts to stretch his conscience so he could not discern the difference between the Light and gradually getting used to the dark.

When he was about to leave God's House of Hope after his testimony, a man was hanging back, afraid to speak to him, until another man urged him to "Go on. He won't mind."

The timid, hollow-eyed man, who looked like a ghost or a shell of a child his mother wept for, asked, "Could you sign my Bible and the date I heard you?"

Without any guile, he shyly asked with his faint voice, "Could you sign my study material, 'To my best friend, James'?"

Michael looked at the emaciated man and thought of Ezekiel and God's question to the prophet, "Can these dry bones live?"

"Sure, James. Let's not go so long without seeing each other again. Best friends need to keep in touch," Michael said to a beaming new best friend.

As Michael walked away from the shelter, thinking about James, men had gathered on the hillside under the stars. One of them was playing a bottle like a pan flute, his breath breathing out a flawless "Amazing Grace." Time seemed to stand still as stars and lightning bugs climbed ever higher to decorate God's nocturnal palette, a night sky that was neither starless nor Fatherless and seemed to lie over the men on the slope like a cupped Hand.

He stopped to point out planets and constellations to them, talk about Who hung them there, and speak of shepherds and the Star of Bethlehem. The men thought it a great gift from an old man who told them they didn't need a map to get to heaven, that they could get there from anywhere if they followed the Light of the world.

When Michael got to his car at the bottom of the hill, he looked up the rise past the men praying and the lighted shelter silhouetted against the boughs of heaven to the endless luminous ocean of Abba love. He involuntarily reached up to touch the edges of the vastness as he did when he was a child in Florida with his pail trying to scoop up the sea. The star-powdered sky shifted and seemed to come down to dwell amongst these people on the hillside as the Lord had done.

Michael remembered when, like Job, the things he feared most had come upon him. It was worse than he could have imagined, but the pain and penalty had led him to eternal life and an undreamed-of promotion by God to speak for Him in places like this.

With childlike trust and the fount of Christ overflowing, he prayed, "O Love that will not let me go, I rest my weary soul in Thee. Thank You for glory in the ruins, for beauty hidden beneath sorrow. Thank You that when we suffer, we do not suffer alone. Amen."

Then he leaned against his car, trying to catch his breath. The stars seemed to pulse from prayer. He thought of when he pawned all he had to care for Susan before he left for prison, her dying lips that went unkissed, more sorrow than a train can haul or a man can bear without Christ, sleeping on old featherbeds and drinking Living Water, shrouds with no pockets, and the Hand of God in the glove of His redemption.

Then Michael sobbed until he could sob no more.

CHAPTER TWENTY-THREE

"Farther along, we'll know all about it; farther along we'll understand why."—"Farther Along," W.B. Stevens

"If you want to be loathsome to God, just run with the herd. The crowd is untruth. We love our neighbors, not the crowd."—Soren Kierkegaard

Michael stared at the clock and calculated time zone differences as he waited on scheduled radio interviews in Israel and Australia via Skype.

He was in the midst of excavations in a field of memories and viewing bits and pieces from his life like snippets from old 8mm home movies. These were the stubborn patches of unpleasant things he would have to talk about, pivotal moments circling in a churn, swirling above a massive drain that emptied into a lost world.

He picked up a beautiful Japanese fan that his mentor, Cappy Harada, had given Susan long ago. Cappy was a Japanese-American who, against all odds, became an aide to General Douglas MacArthur in World War 2. MacArthur ordered Cappy's family released from the internment camps, and Cappy was with him at critical moments in history but off camera because he "looked like the enemy."

He was with the general when he rebuked the Soviets who wanted to partition Japan, as they had Germany, and told them that this was not Berlin, that he was prepared to kick their fannies back to Moscow. MacArthur ordered Cappy to pull over, and they left the Soviet leader in the middle of nowhere to drive home MacArthur's promise.

Cappy flew to Washington to deliver top-secret messages to Truman and was on a plane that crashed on a jungle-covered mountainside.

Because an officer had ordered Cappy to the back of the plane with the Navajo code talkers, Cappy and the Navajos were the only ones to survive. The Navajos kept Cappy alive until allied troops could mount a rescue mission. Cappy said, "Michael, God bless that bigot."

He was with the general on Wake Island when he got crossways with Truman, and he said it was the only time he saw the "old man" err so badly. Cappy later delivered the order from Truman, relieving MacArthur of command.

One day, while dining at California Dreaming Restaurant in Augusta, Cappy told Michael of Martyr's Hill in Nagasaki. The hill overlooks Ground Zero, where the United States dropped the second atomic bomb in hopes of bringing the Japanese to the peace table and avoiding a costly land invasion. Cappy stayed with MacArthur after the war ended when the general was the Supreme Commander of the Allied Powers during the occupation.

Cappy told Michael that Martyr's Hill was also where Christians were put to death in 1597 for refusing to renounce Christ. Twenty-six Christians arrived at the hill on February 5, 1597, after a forced march for 480 miles with their ears and noses cut off. One of the faithful martyrs, only thirteen years old, said, "Show me my cross."

"The world is complicated, Michael, and Christ stands amidst the complexity. That day when the United States, a mostly Christian nation, dropped the bomb to save lives, we killed tens of thousands of people in one of the major Christian centers in Japan. As General MacArthur said, 'The problem is basically theological.'

"It's hard to grasp, Michael. One day maybe the Lord will show us all of it, and maybe we'll understand why some were strong enough to be martyrs, while others denied Him to save what they cannot keep while losing everything that matters," Cappy said, his sad voice bending beneath the weight of his words.

Cappy said, "As his aide, I accompanied the general to church services, sometimes not far from the front. He was a faithful attendee at services held by the army chaplain. One day after the sermon the chaplain complimented General MacArthur on his regular attendance.

"General MacArthur said, 'I am just a four-star general commanding our forces at this moment, but I am flesh and will go the way of all flesh, but you, Pastor, serve the seven-star general in Revelation 1:20.'

"While occupying Japan, General MacArthur asked for thousands of missionaries to be sent to Japan. Faith in the old order in Japan had collapsed. The emperor was no longer a god, the military wasn't invincible, and the worship of the state had failed. He wanted to fill the void, and thousands of missionaries came. Now, I think we could use them here in America," Cappy said as he brushed the wetness from his weathered cheeks.

Michael wasn't sure he fully grasped all that Cappy told him that day, and it would have to wait. Cappy sent word to Michael at Millington Camp that he would "see him in heaven." It was their last communique.

After his radio interviews, Michael thought about Cappy and all he said about Martyr's Hill, the weak and the strong Christians, and questions without answers in a world that only offered more questions.

Then Judy stopped by with a hug and a letter addressed to Michael. It was postmarked Calhoun City.

Dear Captain Parker:

May I still call you that? Once a captain, always a captain. Someone told me that you had come home, that you fell off that pedestal some folks put you on and broke your halo on the way down. Were they able to put Humpty Dumpty back together again?

You caused me a lot of trouble way back when and cost me a lot of money, like the time you had my drivers from Colorado jailed in Grenada, but you couldn't catch me in the act, though, could you?

You just missed me when you and your boys traveled to the Rio Grande near McAllen, Texas, to catch us coming across with drugs, guns, and precious stones borrowed from a former owner. He didn't mind, though, cause he was dead. I saw you through my binoculars and waited you out, but some of the bundles fell in the river and floated away. People down river got high on our dope, and a couple shot each other with our guns.

You boys were slick, but we had trucks and planes. You couldn't be everywhere, could you? Y'all barely missed me the night I had to bypass that small airfield and land in a cornfield. I saw you boys waiting, was about out of gas, and had to go to plan B, which didn't figure on the corn still standing in that field when I bounced in. It tore up the landing gear some and me, too, but I didn't lose any of the bricks or bales in the belly of the plane. Funny, some military jet had already buzzed me near the coast. I had to drop down to treetop level to shake him, and then I saw y'all...two insomniacs, just sitting and waiting. I thought then, don't these guys ever sleep?

That day on the border and that night at the airfield, when I was watching you, I saw your buddy with you, your intelligence chief. It may sound funny coming from me, but I was sorry to hear of his cancer and death. I was in Vietnam, too, and the chemicals they sprayed slow-killed almost as many of us as the Indochina Communists did, and now we have our own Communists, don't we?

We're old men now, and I'm just writing as one old man to another to say I once wanted to kill you and came closer than you know with your All-American face in the crosshairs once and my finger heavy on a hair trigger, but I knew you had told the agents to go easy on my innocent kid sister, the school teacher, when y'all were interviewing people in Bruce. Now they ain't many of us left who lived the lives we did. It's like a fraternity, I guess.

I got some old enemies trying to settle scores now at this late hour, and the devil wants my soul, too. I guess I'm gonna have to handle it, but sometimes I think I've got a million dollars with a ten-cent brain. In a moment of weakness, I wandered into this revival tent meeting near Grenada last month, and the preacher asked me to sing "I saw the light" with them, but I told him, "There ain't no light. I'm a killer, Pastor. Just lay me out in the field when I die and let the buzzards eat me whole. At least I can give them life."

Anyhow, I'm glad I didn't kill you, and you didn't kill me. Maybe we'll get to die in our beds on clean sheets and have preachers say pretty words over us. If all we have is an eye for an eye, we run out of eyes pretty soon, don't we?

Stay healthy. Stay fit. Don't sugar your grits. Do it for the pallbearers.

Calhoun County Outlaw

As he read the letter, the curtains of time parted for a glimpse of a different time and a different Michael.

People always asked him if he was worried about old gangsters looking to settle scores, but he told them the old politicians and prosecutors were the greater threat. Most of the gangsters were dead, but here was one who wasn't, a tough old buzzard with a square jaw and deep wrinkles on his face, even when he was young from too many days under the hot sun at the border.

He was tall, wiry, and favored jeans, a white shirt with pearl buttons, a white Stetson, and buffalo-hide cowboy boots he imported from Texas or smuggled from Mexico. His mouth looked like it was permanently pinched shut and expressionless as he peered out at a world populated by people who wanted to kill him.

Michael met him face-to-face once in a courtroom in Houston after a man from Louisiana was hired to kill him.

As they passed in the hallway, he said, "Death is a business that must be tended to, not by undertakers and preachers but executioners like this boy they sent to cancel me, a boy who now claims self-defense. I don't take it personally. Death is easy, Captain Parker. It's living that's hard. I ain't afraid of dying, and I ain't afraid of killing. It's men like us who make men like you."

A sudden shaft of sharp light pierced the hallway from an open door, caught the gold shield on Michael's belt, and the reflection made the Calhoun County outlaw cover his eyes.

Michael said, "It was God who made us, James."

The day after the letter came, Michael received a call from Agent Tomlinson with the MBI.

"Mr. Parker, we were investigating the death of someone we think you used to know and found a copy of a letter on his computer addressed to you," the agent said.

"Would that be James?" Michael asked.

"Yes, he came up missing, and we found him in a burned-out car. No offense, but he seemed a little long in the tooth for such a violent end, but people had tried to kill him before. It appeared he drove over a hill between Calhoun City and Grenada and down those woodland roads to no-man's land to meet some man to 'settle up.'

"It looks like he danced one last dance with the devil. IOUs have no expiration date and must be collected, I guess," the young agent said.

"Any forensics?" Michael asked.

"Nothing. Our arson investigators said it was the hottest fire they had ever seen. One said it was like the heat at the core of the sun, or the furnace of lower regions, but a hunter said he heard the roar of a loud truck just before the explosion," the agent said.

Michael thought about life and death and the outlaw who lived dozens of times when the odds said he should have died, but he tangoed one time too many. He was now dead and would forever be, no trace left of his lifeblood or the fabled ice water in his veins, nothing for the embalmer. For men like James, violent endings seemed contagious and spread like a fatal virus from killer to killed and kin and back again. They were sometimes lucky, but one day the luck always ran out, and all the bullets could not be dodged, nor the juggled balls forever suspended in midair.

It reminded Michael he had one less day left to be an ambassador for his faith and for the countless men and women who encountered turbulence when they came home in goodwill to embrace the concept of second chances and to hold on to words like "saved," "born again," and "forgiven."

As required, Michael called Steve Ballard at U.S. Probation to report the contact and the murder.

"Yesterday just won't leave us alone, will it?" Ballard said.

Then he broke protocol and said while finishing the initial background investigation on Michael, he had interviewed former inmates who had known Michael.

Ballard said, "I saw a pattern developing, an image of you the inmate, not the former life. I wondered why hardened men accepted someone like you, who was not the average prisoner and had once been a police officer who might have locked them up. So, I interviewed a former resident of Edgefield, who was about to be released from supervision.

"I asked him if it was your words, your writing, the movies. What was it that made them accept you?" Ballard said.

The probation officer said, "The man thought about it for a minute and said, 'Naw, man. We accepted him because he loved us unconditionally, no strings attached, and when he preached on sin, it wasn't complicated. He was against it, and we were, too.'"

Michael thanked him and thought about what Ballard said.

"I tell you what it was. Amid all that indigestible pain, I got a love letter, not the kind you hold in your hands but the kind you hold in your heart, not the kind that came at mail call but the kind postmarked Paradise. I wished everyone might receive His love letters," Michael said.

"The hour is late, Mr. Ballard, and one day too soon, the race will be run and the evangelist silenced, but the books will remain as dead ministers still speaking, and the scattered seeds will still be bearing fruit. Anyone can count the seeds in an apple, but only God can count the apples in a seed. So, we sow and sow, rest, and then return to the field to sow some more until our time is done.

"The fragrance of Mary's perfume still lingers after two thousand years, the aroma of her love and praise for Jesus. Judas called it an extravagance, but we remember him for his betrayal of the Son of God for thirty shekels and Mary for pouring a pint of perfume on the feet of Jesus at a dinner to honor Him and wiping

His feet with her hair. The books may not last for two thousand years, but I'd like to try to emulate her love for Christ and not lose the wonder of the Gospel in the work of it. I want to remember when I was blind but began to see, the very hour and minute I first believed," Michael said.

"If you could go back and change things, undo mistakes, would you?" Ballard asked.

"I wish I could erase the pain Susan endured and the disillusionment of those who believed in me, but if I could go back and change the genesis of this timeline, it would change the story and the ending. All the people who were saved, me included, might never have known Christ. He has been in charge from the moment I stumbled and was born again. I've thought a lot about this, but as terrible as it was, lives have been changed inside and outside prison. They will do His will long after I'm gone, so I try not to lose life and sight of Him in the seductive what-ifs, lest I miss it when love and revelation brush up against me, and He whispers to deaf ears," Michael said.

"You know you could try for a pardon from the President," Ballard said.

"Thanks, Mr. Ballard. A retired general wrote the President, and I appreciate his efforts, but I've already been pardoned by the only One who matters. His grace is sufficient," Michael said.

CHAPTER TWENTY-FOUR

"Professor Tim Charles' faith and his love for his God, his
family, his country, and the truth made him very brave.
I would be surprised if he was afraid of anything."
—Therese Apel, Darkhorse Press

"Instead of an armed rescue attempt by local police,
Tim Charles successfully negotiated the release of
missionaries taken hostage near Cali, Colombia."
—University of Mississippi News

Tim Charles was always figuring out clever ways to get his students to come to his Sunday School classes, always picking up strays. He could be serious and seriously funny. Tim was one of those professors students never forget, but he was so much more than a criminal justice professor. Tim ran a search-and-rescue mission for the lost students who wandered into his classes, and once upon a time, Michael was one of those.

Michael invited Tim and his wife, Dot, to a sold-out David Jeremiah event in Tupelo, a night to get away from the stresses of treatments and ill health. When they came over, Michael saw Tim's color wasn't good. He was wrestling with a bone marrow transplant gone wrong, and he didn't look like the old Tim. Sickness had diminished the larger-than-life vitality that characterized Michael's old friend and confidante. Michael thought he was holding it together with grit and the steel that enabled him to face down some rough people in his life.

Tim had to go to the men's room just before the event began, and Michael walked with him and waited outside. A man in the foyer was selling items for Dr. Jeremiah's ministry, and he told Michael that he had been given only weeks to live from cancer but here he was two years later. He was on fire for Christ, and Michael told him of Tim's struggle.

When Tim came out of the men's room, he and Michael joined hands with the man, and the man prayed a powerful prayer for Tim. Michael could feel a hush spread across the busy lobby area as people stopped and bowed their heads in reverence.

Michael thought spontaneous prayer and praise should break out at such events, and as they petitioned the Lord for intervention, Michael could feel the shadows lengthening on Tim's life, and he silently strained toward heaven, storming the throne, begging to be heard.

When they made their way back to their seats, a young man surprised his wife on the stage and proposed to her. David Jeremiah's sermon, a night of encouragement, highlighted the cycles of life, hope in Christ and served as a reminder of how fragile and tenuous life is.

After the concert, word came that Margaret Thatcher had died of a stroke at the Ritz Hotel in London on Michael's birthday. Michael had once thanked her for standing shoulder-to-shoulder with President Reagan during the Cold War.

At a speech she gave in Atlanta, Michael wrote a note to her on the back of a program guide, and against all odds and the rules that night, it was passed from person-to-person to her after she concluded her remarks.

The grand lady read his letter of respect and admiration, looked around to find his smiling face, and stunned the crowd as she rose from her table to walk over to him. She thanked him for his words, the history of his English heritage, and his support of her friend, Ronald Reagan.

She said, "Surely all the trumpets sounded on the other side when Ronnie left this sunset and entered heaven's morning." He watched her as she returned to her table that night and neatly folded his note, placing it in the corner of her purse for safekeeping.

As he mourned her passing and Tim's struggle, he saw professional protestors in England who cheered her death, close kin of those already shaking their fists at God in America. They had no room for God and were angry at Someone they said did not exist. It was one more sign the world he left behind was losing its memory markers, that the Creator was being consigned to irrelevance by His creation.

Darkness tugged at Michael, inviting him to dine on despair and sorrow, but it only drove him closer to Christ. Then a last note came from Carl Hunt saying he had encountered the man/demon once more.

Michael,

The demon said to, 'Stop fighting. We're on the same side. You can't cast me out without losing yourself. Call me when you get tired of pretending.'

I'm beginning to feel like the man whose parachute failed to open, and I'm just waving my hanky, trying to slow the fall. Don't get comfortable or lukewarm, Michael. Before prison, I bubbled for twenty-five years without coming to a boil for Christ. Stay hungry for the Word and seek the lost in their coldness, that way you'll hunt for the fire.

Thanks for the ice cream, the letter reading and writing, the prayers, and for talking to me about Jesus.

Keep your eyes on the eastern sky. Redemption draws nigh.

Carl Hunt

Michael answered him with a Scripture Tim Charles often cited, 1 Peter 3:15-16.

God bless you, Mr. Hunt. Let us always be prepared to give the Reason for the hope within us. We are not just answering a question but a questioner.

CHAPTER TWENTY-FIVE

"Many a rapturous minstrel…will say of his sweetest music, 'I learned it through pain.' Many a rolling anthem that fills the Father's throne sobbed out its first rehearsal in the shroud of a darkened room."—Unknown

"I learned very early in life that without a song, a man ain't got a friend…the road would never bend."
—Elvis Presley, Jaycees Speech, 1971

"I've got a couple more years on you…I've spent more time with my back to the wall. You're headed somewhere, but I've been somewhere and found it was nowhere at all."—"A Couple More Years," Shel Silverstein

Michael was plowing the lower forty of his life, subsoiling, digging up bones, and sorting through immortal horrors and everlasting splendors, as the world seemed to be standing on tiptoes awaiting the manifestation of the Lord. He was searching for channels, a way out of puddles.

The publishing team asked to meet and questioned the choice of song references in his book, songs they didn't know. There were also questions about Michael's references to Elvis and the fuzzy line between guilt and innocence explored in media interviews he had arranged.

Michael wasn't sure what any of that had to do with *A Ghostly Shade of Pale*. He began to feel claustrophobic when walls pressed in, that feeling when the buttons on your shirt suddenly bind your diaphragm, but he agreed to address their concerns, though it seemed akin to sweeping water uphill or herding cats for tut-tutters. He had been young and old, and they'd only been young.

A raucous jay fussed and chortled at Michael, and the sky had a raspberry tint when he arrived to meet with those who had questions about him, his book, and his interviews. Through the front glass, he saw them sitting solemnly around a long, tribunal-like table, looking funereal. It was pin-drop quiet, and their heads were bowed in ritual uncertainty before their notepads. Michael could almost hear muffled drums and a distant dirge.

He listened to their prepared questions spoken through tightly drawn mouths, punctuated by three-millimeter smiles, and fixed beneath uneasy eyes. Michael then leaned forward in his chair, the back of his fist resting on his chin, and began to address their concerns.

"Music often speaks when words fail, or it fills in the gaps in the story with context and backdrop. Lyrics or song references will take a reader back to a moment in time with the protagonist and form bonds with him, a kinship of unspoken hurts, a longing for more than mere words.

"Readers remember where they were, who they were in love with, who broke their heart, and how it felt when life was fresh, and all things seemed possible. They are no longer distant, impersonal observers, but fellow travelers who bump into themselves from long ago as the character in the book rounds the bends of life.

"Music can wash into the crevices of the hardest of hearts and heal from the inside out, and memories of singing songs can bring back loved ones separated by time, distance, and death. For a moment, you can hear them again, touch them or their memories, and be drawn to Christ through hymns and even some secular songs to touch our Redeemer Who stabbed death through the heart with the Cross.

"For some, like me, who've been given a second chance, they discover that the old hymns were for them, too. Maybe it suddenly comes to you, what evaded you when you first sang the songs as a young person, the feeling Christ is near us, what have we to fear? As an old man, you can sing it with new meaning and pass it on to children and grandchildren. God can use anything for His purposes.

"I don't think it's important that you don't know songs popular before most of you were born. AM Top 40 radio was gone by then," Michael told them.

"The songs fit the fabric of the era in the book, and readers drawn to this book will know them. Those who don't may find some unfamiliar music that speaks to them. Also, if we were to sell this book for a movie or series, we would already have the soundtrack laid in. The lyrics and tunes in the jukebox of my mind would fuel a playlist for years, showers of musical meteorites, mono and mezzo, metronome memories," Michael said.

"I don't want to give up singing for saying. I want to do both, which may help readers find answers to mysteries the author doesn't understand himself," Michael said.

"As for Elvis, his shadow was cast across the South, a part of the culture and the times, and he was born here, a part of the book's story. How could I not include him? Besides…I just want to," he said with a winsome smile.

"To those who love music, it's a language all its own, just as it was when George Klein, a friend of Elvis, used to play 'I Want to be Free' on the radio and dedicate it to me when I was at Millington. Inmates heard his dedications and wanted to know more, and they came to the movie nights," Michael said.

A young staffer, eyes down, blurted out, "In one interview you gave, it sounded like you were saying you were innocent."

It occurred to Michael that neither his probation officer nor his pastor had ever asked him such a procrustean question, but he tried to greet it as a rehearsal for questions from unfriendly interviewers and audiences.

"No, I never said I was innocent. I did say it was complicated. There were nuances and testimony omitted where Paul Harvey's 'Rest of the Story' hides and resides. The government can be grubby and not without their own sins, but if I had been a light then, I might have lighted the path of others, but I wasn't. I thought I was, but I wasn't. I was maybe a penlight in the darkness but not a reflection of the Lighthouse.

"There was right within wrong that shouldn't be discarded like the baby with the bathwater or ignored like a basket floating on the Nile. That right is higher ground to stand on until the flood recedes, not a place to abandon because there is truth there, a parcel of dignity, inseparable from the wrong, akin to Solomon's threat to divide the child into halves to flush out truth and love. That ground was a place of rescue and resuscitation by the Lifeguard for those who are drowning in this world, the first breaths of redemption that ask nothing but cost everything.

"Sometimes, in sticky situations, the argument between your heart and your mind gets heated, until both just refuse to negotiate or navigate, give up, and leave you to lurch into the desert between courage and stupidity. Then muddled, inexplicable decisions with terrible consequences often result," Michael said.

He thought he was talking too much, but he pressed on.

"You sit there under the sequoia. You see the storm coming. You hear the thunder. You see the lightning getting closer, but you still hug that big tree and stand in water up to your chin to defend people who live and lie like lumpy rugs but act like solicitors for Toys for Tots, forgetting that you are not the guy from Krypton, just Clark from Smallville. Deep down, you knew the fight was never winnable, but you just had to wage it, or so you thought.

"The public's limited attention span doesn't like complications and just wants the bottom line, the headline, not the article, but it is in the details where forgiveness is born, and self-examination begins.

"The public says, 'Well, the newspaper says the government mopped up the floor after the crime.' Yes, but they left the water running, the whole building flooded, and the pipes rusted. The public says, 'Well, the television talking heads said they cleaned out the cobwebs in the corruption closet.' Yes, but they ignored or protected the nastiest spiders, who rebuilt their webs in high places and hatched a million more spiders. It's easy to lose the details within the broader brushstrokes.

"In any life, mine included, the telling of complex stories is going to be corrosive at times. There will be splintered remnants, loose ends, and moments that seem superfluous to some, but it may be holy ground where God is at work, all to be explored in future books, but not in this one," Michael said.

Michael rose to leave, thinking all the querulous queries had been addressed, but then someone referred to the Scriptural incorrectness of the name of his prison ministry, Prisoners of the Lord. It caught him off guard, stunning and wounding him like a hot spear thrust deep into his heart, where the scar tissue was thin and tender.

"That's not what that term means," a staffer with a florid face suddenly blurted out from beneath a sheath of red hair and a blank fish-eyed stare. It was deeply personal to him, a dismissive remark akin to someone labeling your child as illegitimate, dismissing your laboring in the fields and contract with grace as without merit, extralegal, or worse, pharisaical.

Michael felt the remark was not in the purview of a publishing constabulary or germane to a book not drawn from that period of his life. The comment just hung there in the air, like a fly buzzing around in a pensive pause, a fly with the face of prosecutor/ magistrate Alex Martin, who Michael had dubbed Mr. Blind Man.

He suddenly had an image of the football runner who thinks he has broken out into the open field, nothing in front of him but green and the goalposts, only to be blindsided and tackled by someone coming off the bench, his own. He had bumped into the walls of an invisible prison, and he heard the slamming of the door and the thunderous silence of a moment when he had allowed himself to believe he was no longer in exile. He took a step back from it all, bit his tongue until he tasted blood, and raised his shields. When he left, he was lower than a snake's belly in a wheelbarrow rut, and the jay waited to say, "I told you so."

Michael came home to find supper on the stove, but he talked and vented to Judy about those who make life harder than it has to be by tying gordian knots in every situation.

"Sometimes, I feel like a curiosity, a mystery, a dinosaur, a carnival sideshow. People want to undress your mind and examine your heart and seem disappointed or puzzled when they don't find the book of Lamentations or the sorrows of Job clogging your arteries. They don't see a man cowering in the darkness of defeat with broken dreams dangling from his heart, but a remarkably joyous man fresh from the valley via the level ground at the foot of the Cross.

"We were trying to get men to see themselves as something other than prisoners of the state, their addictions, or sin, to redefine who they were bound to. No matter our circumstances, we can define Who we belong to and Whom we are in bondage to. The Lord established our identity, and no one there or here can deprive men of it, and the ministry was successful on a level I could not have imagined, succeeding against all odds.

"The recidivism rate of regular attendees of the Christian movie nights was a third of the average rate of men who returned to prison within three years, and the men of those nights carried on the ministry after I left, after my successor left, and then his, his, and so on. Christ became their Truth and Way, and their destination, where He waited at the end of every pilgrimage. I don't think Paul would find fault with that.

"One day, I listened, really listened, to the melodic score of prison. There were dorms full of men humming different tunes, like a bumblebee convention where all the bees got drunk on some foul nectar. The ministry provided a common identity, and many of the men began to sing out of the same hymnal, off the same page, and hummed the same tune, 'Amazing Grace.'

"It was then that these former addicts and misfits who flirted with putting their heads on railroad tracks and waiting for the train, these new prisoners of the Lord, could see an ocean of mercy with no shoreline. They became kingdom-intoxicated believers, dispensers of mercy, the only requirement mercy has for His liberating gift passed from one bearer to the next," Michael said.

He sighed heavily and patted her hands, which were feather soft. She let him continue his purge.

"What we have here is a failure to communicate. I don't understand it, and I wonder what I'm to learn from this failure to converse and convey. You can dot all the i's, cross all the t's, and still misspell or misspeak words for other readers or listeners. You can be almost right and still be misunderstood and speak right past each other, it seems. Memories to words can be a difficult extraction. I've been called every name in the book in the past, but it's the accusing eyes of allies that sting," he said.

Judy was about to say, "It will take time for people to adjust, people who haven't walked your path. Just trust the Lord and seek Him with all of your heart," but Michael took a breath and started again.

"Sometimes I feel as if I'm speaking a foreign language. Maybe I'm speaking in tongues, or others are. It's all a matter of rhythm, syncing, harmony, and alternate universes. Maybe I was on a prison diet too long and had too much of John the Baptist's grasshopper salad, or it's just a matter of generational or institutional menus, but my afflictions served God's purpose. Prison was the place of apocalypse, fear, and punishment, but also unveiling and second birth, a place where many were defined in the darkness below but my hope came from above.

"These days, the mailman brings my letters to our front door without my government number attached, just the name my parents gave me, not what the government added. I found the dynamite gospel in the fog of bleakness and hopelessness, and I don't intend to live a firecracker life, walk on eggshells, drive with the brakes on, or give in to fit in," Michael said as he paced the floor and then plopped down in a chair exhausted.

They laughed when Judy arched her eyebrow, wrinkled her nose, and said, "I never would've guessed."

Then she spoke ever so softly, "Storms never last, do they, baby? I love you." A warm flush on the same cheek where he first kissed her. They hugged for a long time, saying nothing but sighing everything, as a sudden gust of wind made the windchimes on the deck play a soothing, mellow melody of devotion.

As they leaned into each other, their arms were entwined, their fingers locked, two souls knotted together. Judy's long sigh was unbroken through four inhalations and one long involuntary exhalation while love swirled round them in a heavenly churn.

Michael's joy was undiminished. Christ was his lodestar, his salutary anchor, but he had begun to sense again a waking or warning, a tide rising around him, the discomfort of too many dancing on the head of a pin and the tension between two words of the world, accompanist and soloist, discerning the difference between gilt and gold.

CHAPTER TWENTY-SIX

*"It's time to leave some things behind from yesterday.
You know you can't change the world, but you can
change yourself."—"Soul Searchin'," Duncan Cameron,
Glenn Frey*

*"There are strange things happening every day. Quit
talking and do something about it."—"Strange Things
Happening Every Day," Sister Rosetta Tharpe*

Just when the briny naysayers in Atlanta, who drank from salt springs and brine pits, opined that nothing good would ever happen to Michael Parker again and probably shouldn't, there was a buzz in the air, a fragrance as sweet as Tupelo honey.

Tupelo awakened to an ad in the *Daily Journal* heralding a book signing at the Gum Tree Bookstore for Michael Parker's *A Ghostly Shade of Pale.*

Over local breakfast tables people asked, "Isn't he the one who used to be the head narc?" Restaurant owners asked Judy about the signing. Old men in breakfast clubs asked other old men, "Have you heard?" and ladies in Sunday School classes said, "I knew his family."

Michael traveled the highways and byways of North Mississippi like Paul Revere announcing, "The book is coming." He worked like the old public relations guy he once was, but unlike the obsessions of his former life, Michael knew Who was in charge and Who was opening the doors some told him would never open to him.

Michael met people he had not seen in decades—expectant people, curious people, grayed and frayed friends, and friends of his childhood teacher, Nan, who had spread the word that her little boy was back in town.

Michael tried to entertain the civic clubs with war stories from his former life, paint pictures with words, and speak of promise and purpose. He came to praise and for appraisal, to transcend time with stories that bound the fragments of yesteryear to fuzzy memory, and to warn that it's always later than we think. He spoke of last chances, second and third chances, and seventy times seven forgiveness.

Crowds were warm and gracious, and one man asked, "Wouldn't our English teacher, Mrs. L.B. Johnson, be so proud to know that one of her boys had become an author?"

Michael laughed and replied, "Yes, she would. So proud and so surprised it was me!"

Michael, the prodigal and trespasser from yesterday, said things had changed since he was a young whippersnapper doorman at the Lyric, deputy sheriff, and MBN agent.

"The fairgrounds where Mother took me to see Elvis when I was eight are gone. The old movie theater where I took tickets and ejected troublemakers is no more, and the small hospital on the hill where I was born has spread down the slope and all over town like kudzu. But when I sit at Crosstown, watching never-ending, mile-long trains crawl by in the same old train-car logjam, I feel like I never left. Some things never change, it seems," he said.

The more speeches and interviews he gave, the more people began to remember him. The ads he cut for his dentist, who repaired the damage done to his teeth by years of prison neglect and Mr. Hunt's punch in the mouth, made his face familiar to those who didn't know him.

As the book signing neared, people at the publishing company said, "We know you dream big, but you've been gone for a long time. Even well-known authors who come to Tupelo don't have much of a turnout for book signings. You'll do well to sign twenty-five to thirty books. We don't want you to be disappointed. It's just the way it is."

The night before the big launch, he wondered if he had done enough and if anyone would show up. He dreamed and saw ghosts from a past that would not let him go predicting failure, and fake people talking to fake people about fake things. Faces formed and disappeared. Pearl scolded him about staying out after dark.

Susan kept picking Rose of Sharon blooms from her heavenly garden and mailing him crosses cut from red-stained dogwoods until she was called home to a gated community. Snipers rained down merciless fire on Michael and his agents the day the earth froze, and the razor-blade ghouls digging his grave in Tylertown finally gave up when they hit China.

Ugliness tried to elbow its way into his dreams, and his enemies in Atlanta were dancing jigs on his grave. He felt birth naked, a 65-year-old baby seeing with adult eyes when the stone was rolled away from his prison door. He heard the sweetest voice drift across the ageless cosmic sea, rising and falling, lapping at the shores of his life saying, "Come out, Michael."

Michael woke with a start, a thick headache, grainy eyes, and socks on his teeth. A rooster crowed in the distance to wake the world, stickiness was in the air, but morning light seeped through the shutters and cast a sun path from his desk toward the waiting rendezvous with whatever the day held.

An encouraging mockingbird outside his window was heralding the new day, new beginnings, insisting that Michael rise and shine. He remembered Pearl had once told him that it was a sin to kill a mockingbird, just like in Harper Lee's book. Pearl said they want to sing for us and maybe be an alarm clock when you need one some important morning.

When his feet hit the floor, Michael had an overpowering sense of mudslingers muted, their words buried beneath the Word, some admitting they were not without sin, others forfeiting their casting of stones, laying down their rocks, and going home.

Judy was up early and off to the bookstore to set up the tables and put out homemade cookies and refreshments long before the scheduled start of the signing.

She rang Michael after he showered and dressed and said, "You had better get on down here! People have been lined up for an hour, and Gum Tree said they have preorders for more than fifty books!"

Michael's heart rate was off to the races. Suddenly, his palms were sweaty, and he felt a bittersweet longing for days of innocence. He wished Susan, who believed in him and predicted it all, could see this day. The lump in his throat almost choked him, but just as he hung up, an encouraging email came in from Los Angeles from Jim Clemente. "Congratulations on your book launch today. Soon the whole world will know what we know, what a great writer you are."

When Michael arrived at the bookstore, a line was out the door, the street was jammed, no parking spaces were left, and there was a glint of blinding sunlight reflecting from roofs of cars lining the streets. All of the candlepower of the sun seemed aimed at the Gum Tree Bookstore sign like a spotlight, and the mural on one end of the store seemed to come alive with the sounds of music and commerce from days gone by.

When he saw the scene and heard the creaking of the bookstore sign in the breeze, a part of him thought someone important must have taken his scheduled time, but then he saw Judy at the window, holding a plate of cookies and waving him in. Then all of it entered his heart and found a home waiting there, just as the Lord had promised.

When he peeked in the door, people called him by his name, and there was warmth in their voices. Hands were in constant motion to shake his, show him the books they wanted signed, pat him on the back and congratulate him, and say, "Remember me?"

The faces of famous authors stared down at him from the bookshelves surrounding the signing table, and Michael felt like a midget writer in need of stilts to approach them. A large cutout of Elvis kept vigil to the right of his chair, and Michael was swept along on a river of good tidings and a symphony only he could hear. The veil between the here and now and the hereafter seemed a mere fragile gauze.

He saw smiling faces from Calvary Baptist, Don's collection agency, high school classmates, his former taxi driver, ladies from a retirement home he had visited, and his pastor, who liked to quote Kierkegaard's words on faith, the antidote to hopelessness.

Friends of Michael's mother came, the family of Lonnie Smith, the agent killed in Corinth, law enforcement officers, MBN agents, and a friend of John Grisham dropped by to wish him well.

Amidst the reunions and hugs, the publisher rep arrived at the bookstore and saw the people and the book orders. Her jaw hit the floor, and she left immediately to get more books.

Michael was on an emotional roller coaster, and he sensed he was amid Divine destiny. He was healing, and he wanted it never to end. It wasn't just the love of the people who turned out but the caress of the Holy Spirit. He used to carry buckets of water desperately trying to put out the world's fires, but now a river of living water from a well that never runs dry was carrying him home to the Source.

Judy, a warm light framing her face, moved throughout the room quickly and lightly, and gave him looks of love and encouragement across the sea of heads waiting to meet the author. He whispered to her, "You're the hostess with the mostess."

The publisher's rep returned with more boxes of books, which were quickly depleted. She left throughout the day to retrieve more books from the warehouse as sales passed 100, then 200, and moved toward 300.

Orders came from prison pen pals as far away as New York, and an order came from St. Louis that requested the book be signed *To Frankie, John 3:16*. The mayor came, judges came, and a couple from England drove up from Ackerman with the former district attorney who once wrote the governor about Michael's undercover work in Winston County.

Nan, his teacher with sad eyes, came but brought a big smile for the little boy she had paddled in the third grade. Mary Hairald, a teacher who once nominated him for the American Legion Award, hugged him until he thought his eyes would pop out. When the teachers he loved praised and hugged him, he knew it was all real, and he told them that all he wanted to do was make them proud of him.

Just as he thought he would manage his emotions, he looked up and saw Tim and Dot Charles come in. As he did when he came to Atlanta, Tim came to support Michael and his first book, though he was still struggling with the bone marrow transplant. He looked at Tim and, like the pictures of friends in old pictures that begin to fade away, Michael saw it in his face but looked away, his mind shouting, "No!"

Then Andrew Alexander, Michael's friend from the Millington Camp, showed up. He was still on probation but slipped across the state line to drive under the government radar from Nashville to support Michael. He risked revocation of his probation, but he wouldn't risk asking for permission and being turned down. Sometimes you have acquaintances for a long time who never really become friends, but Alex became a friend the first day they met at Millington.

Jack Reed, Sr., an icon in Tupelo and owner of Reed's Department Store and the bookstore, showed up and pulled up a chair next to Michael to sit with him all day. When the crowds began to thin out at the end of the book signing, Mr. Reed thanked Michael for mentioning Reed's in his book and said, "If everyone worked as hard as you, we'd all be in good shape."

Even in the midst of triumph, Michael sensed that not everyone shared Mr. Reed's view. There were a few who thought the day's success was unseemly excess, a bit of "Who are you to show up from the boneyard, bypass the rigid order, and hurt the feelings of authors kin to the right people, members of the right churches and country clubs, and coveted fraternities and sororities? The gentry sat here for hours without signing more than three dozen books."

Michael thought they carried their congratulations like a weapon as they whispered, "Who are you not to need us?"

The day rushed by like a wild storm full of ritual, reunion, masquerade, promises kept, and redemption. The camera lady's shutter had clicked away, and as the torrid pace of the day began to subside, a bit of "what have we done, and what do we do now?" started to set in amidst the savoring of the blessings of an extraordinary day...of dreams come true.

The sun began to set over Tupelo, and the bright evening star rose in the sky. A breeze ruffled the leaves of a magnolia tree that had survived downtown beautification, and Michael thought of a girl he knew when he was a deputy, Magnolia, who phoned in one of the last book orders. She requested that he sign it, "Bloom where you're planted," one of the last things she had said to him.

Quietude replaced the hustle and bustle of the day, the weight that had dogged him for years took wing and flew away, and restless daydreams drifted past his mind and disappeared. Michael leaned back in his chair, smiled at Judy, and asked her if she knew this place of book signings was once part of the old Woolworth store where he once bought a pet turtle in the '50s for pennies.

He sighed deeply and said a prayer of thanksgiving for this day and for the bitter cups of suffering that had led to eternal life, the conquering of despair, and the days and nights when abstract images and timelines became the footprints of Christ.

He thought of things spectators could not understand without the prism of prison when hardness strengthened but also softened, times when hungry souls were fed. Michael began to see trials as not hurting him but as bouquets from Christ, a Divine ladder to climb, not just liberation within the time of sorrow and incarceration but freedom for all time.

Like John Wayne in one of Michael's favorite movies, *The Quiet Man*, he had found a home to come home to, a journey fraught with discovery, a pilgrim's path littered with stumbling blocks that became stepping stones, always revealing and unwinding, startling and surprising.

At the end of the long day, Michael saw himself as a carefree child again, dipping his toes in salty water, chasing sand crabs, splashing water on loved ones, and outlaughing the laughing gulls.

There were good days, so-so days, and bad days. Michael had plenty of the latter, but this was a good day.

He thought of what was to come, of doing more than just your duty because you love Jesus, of highs and lows, rights and wrongs, and listening so hard for God that it hurt, upward and inward, and he wrote on his notepad:

Thinking about jelly in Mason fruit jars. Thinking about big ole alligator gars. Thinking about my old Mustang cars. Thinking about working undercover in bars. Thinking about skirmishes and wars. Thinking about fights and spars. Thinking about feathers and tars. Thinking about the red dot Mars. Thinking about Who hung the stars. Thinking about all the scars…His and mine, the triumph in trauma…resurrection.

CHAPTER TWENTY-SEVEN

"His eye is on the sparrow, and I know He watches over me."—*"His Eye Is on the Sparrow," Civilla Durfee Martin*

"Thy hast made us for thyself, and our heart is restless until it rests in thee."—The Confessions, *St. Augustine*

"These things—the beauty, the memory of our own past are good images of what we really desire; but if they are mistaken for the real thing itself they turn into dumb idols, breaking the hearts of their worshippers. For they are not the thing itself; they are only the scent of a flower we have not found, the echo of a tune we have not heard, news from a country we have not yet visited."
—The Weight of Glory, *C.S. Lewis*

A startled nightbird flapped at his window when Michael opened the shutters. The saffron umbrella was marred by dark clouds like giant smudges on an unfinished canvas. The sky, like Michael, seemed to be a work in progress.

Jim Clemente had sent word that the Hollywood trip and the visit to the set of *Criminal Minds* was imminent, and he had booked Michael for an interview on Lip TV with Allison Hope Weiner in Beverly Hills.

Word had spread throughout North Mississippi about the successful signing at Reed's and those that followed at Tupelo's LifeWay Christian bookstore and Barnes & Noble. Michael's homecoming was no longer a secret to friends or foes.

An invitation came to sign books at Lemuria Bookstore, the grand old bookstore in Jackson. When they arrived the evening before the signing, on impulse, he took Judy to the once-secret site of the old MBN headquarters in the days of its infancy when all things seemed possible.

It was quiet and nondescript, and some mourning doves policed the parking lot of leftovers from a burger sack someone had thrown out next to a crushed beer can rattled by the wind.

There was no sign of the people he loved there, though he stared at the curtained window that was once behind Clay's desk in the Intelligence section, affectionately called the "Bat Cave." Michael imagined the curtain parted, that Clay looked out, waved, and then saluted.

Michael felt a sudden pang of longing for home, for the familiar, for yesterday. Sitting in the parking lot at sunset, he was not in the present but the past, but this was not a tomb or a substitute for what was or where absent friends reside, nor a place to change timelines or relive yesterdays as if they were only dress rehearsals.

Only God is changeless, the same yesterday, today, and forever. This abandoned spot was a place of shadows and echoes, where there once were shadows cast by friends, faithful shadows with them from birth to death. In some parts, superstition held that when a willow tree grew large enough to cast a grave-sized shadow, a family member would die. Others believed shadows hung around after the person died, waiting for someone like Michael to come along and acknowledge it and who it represented.

In the book of Acts, people brought the sick to the streets in hopes the shadow of Peter might fall upon them as he passed by, and all were healed, according to Scripture, whether by shadow or the full power of the Spirit in the shadows of the Apostles.

Here, the longing for reunion was alongside eternity to come. As they drove away, a solitary wind chime sounded lugubrious notes of farewell and "till we meet again" salutations from across the divide, the intersection of never and always, the now and the not yet, the time being, and as Michael was still learning, the division of all time into before and after, before the birth of Christ and after His resurrection.

Then the red sky spread across the horizon of a fallen world like an incarnadine stain from the Cross.

***

When Michael arrived at Lemuria, named for a mythical civilization that created books, the regal bookstore sat high upon its hill and was all he remembered it to be and more.

Friends he had not seen in thirty-plus years came for vigorous handshakes, hugs, books, and to ask, "What happened?" The Secretary of State, whose ruling made it possible for some former inmates to vote, dropped by. MBN agents like Jack Denton, wounded in the ambush Michael detailed in *A Ghostly Shade of Pale*, pulled up chairs at Michael's table.

As the crowd thinned late in the day, Michael and Jack talked about why he asked him to wear the bulletproof vest that saved his life and about the encounter with the Holy Spirit. Michael was reunited with an old friend who had become head of Cowboys for Christ. Michael and some of the former agents sat quietly in the corner, lamenting on the good they could have done had they known Christ when they were young agents out to save the world.

An agent he hoped to see there had fallen on hard times and left the Bureau. Once the best undercover agent in the agency, the lanky agent with a prominent, broken nose had become addicted to drugs himself, had a stroke, saw his house burned down, and endured shunning by other agents.

Michael learned he was living with his mother and called him from the bookstore.

"Rusty, this is a voice from yesteryear, Michael Parker. I'm in Jackson and want to invite you to come by," Michael said.

"Long time no see, Michael. You want to see me? Didn't they tell you all I've done, how far I've fallen?" Rusty asked, slurring his words; a slight speech impediment from his stroke, Michael thought.

"I know all that, but I want to see you," Michael said.

"Michael, I tried to kill myself by every means possible. Drinking, drugging, you name it. They would pick me up, rush me to the hospital, pump my stomach, and bring me back from the abyss," he said.

"So sorry, Rusty, but you survived. You're still with us," Michael said.

"Yeah, the last time. It was just too much. They left me in a room to die. It might have been best for everyone if I had, but I woke up alone, Michael, but I was not alone. Jesus was standing at the foot of my bed, and He said, 'It is not your time,'" Rusty said as he relived the moment again.

"Do you believe me, Michael?" he asked.

"Yes, I believe you. I've seen too much. I, too, have been rescued at the edge of no return," Michael said.

"They all came into my room, rushing around, shouting, calling people, but they wouldn't believe me when I told them what happened. They said I was hallucinating and imagined Jesus there. One orderly mocked me and asked if Lazarus was with me and if Jesus had raised me from the dead.

"Michael, I've had every kind of high known to man, every sort of hallucination, dream, and vision fueled by drugs. I know the difference, Michael. I know the difference," Rusty said.

"You can't be the same old man after that, can you?" Michael asked.

"Man, that was the thing. That orderly was mocking it all, but he was asking the right question. Jesus did heal me, and He got ahold of me, and I do nothing without Him now," he said as he began to cry.

They both cried and said nothing for a long while, except for an amen now and then and many whispers of "Thank you, Lord, Jesus." These former young narcs, who once thought they had the world by the tail, were invincible and would live forever, prayed and praised.

"Thank you for calling, Michael, and for the invitation. I don't get around too much these days, and I doubt I could make it. If I did, I would spoil your party, and some wouldn't want me there, but man, I've sure enjoyed our talk," Rusty said.

"If you can't make it, don't worry. I will sign this book and all that follow and send the books to you, my treat. You've blessed me today with your testimony, and you and I are on the right road now," Michael said.

"It may take me a while to get through them, Michael. Since my stroke, I don't read so well. It's a slow go," Rusty said.

"Just take your time and find the Holy Spirit waiting for you between the pages. You will understand them better than some who don't know Christ, those who judge you when they are the ones who need mercy and grace. Jesus loves you, and I love you. Christ alone," Michael said.

"Thanks, Michael. You haven't changed. You didn't have hidden agendas and didn't run with the pack. They said you were a goody two-shoes who wouldn't party hearty. I think they didn't understand but suspected you weren't housebroken, not a go-along, get-along guy who might soil their playpen if it needed soiling. The rain falls on the just and the unjust, my brother in Christ."

"Amen, Rusty. Amen," Michael said.

***

The roar of the rain and the crackle of pinkish-yellow lightning surrounded Michael and Judy as they left Lemuria enroute to the Jackson LifeWay store.

The first thing they saw when they entered the store was a tall book rack stacked up toward the ceiling with copies of *A Ghostly Shade of Pale*. Across the top of the display was a sign that said John 3:16, "For God so loved the world."

Michael felt the presence of the Holy Spirit and told Judy that He was there and they should expect the unexpected.

Inches of rain fell as they were signing books, the traffic thinned, and a woman with bent shoulders and dark circles under her eyes came in and collapsed into the chair next to Michael and Judy.

Lois began to share her story of losing her child to sudden infant death syndrome. She looked like a woman who had known hard times and was bursting at the seams to share her story and God's story.

"I almost went crazy, losing my healthy boy like that. You leave a room, and everything is fine. You return, and he's gone. What did I do wrong? What could I have done to protect him? Where is he? Where is he?" she wailed, tears and fresh sorrow streaming down her face.

"They put me on drugs and almost put me in the mental institution at Whitfield. I just lost my mind and my faith. Finally, my husband and I decided to try to have another child. It was unlikely, but we had a little girl. I watched her closely, because I didn't want to lose her, too.

"She was about two when it happened. I entered the room where she was playing, and she was crying. I asked her, 'Honey, what's wrong?'

"She said, 'Mommy, my brother came.'

"'What do you mean, honey? Where?' I asked her frantically.

"'He scared me, Mommy,' the girl said.

"'What? Why?' I asked.

"She said, 'He was at the window, and I know he must be an angel, but he had no wings, and when he spoke, his lips did not move.'

"'What? What did he say?' I asked.

"My daughter said, 'He said tell Mommy that I love her, and I'm okay.'"

There was a rumble of thunder, Judy was crying, and Michael knew a door had been opened to the Divine.

"What was your little boy's name?" Judy asked.

A piercing crack of lightning and a loud boom from the last gasp of the storm rattled the windows, and the woman said, "Michael."

Michael and Judy looked at each other, and Lois said, "Isn't it wonderful to hear God thunder from heaven? I can hear Him again."

After Lois had purged it all, and Kleenex was in short supply, Michael left for the men's room. He passed a woman with an oval face pawing at a bargain book rack while holding a Bible under her arm.

She whirled around as he passed her and asked, "Are you a pastor? I could see the light around you when I entered the store. I'm an evangelist, and I am in a crushing period."

Michael said, "I don't have a church. I'm an author and evangelist."

Michael returned to the signing table with her, and he and Judy listened to her story. Later that night, she told everyone in Jackson on social media that she had met an angel in the LifeWay store, but Judy knew that wasn't so, even if Michael ate angel food cake with icing.

Another woman asked if Michael could stay late to meet her son, who was in a crisis. So, they waited until the young man arrived after dark and talked with him about crooked paths and consequences.

They sold out of the books the store had ordered and signed more books from the trunk of their car for people they met in their hotel lobby.

One of the ladies was an English teacher from Grenada who said, "You look tired, Michael, but you've had a big day for the Lord, haven't you?"

"I hope so," Michael said.

She ran back to the elevator and gave him a card just as the doors closed.

It was a quote from Shakespeare. "The quality of mercy is not strained; It droppeth as the gentle rain from heaven. It is twice blest; It blesseth him that gives and him that takes."

CHAPTER TWENTY-EIGHT

"Dance halls…gambling places…saloons.
Still, there is hope, for I know of two Bibles in town."
—*Judge Wells Spicer*

"Hollywood is a place where they'll pay you a
thousand dollars for a kiss and fifty cents for your soul."
—*Marilyn Monroe*

When Michael returned to Tupelo, a friend called to say, "I hear you are going to Hollywood. You're headed to Babylon, maybe downtown Sodom and Gomorrah thrown in, too. They'll be waiting for you, country boy."

Michael laughed and said, "We have the Jericho plan laid in. Judy and I will march around the city and blow our trumpets until the walls fall down."

Michael viewed Hollywood as the manifestation of the midway, a carnival of barkers and barterers, offering a sawbuck for souls, a slippery slope, and a gateway to perdition. He also knew you didn't have to go to Los Angeles to find these things hiding in plain sight and germinating in the jungles of our own backyards and college campuses.

Once upon a time, he had felt like the main course at mantis feeding time, the black widow's mate who had served his purpose or the target dummy for the world's firing squad. He had run so fast, trying to turn the corner of wrong turns, people gathered just to see who or what was chasing him. He had been in the midst of an abstraction he once thought was middle age gone awry. He was stuck in someone else's game, not knowing the actual script, and asked to ad lib in a case of terrible miscasting.

Now, he wanted to use Tinseltown. If it was hell, he wanted to set up a last-chance mission inches from the molten gates. He knew that God would watch over him along the slant of the searchlights that swept the sky in movieland, inviting all to enter their houses of mirrors.

A friend suggested, "If you're going to Los Angles, you should try to get an interview on KKLA. It's the largest Christian radio station in America, a remnant from better days in the City of Angels." He snickered or horse-snorted, suggesting he thought his suggestion was a long shot, the chances slim and none.

Michael looked at the KKLA website and found no producer who normally booked guests. He saw a dropdown button for all of the station's hosts. He didn't know any of them, but he clicked it, and when he saw Frank Sontag's picture, he knew he was the one.

He saw no contact info for Frank or his producer, so Michael looked on Facebook for a page for his show. He found the Frank Sontag show page and sent a private message. He knew on-air talent rarely checked those pages, but he sent a message saying he was coming to Hollywood at the invitation of *Criminal Minds*, had written a book, and would love to be on the show.

Michael's private line rang a few minutes later, and a big, booming radio voice said, "Michael, this is Frank Sontag at KKLA."

Michael was stunned and said, "Well, hello, Frank."

Frank said, "You don't understand. I'm never in the station at this time of day, but something would not leave me alone. I had to come in early, and when I got here, I had to check Facebook. You must understand. I never, ever check our Facebook page. I saw your message and said, 'I must call this man immediately.'"

Michael said, "Frank, I think this a God thing."

They set the date and time, and Michael told Judy, "Honey, you are not going to believe it, but we're booked on KKLA and Lip TV in Beverly Hills."

Chris McCormick arranged a signing at a LifeWay store in Brea, a suburb of Los Angeles, and Allyson Adams, actress and daughter of actor Nick Adams, recommended Michael for a signing in Malibu at the Bank of Books.

So, Judy and Michael loaded Michael's Murano with so many hardback books that their car was riding just above the pavement as they traversed I-40 west. After stops in Oklahoma, a book signing at a Church of the Nazarene arranged by a former inmate from Talladega, and book cards dispersed at every stop along the way, they arrived at the edge of California and descended into the San Fernando valley, the stuff of "get out of here" dreams for a man fresh out of federal prison.

Getting permission to travel across many state lines was a miracle, unheard-of privileges made possible by Steven Ballard, Michael's probation officer and fellow Christian. Such courtesies would have made federal prosecutors and one magistrate in Atlanta grind their teeth down to the gums.

When they arrived at the LifeWay store, they dropped off 100 books, signed books at their hotel for guests, and began to prepare for the KKLA interview.

CHAPTER TWENTY-NINE

*"Go tell it on the mountain, Over the hills
and everywhere."—Traditional*

*"If faith is real, it must worship. If worship is real, it must
behold. Neither is the eye anything without the voice, or the
voice without the eye."—William Walsham How*

The kids from Tupelo took a look at the gazillion cars on the interstates around Los Angeles and decided to leave an hour early for the coveted drive-time interview on KKLA to make sure they wouldn't be late for what should have been a 44-mile trek on I-5 to the station in Glendale.

The old GPS was tardy with verbal directions when they came to spaghetti junction. They missed the turn and wound up in downtown Los Angeles in places a couple from Mississippi or anywhere else wouldn't want to break down. They passed a government housing complex named Haven Acres, but someone had altered the name to read "Heaven help us."

The traffic was heavy in all seven lanes. They had never seen so many cars, and Michael kept asking Judy, "What does it say our arrival time is now?" The traffic flow was either wide open or topping a hill to find all lanes stopped. A Harley with no mufflers roared between them and the car next to them, riding the white line, rattling their windows, and missing the side mirrors by inches.

Michael was sweating, Judy was crying, the clock was ticking, and "Gertrude" on GPS had developed laryngitis. For a moment, he wanted to get off the barreling boulevards and get back to the dirt roads of Parker Grove.

When they arrived at KKLA after two hours in a traffic jamboree, time was short, and they had to sprint to the station from the parking lot. Michael had been in prison for years and beaten down by life. He had not been on a stage of this magnitude in a long, long time. He was walking by faith, not by sight.

They left the hotel early so he would not be stressed before he went on the air, but butterflies filled his belly. He thought the devil had been riding on the hood of their car at times, taunting him with "What will you do now? You're not going to make it. Give up!" But when they walked into the studio with only moments to spare, the peace and calm of the Holy Spirit settled over Michael like a warm comforter and seeped into the recesses of his heart.

The wide-eyed secretary greeted them and said, "Wow, you're here! Some of us didn't think you would make it, but Frank had no doubt. He said this was a Divine appointment, and the Lord is the Producer today."

Judy went into the control booth with the show's producer, and Michael hurried into the broadcast booth with Frank Sontag.

Frank said, "It's good to meet you in person, Michael."

Michael shook Frank's hand and said, "Well, it wasn't pretty, but we made it. If Moses hadn't raised his staff and parted that sea of cars, we might have drowned with Pharaoh's army."

Frank laughed and his demeanor and voice personified calm. The light around him was intense and enveloped Michael. The producer gave the countdown as Michael and Frank slipped on their headphones, and Judy smiled a "You can do it" smile at Michael from the control booth.

The broadcast booth was a cocoon, and Michael soon forgot about all the thousands of listeners who had tuned in on their commutes home.

Frank opened the show and said, "99.5, KKLA, Los Angeles. This is the Frank Sontag show. A very good Thursday afternoon to you and yours. Every once in a while, we have the good fortune to meet someone who, to say the least, has had a very interesting life and is here to talk about it. He has written a book called *A Ghostly Shade of Pale*, a Christian book good enough to attract the attention of the secular world, he hopes. Michael Parker, welcome to the Frank Sontag show here on KKLA."

The time raced by, just two sinners saved by grace talking about their love for Jesus. Frank told the story of how they met, how Michael came to be on KKLA, and after one break Frank said, "We're coming back from break; better put your headphones on."

When Michael heard the bumper music, it was Elvis singing "Peace in the Valley." The producer and Judy grinned widely with their thumbs up high, and Frank asked, "Recognize that music, Michael?"

Michael said, "Oh, I like that music," a moment that was a metaphor for the whole night, as stars fell on the big radio voice in the night and the wanderer who was finding his footing. It was another reference to music from the book that spilled over into new relationships.

"Can you sing, Michael?" Frank asked, grinning.

"Sure, in the shower, I sound just like Elvis. Outside the shower, dogs howl, and mothers hurry small children inside," Michael said, laughing.

Everyone laughed. Joy crowded every corner of the radio station and surely awakened the angels in the City of Angels, who everyone thought had packed up and left town, never to return. It was a broadcast Michael felt must've been heard all the way to heaven.

After the show, pictures were made, and messages of congratulations came in from Jim Clemente and Michael's cousins he hadn't seen in decades. Goodness and mercy had followed Michael and Judy to Los Angeles, and he was healing by the minute. As they left the station, they looked up at a night sky peppered with stars and just floated down the emptied freeways like the last two people on earth.

The trip to the hotel was calmer than the trip to the station, and they talked nonstop about it all, the improbability of it all, of this night, of finding each other in life, of master plans by the Master. They were giddy through and through and thoroughly exhausted, but Michael and Judy hardly slept that night.

CHAPTER THIRTY

*"From the place where morning gathers, you can look
sometimes forever 'til you see what time may never know,
how the Lord takes by its corners this old world and
shakes us forward and shakes us free…"*
— *"Calling Out Your Name," Rich Mullins*

"My pencils outlast their erasers."—Speak, Memory,
Vladimir Nabokov

*"They stone you when you're trying to be so good.
They'll stone you when you're riding in your car."*
— *"Rainy Day Women," Bob Dylan*

The morning after the interview on KKLA, Allison Hope Weiner sent an email from Rome, where she was vacationing, to say she had read the book and liked it.

She thought she had the main character figured out but discovered that he was not the usual protagonist, and she looked forward to the interview. Her producer emailed to say he looked forward to a costarring role when the book was reimagined for a film.

Kyle Gomez, the LifeWay manager in Brea, called to say customers who heard Michael on KKLA were placing orders left and right and wanted to know when they could meet the unknown author who loved God and seemed to have the favor of the Almighty.

Michael and Judy couldn't stop praising God and were floating on cloud nine as they drove to the LifeWay Christian bookstore to check out the display, make final arrangements, and sign some books for mail orders.

The phone rang as they drove to the store. Michael saw it was someone at the publisher's office who tended to throw cold water on his every initiative. She seemed to see the glass as always half empty rather than half full, the person he had dubbed "Chairman of the Cold-Water Committee."

"Hey, wasn't that a great interview? Did y'all catch it back home?" Michael said as he answered the call.

"Yes, we heard it," the somber-toned emissary answered.

"We were not happy with some things you said, and you made this fictional book sound as if it is true. We've talked about this before," she scolded, accused, and proceeded with a laundry list of sins by their author.

Michael noticed that she didn't like contractions and used "can not" and "will not" frequently for emphasis and words like allow, which Michael had grown tired of in prison.

He wasn't sure why, but he remembered a rooster that crowed before dawn every morning, a dog that barked all night, and a quote about argufiers who put on armor to attack threatening things like hot fudge sundaes and banana splits.

Her acerbic words crowded the car, words thicker than the city smog, darkening his mood more than the sludge and grime that smudged his windshield. No congratulations were offered for what KKLA considered a flawless interview, listened to by people at *Criminal Minds*, movie producers, Allison, and people who turned up the volume all across the San Fernando Valley.

She offered no thanks for seeking and securing such a sought-after interview during the top-rated drive-time broadcast for commuters in Southern California and no recognition of God at work. The call stood in stark contrast to the warm reception and embrace from fellow Christians at KKLA.

Michael felt like he had been kicked in the gut by a field goal kicker trying to make one from midfield, putting his leg into it. He could hear the humming of blood in his ears, that squishing sound as his heart rate ramped up, the huff of the car's air conditioner, and the feel of its cool puff against the sudden beads of sweat on his upper lip and forehead. Someone had blown out the candles on the pretend cake at the pretend party, and he sat on the runway talking to folks in the control tower who didn't want him to take off.

He looked at Judy, who was still fresh from the trauma of her cancer surgery. Her mouth was agape, and a drop of wetness hung near her left eye, and as the car turned toward the sun, the daystar briefly turned the droplet to a shade of mercury.

When the call ended, Judy and Michael had fallen from the heights to the depths. Old wounds were reopened, joy died and dried like autumn leaves, and just for a moment, bridges Michael had crossed were burning. They were no longer on the mountaintops but amidst the ashes and debris, the remnants of hard years, and once again, he was reduced to a fallen and failed hero, an associate of his fellow felons. He remembered a man had once told him that his armor was for all seasons and all camps, for friends and foes.

As if on cue, the oldies station they were listening to played the Animals' "Don't Bring Me Down" for a couple from Tupelo who just wanted to make God smile, to feel the love that had moved over the waters. The band mourned on the radio, "When you complain and criticize, I feel I'm nothing in your eyes."

Michael looked at Judy, gave her his best Elvis curled-lip smile, and said, "Uh, Baby, were we just shushed? Some folks just seem to spite the noses right off their faces."

It was then Michael knew there was real trouble in paradise. The whole structure leaned toward toppling, and new arrangements or clarifications were needed when they returned home. When God gives you a dream, it's best to be careful who you share it with, lest you lose it in their nightmares.

His old acquaintance, Slim of the mixed metaphors, might have said, "They're watching me like I was a hawk, issuing decease and desist orders, and I can read them like the back of my book."

He looked at Judy and said, "Believe it or not, ninety-nine percent of authors never hear from their publishers once the book is published, and they complain because they feel ignored."

They both began to laugh.

Michael began to hum and then sing a song he had sung in prison, and Judy joined in. "I shall. I shall. I shall not be moved. Like a tree planted by the water, I shall not be moved."

Then they got really quiet, staring outwardly in the simmering silence but looking inward, chins up, trying to balance bewilderment with hurt.

CHAPTER THIRTY-ONE

*"Let nothing disturb you. Let nothing frighten you.
All things are passing away; God never changes.
Patience obtains all things. Whoever has God lacks
nothing; God alone suffices."—Teresa of Avila*

*"The kinfolk said…Californy is the place you ought to be.
So they loaded up the truck and moved to Beverly, Hills
that is. Swimming pools, movie stars."—"The Ballad of
Jed Clampett," Paul Henning*

At their hotel, nestled on a plateau in the foothills of Orange County, deep sleep escaped Michael the night before the signing. Too many emotional entrees crowded his plate and dream sequences of standing at the edge of the bottomless tar pits in La Brea where persnickety, lone-wolf authors and other felonious fossils turned up.

When they awoke, he drowned his recycled what-if's, why's, and other rhetorical questions in platefuls of extra helpings from the Sheraton Hotel's generous breakfast buffet.

Judy said, "If everyone ate like you this morning, this buffet would bust the hotel's budget."

As they were leaving their room, a genteel lady named Camilla, who had asked Michael to sign a book earlier, got into the glass elevator with them. As the elevator slowly descended beneath the strange light that flooded the skylight and atrium, she took their hands and offered a prayer for the day: "Today, whether you are sharing your books, a box of chocolates or the Gospel, let the joy of the Lord shine through you, and may the faith that has sustained you and brought you here enter their lives as fully as Christ ordains. Amen."

When Michael and Judy left the hotel for the book signing, the morning skies were tinted a reddish-orange, and distant palm trees were silhouetted against the horizon like black paper cutouts.

The weather channel said it signaled a high-pressure mass, trapping dust particles in the air, which scattered the sun's blue light. Such sights did not dampen the enthusiasm of dedicated bookworms and faithful Christians waiting at the LifeWay store and soon, the blue of the firmaments broke through and even the smog cleared.

Michael reached over and took Judy's hand as they parked at a bookstore almost 2,000 miles from home under a rising sun that was the dawning of a new chapter in their lives. They looked at each other, their eyes speaking in a language all their own. Their shadows joined as they stepped from the car to walk into the store. The naysayers who once misjudged their union had mistaken forever for never when Judy and Michael exchanged I for We.

"I heard you on KKLA. I want four books," the first customer said, sunshine pouring from her face as she burst through the front door of the bookstore in Brea, where Michael sat by a giant castle-like tower the store had made from his books.

The lines were long, and Christians from all over Southern California poured into the store to meet the man on the radio. Michael was excited that cousins Ginger and Margie, whom he had not seen in a very long time, would be coming by for books and that he and Judy would have dinner with them and their husbands, Bob and Chris.

Michael remembered that Margie played a mean boogie-woogie piano and once challenged him to listen and not tap his toes. He remembered Ginger as the little girl he skated with at his uncle's skating rink in Grenada. So many divergent timelines from his past were converging, and at times, it was overwhelming.

The store was a popular destination for well-known authors and those like Michael who were not so well known. As the day wore on, the sales mounted, and the totals passed Karen Kingsbury's signing and the numbers for Joni Eareckson Tada, whose life was changed forever when she dove into the water at age seventeen and was paralyzed.

The movie about her life was released in 1979, and twenty-eight years later, Michael Parker saw it at Edgefield Federal Prison and was inspired to create a Christian movie night ministry. Joni was in a prison she could not leave. Who was he, he wondered, to feel sorry for himself or think that God couldn't use him as He had Joni?

Book sales reached the number two position for the LifeWay store, second only to Charles Stanley. Michael told the store manager he was honored to be in such company. "This will likely be the only time I'll come close to the sales of any of these great writers," Michael said.

As people crowded around his table, an older woman and her grown son came up and looked at his book. The son, whose eyes seemed to be in a perpetual state of dry weeping, said, "We wish we could buy your book, but I'm just out of prison, and I can't find a job. I'm trying to believe in second chances, but no one will hire me."

His mother looked worn down, defeated, and bound by despair. The sorrow in her eyes pierced Michael's heart. They turned and walked out the front door as others in line came to the table for signed books. Michael watched them and the trail of heartbreak they left in their wake.

Michael said to those in line, "Please excuse me for just a second. There's something I have to do."

Michael went outside and called to the woman and her son as they walked to their ancient car.

"I'm so sorry to hear of your struggles. I'm just out of prison myself. Be a victor in Christ, not a victim. Here's my card with my cell number and my email. Contact me if I can help or if you just need someone to talk with or pray with," Michael said.

The mother looked as if Michael had thrown a lifeline to a drowning woman. She embraced him in a rib-cracking hug and wouldn't let go. She cried into his jacket, and the man wept as he pumped Michael's hand up and down like a well handle and thanked him repeatedly.

Michael walked back to the store and turned to watch them drive away as gratitude flooded his heart and mind, grateful that he was here, that he was not the man who had lost hope, that he could offer a moment of kindness.

He remembered what he had dreamed on the way home from prison about the place where his faith had taken him, a place where his deep gladness and the world's deep hunger meet.

At the end of the signing, he had made friends he would have never known but for the grace of God, people who loved the Lord and heard him give his testimony on KKLA. He made pictures with store employees and lightened the weight in their car by 200 pounds, all in a city where no one knew him but his cousins and a new friend, Jim Clemente, whose cousin told Michael he should send his book to Jim.

All the fragments of the randomness of God were colliding for a man whose early attempts to reach up above the blue to heaven was akin to Franklin's electricity experiment with his kite and key. Then Michael learned he didn't have to use a key and a kite to draw fire from above the clouds. The Keeper of the keys already had the key to his heart.

As they reluctantly left the bookstore at the end of a long day, and the reddened light of the sun was casting shadows and lifting the veil on the early evening stars, they saw a homeless man sitting on a curb. He was wearing a name tag that said "barefoot prophet" and a rumpled suit, likely a gift from a shelter or the county for burial, but here he sat, dapper in his emaciation, smiling from the corners of his concrete pulpit.

He had what looked like a meal from the Bread of Angels shelter and was feeding it to a stray dog whose ribs were outlined against mangy brown skin, but it was the look on the face of the man that pierced their hearts. A look of serenity and deep peace framed his smile as he fed the dog and dispensed unconditional love.

It was joy, an echo of something left behind or something to come. He, who had nothing, could finally give something to an animal in need, to pass on his blessings. Michael had seen that same look on the faces of men in prison.

Whatever the man's past, God had parted the clouds of drugs, alcohol, and probable mental illness for a moment of grace and clarity and untangled his mind. The man had done everything his friends of the street, flophouses, and back alleys had done but died in a county box labeled indigent and lie in a field of the unclaimed.

As the man shuffled down a side street, his new friend followed him, tail wagging like a windshield wiper in a downpour. Michael knew he was breathing air he hadn't breathed before, but it was a familiar fragrance to an apprentice laborer for the Lord, the scent of victory, despite it all.

Los Angeles was a big step for a fledgling evangelist, but Michael knew it was not where he was but Whose he was, each step another chance to heal his deep wounds, lest he bleed on those who didn't cut him.

CHAPTER THIRTY-TWO

"We all wanna be a star, but don't forget who you are.
Driving down the Sunset Strip. I see that sign up on the hill.
We all wanna be a star. I got the Hollywood Blues."
—"Hollywood Blues," Reverend Shawn Amos

"Who am I? This or the other? Am I one person today and
tomorrow another? Am I both at once? A hypocrite before
others and before myself a contemptible woebegone
weakling? Or is it something within me still like a beaten
army fleeing in disorder from victory already achieved?
Who am I? They mock me, these lonely questions of mine.
Whoever I am, Thou knowest, O God, I am thine."
—Dietrich Bonhoeffer

A thick cloud cover was breaking up as Michael hurried to Culver City to meet with Jim Clemente and a major movie producer. He could see a line of red behind the city near sunset like the town was sitting on a bed of smoldering coals.

Michael knew his inclusion of faith in his writing and his refusal to trade it for fame and fortune was hurting his chances of selling the book for a major project. Hollywood was not the Bible Belt, more like the Beelzebub Belt.

Some of the folks told him he talked funny, but Michael told them, "No, y'all talk funny." They were mostly polite, but they looked at him as if he had just come from the revival fervor of an all-night camp meeting, where he was likely the man in charge of snake handling, sweeping the dirt floor beneath the tent, and lighting the lamps in the blackness of country darkness.

Culver City was where Elvis recorded many songs for MGM, and Michael never thought he would be invited to dinner in the city where *Gone with the Wind*, *The Wizard of Oz*, and *Jailhouse*

Rock were made, not to mention some of his favorite Johnny Weissmuller Tarzan movies.

The producer asked that the dinner be limited to him, Jim, and Michael. So, Michael set out for Culver City with GPS and his phone to find his way to the dinner with a producer for Mark Gordon Productions, which produced *Criminal Minds* and movies like *Saving Private Ryan*. He hoped it would not be a trip of detours like the trip to KKLA.

There were construction projects he had not counted on. There was a festival planned for that night, and all the exits the GPS directed him to were barricaded. He was lost and in a bit of a panic. He took a last-chance exit and found himself before Sony Pictures Studios, which once was MGM.

He slowed and pulled over. Oddly enough, as he paused before the gates to the studio, he didn't feel lost anymore because he had come home to his childhood memories. He just needed to look for the yellow brick road and click his heels twice, or catch one of Tarzan's vines to swing above it all and see if the movies wanted any part of his story.

Michael finally found a parking garage that wasn't full. He hurried through the crowded streets to the restaurant, fighting a sour wind and failing to leave a trail of visual breadcrumbs to find his way back to the garage from the restaurant with the archivolt over the entrance.

It was a long, intimate dinner at a table with a low lamp, an opaque shade, and a soft piano creating just the right mood. The studio rep seemed restrained and antiseptic, hiding his cards like a dark secret, and Michael felt they had failed to convince the producer of the need to buy the rights to *A Ghostly Shade of Pale*.

Just as they were about to leave, the producer said he would be in touch, but Michael suddenly realized he had no idea where he had parked his car in this strange city. His heart jumped up into his throat and sank to the bottom of his loafers, and he got as quiet as a mouse chewing a cotton ball.

Night had fallen, and Culver City looked like a different city, maybe a different planet, but Michael was not about to ask for help and confirm the opinion that he was a bumpkin from the backwoods who wanted millions for a movie but couldn't even find his car.

Michael walked out with Jim and the producer and said his farewells, but as they turned to walk to their parking garage, he went with them.

The producer asked, "Oh, you parked down this way, too?"

"I think so," Michael said in a hoarse whisper, praying for some sudden unction from on high.

They came to another intersection and said more farewells, but Michael was frantically scanning the buildings as giant searchlights swept the sky like images from old Academy Award nights. So, he went their way again. Here he was, a fish out of water, unarmed in California, except for the Sword of the Spirit. He was walking down a street populated by high-octane, inebriated festival participants who appeared to be looking for bigger brushes and bigger buckets to paint the town red.

The producer smiled and said, "Oh, down this way, too?"

Michael almost gulped when he said, "I think so."

They came to a giant parking garage with many levels, practically reaching up to the bright moon. Michael thought his garage was like that, and he had parked on the top level with nothing above him but sky.

The producer said, "Well, it's been a pleasure meeting you," as Michael turned toward the garage.

"Well, we're in the same garage, too, huh?" the producer said.

Michael cleared his throat and said, "I think so."

By this time, Jim thought all of this was Michael's master plan to be alone with the producer, and Jim peeled off with a wink.

When Michael and the producer got on the elevator, the producer hit level six, and Michael said, "Roof, please."

They shook hands again when the producer exited the elevator. He paused and asked Michael, "So, this metro area is a little overwhelming for you, not like the Parker Grove Jim mentioned to me?"

"Sir, the Grove was so remote that if anyone new moved in, we assumed they must be in witness protection," Michael quipped.

The producer laughed as the doors closed, and Michael's heart pounded as the doors opened to the top floor. When he stepped out, he looked down at the Los Angeles valley and then saw his merlot Murano bathed in the warm light of the moon.

He threw his hands up to the sky, said, "Thank You, Jesus!" and fell down and kissed the concrete.

***

The next morning, Judy and Michael sat at an outdoor restaurant called Matsuhisa in Beverly Hills with Jim Clemente laughing about Michael's distress. They waited for the call from the Media Mayhem studio next door for the scheduled interview on Lip TV.

There was a different smell in the air that day, maybe too many pollutants in the air or a case of tinsel town jitters. When Judy and Michael were driving through Beverly Hills to the interview, they gawked at the iconic landmarks like the country bumpkins they were. Michael turned to Judy and said, "Judy, *we are* the Beverly Hillbillies. All we need is Granny on top of the Murano in her rocking chair to make it complete."

When Michael entered the Lip TV studio, he was sweating bullets but laughed at himself and thought, "What's the worst that can happen? They'll probably kill me off in any film adaption of the book, and no one will remember this interview, anyway."

Will Gibson began to powder his shiny forehead, and a peace began to settle over him, just as it had at KKLA. He signed a book for Will's father, Mel, and settled in for the interview.

Allison Weiner was adamant that the interview be confined to the book and its story. She said prison was irrelevant to the story; she wanted to explore the first drug wars and its consequences. Michael was relieved that the focus would be on *A Ghostly Shade of Pale.*

There would be plenty of time to follow the prodigal son into the pigpen. He did not want to get ahead of himself and risk readers turning on Michael before they had time to make some emotional investments in his story and his journey to God.

The music began to play, the credits rolled, and he could see Allison on the monitor as she opened with, "It's a mystery and a thriller. Stay with us. It really captures the South in the war on drugs. It is not what you think it is."

She turned to Michael and said, "It is evocative of the great Southern writers. You should be proud."

She closed the probing interview with, "It is intriguing. The protagonist is not a character we see that often. He is a questioning character, not one who has been programmed. This character is a product of that time. Something must have happened there with his grandma, Pearl. I want to encourage my viewers to read it. It is not what you think. There are a lot of layers to the book. Be sure to buy it. It is fascinating book."

It was a special kind of validation. Allison asked hard questions, but she asked good questions. As the show progressed, the fledgling writer could feel his confidence growing, feel baggage fall away, the dross burning off, refining him for challenges to come.

After their goodbyes, Michael and Judy followed Jim to the *Criminal Minds* set. Keeping up with Jim was a challenge for a country driver who had been carless for years, but Jim slowed to show them the mansions of movie stars of old and to take them on all the shortcuts to the site of TV's hottest show.

When Michael pulled up to the guard station at Quixote Studios, the man said, "Yessir, Mr. Parker, we've been expecting you. Your reserved parking space is right over there." It was so surreal that Michael thought they had taken a wrong turn to the old lots of *The Twilight Zone.*

Michael and Judy were agog. Over and over, they pinched each other to make sure they weren't dreaming. They wandered past the sound stages and constructed sets that were constantly rebuilt for future scenes, and they sat in the jet plane seen on the show, a hull on the lot.

Actors began to come out of their modular dressing rooms, flanked by the Santa Monica Mountains, and Judy and Michael met them, signed books, and made pictures: Shemar Moore, Matthew Gray Gubler, Thomas Gibson, Joe Mantegna, and showrunner Erica Messer.

Filming began, and Michael and Judy sat in director chairs to watch the action. Michael thought of the many attendees at the Christian movie nights and began to hum the old song, "If they could see me now, that old gang of mine. Holy cow, they'd never believe it. If my friends could see me now."

The crew was gracious, but suddenly, the day ended, and the visit was over. It was hard to pack up the emotions and leave, but Jim had arranged for a visit to *Major Crimes* at the Raleigh Studios. The star, Tony Dennison, was on *Crime Story*, a favorite of Michael's in the '80s.

As they crossed Sunset Boulevard, Michael thought of the famous movie and Norma Desmond, who said, "We didn't need dialogue. We had face. I can say anything I want with my eyes."

Major Crimes was running late on their shoot, so Judy and Michael were invited to have dinner with Dennison and the cast and crew. Going through the buffet line on the studio lot, Michael said, "I never thought I would one day be having dinner with Ray Luka," Dennison's gangster character on *Crime Story*.

They went to the dressing rooms afterward and swapped stories with Dennison and G.W. Bailey, who played Rizzo on *M.A.S.H.* and Thaddeus Harris in the *Police Academy* movies. Michael signed books for them all, and the next day, he signed books at the Bank of Books in Malibu. Allyson Adams, daughter of actor Nick Adams, arranged the signing, and afterward Judy and Michael had dinner with her at the Sunset Restaurant on the beach.

It was an emotional farewell as Judy and Michael were packing to leave L.A. for a signing in Las Vegas. Jim said, "Michael, I can't promise you that we will be able to sell it. We will try, but the way it is out here, they could call ten years from now and say, 'We're ready now.'"

Michael said, "That's not important, Jim. If it is meant to be, it will be. Meeting you and making new friends are the things that matter. I've been in a house of mirrors where I could no longer find the ceiling, the walls, the doors, or the way out. I cried love to sleep when my first wife died. I was lost, but then there was God Who turned the page. Now is not a time to panic but to give thanks."

CHAPTER THIRTY-THREE

"There's nothing in the desert. No man needs nothing."
—Lawrence of Arabia

"May God bless you and keep you safe from harm, and
may this prayer quilt keep you warm. In every single
moment spent, in every stitch, a prayer was sent."
—Unknown

When you take the wrong fork in the road of life and return to the narrow path, you will see many off-ramps along the way, like those in old Florida on the two-lane highways from Pensacola to Panama City, where signs promised free shells to visitors at mermaid and dinosaur attractions.

The billboards that intrigued young Michael said *Snake Farm This Exit*, featuring a smiling serpent, a mermaid he later thought could've been Eve, and complimentary apples. He thought it best to keep on the narrow path in life, avoid the wide gates, and bow down to enter the narrow gate.

Michael thought about those days, inspired by the sands they were crossing enroute to Las Vegas, sands that were a poor imitation of Okaloosa's white sugar-sand beaches.

He had arranged a signing at the downtown Barnes & Noble with the manager before they left Los Angeles, and as they topped a rise, Las Vegas rose from the sand, amidst hidden Mafia graves, like a mirage in the desert. He could almost hear the strains of the Lawrence of Arabia theme, a bit of the sweeping overture and some of "In Whose Name Do You Ride," a question that kept Michael focused and the song he was once drawn to: "Lawrence Rides Alone."

He dialed the bookstore, and a young woman answered.

Michael said, "Hi, this is Michael Parker. We're nearing Vegas and wondered if we could drop our books off before we check in somewhere?"

She was spitting mad, slobbering every indignity she could heap on Michael, like a wet cat that had wallowed too long in the catnip.

"You're not signing here. I saw all those emails while I was away in training, and I'm the one who arranges signings, and you're not signing here! I'm in charge! Me, Cruella!" she declared.

Michael was stunned and felt as welcome as a skunk at a wedding rehearsal and wondered if he had heard her name correctly.

Judy mouthed the word, "Cruella?"

"But we're in Las Vegas, and your boss approved this. I traveled across the desert on her agreement, her verbal contract," he said.

"I don't care," she barked. "We have corporate rules, strict rules, and you didn't give us proper notice, and did I mention we have rules!"

We have rules. Am I living in an echo chamber lately? Michael wondered. He thought her somewhere between hard-boiled and half-baked, not a headache but a migraine and short a few dalmatians.

Biting his tongue, trying not to say something he would regret, striving to turn the other cheek, Michael asked, "Well, is there another Barnes & Noble store in the metro area that might host me?"

"No!" she snapped with a Nurse Ratched sternness and voice to match. "They have the same rules we do. You aren't signing in Las Vegas for Barnes and Noble!"

Michael hung up, looked at Judy, and said, "What is it, honey? I think our charm has expired."

They found a big Barnes & Noble store in Henderson, larger than the downtown Vegas store, whose door Michael felt the Lord had closed for some good reason.

He dialed the Henderson store and talked with an older lady who had the same job title as the young blocker downtown. He could tell she was a light bearer, though he thought he must have misunderstood her name at first.

Heaven Lee Day said, "Sure, Michael, we'll host you. Drive right on out here. We'll set up your table and a date and time for your signing."

He thought he hadn't misunderstood her name after all.

So, Michael and Judy bypassed the snake farm downtown and decided her free apples were probably wormy anyway and her grapes...sour.

The Henderson store, fronted by palm trees, was beautiful. Michael and Judy unloaded the car and were given a choice spot by the front door, where they posted an image of the book cover on the giant Nook screen to get the eBook readers.

"Mrs. Day, this is great! Is there a hotel nearby that you recommend?" Michael asked.

She gave them a name of a hotel just a stone's throw from the store, and when they arrived, a joyful lady named Barbara Peard was working the front desk.

"Mississippi? What are y'all doing in Las Vegas?" she asked.

"I'm an author, and we're going to sign books at Barnes and Noble," Michael said, standing up a little straighter.

"What day?" she asked.

"Wednesday," Michael said.

"That just happens to be my day off. I'll come and bring a friend," she said.

Michael was beginning to think the switch to this location had God's fingerprints all over it.

Readers poured into the store on the day of the signing, and a record number of hardback books and eBooks were sold. Barbara showed up with her friend as promised, and when she learned that Judy was a cancer survivor, she lit up and said, "Along with sixty other women, I make prayer quilts for people with cancer."

She returned, gave Judy a quilt, and the picture of her with Judy and the quilt was shared widely on social media.

Michael's suspicions about divine intervention on store sites were confirmed with the gift of the quilt, which became the template for the prayer quilts Judy and other women would make for cancer patients.

As they were packing up at the store, the staff asked for a group photo in front of the electronic board with the image of *Ghostly*. Hardback books plus eBooks pushed the total sales near 100, and with the books the store kept, Judy and Michael had sold all of the books they took to California.

One staffer looked at Michael and said, "Have you ever thought of working in a bookstore? You sure know how to sell books."

To top it all off, they ended their Vegas adventure over dinner with Sandi Miller, a friend and confidante of Elvis he had always wanted to meet.

After they left Vegas, Michael detoured north from I-40 to take Judy to the Grand Canyon for her birthday. While they walked the rim of the canyon, a giant raven seemed to follow them and sound a gurgling croak, a croak that seemed to come from the back of its throat. The giant bird, twice the size of crows back home, harkened back to high school English classes and Edgar Allen Poe.

Michael told Judy these were strange times, and he felt there was something about the raven encounter, but he couldn't put his finger on it.

"Maybe he thinks we're with Elijah and has come to feed us in the ravine," Michael said as the raven flew off toward the canyon to tap at Poe's chamber door, black plumage gleaming glossy in the sun.

CHAPTER THIRTY-FOUR

"Saw the ghost of Elvis on Union Avenue, followed him to the gates of Graceland and watched him walk right through."—"Walking in Memphis," Marc Cohn

"If you stand near its fountain in the middle of the lobby, where the ducks waddle and turtles drowse, you will see everybody who is anybody in the Delta."
—God Shakes Creation, *David Cohn*

"Preacher, don't stop your preaching. This old world is almost done."—"Keep Your Lamp Trimmed and Burning," Blind Willie Johnson

Fresh home from Hollywood, doors opened and invitations for interviews and speeches rolled in, many from Memphis. The heat and humidity of the dog days of summer had not relented when Michael went to Memphis for interviews and to Beale Street to see if the magic or madness was still there like it was when he went to the Bottom of the Blues Club in 1973 to find a killer.

The neon lights were flashing, and the music was blaring from every open door as Michael strolled down the cobblestone street where rock, soul, and gospel blended into a sort of cousinly harmony, a soundtrack of once-upon-a-time America.

There were street performers but not the kind Michael encountered in days of yesteryear. Even the alleys housed artists with jugs and Delta-style slide guitar licks, piercing harmonica riffs, and wailing saxes, and in one club he saw a rockabilly band with a man slapping and spinning an upright bass like Bill Black. Dueling boogie-woogie pianos ripped it up in another. The walkup bars offered concoctions like the "Walk Me Down" sure to disable the gray matter, and the strands of white lights blending with the pink and blue neon made for a fantastical aura.

Bands played the music of old, a glowing red sign spelled out STAX. Rufus Thomas was gone but still "Walking the Dog." The Bottom of the Blues Club he had written about in his book was gone. Beale was on its last legs back then, and they had begun to tear down the old places in the name of urban renewal, so this glitzy Beale was not the one he remembered. Still, Michael was "walking with his feet ten feet off of Beale," as the song said, and ghosts were whispering lyrics from another time.

He passed a line of vintage hotrod cars on display, and a group of young pilgrims were all dressed up in Elvis-styled jumpsuits. Everyone was taking pictures of them and with them. He passed the camera flashes and revving of muscle-car engines and asked some mature musicians about the old club and its proprietor, James Walker, who some used to call Super Fly. A stately old gentleman, who locals said was the honorary "Mayor of Beale Street," told Michael Mr. Walker was still above ground and where to find him, at the corner booth where he always sat in B.B. King's club on 143 Beale.

Michael walked in and scanned the club. The bass and the brass of the band made it hard to think or hear, but over in the corner, his eyes fell on an old man who was nursing a drink and nibbling on a plate of soul food. He wasn't the giant man Michael remembered, no longer 300-plus pounds with massive hands but lean and a bit on the frail side. Could this be the same big man who once hung out with Howling Wolf, who sang "Three Hundred Pounds of Heavenly Joy" before he left Memphis and Sun Records for Chess Records in Chicago?

Michael looked again. It had to be him, and Michael wondered how old he would be now. He was always someone who could be plus or minus twenty years.

Michael walked over to the table. The man finally looked up at the gray-headed man standing before his table, just as the band took a break and the decibel levels dropped enough to carry on a conversation.

"Mr. Walker?" Michael asked.

"Who's asking?" he said.

"Michael Parker, someone you used to know," Michael said.

The man looked at Michael through what appeared to be the white of cataracts.

"Come closer," he said.

When Michael stepped up to the edge of the booth, the man turned his head back and forth and up and down, and Michael could see the moment the light went on in his hazy eyes.

"Well, I'll be, a bolt out of the blues," he said, his eyebrows arching as high as a cat's back.

"Well, bless my soul! The crow has turned white, and the egret has turned black. Agent Michael Parker shows up in the thick of the signs of these times. I thought you was dead, son," he said.

"No, sir, not yet. May I sit and talk a bit?" Michael asked.

"Surely, Mr. Parker. What are you doing down here at this pretend Beale Street?"

"Looking for you, Mr. Walker," Michael said.

"You came looking for me once when you were a hunter, a man with a badge who seemed more vigilante than lawman. You still hunting?" Walker asked.

"Not that kind of hunting. A lot of turbulent water under the bridges," Michael said as he began to tell him his story.

"So, that badge didn't save you, and that white-boy complexion didn't either," Walker said.

"No, only Christ could save me, and that pigmentation is just a figmentation, Mr. Walker. Doesn't mean a thing to the Lord or the devil, for that matter," Michael said with a smile.

"Well, Michael Parker, I always suspected you would never give in to fit in. You were the kind who just dug in," Walker said.

He looked far, far away, seeing something only he could see, and then shook his head and pursed his lips.

"I hung on as long as I could and watched the old Beale Street die. There was no more room for an entrepreneur like me. It was just too civilized and controlled. They ran off everybody worth a cuss. I just come down here for good food, good music, and because I'm a sentimental masochist. Some of these tourists from Europe ask to have their pictures made with me. They don't know me, but they think I look...genuine," Walker said as he laughed long and hard.

"You *are* genuine, Mr. Walker. They broke the mold when you left, and even Lansky Brothers had to move from 126 Beale," Michael said.

Walker drained his glass of liquor and asked, "What are you really doing down here?"

"I'm not sure. Taking a last look at things left behind, maybe, and I've written a novel and have an interview tomorrow in East Memphis. There's a character in it who bears a striking resemblance to you, Mr. Walker," Michael said.

"Is that a fact now? Is this character all that I was?" Walker asked.

"Every bit genuine, the mystique and the man who parted crowds when he walked down Beale and Union, too, like Moses and the sea. I'm just back from Hollywood and thought we might ask Morgan Freeman to play you," Michael said.

"Mr. Parker, you won't do, but Morgan is not bad enough, mean enough to play me," Walker said. For a moment, Michael could see the man he once knew, the man with bodyguards and guns and girls who bought powder and paint by the pound.

"All the greats and their greatness are gone. Our beautiful brush pile got manicured. Memphis Minnie, who once worked the Beale Street bars when I was a child, left here and made it big in Chicago playing the blues before time passed her and me by. They brought her home and buried her there in Walls in an unmarked grave just down the road from Ace's setup the same year you raided his place," Walker said.

"I didn't know that then, but I did later. There's a marker there now. I guess we all need something to say we passed through this world," Michael said.

"Michael Parker, you were always different and fell between the stools of this crowd and that one, not that that's a good thing or a bad thing, but there is something different about the you sitting before me, and it's not just the gray hair. You're the same, but you been made over. You seem like you could smile even as the tears were drying on your cheeks. You got the Light. I don't have it, but I know it when I see it in someone else.

"I'm not of your tribe, but I recognize the good it's done for some people who would've died young, but it no longer seems the world wants to live and let live, to give your people any space. People once thought maybe there was something else, but they don't come to your churches now. They hate you folks, and there's no middle ground. Everything's frayed around the edges, and nothing seems off-limits. Do you feel the stirrings and shakings lately, man of God?" Walker asked.

"People keep asking me that, but yeah, I do, and it is strong and getting stronger. Sometimes I get a whiff of it when an ill wind blows, and it smells like the darkness of a devil we once knew," Michael said.

"Did you know his poor mama had Fredrick's remains buried out on that big spread of theirs? No one would take him, and she finally had to move him to an unmarked grave in parts unknown because all the devil worshippers came at midnight to worship him and perform animal sacrifices at his graveside," Walker said.

Michael shook his head.

"She was a fine lady. It made me want to go out there with my gun and pick off Satan's ghouls one by one," Walker said.

"I think I would have gone out there with my Bible, armed with the Word, and picked them off one by one," Michael said.

"You have changed, Mr. Parker, but I hear you," the former king of Beale Street said.

"I tell you, Michael, these are strange times, maybe the end of times. It feels like someone left the oven door open, and it's a hundred and fifteen in the shade. It's like Sister Rosetta Tharpe used to sing in the clubs and revivals I frequented as a boy. Strange things are happening every day," Walker said.

"She also wrote, 'Up above my head, I hear music in the air. I really do believe there's a heaven somewhere,'" Michael said as he shook his hand.

"It's too late for me, Michael Parker, but I sure enjoyed shaking hands with yesterday tonight. It's been the best chin-wagging I've had in a long time," Walker said.

Michael said, "It is later than we think, but as long as we're breathing and repenting, it's never too late, Mr. Walker. Even Memphis Minnie was baptized before she died."

As Michael and James walked out together, a woman was weeping, then wailing at an outdoor table. A pall fell over the festive nightlife, the horns and strings began to go silent, and one by one tourists and artists alike began to come to her side to comfort her. There was something in the air. Time seemed to slow to a crawl. Musicians came out of the clubs, and someone in the crowd began to sing solo, unrecognizable a cappella at first. Then others joined in, and sorrows mixed and mingled in a group mourning and petition.

Someone banged a tambourine, a saxophonist joined in, and the collective joining of the woman's unknown desperation consumed Beale Street. More gathered and held hands and sang, "Pass me not, O gentle Savior. Hear my humble cry; While on others Thou art calling, do not pass me by."

Walker turned to look at Michael, and the light reflected off the tears overflowing the well of his eyes. Walker dabbed at the runaway water and said, "Well, I'll be. Maybe it's not too late for folks like me, Michael Parker."

The big tower clock down the street began to chime thirteen, and Michael said, "It's later than it's ever been. Why not tonight? He's always up, always waiting, knocking at the door. Normal is not returning, but Jesus is. Think of Him as 9-1-1."

Just then, a blues singer down the way began to sing a bit of Howling Wolf's "Moaning the Blues." "Well, somebody knocking on my door. Well, I'm so worried, don't know where to go."

Walker said, "Signs everywhere tonight. I'll think on it. I will."

After Michael left Beale, he went to the Peabody Hotel, where ducks walk, where Hal Lansky once said the Delta began right there in the living room of Memphis. It was a warm night, but Michael went up to the roof where all that was left at ground level in exchange for an imagined foretaste of fall. It was where he and Susan once dined under the luminosity of the moon and stars next to Elvis' confidante, Red West, and listened to Jason Williams pound his piano and appear to be a reincarnation of Jerry Lee Lewis.

Memories overwhelmed him, and he went down to the river and parked on the bluffs. He watched the lighted tugboats go by, thought of the concerts he and Susan had attended on Mudd Island, and riding on the *Memphis Queen* riverboat with Clay and his wife, Pat. As the moon skimmed lightly over the rippled surface of the Mississippi, he sang, "Long distance information, give me Memphis, Tennessee. She could not leave her number, but I know who placed the call."

CHAPTER THIRTY-FIVE

"Willoughby? Maybe it's wishful thinking nestled in a hidden part of a man's mind, or maybe it's the last stop in the grand design of things—or perhaps, for a man who climbed on a world that went by too fast, it's a place around the bend where he could jump off."—Rod Serling

"On a hill far away stood an old rugged cross, the emblem of suffering and shame…where the dearest and best for a world of lost sinners was slain. So I'll cherish the old rugged cross till at last my trophies I lay down…"
—"The Old Rugged Cross," George Bennard

"He who watches over you will not slumber."
—Psalm 121:3

Michael rose early after a night of lucid fever dreams.

In his first dream, he had fallen asleep on a train and awakened to find himself on a 19th-century rail car in 1888. The conductor walked the aisle calling, "Willoughby. Next stop, Willoughby." Michael looked outside and discovered he was in a town called Willoughby, a peaceful, restful place to start over, a place of sunlight and serenity appealing to the boy/man people said had been "born too late," nothing but a dreamer.

People greeted him, waved, and tipped their hats as he walked through Willoughby, and a band under an open pavilion in the park was playing the popular song of the day, "Beautiful Dreamer." The pace of life was slow and idyllic where dreams were exchanged for answered prayers, and the wind sang hymns you'd never forget.

Michael began to recognize Willoughby from a favorite show he had seen when he was a boy of twelve in 1960, but dream or not, he didn't want to wake and leave Willoughby. He wanted to stay and play hooky from the world where he felt misassigned.

Kids were playing softball in the park, and one little girl stopped to greet him after she rounded the bases. She took his hand, gave him a peppermint stick from her pocket, and told him she was nine. She said her name was Annie Pearl, but people called her Pearl.

Pearl said, "Willoughby is not what you seek. You are searching for heaven. You were a little boy who wanted to be a hero in a world that pretended to like heroes but really hated them. You wanted to fix everything and everybody, but your armor was only held together by one bolt. The world removed that bolt and you collapsed, but He came to your side with the full armor of God."

Willoughby and Pearl began to fade as the train pulled away, but he heard her call to him, "I will see you in heaven. He loves you, and I love you too, Michael."

As Willoughby receded, he found himself lost atop Golgotha, where men had gathered to murder their Maker. Michael wandered through a dense, swirling fog and residuals of shame until he was standing at the foot of the empty tree plucked from the forest to hold Christ in His crucifixion. The blood-stained tree swayed and creaked on the hill of suffering and sacrifice and groaned, "It wasn't my fault. I was brought here to the Skull, this place of death, but I'm not that tree where men still eat and think they will be as gods. I am the symbol of an undeserved gift, the crux of history. I held Him as tenderly as I could. You believe me, don't you?

"You have been in the desert, but He gave you a voice for the lost in the infirmary, and the tears dripping down your cheeks are water for your parched lips.

"You wounded Him with sin, but He spoke on your behalf while on this cross full of God. He climbed this hill on purpose for a thankless mob and said, 'Weep not for me. Weep for yourselves.' They did this to the tree always green, but see what they do now that the tree is dry. He fed the multitude, but they couldn't understand Him when He said, 'I am the bread of life.'

"The barbarians are inside the gates. The world is perishing, but there's a new world coming. Hang your harp in the willows, weep, and watch for the signs, Michael Parker."

Michael awakened in a sweat. A loud siren wailed by the hotel, while the housekeeper's cleaning cart squeaked in the hallway. Outside his room a small flycatcher in a willow tree sang his plaintive pee-a-wee, a petition once called a little bit of heartache set to music.

Michael wrote down everything he could remember from the haunting dreams and then drove out Poplar Avenue to KWAM radio in East Memphis. He saw so many familiar landmarks where he and Susan had once shopped and watched movies. Beale Street was famous, but Poplar Avenue was one of the original streets when Memphis was formed, a vital corridor for the city.

Earle Farrell, the veteran newsman and Memphis fixture, allowed Michael an hour to tell his story, and friends sent emails to say hello during the show. During the show a man called in and said, "I sure do like your guest today. I used to know him in another life."

The producer said, "Well, tell him on the air."

"We have a call, Michael. Go ahead, caller."

"Hello, hello, am I on the air?" the caller asked.

"Yes, we hear you," Michael said.

"Agent Parker. This is Otis, 'Bad Eye.' I just wanted to tell you that the girls are doing fine. They married and had babies who look just like Sheler. I still set off them metal detectors because of that plate in my head, but my traveling days are done. I sure hope your book is big for you. You was a straight-shooter.

"One of my grandsons is named Parker. Hope that's okay. Well, I gotta go. Thanks for everything. If we never meet again this side of heaven, we'll meet on that beautiful shore," he said as he hung up abruptly and the dial tone roared in their headphones.

Michael adjusted his headphones, rubbed his ears, and shook his bowed head.

"You okay, Michael?" the producer asked.

"Yeah, something in my eye," he said, clearing his throat.

"Someone you know?" she asked as they went to break.

"Yes, a long time ago. Strange things, wonderful things are happening every day, it seems," Michael said.

CHAPTER THIRTY-SIX

*"It's a long way from Graceland across Jordan to the
Promised Land."—"From Graceland to the
Promised Land," Merle Haggard*

*"This one is for Michael and all his friends at the Gray Bar
Motel in Millington."—George Klein, The Elvis Hour*

When Michael left East Memphis, he decided to swing by
Marlowe's B-B-Q on Elvis Presley Boulevard, where he had a
book signing scheduled the following week during Elvis Week
activities.

On the way to Marlowe's, he turned on the Sirius Radio Elvis
channel and heard George Klein on the air. George and Elvis
became friends when they met at Humes High School in 1948, the
year Michael was born.

Michael attended George Klein Day in Memphis when he first
came home to thank George for his many kindnesses when
Michael was at Millington Camp. He gave George a draft of
A Ghostly Shade of Pale before it was published and told him he
was in the book.

As Michael passed Graceland, the leaves on the giant trees on
the hill seemed to wave at him in the gentle summer breeze, and he
had the urge to stop at the gates and ask if Elvis was home. He
thought of seeing Elvis at the fair in Tupelo and the college nights
when he and Susan went to sleep listening to Elvis sing about
bridges over troubled waters. He remembered "Softly as I Leave
You" playing on the radio when Clay died and long lines of
mourners for Clay and Elvis.

Riding a wave of memories, he turned into the plaza and
parked across the street to see if any friends were in town early for
the annual Elvis Week in August. He half hoped to see people like

his friend Mary Logan, head of Shreveport's Burning Love fan club, who had gone home to be with the Lord.

As he neared the Sirius XM booth, he saw George Klein outside talking to some fans. Michael stopped at a respectful distance and waited. George saw him and motioned him to stand by. He stepped into the booth, came out again and said, "You're on the air, Michael."

Suddenly, the prized interview he had wanted for so many reasons was underway with no preparation, just a window opened and an invitation to step through and wing it. So many memories flushed up of George playing songs for him on the syndicated Elvis Hour radio show while Michael was at Millington Camp, what George called the "Gray Bar Motel." George had dedicated "I Want to be Free" by Elvis to Michael, and inmates kept asking him, "Do you know George Klein is talking about you on the radio?"

"So, Michael, you've written a book and been to Hollywood. Tell us about it," George said.

"Well, as far as Hollywood goes, I think it is a different place than when you went there with Elvis, but yeah, we have this novel, a big crime story, and you and Elvis are in it," Michael said.

"Is that right? So, you're going to sign at Marlowe's next week?" George asked.

"Yes, looking forward to signing on EP Blvd," Michael said.

They talked for a bit, made pictures, and Michael's feet were ten feet off Elvis Presley Boulevard when he left the Sirius booth.

Michael stopped at Marlowe's, and like a kid who just left the candy store, he told everyone he met that he had just come from George Klein's show. He returned the following week for a signing at Marlowe's, a place of great food and wraparound Elvis images and music everywhere you looked or listened.

He signed books for Elvis fans from across America and around the world. A young woman with red hair named Nancy, one of Dixie Lee Carter's sisters, came to help him pass out book cards, to tell people about his journey, and why they should care. She cried a little before she left.

Just before he left for Tupelo, Marlowe's brought the giant "hunka-hunka apple pie à la mode," courtesy of the house. It was what apple pies used to look like when cooking was artistry, and the title of "cook" was revered and almost a holy calling, when "yum" was a sort of amen. He could almost feel the rich ice cream clogging his arteries.

Late that night on the lonely, sleepy way home, dodging deer and waddling possums, he heard the replay of his interview with George. As his headlights cut through the night, he turned up the radio, opened the moon roof on his Murano, and saw the firelight of distant stars that seemed to grow brighter as he watched them, drawing him up to their pulsing light, a light so bright that it seemed to burn the moon with sparklers of tender mercies, while writing grace on his eyelids.

He thanked the Lord for it all, and just as the interview ended, George played a song for old times' sake.

"I sit alone in the darkness of my lonely room, and this room is a prison to me. I look out my window, and what do I see? I see a bird way up in a tree. I want to be free, free, like the bird in the tree."

CHAPTER THIRTY-SEVEN

*"There's a long line of mourners driving down our little
street... Through tears I watch as you ride by. You're
riding in that long black limousine."—"Long Black
Limousine," Bobby George, Vern Stovall*

*"Bring my flowers now... Don't spend time, tears or money
on my old breathless body. If your heart is in them flowers,
bring 'em on."—"Bring My Flowers Now," Tanya Tucker*

The phone rang in the fading light of evening, just as the
flickers of lightning hiding in ominous thunderheads split the sky.

It wasn't the hotel phone ring that could wake the dead, but it
was one of those demanding rings that you dread, like death
knocking at your door. You think you won't answer it so the bad
news it brings won't happen, but when sorrow comes, it brings
its own key to your door and its own chair to sit uninvited at
your table.

When he heard the voice of Dot Charles, Michael knew that
Tim was gone. The bone marrow transplant had gone all wrong,
and Tim's immune system never regained its footing.

Tim protected him from his enemies when Michael left the
MBN and held him up in Atlanta. Now Tim was going where he
needed no one to stand with him, where he would stand before the
Lord to receive his "Well done, good and faithful servant."

Michael looked at an old picture of a last MBN picnic at
Sardis Lake, a day of softball games and homemade ice cream with
Tim, Clay, and Susan. Now they had all gone home, and soon he
would join them there.

When Michael entered the funeral home for visitation, he saw
Tim's wife, Dot, sitting alone. It was difficult to imagine one of
them without the other. Michael had seen her without him, but she
was still not alone. Tim was always in her eyes and heart.

Former agents, some Michael had once supervised, kept their distance, stared at him across the room beneath hooded eyes, and whispered in hushed tones. He wanted to tell them that it was okay, that his sins were not catching, that he was not "unclean."

Someone Michael didn't know, a former student, came up and asked, "You were his friend, weren't you?"

"Yes," Michael said.

The man tried a brave smile and said, "Tim was a character, but he just had so much character, how could he not be a character?"

A young woman who was also a former student said, "I loved him for many reasons, but he always drilled into us that if a child tells you someone makes them uncomfortable, listen to them. I tried as an abused child, but no one would listen. I loved him for trying to protect vulnerable kids like I was. I'm passing his warnings on now."

It was a beautiful service. Michael was a pallbearer. When "Praise You in the Storm" was played, Tim's family stood together, hugging and holding each other. Tim's son, Chuck, preached and praised through tears, making the service all the more poignant and Christ-honoring, as loss and grief ripped at his heart.

Anyone who looked at the children of Tim and Dot knew all they needed to know about their parents. Their children testified to their parents' faithfulness, a home in Tula filled with love. There was an altar call that Tim had requested, a chance for someone to come forward and surrender to the Lord.

Despite how they treated Tim when he was alive, Ole Miss wanted to do an article on Tim, and Dot asked Michael to speak for them, one last vote of confidence from the people who loved Michael when few did.

Michael thought of the students Tim mentored and the joy he brought them. He also thought of the day of his oral exams for his Master's when he sparred with one of his other professors.

Michael knew he had overstepped, and he waited for the judgment by the professors. They opened the door and congratulated him. As Michael walked down the hall with Tim, Tim looked at him and said, "Why did you do that?"

"Because he is a liberal academic who doesn't understand the real world, and I guess all of that tongue-biting for years just bubbled up," Michael said sheepishly.

"Well, we all know that, but why did you do that?" Tim said, half scolding, half teasing.

These were the moments Michael remembered; the moments taken together made Tim Charles who he was and made it easy to tell Ole Miss that he was the best of what Ole Miss once was.

Tim was a friend to the end, but the end came sooner than expected.

Like Tim, we come on the crest of a wave that climbs high on the tide and then recedes into history and memory, as all flesh must one day.

***

The quilt Judy received in Las Vegas became the template for hundreds of prayer quilts to come for cancer patients. Ladies at Calvary Baptist worked with Judy to make the quilts, which were in great demand. The *Tupelo Daily Journal* did an extensive article on the quilt ministry, and she told Michael that everything was going well, except they were running out of fabric.

Enter the Lord.

Martin Falkner, a man who had told everyone about Michael's books, called to say his mother's cancer had returned, that she was in the hospital, and it didn't look good.

"Mama has one request. She wants to meet the real man in the books she has read. Would you come to the hospital?" he asked.

Michael bundled up on a cold night and went to the hospital. When he knocked at the door to her room, he heard a small voice say, "Come in."

Dianne Nabors was a tiny lady, hair almost gone, and she looked like a strong breeze might blow her away, but there was a light emanating from her whose origin was unmistakable.

She was propped up in her bed, smiling from ear to ear like she had just discovered she had teeth, and Michael's books were all around her.

They talked and prayed for almost two hours, and she had many questions about things in the books. Michael thought he was on a mission of mercy, but it turned out that he was the one who received strength and clarity from her and her faith, even in the shadow of death.

When he finally left, he told Martin, "I don't know if I blessed her, but she sure blessed me."

Later they found Dianne in her bed. She was gone where the saints long to go, and Michael liked to think that Tim, Clay, and Susan were there to greet her.

Shortly after her funeral, Martin called Michael.

"Michael, Mama had an obsession…fabric. She has two homes full of top of line bolts of fabric. I know she'd want Judy to have the fabric for her quilt ministry," Martin said.

Martin brought a trailer load to Calvary Baptist, and Judy and another lady loaded up more to bring to the church. Judy had enough fabric to supply her group, other churches that wanted to start quilt ministries, and to give some to women sewing for missionaries in Central America.

In the rearview mirror, Michael could see God orchestrating it all. Don't go to this bookstore; go to this one and meet the woman there who gave Judy the first quilt. Meet Martin and Dianne through your books. Go to the hospital and do what you're called to do.

CHAPTER THIRTY-EIGHT

There's nothing left to do but go our separate ways."
—"Separate Ways," Bob West, Bobby West,
Richard Mainegra

"There are two kinds of non-conformity, and only one of them wears hipster glasses. The kind that does wear them is a very popular form of pretending to be out of the mainstream, in order to be the envy of it, and the other is a radical form of unpopularity, calculated to get you slandered and viciously attacked, on the way to changing the direction of the mainstream. One kind of non-conformity requires courage, while the other kind requires nothing more than vanity and a five-dollar cup of fair-trade coffee."—Rules for Reformers, *Douglas Wilson*

The sun was a pale sulfur yellow, and acorns were falling like rain, perhaps hurled by mischievous squirrels launching tiny missiles from the oak trees around Tupelo's old library. The nuts bounced like BBs in a barrel on the sloped parking lot as Michael arrived to speak at "Lunching with Books," sponsored by the "Friends of the Lee County Library."

Dodging the errant nuts, he thought about the path forward, the mediocrity of conformity, and the intersecting paths that brought him to this intersection, to the library just up the street from the first apartment he and Susan shared when they were as poor as church mice. He used to walk to the library to do research when he was commuting to Ole Miss and found that his library card from his childhood days was still active.

The country boy, whose library card was a treasured passport of admittance to the world of literature, would now speak words in a building that housed some of the greatest words ever written. He felt like Linus in the *Peanuts* comic strip who showed Charlie

Brown and Lucy his library card and said, "I have been given my citizenship in the land of knowledge!"

After his speech to the library patrons, Michael negotiated access to Kroger grocery stores for his books, and he contacted STL (Send the Light), a Christian book distributor, to extend the reach of the books. He had learned that distribution was the key to visibility, not so much the publisher, but the "Cold Water Committee" chairlady said neither was in their business interest, and Michael should leave such things to the professionals.

It had become evident that Gershwin was right: "You like this and the other. I like this and that. Tomato, tomahto. Let's call the whole thing off." It had become more than just pronunciation and hair-splitting semantics. The nuts and bolts of the venture were rusting, and the blurred vision had passed "agree to disagree" and "neither of us is necessarily wrong." Some haystacks just have no needle within them to find.

Michael thought of the sunsets he watched on Okaloosa Island when it seemed the water held the sinking sun as long as it could until it seemed to simmer no longer but to boil when there was more heat than light.

A meeting was held, and everyone decided that an amicable separation was in the best interests of all concerned. Oil and water just hadn't mixed well.

When the flood waters rise, and Johnny Cash asks, "How high's the water, Mama," new channels have to be created to give the tide somewhere to go. A means to separate was put on paper, and Michael bought the entire stock of hardback books to use and to save them from an unknown fate.

When the meeting to sign paperwork ended, and he and Judy rose to leave, the "Cold Water Committee" chairlady couldn't make a clean break and just leave it there. Like the boxer who jabs or lands low blows on the break, she sardonically snapped at Michael and said, "You just don't like anyone telling you what to do, do you?"

He looked at her and said, "No, I don't. I've had too many years of people telling me what to do, and like black eyes and busted lips, they were enough to last a lifetime. I have a mission, a calling, and no time for diversions. I'm just swimming to shore like Paul at Malta to preach the gospel and keep God's appointments before time runs out," he said.

When they walked outside, someone next door was playing a radio too loud, and a boy across the way was playing fetch with his barking dog. Leaves rattled across the parking lot, chasing each other in a rush to nowhere. An early pale moon peeked full-faced through the tree branches and crowned the old oak.

Autumn was in the air, the scent of a cleansing rain was chasing the wind, and a raucous blue jay was loudly alerting everyone in earshot with its demanding, megaphone voice, tinged with melancholy.

Michael looked at Judy and said, "How far we've come from how close we were. Sometimes it's just not best to go the wrong way together. We may take different paths and arrive at the same destination, but it's better to be a lean bird on the wing than a fat bird in a cage. A caged bird is heartbreaking, but a caged evangelist is sadder still."

Michael closed his eyes and looked up to feel the first spray of mist on his face. He sighed deeply, felt the pause of creation, the seasonal rotation, and could almost see God out and about, painting treetops and sprinkling the world with melodies of hope. He caught a gilded leaf of gold in his hand that looked like a flake off the streets of heaven. These were the days of high cotton. Summer had done its work and the heat was gone, but the living wasn't easy.

He turned over the old leaf and thought of the days when he was a leaf blown by ill winds and the day God turned the page in the leaves of his story.

Judy leaned into him, and Michael said, "It seems like good weather for sweaters and porch sitting and maybe a first fire to take the chill off the house."

CHAPTER THIRTY-NINE

"If, in the quiet of your heart, you feel something
should be done, stop and consider whether it is in line
with the character and teaching of Jesus. If so, obey
that impulse to do it, and in doing so you will find it
was God guiding you."—Eric Liddel

"The 'senses' of Scripture are woven together as the
Seamless Robe of Christ. No 'spiritual sense' may be
divided from the 'literal,' yet together they form a unified
whole. To find the 'meaning' is to be clothed with the
garment of Christ, not to go about picking at threads."
—Canon Theologian of the Bible Belt

Freed from the constraints of his publishing deal, Kroger offered a contract for his book and books to come. Michael began to sign at their stores around the South and meet people who never went to bookstores.

In this milk-and-bread mission field, Michael told shoppers about his books, about how to never be hungry or thirsty again. He told them about the Bread of Life, the Great I Am.

It was raining like the days of Noah when Michael ran into the Tupelo Kroger store to pick up something for Judy and check the stock of his books. The floodgates opened, wind whipped shopping carts across the parking lot, and thunder rattled the rafters.

The rhythm of the rain covered the roof like a comforter, and the moment he entered the store, a wave washed over him, and it wasn't from the storm. He sensed the Holy Spirit's presence and felt as though he was walking through molasses in slow motion. He realized people were speaking to him, but he seemed out of sync with their time and speed, like 45 records played at 33 or 78 speeds, and he could not understand them.

He walked down the aisles, looking left and right, and then he saw a distraught woman sitting on the floor, sprawled in a pool of defeat, near prostrate, and crying as she stocked the shelves.

He approached her and asked, "Ma'am, are you okay?"

Through red and swollen eyes glued together by brokenness, she looked up at him and said, "My husband left me for a younger woman, and now I'm working two jobs to feed my kids and keep a roof over our heads."

There was a stillness around them, an invisible wall where shoppers could not intrude on a Divine appointment. Michael had a knot in his stomach as he listened to her purging of all that seemed too much to bear, all the unspoken things bottled up within her bruised heart.

Michael told her he was sorry, that he had once been in a deep valley and felt hopeless and abandoned.

"I learned to seek God's purpose in all things, no matter how crushing they might be, to look for His light to find the way out of despair. You feel lost right now and unloved, but the Lamb knows where you are, and He loves you," Michael said.

He prayed with her and she rose from amidst the mountain of cans that surrounded her to wipe her eyes and hug him. She asked if any of his books were in the store and went in search of them.

His footsteps made no sound as the Holy Spirit pulled him along through the crowded store. From seafood to milk to eggs, Michael began to talk about God with refugees from the storm outside, releasing the joy that overflowed the well of his heart to a captive congregation.

Then, someone walked up behind him and tapped him on his shoulder. When Michael turned around the man asked, "Are you Michael Parker?"

Michael smiled and said, "I think so. What did I do?"

T.K. Moffet, lawyer and retired major general in the Army Reserves, said, "I just read *A Ghostly Shade of Pale*. It was the best book I've ever read in my life."

Michael thanked him, and their talk took on an importance all its own. Moffet said, "I'm thinking about running for Congress."

"Before you make your decision, you should read *A Rented World*. It's my new book about the imitation of life offered in Washington, where honest men are viewed as traitors, and dissent is not tolerated," Michael said.

When Michael finally left the store, the rain had stopped and the air was clean. He was drained but on fire for the Lord. He looked at his watch. His five-minute shopping trip to the store had turned into two hours.

When he arrived home, Judy asked where he had been, but she looked at him and said, "Either you've had an encounter with the Holy Spirit, or you've been struck by lightning."

After that night, STL Distributors picked up the books and opened the door to many outlets, including Christianbook.com, the catalog Michael used at Edgefield to find movies for his fledgling Christian movie night ministry.

Barnes & Noble manager Scott Jackson announced *A Ghostly Shade of Pale* had become his store's all-time bestselling novel, and he placed Michael's books in the store's coveted center display.

Itawamba Community College then chose *A Ghostly Shade of Pale* as required reading for all English students, a vote of confidence from the English department at a college Michael had attended. ICC purchased 500 books, and Michael spoke to all English students.

High school English teachers, who liked the books because they were written as literature and contained no profanity, began to use them from grades eight through twelve. Schools from Memphis to Mobile picked up the books, and the top academic freshman at Ole Miss chose *Ghostly* to profile and dissect for his presentation to the Honors College.

Michael was invited to speak to a journalism class at Ole Miss. A student came up to Michael after his presentation and quietly said, "Thanks for talking about God. No one talks about Him anymore."

God was opening doors at an accelerated rate.

CHAPTER FORTY

"I am the prodigal son every time I search for
unconditional love where it cannot be found."
—The Return of the Prodigal Son, *Henri Nouwen*

"Quoth the Raven, nevermore."
—"The Raven," Edgar Allen Poe

"Between my finger and my thumb, the squat pen rests.
I'll dig with it."—"Digging," Seamus Heaney

T.K. Moffet took Michael's advice and declined a run for Congress, which left him available for an appointment as Chancery Judge. He used his courtrooms to point to the One Who offered true healing, not the Band-Aids of government. He invited Michael to open his court proceedings and speak to fractured families who had tried everything but Jesus.

Judge Moffet ordered cases of books for retired army officers and for people in prison, all because of a "chance" meeting in Kroger.

T.K. called one day and said, "I talked about you with my staff and other lawyers at lunch. Know what I said?"

"I'm afraid to ask," Michael said.

"I told them that when it comes to mastery of the English language, John Grisham is a one, and you are a ten!" he said.

"I love you, T.K.," Michael said.

Things were going well, too well.

Michael sat on the ramparts, dangling his legs over the edge and wiggling his toes at the world, like his days as a barefoot kid sitting in his treehouse on the outskirts of the sky in the deep forests of Parker Grove.

Then the worm turned.

The ICC English department chairlady told him they had received such positive feedback from his presentation to students and wondered if he would speak at a special honors banquet and inspire more students and parents.

Michael was thrilled to be invited. It would give him a platform to speak to young people about the goodness of the Lord and put him one step farther away from the drag of prison.

He was excited and waited for the particulars, but none came. He left word, but his messages were not returned. When he finally hemmed up the embarrassed head of the English department, he heard the regret, pain, and resignation in her voice. She had been overruled, and Michael's invitation had been rescinded.

"I'm sorry I haven't called you, but I didn't know how to tell you. I didn't want to tell you. You've been disinvited. The college president said he wanted someone else to speak at the banquet. I'm so sorry," she said.

Michael felt bad for her and others at the college who supported his books and paved the way for thousands to read *A Ghostly Shade of Pale* on campus and in pre-college courses at area high schools. The president knew of his past, and Michael suspected the devil used him to yank the prison tether once again. He had always struck Michael as the kind of man who would snatch the last Oreo in the bag just as you reached for it.

Scott Jackson transferred to Florida and the support Jackson had extended left with him. Then someone in the store tearfully told Michael it was because he was a Christian. Whatever the real reason, his books were removed from the center placement because "it wasn't fair to others, you know," and books that once flew off the shelves eventually disappeared from the store.

Then Steven Ballard, Michael's probation officer, called.

"Michael, I wanted to tell you that I am transferring to another assignment, and a new officer will add you to her list of case files," he said.

Michael groaned, but Ballard said it would be all right.

"Thanks for allowing me to go to California and Las Vegas. It accelerated God's plan. You are part of everything that has happened, a part of His purpose," Michael said.

"She hasn't dealt with probationers in a long while, but she'll be all right when she adjusts," Ballard said as if he was trying to convince himself.

Mary Jackson, the new probation officer, said she wanted to meet with him, and Michael went to the office as he had before, full of good cheer.

She was an older woman who looked like her face might break if she smiled. Her eyes were set back into her face with skin the hue of dark charcoal, and her lips were pursed in the sneer of someone who had just smelled something or someone foul. He thought for a moment that she could have been the mother of the halfway house director.

Michael smiled, introduced himself, and stuck out his hand, which she refused. Then he told her of his trip to Hollywood and the many places he had given his testimony, thinking she would see the fruits of his labors for the Lord.

Her face contorted in anger and the look of someone having an amputation without an anesthetic.

"You were allowed to cross state lines without supervision? I wouldn't have let you out of the Northern District if you owed money," she said as she thumbed through his file, and a sudden rage began to bubble over like the froth of scalding hot cocoa fresh out of an airport vending machine.

"You don't owe the government any money?" she said.

"No, ma'am. I settled up before I left for the monastery. I didn't want to be beholden to anyone when I came home," Michael said winsomely as he began to suspect this visit would not be a routine bagatelle.

"Who do you think you are? You mess with me, and I'll have you in handcuffs and chains again, file a probation violation on you, and send you back to prison and wipe that smile off your face. Where will you be then?" she barked in a voice like a rusty hinge opening and closing, a grimace under dark eyes that didn't quite track properly. She hurled angry words at him like a child throws stones, using them to shrink and diminish him.

Michael was stunned and taken aback, but he looked her in the eye and said, "Where I am now in this awkward moment between birth and death...in the hands of God."

As he walked to his car, he wondered what had just happened and thought of Percy Sledge's old song, "Out of Left Field." Michael could feel the darkness dogging him. He felt eviscerated, gutted from stem to stern, and wondered what he had done to provoke such an outburst of wrath and disrespect, such an attack on his self-worth delivered with the surgical precision of a sling blade.

Then Jackson came to do a home inspection. Judy and Michael were on their best behavior.

By the end of her visit, she seemed to have mellowed some, and she stopped to look out the patio window at the deck and flowers. At that moment, the largest crow Michael had ever seen swooped down like a messenger of death, a harbinger of malaise and sorrow in some cultures. It was raven-sized with a broad wing span and the glossy black color that ravens, not crows, show. Michael thought it looked like the raven they had seen at the Grand Canyon.

It perched on the rail, rocked back and forth with wings spread for balance. The giant bird was imposing and challenging, its beak opening and closing, as it threw its head back and made a gurgling croak. The probation officer's mouth was agape, her eyes wide, and she was clearly terrified.

"What...what *is* that thing?" she asked, her sweaty hand gripping the top of the breakfast table chair. Her raspy voice sounded like a lifelong unfiltered Lucky Strike smoker.

"It's just one of our locals checking on us," Michael said as if it was a daily occurrence.

Officer Jackson suddenly said she had to go. She couldn't get out the door fast enough, yet she looked like she was sleepwalking toward the door. When she got to her car, she shook herself like a dog coming out of deep water. She sped away, looking up as a giant shadow passed over her car.

Jackson met with Steve Ballard to tell him what had happened in her first meeting with Michael, where she thought he was not sufficiently submissive to her authority, about the home visit where this apparition from her nightmares swooped down from the sky.

Ballard said, "They called him Bird Man in prison. You never know what you'll see at his house, but he's all right. Cut him anywhere, and he bleeds evangelism.

"The world he lives in is not the world he longs for, so he writes and creates a world where it is just him attuned to the thrumming of God. He's a fish out of water, a man born too late. He is in self-exile and rebellion against conformity, but it's not rebellion he seeks but restoration of what was and might be. You can see his rebellion and submission at the same time. I sometimes think he is looking for a place of solitude to ride out the storms and rediscover his identity, but then God calls him to speak amidst the storms with cruciformity.

"To him, the past is not dead as long as he has his pen and prayer. He was always over here walking the perimeter, while the world was over there. He's a wonderer in an impoverished world, who yearns for the God of wonder, part poet and part historian, collecting time in a bottle. He sees this time as populated by those who don't know they're spiritually dead. His nostalgia is more than a longing for happy times and loved ones lost. It is the nostalgia from the Greek that speaks to the suffering, the aching to return to his point of origin, a place left unguarded, that he might see his destination through the eyes of a child as Jesus instructed the twelve.

"He dreams. He regrets. He remembers. His heart will break for what was lost until he has no heart left to break, bleeding internally for those whose hearts have been hardened and encrusted by the world. He is still finding his way to God, making up for lost time. Though you can see the sadness when he looks a certain way, his joy is increasing exponentially, and that is what you mistook for irreverence in your first meeting, an ever-fresh, newborn joy he cannot restrain. He is a cave Christian trying to reconcile his faith with the Twitter and YouTube Christianity he sees. He sees the cracks spreading beneath him in the foundations, but he found his footing in Christ and sees the culture trying to dethrone Him," he said.

Ballard tilted his head to the side and said, "Sometimes his smile reminds me of how the sun can sparkle and dance all over water spilt from a broken vessel and how the light on the water then migrates to create puddles of the Gospel.

"A lot of sticks were thrown in his life to test him, to gauge his subservience, but he was never good at fetch. He was farsighted, some things up close got blurry, and he made mistakes and enemies. Prison was unexpected and crushing, but he is tireless and I guess someone has to be. His mistakes imperiled his life but not his soul. He learned how little he knew and how dependent he was on God. Love him or hate him…he is who he is all the way down to the ground. His humility is not counterfeit.

"He runs so fast and hard that he sometimes has to pause and let his soul catch up with him. Those who don't wish him well think his faith does not conform to the modern church, that he is lucky and has just caught lightning in a bottle, but when he wakes up in the morning, he knows what he thinks, what he believes, and Who he is willing to die for. Whatever caused him to stumble was an aberration used by God, and that is why I let him go on his way to Hollywood, Timbuktu, or wherever Christ sends him," Ballard said.

Mrs. Jackson wiped at the corners of her eyes, huffed out a deep sigh, and said, "I understand now."

Michael soon submitted a request to terminate his probation early, and Officer Jackson, who never visited Michael and Judy again, concurred and forwarded her approval to the federal judge in Atlanta.

The federal judge was the same judge who had ordered Edgefield prison to escort Michael to Susan's funeral. He made a routine referral of the request to the U.S. Attorney's office to see if they objected to shortening Michael's probationary period.

They did not respond to repeated queries and later denied receiving the referral, but there were liars on the loose. The federal judge finally had to issue a formal order forcing them to respond.

The judge didn't know the U.S. Attorney's office was purposefully stalling on answering at the request of another judge, a magistrate judge with a grudge, whose anger only grew worse when he learned Michael had been invited to Hollywood, and the government had allowed him to go and to go unescorted. Sometimes, the honorific of "Your honor" is forfeited.

When the order terminated his probation, Officer Jackson called Michael with the good news. She told him she was happy for him and asked how she might find his books. Michael was finally free of supervision, free of all the artificial restraints.

As Michael and Judy sat on their deck talking about it all, a flock of crows flapped lazily along in the distance. They were normal-sized crows that cawed, not croaked.

They watched the crows until they disappeared and then Judy said, "I wonder if we'll ever see that giant bird again."

Michael smiled and said, "Nevermore."

With the smile still on his face, he added, "Nor prosecutors, magistrates, college presidents, Barnes and Ignoble book peddlers, or scapegraces of yesteryear."

CHAPTER FORTY

*"I have but one passion: It is He, It is He alone. The world
is the field, and the field is the world; and that country
shall be my home where I can be most used in winning
souls for Christ."—Count Nikolaus Ludwig Zinzendorf*

*"You must talk to God about people before you
talk to people about God."—D.L. Moody*

*"Run, John, and work, the law commands, yet finds me
neither feet nor hands, but sweeter news, the gospel brings.
It bids me fly and lends me wings."—John Berridge*

Michael stayed up late for a ninety-minute video interview on "Caravan to Midnight," a subscription podcast with former Coast-to-Coast host John B. Wells. The show had listeners in the far corners of the world.

Listeners from as far away as New Zealand commented on the interview, and as the show ended, goodbyes were said. As the link was dropping, Michael heard Wells turn to his producer and say, "Wasn't that something?"

Then an email popped up in Michael's inbox from a listener in Arizona.

I heard you on "Caravan to Midnight" tonight. I am originally from Mississippi, one of the last independent seed producers that Monsanto hasn't crushed. Things were looking up for me overseas and a deal is in the works with customers in Europe. While there, I met the love of my life, and we are to be married.

Then my health took a downturn, and I had a battery of tests. I get the results in the morning. I am alone and afraid in a hotel room in Arizona tonight, but I know God wanted me to hear you tonight. God bless you.

As Michael read the note, he could almost hear the man's voice, his anguish and uncertainty. It reminded him that he was part of a larger plan, maybe a bit player, but something that made him feel useful.

Tears stuck like glue to the puffiness beneath his eyes. He looked out his window, and the constellations all seemed in the wrong places, and cows could never jump over the giant orange moon that seemed to sit on the earth. The night sky seemed to inhale and exhale, and he again felt Someone was calling his name.

He answered the man's email, prayed for him, and passed out from the draining interview and the shrinking of the world to bring two men together via terrestrial radio. Though there were no breaks for station identification anymore, there was no doubt who the Broadcaster was and where the link originated.

***

After a few hours of restless sleep, Michael stumbled out of bed and saw the light from his computer. He thought it strange because he never left it on. Amazon said his books had sold out after the "Caravan to Midnight" show, and a Facebook private message box was open.

Rubbing the sleep from his eyes and the cobwebs from his brain, he leaned over and looked at the private message.

It read, "I don't know if you remember me, but you arrested my husband forty years ago."

Michael paused for a minute and peered through the fog of time. "Yes, I remember. How is he doing?" he asked.

She said, "He's gone now, but he was finally sober for those last two years."

"I'm so sorry," Michael said.

"Those were hard days. I was in nursing school at the Mississippi State College for Women, and they thought I was involved in his drug trafficking and would bring bad press on the school," she said.

It was all coming back to Michael.

"You were so kind to me. You contacted the school, told them I was not involved, and to leave me alone. I was a good caring nurse to people for forty years, and I just wanted to tell you that I owe you my life," she said.

A tear caught Michael off guard, then another until the dam broke, and God gave him a glimpse of yesteryear and residuals still paying dividends.

He told John B. Wells the night before that real men cry for Jesus. And so he did, until the river ran dry.

CHAPTER FORTY-ONE

"It is the image of God in you that enrages hell;
it is this at which demons hurl their
mightiest weapons."—William Gurnall

"All the cunning of the devil is exercised in trying to
tear us away from the Word."—Martin Luther

Michael was listening to Mahalia Jackson's soulful rendition of "Sometimes I Feel Like a Motherless Child" when Judy announced, "Mail call. Another letter came for you."

The letter, postmarked Costa Rica, was from an inmate Michael knew at the Millington Camp, an intense and sometimes intolerant man who just walked away and disappeared one day. He had served years and only had a year or so left when he just slipped out of the government stream. Michael guessed he must have stood all of it he could and had just hit the wall.

Dear Michael:

I am not in Costa Rica, in case the Marshals ask you. I am not dead, killed by a Mexican cartel as some have said, but I do move around quite a bit.

I was ready to leave that last day in Millington when we walked together early in the morning, but one last walk seemed the thing to do.

I don't know why, after all the time I served, I decided to go on the run. I guess it seemed the thing to do, too.

You almost talked me out of it, though you didn't know I would hop the fence and leave. All that stuff about Jesus and second chances burrowed into my mind that morning. I listened to you on shortwave when you were on "Caravan to Midnight" with John B. Wells and decided to write you and tell you that I went straight to the airport and was out of the country before they did bed count that night and found me missing. That was the plan to get a head start, and it seemed to work from what my sources said.

The federal boys will be watching my relatives and old girlfriends forever, I suppose, to see if I contact any of them, but it will be a long wait because that life is over; that man is dead.

I wish I could tell you what I'm doing, but just in case they intercept this letter, I won't get too specific. I think you'd approve. Suffice it to say, I found a good woman, and she insisted that I get to know the Jesus you were always talking about.

I always enjoyed our talks. You weren't a shallow person, unlike some of our fellow detainees. There were depths to be plumbed until our brains ached.

Sorry to leave without a goodbye, but I bet they interviewed you to see if you knew anything. I protected you and me. They didn't like you too much anyway. They were looking for an excuse to transfer you to the prisons in the deserts of Arizona or the cold winters of Maine so you'd get no more visits. They might have put you in "diesel therapy" and rode you all over America, napping on dirty floors of local jails, until they woke you to ride the bus again, so you'd relent and promise to bow before them. I couldn't tolerate one more day or hour around people who would do these things to other humans.

I will tell you this. For a while, I led a bird tour on the Amazon River, and I sometimes thought about how the "Bird Man of Millington" would have loved that gig. That trail is so cold it would mean nothing to them to run it now if they could, and people on the big river don't talk to the police. I'm like those guys in the movies, brushing out my footprints and spoor behind me as I go.

I'm not well now. I'll die in the jungle one day and no one will know, but I will be a free man when I do, free from the government and free in Christ. Some of your faith rubbed off on me, and I scrubbed and scrubbed but couldn't wash it off.

God bless you, Michael. If you ever pass a closet full of stuffed animals, look closer. I might be hiding in plain sight in their midst like E.T. in that movie.

Ponce

Michael could see him in the jungles, ports, and places he once talked about, places where expats could live well for very little. Before Michael and Judy were reunited, Michael had considered a possible move out of the country.

He saw the dark clouds on the nation's horizon, a faith encrusted with corruption and preached so long by so many that too many believed the corruptions to be truth and no longer saw the rotten eggs in the omelet.

So, Michael researched what countries were hospitable to Christian Americans. He looked at several countries in Central America, places he could serve God and possibly lead birding tours in Costa Rica or in Nicaragua, where his friends Rick and Mary Erwin moved to serve the Lord. Michael didn't move to Nicaragua, but he and Judy sponsored a child there, and Rick and Mary donated his books to the library in Managua.

Michael wished he could respond to Ponce and tell him how much his departure upset the applecart at Millington, how many people were called in for interviews. He wished he could tell him that the only thing they got out of the interrogations was a report from one inmate eager to please and to curry favor.

The inmate said he saw Ponce walking with Michael early on the morning of Ponce's departure and had passed them on the walking track.

They asked the man, "What were they talking about? Did you hear?"

"Well, yeah. Ponce was, uh, talking about philosophy and other deep stuff, and Parker was talking about Jesus and pointing out birds in the trees to Ponce," he said sheepishly.

Michael wished he could tell Ponce that they never even bothered to interview him, but after his escape, the food in the chow hall became sparse and foul, worse than usual, until the official temper tantrum passed.

While he was thinking about Ponce's letter, Judy came in with a wrinkled draft copy of *The Redeemed* she had taken to proof.

She had watched him cry at his keyboard while writing the book and told him, "You're killing yourself."

"I know, but I promised God, and I can't break that promise," he said.

She stood beside him with the draft, wiping her leaking eyes, and said, "The enemy is not going to like this, Michael. He's going to attack you."

Michael usually was the one warning Judy that attacks from the enemy were coming, but he knew what she was saying was true. The book had opened old wounds, and he had bled pain, but he cleansed the wounds with the Word, lest the infection of bitterness set in. He knew he would be no good to God then.

The Redeemed went to print and was finally released. A book signing was held at the Gum Tree Bookstore. It was a good turnout, but not like the first book. Some said they didn't want to see the hero suffer. People wanted more of the shoot-'em-up, true detective stories, not a book about prison, but it was unfolding as God planned.

The night after the signing, Michael sat straight up in bed at 3 a.m. on a Sunday, tearing at his shirt and shouting, "No! No! No!"

"Michael, what is it? Are you alright?" Judy asked, startled from her sleep.

"The enemy was attacking me, but it was more than a dream or nightmare. It was vivid, textured, and nuanced, and I could see, smell, hear, and taste everything. I was in an apocalyptic world, like the aftermath of a nuclear war, and everything was dead or dying in a land of ruin.

"The trees were bare and dying. The air was thick with suffocating gray dust, and the sun couldn't shine through the hoary fog. Sunlight was just a memory, a ghost. The ground was covered in sooty silver ash, and each step caused more fine powder to rise into the air. It was a sin-dusted world.

"The walking dead, zombies with their heads down, were plodding alongside me as we walked down this road of death, and one hollow-eyed man reached for me from the roadside with bony fingers and asked for water. Up ahead, when a zephyr stirred the dust in the air and opened a clearing, I could see a ghost town, like in one of those old western movies. There were signs as we entered, old wooden signs with smeared paint dripping down the boards.

"It was the gateway to hell, and I seemed to be the only one on the long train of souls who was not lost or dead. Ghoulish clerks and accountants were counting new arrivals and checking names. I was cut out of the throng and taken to a room in what looked like an old hotel. I could hear the shrieks of the lost in the distance, then a muffled and deep rumbling sound, then silence.

"I was sitting on a cot in the room when the door suddenly flung open, and there stood this tall, immaculately dressed and meticulously groomed man with every hair in place and wearing a sardonic grimace.

"Though he had the bearing of an angel of light, it masked someone who could steal or devour everything forever, and I thought of what Shakespeare had said, 'The devil is a gentleman.' I knew he was the seductive serpent and the frightful, powerful dragon, the roaring lion and the destroyer, and out of billions of souls, he had come for mine.

"I looked at him and said, 'Satan, I presume.'

"Then he changed into man's image of him, a goat-like creature with a red-hued face and blazing eyes that appeared to be on fire. His breath was acrid and reeked of rotten eggs. I knew this was the spirit that had led a rebellion against God in heaven, and I was out of my league and helpless without Christ.

His claws came out and raked across my chest in a sudden attack, tearing away my shirt, but at that moment, a blinding light burst forth from dozens of small flaming crosses exposed on my body. It was like a sun going supernova. I raised my hands to shield my eyes in that dimension and this one. The Light burned away the devil and the gateway to hell, showing me that I was covered by the blood of the Cross, and from within the Light, I heard a voice say, 'Fear not, for I am with you always.' Then I woke up screaming with the smell of sulphur in my nostrils and claw marks on my chest," Michael said.

Judy and Michael stayed up until dawn, talking about what had happened. They went to church at West Jackson Baptist and separated to go to their Sunday School classes. Judy encountered a friend in the middle of the church. It was Anita and she was crying.

Michael always said the Holy Spirit perched on Anita's shoulder, and when she spoke, it was like the old E.F. Hutton commercials where everyone listened. Today she looked wilted, tired, and hueless.

Judy asked, "Anita, what's wrong, honey?"

Anita said, "I don't know what was going on with you and Michael at 3 a.m. this morning, but God woke me and said I was to get up and pray for Michael and Judy, that you were under spiritual attack."

When Judy told Michael Anita's encounter with God that morning, he was surprised but not surprised. He had seen too much.

The bond that binds believers together passes hope and empathy along the line of saints like a gospel flu, what Michael called the "good infection."

The story of that night became a part of Michael's testimony, and it was confirmation for skeptics who doubted spiritual warfare was real.

Michael's friend and spiritual advisor Pastor Danny Bell said, "The devil hates your guts. He has a dartboard with your picture on it."

CHAPTER FORTY-TWO

*"I had no real communication with anyone, so I was
totally dependent on God. He never failed me."*
—Things We Couldn't Say, *Diet Eman*

*"There's a Greystone chapel...the touch of God on
every stone. Inside the walls of prison my body
may be but my Lord has set my soul free."*
— *"Greystone Chapel," Glen Shirley*

*"But the Lord was with Joseph and showed him mercy,
and He gave him favor in the sight of the keeper
of the prison."—Genesis 39:21*

The phone on Michael's desk rang, and he could see it was
Dr. Tanya Broder, the psychologist at Edgefield Federal Prison in
South Carolina.

"Hello, Michael. It's been a long time. How are you doing?"
she asked.

"I'm blessed, Dr. Broder. I hope you're well," Michael said.

"I wondered if you'd consider returning to Edgefield to speak
to the inmates. We've got a new warden who loves success stories.
The Christian movie nights you started are still going strong,
bigger and better than ever. They are in English and Spanish now,
thousands of men have attended them since you left, and your
books are in the Drug Abuse Program library. You'd be surprised
how many current inmates know who you are," she said.

Michael was thrilled to hear from her. Maybe he wouldn't
have survived without her kindness, and he certainly couldn't have
done the things he did without her help. She allowed him to bypass
the official channels and send the movies straight to her library for
the inmates in the drug program and then show them to the entire
compound.

The invitation was a validation of sorts, an answer to prayers, but his joy was tempered by the thought of returning to the dungeon on a hill, a likeness of Dante's Inferno, where he suffered untold indignities, the loss of Susan, and the loss of liberty, civility, and normalcy. He remembered what one old man there told him about Edgefield: "If I owned hell and Edgefield prison. I'd choose to live in hell and rent out Edgefield."

But God was there. Fences and razor wire couldn't keep Him out. Christ walked the aisles, listening to men cry for their mothers, men who never called on Him now begging for Him, row after row of beds feeling His presence as He passed by, hands reaching to touch the hem of His garment.

Some of the men swore to their relatives that the prison used a post office box because the actual address was on Cemetery Road and that would have been too much for loved ones worried their kin might not come home. Of course, none of that was true, but it made for a good story. At the big prison next door, there were men whose files reflected release dates of "Deceased" stamped in big red letters.

The most popular song inmates listened to over and over on the local oldie station was "Hotel California," which some renamed "Hotel Edgefield." It seemed to play incessantly, and you could often hear a chorus of men singing about stabbing something or someone with "steely knives, but they just couldn't kill the beast," and everyone joined in on "You can check out anytime you like, but you can never leave."

When some men sang along, others thought they were intentionally off-key or doing a Pentecostal version, speaking and singing in tongues, but the men were just gumming it, forgetting to put their false teeth in when the unofficial choir assembled across the dorms. One of these toothless wonders put a captured rat snake in the bunk of one of his critics, and officers at their stations a hundred yards away said they could hear the screaming and the expletives echoing down the hillside.

There was a seesaw loneliness embedded in that haunted castle. Mr. Hunt said he had no one to play with him in the small Tennessee mountain schoolyard when he was a child, and he just sat on the old plank waiting. In his prison dreams, he was still running back and forth from one end to the other, exhausted but looking for a friend to balance the seesaw of life.

Michael came to think there were two kinds of men at Edgefield: the potatoes who arrived hard as rocks but softened by floating in the heat of the boiling water of stress and resignation, and the soft eggs who were hardened by the same boiling water seasoned with lies dressed up as truth. In a sea of strangers, both were alone with themselves for the first time, forced to confront their demons and discover just who they were.

Some days, Michael thought it was what T.S. Eliot called the still point of the turning world, a suspension of to and from, neither up nor down, just a silent dance where past and future gathered in a timeless timeout zone to sort things out.

But it was also a trysting place for Michael, an appointed meeting place where Agape love waited to embrace and heal him. It was where he weakly tried to say, "Here I am, send me," but found he first had to acknowledge his dependency on God and say, "Oh woe is me." It was where he found blessings wrapped in thorns, thorns that plagued Adam and became a crown of victory for Christ.

It all passed through Michael's memory in overdrive, but it seemed he had waited forever to answer Dr. Broder.

"That would be great! Thanks so much for inviting me," Michael said.

Michael and Judy brought books to sign at local Augusta bookstores before his scheduled talk at Edgefield, but Michael, who was once called "Mr. Augusta," was not given a warm reception when they arrived.

The library on Ronald Reagan Drive, a street so named when Michael was chairman of the Reagan Legacy Project, refused to host him for a book signing, a courtesy extended to most authors.

Two businesses agreed to host him for signings but rescinded their invitations when politicos complained.

Then, a lady named Mary Ann contacted Michael and said the Lord had told her to help him, to go before him, run interference, and open doors for the prodigal son home from the pigpen.

She donated Michael's books to local libraries and prisons, arranged a television interview on Watchman Broadcasting and convinced a local church to allow him to give his testimony. Michael had successful book signings at three bookstores and Kroger, and people gathered at Pineview Baptist to hear his story. They cried, and Michael cried. Thanks to the Lord's emissary, he also interviewed with a daily paper columnist who wrote of Michael's desire to serve Christ.

When his rounds were complete and friends had drawn round him at a reunion dinner, a quilt Susan had given her nurse, Melinda, was returned to Michael by Wayne Thatcher, the friend who took him to surrender at Edgefield in 2006 and had married Susan's nurse. Melinda said she was but a temporary custodian of this bit of Susan and wanted it returned to its "rightful owner."

Michael felt the nearness of the Lord in it all, days when he was asked if he was willing or willing to be made willing. Michael was the bird chased away, returned to sing from another bough, enter Edgefield, face his ghosts, and feed His sheep again.

***

It was dark and dreary the day Michael arrived at the prison where he had been strip-searched on December 6, 2006. The leaves were dying, and a curtain had been drawn over the sun. A cold rain smeared his windshield, the kind that brings on a post-nasal drip and scratchy throat.

The prison seemed to be submerged in shadow, a mirage at the bottom of the world, and as he drew closer to the drive, he felt he was crossing a boundary between reality and nightmares. He felt something was there waiting for him, some unfinished business with the phantoms of the shadowlands, where a battle raged between light and dark, where saints commissioned by God hacked away at the strangle vine of sin.

As he parked, Michael remembered this was the last place he saw Susan alive, the last night she came to see him to say farewell, to let him know he must go on without her. He was shivering from the cold, maybe a low-grade fever and a high-grade dread, but she had told him that night she would look for him in God's furrows, and here he was after her homegoing in a homecoming of sorts, though he once wanted to stay as far away from his old self as he could.

He stepped out of his car and looked at the spot where he last saw the disappearing taillights of the old red Caddy that bore her out of his life. He thought she was with him still, cheering him on from the balconies of heaven, saying she knew all along that this was the path he would take.

Michael could see Dr. Broder's face at the front door to the visiting room area. He walked past the razor wire toward her, uncertain how to greet her. He thought for a moment that he should have worn a suit and tie, maybe one of those clip-on ties from the 1960s, a shirt with a button-down collar, something to make him look serious, official, and buttoned-up, but he wanted no barriers between him and his audience.

Inmates were strictly forbidden to touch staff, and that was deeply ingrained. He wasn't sure what to do, shake hands, maybe, but a hug seemed too far. It was awkward, but she opened the door and embraced him. More shackles fell at his feet, and showers of grace rained down on him. "If the Son sets you free, you will be free indeed."

"Welcome back, Michael. I won't say welcome home, but we are glad to see you again, triumphant after your resurrection," Dr. Broder said.

"I'm thankful you asked me…home," Michael said.

He followed her into a packed room of inmates, mostly men imprisoned on drug charges. All were clad in the dull federal avocado pants and shirts that forever turned Michael against any shade of green.

He could feel the anticipation, hear the sounds embedded in their silence, the presence of the divine, and a sudden affinity with men who had traded their souls for fool's gold and were out of tune with God. They had fallen for the lure of boom times, fun times, money times, and rough times. Many were the fall guys for bigger fish that always seemed to swim away before they were netted by the anglers of the law, leaving officials to find new sucker fish and the game to continue unabated.

Though he was not well and felt like a pale shadow of the titans of the faith, he reached down deep to find energy and conviction to jolt the men from the grip of whatever demons haunted them. Dr. Broder solemnly introduced the visitor from the land of ironic reversal who had come when the prison gates were opened to talk about resurrection, to tell men of the day when the gates of pearl would open to men such as him and them.

He watched the pallid faces of the men who were restlessly sitting on the rims of their chairs in their government-issued uniforms, wearing the black boots that would ruin a man's feet. Their pallor was dull and lifeless, like their deep-set eyes and elongated jaws.

Some looked like fugitives from blood banks. Sorrow was sutured onto wizened faces aged and weathered by prison and bad choices, but today their uniforms were pressed with sharp creases showing. Their shirts and pants were so ironed and hard starched they looked like they could stand up on their own and walk away.

Michael walked to the podium with the ghosts of familiar surroundings dogging each step, and when he looked out at the audience again he could have sworn he saw Susan sitting in the back, smiling at him.

"I miss the green. Y'all have any spare outfits you might share?" Michael asked, smiling. Everyone laughed, the distance between him and his audience shrank, and the ice began to crack beneath a warm embrace.

"I know that some of you just hang around here because of the good food they serve, especially when there's fresh roadkill seasoned with asphalt," he said to more laughter and some head-nodding and tentative knee-slapping.

"Any fans of *Criminal Minds* here?" Michael asked. Those still slouched in their chairs sat up straight and smiled, and fluttering eyes suddenly popped open. The reference to *Criminal Minds* worked everywhere, including prison.

"I just got back from Hollywood, where I signed books for the *Criminal Minds* cast and did radio and television interviews. Once, I wouldn't have believed that could happen but it did. They were very nice to me and very impressed I had been in prison," Michael said with a smile.

"When I came here years ago, I thought it was the end, but it was not. It was the beginning. I know Dr. Broder misses the sad-sack scarecrow who came here, full of self-pity, the guy the 'doctor' drugged to ease me into this world, robbing me of the ability to think. I once asked Dr. Broder if she thought I could ever think again, and she assured me I would. Then the Christian movie nights, which many of you attend, were born from the prayers of a man who found God's purpose in pain, the threads of good woven into crushing blankets of pain.

"I'm happy to hear you read my books. They are a means to testify, books for men who won't read the Bible but may find Christ in my story and His story. They are in Dr. Broder's 'Book of the Month' club, but they point to the Book of Ages.

"It was in this room where I last saw my first wife. She stood up from her wheelchair to walk to me. Everyone was crying. She believed God was going to give a blind man sight, that He was going to use me, and He has, and He can use you, too. We know things comfortable sinners on the outside don't. We understand the smallest of His blessings. We forge friendships out of pain our people back home could never understand," Michael said.

Every time Michael said "we," each time he showed them his scars, he was saying, "I am one of you," and walls dropped and men whispered in sweet harmony, "Amen." Even the one in the back who lived in his private cave was stirred and looked at Michael as the demons did who asked Jesus, "What have you to do with us? Have you come to torture us before the appointed time?"

"There were lots of sleepless nights spent here, waiting on the dawn, but hiding in the dark, dreading the sun that would rise and reveal the reality that wouldn't go away. He put me to bed in the dark but got me up in the morning light of the Son. I remember the Son's warmth that cold morning I learned of Susan's death. I stumbled down the stairs to the chow hall and heard the loudest whip-poor-will I had ever encountered. You don't forget things like that," he said, with a catch in his voice.

"But it was here that I found the bridle that guides, the wings that lift, and the map to a life serving Him. I learned that hardened hearts need to feel His love and the tutelage of hard lessons, the jackhammer of God, to break up layers of pride, confusion, and obsession. As tough as this place was, I was finally able to view it as a rescue mission where God was tearing down the old man and building up the new, where He put the brakes on a life galloping through a dry gulch with bushwhackers all around, a blind man riding lickety-split toward the abyss," he said.

Michael yielded to the Holy Spirit and began to move in and out of the chapters of his life, things in the books, brushes with death, surrendering to the Lord, miracles on Christian movie nights, and standing on holy ground.

"Trying to hold on to false friends and counterfeit happiness bought with illicit money is like holding a greased pig in the contests they used to have at the old fairs. I didn't find happiness while looking for it but stumbled upon it while serving Him and woke up from a long sleep with peace in my heart.

"It's late, later than it's ever been. It's time to get right with the Lord. Forever is a long time to be wrong. We all have a lot of holes in our lives, but He owns all the spaces and fills them all. His footprints are already on the shores of our tomorrows. We were captives of sin, but He has taken captivity captive and offers us the liberty of the sons of God to make us whole in body and soul.

"He can use you like He is using me. Not many will risk comfort and reputation to take the gospel into all the world, but we don't have much reputation left to lose, do we? The world has probably made up its mind about us, but we can be examples for some on the front pews who've never confronted their sins and are hiding their scars beneath designer phylacteries.

"We don't have to be eloquent to be delivery boys, field medics, and stretcher-bearers for Christ, till the Man comes around…just eyewitnesses to tell them there is a Fountain of Living Water, not made by man," Michael said.

"I learned to not question God. If old Adam were here, he'd tell us that if God tells you to stay away from a certain tree, you best listen. If He tells you to build an ark, you best get to hammering," he said with a smile.

The men laughed. Then it got pin-drop quiet there in the shadow of yesteryear, and church broke out.

"There's another tree, a tree where Christ died for us…tree and true, only one letter different. When the world presses us, remember to return to the tree to touch the True and find our names written there in His blood, the blood that sights the blind," Michael said, stifling a sudden urge to sob.

"Thank you. God bless you. We can repent of mistakes in our lives right now. We can't when life ends sooner than planned, or we resume old lives and die of a thousand nicks of sin.

"If you aren't already, go to the Christian movie nights and find fellowship there with some tough guys who cry in the dark and come to peace with their Maker. That ministry belongs to the Lord.

"Thanks for having me back. It seems I just can't say goodbye," Michael said.

Spontaneous applause broke out from men who were hard to impress, and they stood to their feet in a standing ovation. Dr. Broder asked if the men had questions, and they did…endless questions about reentry, Hollywood, books, Michael's case, why someone like him got such a long sentence, why he wasn't bitter, about finding Jesus amidst the ruins of life.

Dr. Broder finally had to end it but allowed the men to line up to shake Michael's hand and ask personal questions. One man said, "The things you said were right out of our Bible study." Another said, "I'm writing a book, but after hearing you, I'm taking out all the profanity!"

One man was allowed to bring a copy of one of Michael's books his wife had sent him to be signed. He asked if Michael would come to his church in Florida to speak when the man made it home. Michael said he would and said, "I can now say I've signed a book in prison!"

Michael looked them in the eye, one by one, and saw the tears, the potential. Some held tightly, desperately to his hand. He repeatedly said, "Reach out to Jesus. He's reaching out to you."

By the time Michael shook the last hand of the last man and the room had emptied, the lambent light that had flooded the room began to recede, and with it, the presence of Susan. He felt it would be the last time he would sense her near. Her prayers had been answered. Her prophetic words had come true.

The earth had gone around the sun seven times since he left Edgefield, but as Michael walked to his car, he could almost hear the whine and hiss of radios as men tuned the static to find clear channels, Christian instruction that almost seemed to emanate from heaven, broadcasts that ebbed and flowed like the tides at night when groundwave ended, and skywave began.

He remembered the nights when men found the same station and didn't use earbuds. A stereo sound drifted above and across the bunks when it was lights out in the dorms. The Word wafted over the brokenhearted and settled like a warm comforter to soothe troubled minds and muffle tearful petitions aimed above the terrestrial on a different kind of Skywave, prayers just piling up on the doorsteps of heaven.

Michael leaned against the roof of his car and paused to praise God for this miracle and scan the landscape one last time. Over there near the back fence were the woods where men once fed another three-legged fox and a crippled raccoon, just above the Greystone chapel where Christian movie nights were the hottest ticket on the compound.

Down in the depression was a tiny pond where Canada geese raised their young in the spring, where the willows draped over their nests. The high point of the ridge overlooking it all was where Michael sat when the purple dusk yielded to the white beam of the moon, where he watched the stars rise in the night sky, and planets take their place, where his loneliness was salved as he felt the One who hung those stars staring back at him, telling him that he was halfway to heaven.

He was but a wanderer always on his way home, who had to return here for a moment, as a trustee of the gospel, to say final farewells and testify to the presence of Christ Who looks upon His beloved in a fallen world.

CHAPTER FORTY-THREE

"...do not concede one square millimeter of territory to falsehood, folly, contemporary sentimentality, or fashion...speak the truth and let God be our judge."
—Touchstone, *Anthony Esolen*

"There's a long, long trail a-winding into the land of my dreams...there's a long night of waiting until all my dreams come true; Till the day when I'll be going down that long, long trail with you."—*"There's a Long, Long Trail," Zo Elliot, Stoddard King*

After his trip to Edgefield, Michael's stamina was suddenly not what it used to be. He lost some of his focus and seemed to be in what some called Hashimoto's fog. He took prescribed medicine, but it hadn't restored his vitality or eased his angry innards.

When he and Judy were about to leave Nashville after a brief trip there for rest, relaxation, and some concerts, he met a teacher from New Mexico when he was checking out of the hotel. She asked him if he had any books with him. When he said he did, she asked for thirteen sets for classes in New Mexico. Michael was thrilled, but when signing and personalizing the books, he lost track of how books should be inscribed, something he had never done.

When he spoke to Gray's Creek Baptist Church in Hernando, he struggled at times, his thoughts were jumbled, and thought some of the power of his testimonies had withered. He was suddenly anxious to abandon the pulpit that Pastor Danny Bell had so graciously lent him for his second appearance at the church.

Just as he thought he had failed, he looked to his left, and there, illuminated by the light filtered through the window above her, was a woman who was crying. He looked and looked again, surprised words he thought insufficient were what she needed to hear, and she told him later that she thought he was speaking straight to her about her burden.

He came home to rest and await the test results doctors ordered. He wondered if his fast sprint was over, if he had run his race. His eyelids were heavy as he slumped in his chair and read feedback on his testimony at Edgefield, inmate comments Dr. Broder sent along with her thanks for his return to Edgefield.

A steady rain began to rattle in the gutters, and the wind caused the crepe myrtles to rake the windows near his desk. The sun hid its face, and the gloominess matched his mood.

"Here are some of the comments, Michael. I know you didn't feel well, but your trip was not in vain. It must have been wonderful to see that the seeds you planted in 2007 had taken root and were blooming in the desert, fully matured," Dr. Broder wrote.

"We're all herd animals except him. I don't think he's one."

"He didn't come to serve cool whip or speak empty words."

"I'd rather go hungry than eat one more serving of sin stew."

"I thought of things I wished I'd done and things I wished I hadn't."

"He's not in the Who's Who, but he knows what's what."

"God sent him with the clean water of forgiveness."

"He didn't measure out love and kindness by the cc."

"I wanted to confess something, everything, to somebody."

"He's not hiding in the suburbs. He's here, slumming for Christ."

"I dreamed of a key to unlock the gate, and now the key looks like a cross."

"He wasn't wagging a finger at us. He was pointing to himself."

Michael read their words and reread them. The wariness, suspicion, and resignation he had felt at first with the men at Edgefield had given way to Christ.

They were men who had gorged themselves on the things of the world, a spiritual gluttony that bloated but never filled, and they had to come to prison to realize how empty they were, to know they were in debt, a debt that could never be repaid, though some would try for the rest of their lives. Each man was a unique individual with all the emotions, doubts, and sadness of men on hold, but it was in prison where many understood that their lives hung by a thread held only by Him Who paid their debt.

They were leaving a place of hard order on an island of confusion and preparing to start over in a world filled with a different kind of confusion and fresh temptations.

He thought of a line from *The Wild Bunch* where the character says, "We all dream of being a child again, even the worst of us. Perhaps the worst most of all."

He laid the comments aside and picked up the phone to call his partner when he was a deputy to let him know that, health permitting, he would soon be speaking at Moselle Memorial Baptist Church's annual Wild Game Dinner to raise funds for missions and outreach.

At that moment Sarge was walking across his property near Moselle, where he had retired from the Hattiesburg Sheriff's Department. He suddenly wondered what had happened to his young partner at the Lee County Sheriff's Department. He hadn't seen Michael Parker in decades.

His cell phone rang and the display said *Michael Parker*.

"Hello?" Sarge said, answering with a bit of uncertainty.

"Hey, buddy, this is Michael Parker. Long time no see," Michael said.

"Michael, you won't believe it. I just thought of you, and the phone rang with your name on the screen," Sarge said.

"Sarge, things like that happen all the time since I went under new Management," Michael said.

"Son, it's good to hear from you, and I'm so happy to hear that you're serving the Lord. I wasn't a Christian when we rode together," he said.

"I wasn't either, Sarge. I was raised in the church but didn't understand what it meant to have a personal relationship with Christ," Michael said.

"He sure got hold of me, too, Michael. On July 13, 1975, I was at church with my wife and heard the call. I almost ran down the aisle to surrender. People were shouting. Others were weeping. I gave up all the old ways. No drinking, no cussing. We had a big old washpot at the jail in Hattiesburg, and I began to baptize inmates in it! Some of 'em, we had to dunk two or three times to make it stick," Sarge said with a chuckle.

"I want to hear all about it. I tracked you down to let you know that I will speak at Moselle Memorial Baptist Church at their Wild Game Dinner, and I'd love to see you if you'd like to come. They say there'll be seven hundred or eight hundred folks there," Michael said.

"You tell me when, and I'll be there," Sarge said.

When Michael hung up, he felt like that young deputy again, like he had been here before, winding up where he was always going. He knew then that God had known all along that two sinners would meet, part, and come together again in Moselle as servants of the Lord.

***

Test results came back and confirmed Michael had Hashimoto's. A doctor gave him thyroid meds and pronounced him cured, but Michael could barely get out of bed some days.

Medical facilities were fast becoming his mission field, and he signed books for doctors, nurses, and patients wherever he went.

A young man and woman came in as he sat in a doctor's office in Corinth to see an obstetrician who treated Hashimoto's patients on the side. The man looked stern, and she was pretty, very pregnant, and jumpy, like an addict just a step away from her next relapse.

Michael knew he was supposed to meet her.

"When are you due?" he asked her.

"June," she said, flashing a big, nervous smile.

"You'll have some time on your hands then. Do you like to read?" he asked.

"Oh, I love to read," she said, beaming.

Michael gave her his book cards and said, "I'm an author. These books are written as fiction but drawn from my life, and you might find them interesting."

Her jaw dropped when she fanned out the cards, and her eyes were suddenly like dinner plates.

"I know this book," she said, pointing to *A Ghostly Shade of Pale*. "It was in my rehab facility in Columbus," she said of a facility a hundred miles and a world away from where they sat.

The man spoke up from behind a dark beard and said, "But she's clean now."

Michael wasn't so sure, and when he looked for them after his appointment, the couple had left. He drove around Corinth to see if he might find them. Just as he was about to give up, he saw them. He picked up his books and walked to their truck. They were stunned to see him across town.

"I'm not following you, and I'm not here to preach at you, but you need a friend, and that Friend is Jesus Christ," he said, handing her his books.

She clutched them to her like they were a great treasure, and months later, as he was leaving the doctor's office, he heard someone blowing a horn with gusto. He looked up to see the two of them passing by in their truck, and she was hanging out her window, waving and calling his name, "Mr. Michael, it's going to be a boy."

Michael was sick and wobbly, but each time he remembered her waving at him, the wind blowing the former addict's hair around her head like a halo, and the radiance of motherhood in her face, he booked more testimonials in the hidey-holes and alleyways along the road to a rendezvous with the Holy Spirit in Moselle.

CHAPTER FORTY-FOUR

"Come unto me, all who labor and are heavy laden,
and I will give you rest."—Matthew 11:28

"I've seen a dead man rise and a blind man see.
Yeah, but that ain't the reason I'm a devotee.
No, I believe in Him because He believes in me."
—"The 13th Apostle," Sean McConnell

Michael crossed old rail line used to transport the products of prison labor to market and entered a world on the wrong side of the tracks, but as he and Judy stared up the hill at the sprawling prison complex, he thought anywhere in a fallen world was the wrong side of the tracks.

The Oakley Training Center, the state correction facility for juveniles, was situated on a thousand-acre facility surrounded by fields and farms near Raymond, Mississippi.

The residents were male and female, and most were felons or repeat misdemeanor offenders. Some were sent here for a second chance, escaping the harshness of incarceration at Parchman Penitentiary, though some dangerous or chronic incorrigibles were housed in a maximum-security unit within Oakley.

The warden was cordial but seemed tired and listless, like he had seen it all. His command staffers were openly skeptical of the mild-mannered evangelist but rode over to the packed auditorium to see Michael fall flat on his face with tough kids who were required to attend. Social workers and psychologists were also in the rear of the giant chapel, but they were not scoffers, just tired and worn around the edges by too many social programs that failed, too many kids they felt the system had failed.

Michael peered down from the stage at his audience of hardened young faces, some jabbing each other and mocking the old man who came to "save them."

Michael launched into his past, redemption, Hollywood, and the story of the gospel road that led him to Oakley. In the pictures taken of Michael that day, he didn't look mild-mannered. He was bathed in light, hands outstretched, hands above his head, a sermon in his gestures and hand talking. Michael was using up energy from his reserves, but he was knocking down barriers. The whirlwind of the Holy Spirit was pushing him to the limit one more time.

He saw the warden and his team look at each other in disbelief, mouths agape. The social workers were awake, wide-eyed, and raising their hands as if they were in a holiness revival. The young inmates were clapping their hands, and Michael could tell they were being baptized in the gospel and had laid down all of their assumptions and cynicism, just as the inmates at Edgefield had.

"How many of you love Jesus? How many of you are never coming back here or to any prison? How many of you are willing to lay down that junk in your trunk and crawl to the foot of the cross as I did and ask for a new life, to be born again?" Michael asked them in an altar call of sorts. The only thing missing was a choir softly singing "Just as I Am" and a pastor saying, "Let's sing just one more verse, just one more verse. Someone is hurting."

When Michael finished, the young inmates rushed the stage, asked him about Edgefield, about Hollywood, about his time as a narc, the ambush, and the kidnapping.

One young girl named Kelly fought her way to stand sobbing before Michael. Tears were streaming down her face in salty rivulets. Her eyes were reddened and swollen, and Michael could see that the Lord had hold of her.

"I know it was God who sent me here, not to Parchman, to give me a second chance," she said, gasping and sobbing.

"Jesus loves you. Take this chance He's given you, and never let go of His hand. Call me when you get out if we can help you. Let me know how you are," Michael said.

"I picked up a Bible once, and I saw words meant for me. It said, 'And it came to pass,'" she said.

Michael looked at her and she said, "You know, I figure that means my troubles and sin didn't come to stay, just to pass by. There's hope for me."

Michael smiled and said, "Close enough, Kelly, close enough. Just run to Jesus when they pass by."

When the crowd cleared, the social workers said, "You not only blessed these young people today. You blessed us, too. Today is a day we won't soon forget."

Michael left the books for the residents to read and walked to the car where Judy waited. She said, "You look exhausted. How'd it go?"

"A social worker said I looked pale but on fire. She asked me if I was okay and how I maintained this pace. I told her that the Lord shovels it in as I shovel it out, but His shovel is bigger than mine, and sometimes you just have to get off your blessed assurance and do what He has commissioned you to do, no questions asked," Michael said with a mischievous smile.

"I told her that the law bids us to run but gives us neither feet nor hands, but the gospel bids us to fly and gives us wings. The Holy Spirit moved through the crowd, and I just followed His lead. I was so-so, but they asked me to come back. That's always a good sign," Michael said as he reached out and caught her hand, kissed each of her fingers, rested his head on her shoulder, and snored through a quick catnap.

CHAPTER FORTY-FIVE

"There's a sweet, sweet spirit in this place, and I know it's
the Spirit of the Lord; There are sweet expressions on each
face, and I know they feel the presence of the Lord."
—"Sweet, Sweet Spirit," Doris Akers

"Sweet Holy Spirit, I'm down on my knees. I am low in the
valley, I am so weak you see. But I know I will make it, for I
trust in Thee. The sweet Holy Spirit is falling on me…don't
ever leave me."—"Sweet Holy Spirit," Joe Isaacs

"God is the forever bridge that creates impossible
reunions."—Craig D. Lounsbrough

The good people of Moselle Memorial Baptist Church knew Michael was ill, and they were praying without ceasing for him, not only because that's what Christians do but because they had advertised for months that he would be the speaker at their annual Wild Game Dinner to fund Kingdom work.

When Judy and Michael arrived in rural Jones County, Michael was white as a sheet. Someone in Jackson had told him that he was a ghostly shade of pale. Though he had never been to Moselle, he felt he was going home.

When Michael and Judy pulled up in front of the beautiful church in the vale, the leaves were off the trees, but the bloom was not off the church's love for the Lily of their valley, and the promise of spring and renewal was always just over the horizon.

Michael asked some young men to help unload books to a table set up for book signings, and as he walked through the life center, he felt he had gone back in time to the days when people didn't leave their faith in the pews when they left church. The tables lining the walls were filled with paintings, quilts, crocheted items, rods and reels, crafts of all sorts, and homemade cakes and pies.

Here in winter, the parishioners shared the bounty of summer and fall. The shucked corn, peas and butter beans, squash, and okra made for some tasty casseroles for the attendees to bid on and take home, and the jams and jellies were delicacies sure to fetch top dollars to fund mission work and local projects of God's people. They had gathered for a feast of food and fellowship, to remain faithful to the legacy and grit of their ancestors, and to hear an itinerant evangelist strum heartstrings.

As he moved through the gathering crowd, he could hear how they greeted one another, feel the warmth on a cold winter's night, and hear the remnants of old sayings, adages, and idioms the world wouldn't understand. Within the fragments of conversations, as he passed by, there was a treasure trove of the language he grew up on, and a faith he feared was an endangered species.

Michael thought that no stained-glass faith was practiced here. It was the old-time religion built on the Rock of Ages by people who lived and loved the Word, listened to tapes of sermons and Scripture on their commutes to work, and delivered meals and Bibles to shut-ins. It was old Americana, and Michael felt again that he had been in this place before and was destined to limp to this stage on a fluttering wing and a fervent prayer to share his story and God's story of second chances and redemption.

Towering above it all was a makeshift platform of bare wood for the speaker, built by church carpenters for the Carpenter's emissary, a temporary custodian of the gospel, but Michael was dizzy and didn't know if he could climb the stairs.

He thought it looked like gallows out of an old Western movie. He didn't see a crossbeam, so he thought he was safe. He smiled at his vivid imagination and wondered what he would say to the people gathered in the church by the wildwood. He thought of the difference between things accidental and things Divine, the space between unpopular truth and celebrated wrong. He thought of words by James Russell Lowell, "Truth forever on the scaffold, wrong forever on the throne. Yet that scaffold sways the future, and behind the dim unknown standeth God within the shadow, keeping watch above his own."

As the crowd poured in for the Wild Game Dinner, mostly catfish, hush puppies, and all the fixings, he saw Sarge coming his way. Time evaporated, and it was as if they were about to go on patrol again.

"Hello, Michael. You haven't changed a bit," he said, laughing.

"You either, and we're still dragon slayers. Well, lizards or salamanders, maybe," Michael said, and they both laughed like old times.

As Michael and Sarge reminisced and told war stories, Jeff Boudin, who had worked with Michael in Bell Security, joined them. Michael hadn't seen Sarge in forty-five years, and he hadn't seen Jeff in thirty-five. They were older like Michael, but they also now bore that unmistakable spark of Christ. Michael introduced them to Judy, and all three had a seat up front with the local sheriff.

The time came to ascend to the mile-high platform God had provided. He gripped the two-by-four rail and measured each step carefully on the creaking boards as he climbed to where the pastor was waiting.

After Michael was introduced, he approached the podium and looked down on the room from an elevation that seemed to brush the clouds. He could see people visiting and talking at their tables. Some had not seen each other for a while, and it was social time, a bonding event for church members and guests who came to catch up and savor good food and a good word.

Michael's tank was empty. He had a death grip on the lectern and was struggling. Something was about to happen, but he didn't know what. He had gone from the pit to the pulpit and had come too far to fail his Redeemer now. He knew this was the tightrope without the net, surrender and trust taken to a new level, an admission he was not enough and had never been enough. He needed God tonight and had always needed Him. Michael said a prayer at that moment. "Lord, I can't do this. You are going to have to take over."

Michael said, "I'd like to tell you a once-upon-a-time story about the time I thought I had been buried but discovered I had been planted."

He looked again and saw that they had stopped talking. He looked again, and they were leaning forward in their chairs, locked in on him. It was so quiet he could hear himself sweat. He looked again, and the room was fading to gray. Everything was vanishing. That was the last thing Michael remembered until he said, "Thank you. God bless you."

As he carefully turned to his left to find his way to the stairs, Bo Thompson, head of the men's ministry, was bounding up the steps, hand outstretched. Michael thought he looked dazed and moving in slow motion, like people who run across golden meadows in movies.

He grasped Michael's hand and said, "We've never seen anything like that!" Michael wondered if that was a good thing because he didn't remember anything he had said. Then he turned and saw the crowd on their feet in a standing ovation, something the church later told him had never happened in the history of the Wild Game Dinners.

He saw the faces of the people who came forward to shake his hand. In the distance, he saw Judy at the book table, but he knew he wouldn't be able to get to her through the surge of the crowd.

Some were crying, some brought their children, and others worked their way through the throngs of fellow Christians to bring books from the author table to be signed. Some looked like prisoners who had been set free.

God had answered his prayer.

CHAPTER FORTY-SIX

"Give me the love that leads the way, the faith that nothing can dismay. The hope no disappointments tire, the passion that will burn like fire… Make me thy fuel, flame of God."—Amy Carmichael

"No man can have the moral high ground on any issue, unless he, by the grace of God, is chosen to stand on the ground God has assigned to him. That ground is high ground only because it is on top of mountains of grace, and from the vantage point of that grace, from the promontory of grace, we can see it all."—Doug Wilson

Michael and Judy slept the sleep of the exhausted and pushed on to Biloxi and Gulfport for book signings and then to Okaloosa Island to rest, write, and see a functional medicine doctor in Destin.

As they passed Pensacola Bay, they pulled into a rest area by the water where shorebirds gathered, and the white foam of the breakers crashed on the rocks.

There they met a young boy and girl who appeared to be traveling with just the clothes on their backs. They looked naïve and vulnerable, somewhat like hippies Michael met in the early days of the MBN, but they were clear-eyed and bore none of the telltale signs of drug use that the old narc could see.

His name was Tom and she was Penny, Pennsylvanians, young and in love, runaways off to see the world, to cross moon river, wider than a mile. Tom looked like he knew a secret he would trade for a rusty nickel, and Penny gazed at him like he was her knight in shining armor, perhaps someone who had rescued her from abuse.

"Where are y'all staying?" Michael asked.

"We stayed at this great shelter in Pensacola last night," Tom said as Penny hung on his every word.

"What are your plans? Where are you going?" Judy asked.

"We left plans behind. We just put on our traveling shoes and go where the wind takes us, to places we ain't never been. We're free," Penny said, turning to beam stars into Tom's eyes.

"Do you know Jesus?" Michael asked.

"We heard somebody on the TV in one of the shelters talking about Him," Tom said.

"He loves you very much, and we do, too. He is where real freedom lies. I want you to be very careful as you travel all alone. There is a lot of darkness in the world, and not everyone is as nice as y'all are," Michael said.

Michael gave them one of his books, which they promised to read, and Judy gave them some money, though they asked for none.

As the young nomads headed back to the shelter in Pensacola, a bell clanged somewhere far out to sea. Michael and Judy watched the spiritually malnourished kids walking along the edge of the water, holding hands. The spray of the crashing waves cast a silver mist over them, finally absorbing them in a churn of eventide and purple twilight.

They had promised to be careful, but Michael had a strong foreboding and worried for them. All of their connectivity and meaning were vested only in each other, a shared itch for what they did not know in a rootless world, an itch that could only be scratched by Christ.

He felt inadequate and thought he had been unable to penetrate the fog they lived within, a lostness that doesn't know where home is. He watched them and thought that to pass the lost without sharing the gospel was to pass people dying of thirst without sharing a drink of water.

After a long silence, Michael and Judy moved on toward Ft. Walton, but Michael couldn't get the couple out of his mind and said what went unsaid the night before after Moselle.

"I wish we had taped my testimony. I would've loved to have heard what the Lord said through me; maybe there was something, one entreaty, that might have resonated with Tom and Penny."

***

The first morning on Okaloosa, Judy threw open the blinds, and the grandeur and magic of a long-lost friend whooshed into Michael's heart. The weight on his chest melted away, and he could breathe again.

The sun was a sherbet orange, the Gulf was a pristine aqua blue, and sparkling diamonds of sunlight danced on the water. A heron stalked the shallows for lunch, and the swarming terns were as white as whiteout fluid as they dipped and hovered, chattering like quarrelsome children.

After a week of sleep, surf, and recurring dreams of walking in the shadow of the Holy Spirit in Moselle, Bo Thompson called to check on Michael.

"Michael, we're just checking on you to see how you are," Bo said.

"Thanks so much. I'm seeing a new doctor. I'll be all right. I'm taking beach therapy right now," Michael said, punctuated by a weary chuckle.

"Well, I just wanted to tell you that the night you were here, that's all people talk about. It was the biggest fundraiser we've ever had by far. There are so many projects we can fund now, people we can reach," Thompson said.

"Oh, that's great!" Michael said.

"We have an older man here who can't do much but is always the first to volunteer for church projects. His hearing is bad, too. I saw him after your testimony and asked him, 'Wasn't that something the other night?'" Bo said.

"He told me, 'Aw, I couldn't hear a word that man said,'" Bo said.

"'You mean you missed that?' I asked him.

"He said, 'No, my ten-year-old grandson repeated it to me, saying, 'Grandpa, that man was something.'

"Michael, do you realize what that boy may do with the seeds you planted long after you've left this world?" Bo asked.

Seconds that seemed like minutes passed without a word. Bo and Michael were caught up in silent reverence, and both knew they had been part of something bigger than they were.

When Michael hung up, he stared out at the waters rushing to shore on Okaloosa Island, then dropped his face into his hands, where the salty water was not from the Gulf, and the grace he felt lifted him a little closer to heaven, a little farther from a lost world.

CHAPTER FORTY-SEVEN

*"To know that nothing happens in God's world
apart from God's will may frighten the godless
but it stabilizes the saints."—J.I. Packer*

*"God's plans reach from an eternity past to an eternity to
come. Let Him take His own time."—William S. Plumer*

Michael stood before the impatient fourth-graders at Destin Elementary School, wearing his official author blazer and slacks. The school required students to write books to share in class, and the principal asked Michael if he would come by and speak to the kids.

"Good morning, students. How are you?" Michael asked.

One boy to his left dramatically fell across his desk and said, "I'm inspired already!"

A little girl to his right seemed to be hyperventilating and gasping for breath as she said, "I was so excited about you coming! Um, um, I was bouncing all over the house last night, and my mama just couldn't keep me still."

As the love and innocence washed over Michael, he could almost hear God say, "See what I have done."

Michael looked at their compositions, advised aspiring writers, and complimented them all. Then they lined up for autographs, and one sad-faced little boy said his father was in the military and deployed far from home.

Michael said, "You miss him, don't you?"

The boy said, "I sure do."

"I can tell you that he misses you more than you'll ever know. He wouldn't leave you if he weren't protecting our country," Michael said.

Then Michael looked down at the tiniest little girl with huge eyes, her arms upstretched to him. "Can I have a hug, Mr. Michael?" she asked.

"Sure, honey," Michael said and he hugged her as Christ hugged him.

As he left the school the principal said, "I'm sorry we can't pay you for coming."

Michael said, "I should pay you for these precious memories."

A man who just happened to be there asked Michael if he would like to come to Panama City and speak to a senior group at the Gulf Coast Regional Medical Center where he worked. He warned Michael that they had no money for books and would just walk out if he ran long or they lost interest.

Michael spoke to the group, but no one left. They all lined up for signed books, and as the word spread, hospital staff gathered to see the emissary of God who could glue impatient seniors to their seats.

Michael took Judy to see Captain Anderson's fishing fleet, where Michael went deep sea fishing with his father as a child.

He could almost smell the suntan lotion, the diesel fumes from the boats, the buckets of bait fish, and see his father with his prized red snappers.

***

While Judy and Michael sat in Hardee's near Ft. Walton Beach, Michael wondered what the tests ordered by the local specialist would reveal and what the future held for him and Judy and the ministry.

He couldn't eat much of the food and began to watch a group of homeless men outside in the cold rain. He wondered about these men and how they came to this point in life. Drugs, alcohol, mental illness, or maybe they zigged when they should have zagged.

One man seemed eager to please the others. Where they seemed coarse and volatile, he seemed vulnerable and childlike. His face was the color of old paste, and he stood beneath the eaves of the building in the rain, where raindrops kept falling on his eyes.

One huge drop seemed to hit his brow and cheekbone every few seconds, clinging to his lashes and blurring his vision until he wiped them away.

Michael's stomach was so tender that he could no longer eat without the pain overwhelming him. He bought biscuits and gravy, sausage, bacon, and cartons of milk and walked outside.

"Hey, buddy, are you hungry?" Michael asked the man.

"Yes, sir, I'm always hungry," he said as he took the food and tucked his long blondish hair behind his ears and beneath his toboggan.

He looked up at the drizzling rain and asked, "Can you stop the rain, mister?"

Michael said, "No, but I know the One who can.

"What are you doing out here? Where are you from?" Michael asked.

"Arkansas," he said as he wolfed the food down like he hadn't eaten in a year.

"I had an accident and was brain damaged. Then I got on drugs. Then I became an alcoholic to get off the drugs. Then I just started to roam, and here I am," he said as he drained a carton of milk and shrugged his shoulders.

"Are you in a shelter?" Michael asked.

"I'm in line to get in a good one here," he said.

"Do you know the Lord?" Michael asked.

"Oh, yes, sir. I know the Bible, and I took a course in another shelter, but someone stole my Bible. My name is John, like in the good book," he said as he began to quote Scripture and looked to see if his group had left him.

"Will you be here tomorrow?" Michael asked.

"Yes, I'll be here, I think. I'm pretty sure," John said.

"I'm going to bring you a Bible and a wrap. It's cold and wet out here," Michael said.

"Thank you, sir," he said, punctuated by a dry cough.

When Michael and Judy returned the next day with a Bible, some more food, and a thick comforter for the man to wrap himself in, they saw him leaving the Hardee's parking lot in the pouring rain, chasing the men who were family to him.

"Hey, John! John!" Michael called.

John turned, and his eyes went wide. He looked past the food and the blanket and said, "You remembered my Bible. Thank you, mister." The look on his face was that of a child on Christmas morning.

"Jesus loves you, John, and we do, too," Michael said.

John smiled as he tucked his food and Bible beneath the wrap and disappeared into the grayness of the rain, there one minute and gone the next, as a bolt of lightning glinted off the thick wall of the dirty, silver rain.

Michael felt once again, as he had when he walked in the rain at Edgefield, that God was speaking to him in the storms, telling him that His grace was sufficient and all of his questions would be answered.

***

The grim-faced doctor looked at the test results and then looked at Michael with sad eyes as they sat in his office in Destin.

Dr. Chase was a young man with black hair and eyes, a doctor who wanted to get outside the box of the medical schools, a doctor who wanted to be a healer.

"Have you been under a lot of stress?" the doctor asked.

"Yes, day and night for nearly six years," Michael said.

Dr. Chase looked up from the test results and arched his eyebrows.

"Have you been overseas or eaten bad food?" he asked.

"Yes, for almost six years, I ate out-of-date food, cornbread drenched in sugar, rice from rodent and roach-infested kitchens, green baloney, and food bought for pennies on the dollar from bankrupt food manufacturers, food stamped not fit for human consumption in some cases," Michael said.

The doctor paused and furrowed his brow again, question marks in his eyes, sudden deep creases showing in his frown.

"Well, did you ever get sick during that period, really gut-sick, and antibiotics couldn't cure or kill what was inside you, but you thought the meds might kill you?" he asked.

"Yes, that was a rough period just before I married Judy in prison. They had to kinda prop me up on my wedding day," Michael said.

"I see," the doctor said, nodding.

"I think you have yeast overgrowth, candida, and maybe some nasty parasites left over. Your guts are very angry. Your immune system fought through it when you were younger and it was stronger, but now it is worn down and struggling. There has been a resurgence of it all, and your iron markers are very low. That's why you are so pale. You need an iron infusion, maybe many infusions. Your tank is out of fuel. It is only going to get worse without treatment. Your diet will have to change, and we'll see what you can tolerate after we eliminate it all and start over," he said.

Dr. Chase paused and said, "You project peace, but your body is suffering from post-traumatic stress. How did you get through it?"

"When they removed all the guardrails of life, there was no more familiar, nothing was out of bounds, and I found myself in the middle of 'what's the worst that can happen.'

"When they slammed that door behind me, and I accepted that this was not a dream but an ongoing, consuming nightmare, I had to step up and show what I was made of, but without Christ, I wouldn't have made it through the first year, the first month, or the first week," Michael said.

"We're going to do what we can to make it better, Michael," Doctor Chase said.

Dr. Chase suddenly stared at Michael's chart for what seemed near forever, cleared his throat, and said, "I admire your commitment to telling your story."

"Too many folks talk about the goodness of God in private, but I think He's looking for people who will talk about Him in public, not people with a 'Santa Claus' faith but those who have a 'Though He slay me' kind of faith.

"Some things are just not negotiable, and some hills are worth dying on. This ministry is mine. Just keep me going for a while longer, Doc. There is much to do," Michael said.

CHAPTER FORTY-EIGHT

"Nourishment for the malnourished soul. Food for those hungry for beauty. Manna in the desert of our postmodern wasteland. Lembas for sojourners in Mordor. All we need to do is taste and see that it is good."—Joseph Pearce

"I owe my life. I owe my all. So I come to tell you that He's alive. To tell you He dries every tear that falls. So I come to tell you that He saves, to shout and proclaim He's coming back for you."—"This Blood," Paulette Wooten, Rita Springer

On the "Isle of Okaloosa," Michael worked on his new diet and sought words from the dusty mantel of memory for a new book.

Mail forwarded from home included a long letter from a lawyer in Macon, Georgia, who said his girlfriend found *A Ghostly Shade of Pale* at a Goodwill store, and it had changed his life.

There was also a letter from an inmate serving a life sentence that began in Chicago.

I roamed the South in the old days and knew all the characters in your books, the real people, from Chicago to Memphis to New Orleans. Most of them are gone now. I tried to make a break from the dark and went over to what I thought was the light side but found there was darkness there, too, masquerading as light.

I heard about you back then and feel I should have known you, but I do now after reading your story, which was also my story, and now that we are brothers in Christ.

I survived two dozen assassination attempts and never thought anyone could imagine my life until I read your book. Your writing is creative, factual, and displays a "hidden self," or I should say "Genesis." Your passion, kindness, and rough, tough truth are appreciated.

"Pray for me, Michael. I need it. I'm the thief on the cross asking Christ to remember me.

Michael read and reread the letters and tucked them away to read again when the enemy knocked loudly at his door.

Word also came from home that Jim Clark, the publisher of the *Lee County Courier*, wanted to serialize Michael's novels in his newspaper, good medicine for an ailing author.

Michael leaned back from his computer, rubbed his belly, and tasted the acid in his throat. He quietly hummed, "Nothing but the blood of Jesus," and stared out his condo window at the rolling Gulf, where time seemed to slow down to one long mood and moment that defied the clock and the tides.

He sometimes thought he felt closer to God on the island than anyplace in the world, and he wondered at conquistador Hernando De Soto, who once told the King of Spain that Florida was "an uninhabitable sandspit."

Though his stomach felt like someone had lit a bonfire and tossed in some hot coals, he randomly hummed tunes wedged in the jukebox in his mind. He stood, stretched, and wrestled with the burning in his belly.

He wadded up a page of writing he didn't particularly like and looked at the waste can far across the condo. He aimed for the basket shot. Like the games he played as a child—if he made it, his team would win the big championship of something. The shot bounced on the rim and rolled over into the can. The crowd roared, confetti fell, music played, and he was once again the imaginative child in Parker Grove.

He smiled and looked at the bundled people walking in the cold on the wet sand. They paused life for photographs of fixed smiles over chattering teeth, pictures from the passing parade on the beloved beach of a boy's dreams, the timeless refuge he wanted it to be, America as it ought to be.

He saw one beachcomber with long legs and named her Mrs. Heron. He saw another with heavy jowls, and Michael dubbed him Mr. Pelican. Smiling children danced down the edge of the foam like sanderlings and played hide-and-seek under a large piece of driftwood. He thought of the line from the song: "All the lonely people. Where do they all come from?"

He looked at his Bible, which was open to Jeremiah, and asked the weeping prophet, "How lonely does it get?" Then the former knight errant, who once tilted at windmills, decided to abandon melancholy and see more of the "sandspit." Judy was at the fabric store, finding treasures for new prayer quilts, so he left to visit friends at the Barnes & Noble store in Destin with the giant palms out front.

When he crossed the bridge into Destin at the Pass, the water was whitecapping, and the sky had a silvery tone. A brave osprey fought the wind to hunt for lunch and floated on the currents right up to the bridge and Michael's car. The piercing eyes of the raptor looked right at Michael and seemed to be a testimony to surviving the storms of life.

As Michael scurried across the parking lot to the bookstore, the wind whipped the palm fronds and whisked debris through the air like an errant broom. The limb of a small tree was raking the window of a store next door, producing sounds like long, screeching nails on a chalkboard.

A man was standing outside the bookstore, holding a flopping sign that said *We are living in until*. He looked familiar, and as Michael passed him he said, "We are living in until, Michael Parker...until He comes. Doubt your doubts." He looked like the man outside the halfway house, but when the man mentioned his name, Michael looked back and he was gone.

Looking back for the man, Michael almost ran over Dee Schultz, a local teacher coming out of the store. She had used *A Ghostly Shade of Pale* in her middle school English classes in Destin.

"Michael, I was just thinking of you. I am teaching senior English now at Niceville High School. *To Kill a Mockingbird* is required reading for my seniors," she said with an anticipatory smile that indicated she knew something he didn't.

"That's a great book," Michael said.

"I thought you'd like to know that I made your book *Deputy* the required companion read," she said, beaming under her mop of blonde hair.

"Wow, Dee, I don't know what to say. I'm not worthy. I can't even go there except to say thank you and praise God," Michael said.

When she left, Michael stopped by the information desk to talk with friends. He sensed a presence enter the store. Michael turned to see a tall man standing just inside the front door. He had a chiseled face that looked like he might have been a Founding Father mistakenly left off of Mount Rushmore.

Michael thought he was a man who was accustomed to power, prestige, position, and wealth. The man looked left and right as if he was looking for someone. Then he saw Michael and walked directly to him with certainty and purpose.

"Hello, I'm Charles Billingsly. I've known the rich and famous and experienced things most men can't imagine. I've had wealth and notoriety and everything the American dream is supposed to be all about.

"My wife died suddenly, and I realized it was all for nothing. I'm lost and don't know what to do. As I sat alone in my car in the bumper-to-bumper traffic jam out front on Highway 98, I cried out to God. He said, 'Go in that bookstore and see the man who writes books, and he will help you.'

"Are you the man who writes books? You look like him," he said.

"Well, sir, I am the only man here today who writes books. I don't have the answers, but I know the One who does," Michael said.

So, Michael talked with the wounded tycoon, as he had with the inmates at Edgefield, and the homeless man who needed a blanket and a Bible. Grief and loneliness were the great equalizers, a plain of hard common ground where we realize we don't have the answers and don't even know the questions, where the similarities of the human condition override our differences, no more me and thee, just us, sinners huddled neath the shadow of the Cross.

CHAPTER FORTY-NINE

"Visit us with thy salvation; enter every trembling heart.
Breathe, breathe thy loving spirit into every troubled
breast."—"Love Divine, All Loves Excelling," John Wesley

"Jesus paid it all. All to Him I owe. Sin had left a
crimson stain. He washed it white as snow."
—"Jesus Paid It All," Elvina M. Hall

Michael prepared for a talk to the Sunday morning service at Faith Assembly in Miramar Beach. Some called it the Rock and Roll Church due to the talented band and choir members who once played in secular bands.

Duke Bardwell had played with Elvis, and Tareva Henderson was a well-known singer in Nashville and Louisiana. Many of the musicians had seen hard times like Michael, and forgiveness, redemption, and salvation were not abstract words to them.

Pastor Toy Arnet had invited Michael to speak to the congregation. The church was packed to the rafters during the winter months with "snowbirds" who wintered in Florida and came to the "church by the sea" to thaw out and warm their hearts on the hymns, love, and sermons at Faith Assembly.

When the day arrived for Michael to speak, he prepared as best he could. As his health issues worsened, he timed his small meals around his presentations, trying to purge his body of pain, sickness, and distraction long enough to give his testimony, sign books, and then retreat to the condo to rest and sleep. People thought he was in command, but he was hanging on by the hair of his chinny-chin-chin, keeping the wolf at bay.

Pastor Toy advised him that the congregation got restless around lunchtime and would likely get up and file out if he ran long. It wouldn't be personal, he said. They just wanted to get to their favorite restaurant on time.

A missionary bound for the Holy Land spoke briefly about leaving for Jerusalem. Michael sensed she was headed to Israel on a wing and a prayer, but she was confident "the Lord would provide."

As the band played "Greystone Chapel" at Michael's request and Phil Calhoun's deep voice made the song personal and moving, Michael saw a group of young women slip into the last balcony seats. They were from the Path of Grace thrift store and shelter for women wrestling with drug and alcohol addictions.

Phil closed with, "Inside the walls of prison my body may be, but my Lord has set my soul free," and Michael worked his way up to the pulpit. He looked out at the people in the church, sitting side by side, packed like sardines into the crowded pews. They were from states throughout the North and Midwest and looked eager or curious to hear this pale speaker. The warden from the Walton State Prison, where Michael had spoken to inmates, also slipped in at the last moment.

Michael took a breath and began.

"There is so much love in this church, and the Holy Spirit is all around. There are so many stories to tell and so little time. Brother Toy said I had until 1 p.m. Is that okay?" he joked. The congregation laughed with him, and it was the beginning of an intimate sharing among friends.

"When I left college and entered the first Drug Wars, I was very naïve and had a fixed view of the world. I was ready to slay dragons and tilt at windmills like Don Quixote, right wrongs, and rescue damsels in distress, but I found the world was not a neat and orderly place.

"I was a nominal Christian, raised in the church, but I didn't have a personal relationship with Christ. I was engaged in full-blown works-based salvation, being as good as I could, hoping the good would outweigh the bad, and the pearly gates would swing open one day and let me slip in the back door," Michael said.

He worked through the kidnapping in Tylertown and told the congregation about God delivering him from the razor-blade-eating, fire-swallowing drug dealers who held him at gunpoint.

"My whole life flashed before my eyes that night, and God delivered me from what looked like the end of the road. I did something I never did. I prayed, and my prayers were answered. Then I jumped from the frying pan into the fire. The Dixie Mafia hired assassins to lure me out to kill me near Memphis, but the Lord delivered me again from harm's way.

"When I became the captain for North Mississippi, we were doing a large heroin deal. When I left the office to meet the agents, the Holy Spirit filled my car. I heard, 'Go back for the bulletproof vests,' and then a deafening silence. I thought I was losing my mind. No one wore vests in those days. We only had two vests, both with no armor.

"I tried to leave again, but the presence returned, massaging every molecule of my body, all around me, all through me, and infusing me with the same command. It wasn't optional. I said, 'Okay, okay!' and returned to get the vests.

"On a day when it seemed every last ounce of light had been squeezed from the earth, we were ambushed by a sniper guarding the deal from his perch high on the ridge by the railroad trestle. As the chief of intelligence and I came across the levee where a firefight had erupted, it was a scene of horror. Gunsmoke was hanging in the frigid air like clouds or disembodied spirits. One agent was hit three times, and another agent wounded one violator.

"The sniper fled, and I went to the hospital to check on my agent. When I walked into the ER, I could see the white vest the Lord sent me back for was crimson-soaked in blood. The agent had been hit three times. The doctor showed me the wounds and said the vest had deflected the round to the chest. The bullet had skittered around the barrel of the agent's ribcage. The doctor said if he hadn't had the vest on, he would've been dead before he hit the ground.

"Chill bumps to my toes, then and now. I could feel the shuffle of angels' feet and knew that I, that we, were not alone. God was there, and He is here now. He walks incognito all around us, but we aren't listening for the sounds of His footfalls.

"After some political skullduggery, I left the MBN for the corporate world but even there I found an unholy trinity of politics, crime, and business. They gave me all of their awards, but they didn't fill up the hole in my heart. I took chances and openly opposed a member of the political establishment who had threatened a woman running against him.

"That unholy trinity threatened me, but the incumbent lost, the biggest upset in fifty years. The politicos told the company that no more legislation would pass until I was punished and muted. It was brutal, and I left the company for an appointment in Atlanta as Deputy State Superintendent of Education. I was looking for one last battle and more dragons to slay, but those T-Rexes were bigger and nastier than I could have imagined. They were waiting to gobble me up.

"We were battling the governor over the diversion of federal education funds. State troopers warned us that the word had gone out to 'stop us, fine us, arrest us...hurt us' when we were on the road. Don't think it happens? Happens all the time. Federal education funds were illegally diverted by the governor's people, and the White House threw us and the Constitution under the bus. My boss ran for governor and lost, and they indicted us. They never sought recovery of tens of millions stolen by favored politicians.

"People always said I could fall in a briar patch and come out without a scratch, but my miracles weren't working anymore. I wondered where God was, but He wasn't lost. He was right where I left Him when I thought I didn't need Him. Then He used the megaphone of pain C.S. Lewis wrote about to shout at me, 'Can you hear Me now?'

"'Yes, Lord,' I said, 'I hear you now.'

"I defied the federal prosecutor. They threw me in a terrible jail so I couldn't testify. They put me in isolation because they feared inmates might kill me since I was a high-profile case, but it was there that God worked His will on me.

"Someone brought me a Bible, and the Word leapt off the pages and into my heart. He called my name, and I was born again in the darkness and dankness of that cell. Suddenly, men came to my door...Nigerians, Cubans, crack addicts, and more. They looked at me through the hole in that steel door and confessed their sins and their crimes to me...murder, horrible things I can't talk about here.

"I told the Lord that I didn't understand, and He showed me that He would bring me down into a world I would have never known to tell people about Him. I didn't know Him, but He wanted me to tell others about Him. He comes on His own terms and His time, but I didn't run from Him anymore. I realized He was the missing piece in the giant jigsaw puzzle I could never complete. I yielded and exchanged control for obedience. I learned to say, 'Speak, Lord. For your servant hears.'

"The guards passed by me carrying a man. They took him to an empty cell in the back, and I could hear the four of them beating him, the slaps of fists and clubs on flesh. I shouted, 'Stop. In the name of Christ, please stop,' but it continued until they finished and warned me to mind my own business.

"I wrote a letter and smuggled it out, and one day all the brass showed up on the floor with wardens, chaplains, psychologists, and cleaning crews. They cleaned those torture cells, brought in a new team, and a guard came to my door and said, 'See what you caused.' It was my first test, and I learned that He could use me, even when I seemed powerless. When we don't speak, our silent words fall to the ground. When we don't obey Him and step into the gap, people pay.

"They gave me eight years to make an example of me, to show others what happens when you cross the government. It was bad. I can't tell you how bad it was to know I would be separated from my terminally ill wife, that I was facing over 2,000 days and might never see her again.

"I learned that fences and razor wire can't keep the Lord out. He was there walking down the rows amongst the bunks and broken men. My wife died, and they wouldn't escort me to the funeral, though it was thirty minutes away, and a federal judge had ordered them to take me.

"As I told a friend recently who was thinking of giving up and checking out, I was crushed and lay in bed listening to a small radio but could only receive roaring static. Then a voice broke through, 'You there! You there! Yes, I'm talking to you. It's not noble lying there, wallowing in your pity. Now you get up and get about your Father's business.'

"And I did, and we started what became the most successful inmate-led Christian ministry in the history of the Federal Bureau of Prisons. They use my books there now, and I spoke to the men there recently.

"It was a long, hard journey inside, and some nights I went to sleep clutching a little cross around my neck, not knowing if I would live to see morning. It was the Lord and me, but that was more than enough. I just scrunched up against Him as close as I could get until there was no room for anything but His wells of salvation, where I learned to hang my hopes on Christ who hung on the Cross for you and for me," Michael said.

"In 'The Hound of Heaven,' Francis Thompson wrote, 'I hid from Him. I fled Him for a long time, but He was always following after me, following, following ever after, that Voice around me like crashing seas.' Then everything changed between us when I stopped begging Him for relief and asked Him to show me His threads of good and purpose in the midst of unbearable pain so I might understand and become a better servant of Christ. Then the Holy Spirit drew close to me, opened my eyes, and showed me that He had good things waiting for me... Hang on, hang on.

"There is no testimony without a test, no crown without a cross. God's grace was greater than my sins, and on my tear-stained pillow, repentance drowned shame," Michael said as a chorus of Amens broke the silence and the young women from the Path of Grace shelter dabbed at their leaking eyes.

"Since I've been home, I've talked with many nonbelievers. When I debated a Satanist, he called me names I didn't even hear in prison," Michael said. The congregation had been crying with him, but finally took a breath and laughed with him.

"The Lord showed me that this is not about me but Him, that I might be the only Christian some ever meet, the only Bible they ever read.

"The man who had sold his soul said, 'Old man, no one wants to hear about a man in the sky with a book of rules. You'll die soon, and me and my offspring are going to tear down everything you Christians built.'

"I smiled and said, 'You sure have a winsome way of winning people to your point of view. I sense a lot of anger from you, but I suspect it's masking a lot of pain. You miss Him because deep down, you know He's the only One who can fill that big God hole in your heart. I don't feel any love from you, but I love you because He loved me when I thought I was unlovable.'

"He was speechless, and you could feel listeners buying in and asking, 'What kind of love was that in the face of such hatred, and Who makes that possible?'" Michael said.

"One holdout asked, 'Look forward, not back. Science and technology are creating our gods. Aren't you just trying to revive the corpse of Christianity?'

"'That's just it, my friend. There is no corpse. He has risen,' I said."

The shadows of yesterday washed over the pulpit and Michael's life, and he paused and blinked away tears.

"That awful day when I paused to climb the steep hill to the house of horrors that awaited me in Edgefield, I turned to the kindly old guard who had escorted me as far as he could, and I asked him if he had ever seen the movie *The Natural*. He said he hadn't.

"I told him that Iris tells Roy Hobbs that we have two lives, the one we learn with and the one we live with after that. I told him

I had been born again and planned to go and live that second life now, and I have.

"I got nothing I asked for in life but everything I could have hoped for. Among men, I count myself most blessed. I took a walk in the woods with God. I came out taller than the trees, and I could see all the way from prison to Hollywood to this day right here at Faith Assembly. There are no accidents.

"We love Brother Toy, and we love this church. Thank y'all for having us," Michael said.

The applause was long and loud. Michael signed books for visitors from the "Big Apple" to the Carolinas and the "Motor City" to the "Windy City." Beth, an eleven-year-old girl once left as collateral with her mother's drug dealer, took orders for the books and made pictures. Over burgers and shakes with her and her grandmother at Johnny Rockets in Destin, Michael told her she was his Florida book agent.

She gave him a late birthday card at the church that read, "Mr. Michael, you are funny, super cool, and an amazing person." Michael wished Jimmy Streeter had been there to see someone thought he was not just cool again but "super cool." Michael wondered if Beth, a child who had seen things no child should ever see, would be surprised to know he kept her card forever.

Judy met the missionary who needed provision for her trip to the Holy Land and whispered, "Michael, I think the Lord wants us to give money to help her."

So, they gave her all the cash they had.

Dawn flushed red against her fair features and said, "Oh, I can't believe it."

Michael said, "You said the Lord would provide, and He just did."

They hugged, and Michael gave her books to take to Israel if she had room in her luggage.

"I'd love to seed the books in the Holy Land," he told her.

The young women from Path of Grace pooled their money to get books for their transition homes and told Michael the Holy

Spirit led them to Faith Assembly at the last moment to hear his message.

One young woman, who looked like she was on the road to recovery, said, "Mr. Michael, you're like the old metal alarm clocks in our shelters with a hammer striking two bells, like a fire alarm to wake the spiritually dead, to stir the sleeping children of God, to get us to heaven on time.

"No one can sleep through those alarms or your testimony," she said.

CHAPTER FIFTY

"Most blessed, most glorious, the Ancient of Days.
Almighty, victorious, Thy great name we praise."
—"Immortal, Invisible, God Only Wise,"
Walter Chalmers Smith

"Down in Eutaw, Alabama…a young man no different than
you or I…catching catfish."—"Big Time in the Jungle,"
Old Crow Medicine Show

"If it were possible for me to alter any part of His plan,
I could only spoil it."—John Newton

After a long rest and a trial elimination diet going nowhere fast, Michael paid another visit to Walton State Prison. He first went to the prison by invitation from two dedicated prison evangelists.

In an abundance of generosity, they let the mild-mannered visitor go first. Inmates embraced him as one of their own because he had voluntarily come behind the steel doors for them, which no one could understand who hadn't been in prison. Praise broke out, the sleepy chaplain almost fell out of his chair, and Michael's fellow evangelists were stunned.

For his second visit to the prison, a lifer, who looked like the historian Shelby Foote, escorted Michael to the chapel. He was an older man with kind eyes. The chaplain used him to shepherd new arrivals and help the staff keep the peace. He would never leave the prison unless it was in his coffin. He was one of those forgotten men in the world of quick forgetting, but he had the unmistakable joy of a believer.

The inmate, convicted of a crime of passion long ago, fingered a wooden cross around his neck and asked, "We hear you have a new book. Is it as good as the others we've read?"

Michael was overcome with sadness for him and those like him, but looked up as they walked and felt grace faintly falling like a fine mist from heaven.

He shook the man's hand and said, "I sure hope so."

Michael told the men, most of whom had chased away everyone they had ever loved, "Many are on the highway to nowhere but making good time, but time is short, and eternity is long. You are fleet of foot, but why try to outrun the Lord when you are on the wrong road? It is past time to stop yelling at Christ and start yielding. As I told a lost man, a violent man who became a friend, it's late, later than it's ever been."

He looked over at "Shelby," and he was praying. His eyes were closed and his arms folded across his chest, a glimpse of the way it would be.

As Michael bid them farewell, he told them his health was not the best. He might not see them again, but he would pray for them.

As they filed by to ask for prayer, some were old and feeble, blind and led by the arms of others. Two men with raspy voices told him they were afraid to go home after a long period of incarceration because they no longer knew how to live. There was some nervous laughter like the breaking of glass and acid perspiration pooled in palms as he shook hands with each man, but he saw eyes once as cold as winter gravel now warmed by the fires of the gospel.

He left them with a Puritan prayer.

"Kill my envy, command my tongue, trample down self. Give me grace to be holy, kind, gentle, pure, and peaceable. Amen."

Michael's escort walked with him to a line he could not cross. The permanent resident paused to turn back toward his life of bareness and sameness and said, "I've picked out my box. They make them down at Angola, and the warden arranged it. Don't be sad for me, Michael. I'd rather be here with Him than in the world without Him. I once embalmed myself with bitterness, but Christ changed all that, and I am bound for that city built foursquare. If you get there before me, please leave the porchlight on for me."

As the man with slumped shoulders shuffled down the graveled lane toward the dorms, streetlamps sputtered and fluttered to life before him, lighting his way, and Michael felt again a great unsettling, a stirring of Divine intervention and invitation.

A surly guard mocked Michael and said, "You know you're wasting your time with these men." The pot-bellied officer had the fixed stare of a dog looking at your dinner, waiting to make his move.

Michael watched silently as the creaking gate slowly opened a path for his departure. He turned to the guard, met his permanent scowl with a smile, and said, "If so, it was time well wasted. Christ died for them, too."

***

With the Okaloosa pier in their rearview mirror, Judy and Michael left for Eutaw, Alabama, where he was scheduled to speak in a small town full of old homes and ancient churches on the National Historic Register.

Eutaw was tucked away between Tuscaloosa, Montgomery, and Selma, cities where Michael had spoken and signed books, but this town seemed remote and isolated to Michael, a place where time had stood still.

As they passed the Welcome to Alabama sign, Michael told Judy he was bone weary, felt as if he was sleepwalking, and just wanted to go home. He said he didn't know why God was sending him to a place called Eutaw, Alabama. Just then they passed a small church called Pilgrim's Rest, and on the marquee was Matthew 11:28. "Come to Me, all ye who are weary and burdened, and I will give you rest."

When they arrived in Eutaw, originally named Mesopotamia for the early home of Abraham and the possible location of Eden, Michael saw signs with Scripture references. One big sign outside a barbeque house said *Pray for Johnny*, and church signs advertised peanut brittle sales to benefit missions. Eutaw seemed to be a town that had synched up its "Bible Belt," so Michael sat up a little straighter in his seat. He began to rethink his desire to crawl into bed and pull the cover over his head.

First Christian Church was over a hundred years old and felt like an above-ground sepulcher. A tidal wave of yesteryear's murmured greetings washed over Michael when he stepped through the door, welcoming him "home," and his senses were overwhelmed with stories and secrets the Lord had sent him to find.

It was similar to the night in Kroger, bore the same intimacy and caress of the day of the ambush, and the presence of Someone he leaned on in Moselle.

He could feel the echoes of yesterday, the residuals of people who had laughed there, cried there, birthed there, died there, wed there, and found eternal life in a cocoon of faith that had nurtured their forefathers.

He knew immediately he was standing on holy ground and that the Holy Spirit was in the stately church with the high ceilings and the pulpit with the giant Bible. People poured into the church, and like in Moselle when Michael was struggling, the Holy Spirit made him more than he was. He forgot about his books and just talked about what the Lord had done in his life. Then he looked out and saw people crying.

One man who was crying was a local reporter. When he got to Michael in the line for signed books he said, "A long while back, they told me that I had a month to live, and when I didn't die, they called me a miracle. They wouldn't believe me when I said Jesus had appeared to me in my hospital room and said, 'It is not your time.' No one will listen. No one understands. No one understands, but you…you understand," the man said.

"Yes, sir, I do understand," Michael said, as his soul sighed from the warm weight of the Lord.

Michael thought he had more than enough books for a small town, but he signed all he had and filled more orders by mail.

As they were leaving Eutaw, they stopped by the ancient Mesopotamia cemetery, established in 1822, and walked under the shadows of the giant oaks and through the graveyard where, like Eutaw itself, the past meets the present.

One gravestone still had visible words etched into the marble: *Bury me face down over the underground spring that I might drink of the Living Waters.* Underneath his request was Scripture, John 4:10.

The headstone next to his read: *Under Eutaw's trees lieth Charles Pease. Pease is not here, only the pod. Charles shelled out and went home to God.*

He stood before the headstone and then turned to see a plaque erected in 1937 near the entrance to the old cemetery: *They are not dead who live in the hearts of those they loved.* Michael thought of God, eternity behind Him and eternity before Him, and his heart swelled.

On the way home Michael said, "When will I learn, Judy? If He is sending me somewhere, there is a reason. I know I am not well, but He will not let me drown in shallow water."

When they arrived in Tupelo, Michael checked his email before he gave in to fatigue, and vivid pictures from Israel filled his screen like a live feed. It was Dawn, the missionary from Miramar Beach, sitting in front of the Jaffa Gate in old Jerusalem. She was sitting with the man who became famous for saving Christians from ISIS in Iraq, Andrew White, the "Vicar of Baghdad." He was holding up a copy of Michael's book *The Redeemed: A Leap of Faith.*

Her note said, "Hope you like this. He has your books, and a set will be available in the library attached to Christ Church, the oldest Protestant church in the Middle East."

Michael fell back into his chair, clicked through the pictures again and again like a slideshow. Through a driving tear storm, he opened Facebook and saw that the good people of Eutaw had posted a message about his visit.

Eutaw, Alabama, loves Michael Parker. The hand of God is on him.

CHAPTER FIFTY-ONE

"…God writes straight with crooked lines."
—Jermiah Denton

"Truth is always strong no matter how weak it looks, and falsehood is always weak, no matter how strong it looks."—The Joy of Preaching, *Phillips Brooks*

"Streams of mercy, never ceasing…"—*"Come Thou Fount of Every Blessing," Robert Robinson*

Each time Michael and Judy came in from the road, a little red-haired boy, who looked a bit like a young Opie Taylor from Mayberry, waited at church for Michael, and this time was no different. Carson came barreling down the center of the big church and bear-hugged Michael with enthusiasm usually reserved for family and superheroes.

Carson came to book signings with his grandfather and kept a signed poster of *A Ghostly Shade of Pale* on the wall of his room. Carson believed in Michael so much that he made Michael believe in himself.

Michael invited him to his last signing at the LifeWay Christian Bookstores in Tupelo. Lifeway had decided to close all brick-and-mortar stores in America. It grieved Michael because going to LifeWay was more than selling books. It was like going to church, a church filled with the Holy Spirit. When he entered the store, the staff always greeted him in unison with a warm and loud, "Brother Michael!"

One night, he stopped to say hello to staff just before closing and noticed an elderly couple looking at Bibles toward the back of the store.

He approached them and said, "Excuse me, I don't know if you read Christian novels, but here are my book cards in case you do. I hope you find the Bible you're looking for."

As he turned to leave, the woman looked at the cards and began to cry. She looked up at Michael, held up the card for *The Redeemed*, and said, "I know this book. My pastor, Bobby Douglas, gave it to me, and it changed my life."

Michael stayed until closing time talking with them, and he signed all of his books for the couple he met by "accident." The LifeWay store was an outpost for the gospel, the hub of his diminishing book world.

A family once drove up from Bruce to see him at a signing. "We gave our father your book. He has Alzheimer's and hasn't spoken in a long while, but he lived through those times when you were in the Bureau of Narcotics. He looked at the book and began to read.

"Daddy looked up at us and said, 'I know the real people he's talking about.' He talked to us for hours, reliving those days. We just wanted to drive up here when we heard you were signing to thank you for giving us back our father for a while," they said.

It was that kind of place, the right kind of place to close out a ministry, to proclaim that an ailing evangelist had kept the faith and finished the race.

Michael was signing books for the last time at LifeWay when a devout Christian entered the store with a young man. Licia Hudson Kennedy had asked if she could bring an inmate by to meet him, a man just released from Texarkana Federal Prison in Arkansas. She said he had read Michael's books in prison and wanted to meet him.

Charlie was nervous, but Michael told him not to be, that they were just two former guests of the government who loved the Lord.

Charlie said, "Your books are in the Texarkana prison, worn and tattered from so many men reading them."

"Oh, that's great to hear!" Michael said.

Charlie took a deep breath, sighed, and said, "I had some standing with the gang there, and I risked my life to leave *A Ghostly Shade of Pale* on the bed of the head of the Aryan Nation. He came to me later, and I could tell he was wrestling with the Holy Spirit.

"He was furious and nose-to-nose with me, nostrils flaring, spitting on me, and cursing. 'Why did you leave this book on my bed? This can't be true. God couldn't love me like this, and wouldn't protect me like he did this agent.'

"I thought he was going to kill me. I said, 'God does love you, and He can protect you.'

"He turned and stormed off, but later he accepted Christ and left the Nation. They beat and stabbed him because once you are in, you don't leave. He survived the attack, and they transferred him to another prison. The last we heard, he was leading a Bible study built around your book," Charlie said.

As Charlie shared his heartfelt witness, Michael noticed a man eavesdropping. He had entered the store with his wife and daughters. Michael felt something was coming, another train coming down the track, and the Holy Spirit was about to move again.

Michael thanked Charlie for his testimony and urged him to stay clear of anything that might invoke a probation violation and send him back to prison.

As Charlie and Licia left, the other man stepped up and said, "I'm sorry. I didn't mean to eavesdrop. Would you like to hear my testimony?"

"Yes, very much," Michael said.

"My name's James Beachum. I'm working in Columbus. When I got up this morning, the Lord directed me to come to this bookstore in Tupelo with my family, who is visiting me this weekend. I'm not sure what that means or why we are here," he said.

Michael saw his wife and children wandering around the store, and he looked closely at James. James had scars on his arms, some from violence and others possibly staph in meth, and Michael thought he looked like a man who had been to the brink of hell and back.

"I was out on the street at an early age. I was doing dope, selling dope, mugging and being mugged. I had so much meth in my body and so much staph doctors said I shouldn't be able to live. I was barreling toward hell, and then I sold drugs to an undercover cop in Hattiesburg. They arrested me, and I figured that was it. I was on my way to Parchman, a hell as bad or worse than the one I'd been living in," James said.

"Then they found out that the cop was selling drugs, and they threw out all of his cases. Jesus reached down and collared me. I got a second chance at life. I went from being high on drugs to hooked on Jesus. I began to go into the drug dens and the flophouses and tell the addicts about Jesus and what He had done for me. I knew where they were. They couldn't hide from me. I go all over the state and tell people about my Redeemer, but I don't know what I am doing here at LifeWay in Tupelo," James said with shrug.

"You said you were arrested in Hattiesburg, and you're working in Columbus, but where are you from?" Michael asked.

"I'm from Moselle, about two hundred miles from here. Do you know where Moselle is?" James asked.

The train was pulling into the station, and Michael's heart began to race. "Yes, I know where Moselle is," he said.

"I go to this big church, the Moselle Memorial Baptist Church. Every year they have this big Wild Game Dinner and auction to raise money for Kingdom work. Brother Bo told me a man was coming to speak and that I needed to hear him. Something happened, and I missed him. I've heard about that night ever since and always regretted not being there and meeting the man they talked about," James said wistfully.

Michael's heart was in his throat, his mouth was dry, and he could see the room growing brighter.

"James, I was that man," Michael said, swallowing hard.

The former addict's chin fell to his chest, and his eyes were wide and wet. Everyone around them, including Chris McCormick, the store manager, was rubbing the chill bumps on their arms.

They talked, embraced, and took pictures. They praised God Who does the impossible. They shook their heads and said, "But God."

Everyone knew they were part of something unconstrained by doctrines and denominations, a living Christ for a dying world, and these were stories that needed to be put on paper so people would hear the gospel through storytelling that invites the lost to meet the Gatekeeper.

As Judy and Michael were packing to leave the bookstore for the last time, a widow arrived late. She told Michael she had read *Ghostly* several times. The last two lines of the book where the pain of loss was finally subsiding for the wounded hero gave her comfort.

She took Michael's hand and said, "I just can't get that book out of my mind."

CHAPTER FIFTY-TWO

"I was standing by my window on one cold and cloudy
day, when I saw that hearse come rolling…
Undertaker… Please drive slow… There's a better home
a-waiting, in the sky, Lord, in the sky."
—"Will the Circle be Unbroken," Roy Acuff

"Going home, going home. I'm going home.
Shadows gone, break of day, real life just begun."
—"Going Home," William Arms Fisher

Michael limped in from a presentation to the Academies of West Memphis, where the charter school and feeder middle schools used his books.

Michael looked at a gift they had given him, a sign from an old Christian Almanac that read *Give me, of all mottoes 'God with me.' Oh, that I might write on my child's cradle, 'Immanuel, God with us.'*

He picked up a pile of mail and opened a big envelope from Gary White at the federal prison in Montgomery, Alabama. Gary read the books and used them to help others. Michael always thought he needed to come home to his wife, who was also named Judy.

Gary didn't need to be in prison, certainly not for the long sentence he received. Gary was hit by a ricochet from a salvo fired from Washington, when rules were changed and politicians decided there would no longer be signs, lanes, or speed limits in their demolition derby.

In the envelope was a drawing of Michael and Judy that Gary had done, and Michael could feel the love and care that went into each stroke of Gary's pen and pencil to create a lifelike portrait, the kind and quality people would pay to have drawn or painted. Gary created his beautiful rendering from a photograph, a testament that the Shirriffs, the two-feather hobbits who accused him of "tearing up of rules," had not broken him.

There was also a letter from Nettleton waiting for Michael. Inside was a black-and-white grammar school picture of him in jeans and a plaid shirt, sporting a flattop haircut that never did well with his curly hair. Standing beside him was a young girl with a shy smile and a long skirt that billowed from the petticoats beneath.

On the back of the picture was a note written long ago, identifying him and Linda Patterson, who was smiling the big innocent smile of a girl on her way to heaven. She was the first young person Michael had ever known who died. She was there one week and gone the next, and he wasn't too sure where she had gone, just that the teacher and others were crying. He rushed out to the playground to see if she was there and called her name, but she didn't answer, and there seemed to be a hole in the world. Mrs. Berryhill told him to come back to class when he was ready.

Her sister enclosed a note:

Dear Mr. Temple,

Mrs. Berryhill took this picture of you and my sister on the playground not long before Linda died of cancer in 1960, just shy of her twelfth birthday. Our mother gave her a camera when the doctors said she had only a short time to live. My sister told Mama that you were always so nice to her, and Linda wanted to have her picture made with you before she went to the hospital for the last time.

There was a picture of Linda with a doll and the picture with you. This photo was developed after Linda died. I think it would make her happy knowing you have it.

Wanda Morris

Michael stared at the picture until he was there on the playground, and the black-and-white images assumed the color in the clothes and warmth came from the smiles, until he could hear Mrs. Berryhill ringing her bell to call them back to class. He stepped into the scene until he held Linda's hand so tightly that she couldn't leave, until he could speak to the Man in charge to ask why little girls had to die, to see if she left by train, boat, or plane for heaven. He walked with her a little way over the rise to see where people go when they die, to say goodbye when she let go of his hand, and he could no longer hear her footfalls.

The picture from the family's treasured memories was like a portal in time. There was such joy in the image, yet a sense of foreboding, a cry of 'surely not yet' for a life just beginning, and Michael wondered what he said to her, why she wanted her picture with him, if she knew she was dying, if she was afraid, and if some bright morning he might see her again.

Michael stared at the haunting image and didn't realize he was down some distant, winding trail trying to retrace his steps home until his friend Andrew Alexander, from the Millington Camp, called and summoned him back from yesteryear.

Andrew called to say how much he enjoyed visiting with Michael and Judy when they came to see him in Muscle Shoals.

"I hope you liked the plastic, pink flamingos I put in the yard. I know you like birds," Andrew said with a chuckle.

Andrew also said that he was about to have heart surgery, but Michael wouldn't be allowed to visit due to the Corvette, as he called the virus.

Andrew, who was always full of mischief, joy, and jokes, owned a company that helped inmates with appeals and petitions for sentence reductions. He wasn't a Christian, though he knew a great deal about the Bible and came to the Christian services and movie nights at Millington. When he left prison, Andrew worked Michael's books into prisons across the country, prisons like the one where lives were changed in Texarkana.

After the surgery, recovery, and updates from Andrew's assistant, Andrew called Michael when he was allowed to go home.

"Michael, it was a rough ride, buddy. During the operation, I was up above it all, the doctors, nurses, and me. I was looking down at them working on me, and God began to show me my life on a graph of sorts. We took a little trip, just me and Him. He's like the best Daddy you can imagine.

"When He spoke, it was like a rushing wind, a whisper inside my heart, the world awakening, birds singing, rainbows after a spring rain, this warm embrace of peace and rest, and then a feeling of being immersed in the Jordan where He was baptized, but the water was red like blood and made me as spotless as a newborn babe," Andrew said as he choked back emotion and cleared his throat.

"It was sorta like watching home movies with your parents. You know, look at me as a baby, a boy on a tricycle, family all around, but I sensed they were waiting for me somewhere, too, and then He showed me milestones in my life, the turning points, with the date and time by each point, plus one second," he said.

"What was that like? Was it good, bad, scary, or comforting?" Michael asked.

"Not bad at all and not painful, either, not a dream or a nightmare but like an episode of 'This Is Your Life.' No, no, that's not what it was. It was like, 'This *Was* Your Life.' It was a feeling you get on the road after driving all night, suddenly drawing near to a bright light that grows brighter and brighter until you arrive home and become part of the Light.

"I did hear a nurse say, 'The sugar got him.' So I thought I was dead, that my diabetes did me in. Then I was sitting on a bench, kinda like Forrest Gump in the movie, waiting for the bus to see where I was bound, up or down. Then a nurse woke me in my room, and I said, 'Well, I'm not dead!'"

"How do you feel about your experiences?" Michael asked, wiping the wetness from his cheeks and dabbing at his runaway nose.

"Michael, it's caused me to rethink my whole life, my relationship with God. I see Him up close and personal now, not distant," Andrew said.

"Prayers answered, my friend. I want to hear more about your guided tour with the Lord after you get some rest," Michael said.

"Yeah, boy. You know, I once thought heaven was going to be like one of those potluck Christmas dinners where no one communicated, and all your aunts and cousins brought pots of dry, crunchy string beans, pork chops you needed a chainsaw to cut, and bedeviled eggs that tasted like Beelzebub himself made them, but Michael, I think it's going to be a feast that never ends," Andrew said.

Later that night, Michael called to check on him but got no answer or response to voicemails. It wasn't like Andrew and Michael was worried.

Then Michael's private line rang. It was Andrew's number. Michael answered, "Hey, buddy, I was getting worried about you."

It wasn't Andrew but Josh, who worked for Andrew. "Michael, I'm sorry to tell you that Alex is gone. He got up to go to the bathroom and had a massive heart attack. The emergency responders said he was likely dead before he hit the floor," Josh said.

It was like a punch in the gut, a fist to the heart that rattles the fragile frame that holds us together. Michael slumped in his chair and felt the piercing of his heart. Then the funny stories for which Andrew was legendary began to flood Michael's mind and displace sorrow. Despite himself, he smiled. With Andrew, there would always be humor hiding beneath every heartache.

Michael remembered Andrew used to pull up next to cars at red lights, fake his best sophisticate accent and ask, "Pah-don me. Might you have any Grey Poupon?"

Andrew once told Tommy Lasorda, the L.A. Dodgers manager who did commercials for Ultra Slim-Fast, that they should hire Andrew for a success story ad.

Lasorda looked at Andrew, who weighed near 400 pounds then, and said, "Huh? What're you talking about?"

Andrew grinned and said, "Well, you could say I weighed six hundred pounds before Slim-Fast and look at me now!"

Lasorda laughed until he bent forward with his hands on his knees and said, "Son, you won't do."

Michael remembered the time Andrew had a date with Miss Alabama and was running late. After drying his hair, he mistakenly grabbed the bug spray, thinking it was hair spray, and fogged his hair. His car was dirty, so he stopped in one of those do-it-yourself car washes. The water wand, a cousin to a writhing boa constrictor, broke free, hit Andrew in the head, and soaked him, not his muddy car, from head to toe. So, he arrived at Miss Alabama's house late, wet and smelling like a giant can of Raid.

Andrew said, "Michael, that was our only date. I can't figure it out."

Soon, tears of sorrow were mixing with shoulder-heaving, belly-jiggling laughter, until Michael didn't know where one ended and the other began.

After he laughed until he hurt, he cried some more before calling Andrew's young daughter, Emma, who had a life-threatening illness. He used to see the frail beauty at Millington when she visited her daddy.

Michael used to watch her as they called Andrew's name. When he appeared, she held herself to her chair with all of her might like she had been gorilla-glued to her seat because the government wouldn't allow her to run and throw her arms around him, but her eyes sparkled like newly minted money when his face appeared at the door. To say she loved her daddy would be an understatement unless the phrase "the ground he walked on" was added.

After Emma and Michael talked a while about Andrew and his God encounter, he told her stories about her father and what a good man he was. She asked Michael if she could get a copy of *The Redeemed: A Leap of Faith.*

"Daddy told me a character based on him was in that book. He told me that if anything ever happened to him, you would call...that you were a good friend, a good writer, and a real Christian," Emma said.

Michael wrenched his emotions back from the brink of total meltdown and said, "In the mail today. Inscribing it now to Emma,

Andrew's little girl, the apple of his eye. Psalm 17:8," Michael said.

"Thank you, Mr. Michael. He told me you would talk about God and the Bible. I'm glad you did," she said.

When they lowered Andrew into the frozen ground of North Alabama, white smoke curled from the chimneys near where he once dated Miss Alabama herself. Forrest was no longer waiting for the bus, and Michael knew again that grief was the price of love.

CHAPTER FIFTY-THREE

*"As a lamp brings forth its light in a dark house, so truth
rises in the midst of faith in a person's heart.
When it rises there, it casts out four darknesses: the
darkness of paganism, the darkness of ignorance, the
darkness of doubt, the darkness of sin, so that there is no
room for any of them there."*—Colman mac Beognai
(early seventh century)

*"No matter how many of them we kill, they won't lose
hope. We're losing, Lucifer. We are losing."*
—Winter's Tale

The phone rang when Michael was taking his daily regimen of meds and reading a letter from Selma, Alabama. Morgan Academy adopted his books after he spoke to students and interviewed with the local paper.

When he saw that the call was from Carl Hunt's niece, Hanna, he feared the news would not be good.

"Mr. Michael, you know Grandaddy Carl was staying with us. He had no one else. He had been out giving his testimony to all who would listen, and lots of folks who remembered him from the old days came to see what the Lord had done with such a sinner. The altar calls were something to see. When he got wound up, whacking the pulpit with his cane like a conductor with a baton, the thunder rumbled over the mountaintops like drummers announcing a coming parade. Everyone in the mountain country talked about those nights, even some who used to be scared of him," she said through dry sniffles.

"Then he fell ill and went down quickly. One day, I heard him shouting, and I ran into his room. He was swinging his cane wildly in the air at someone or something only he could see. He was yelling, 'You get out of here now, Satan. I ain't going with you! I'm going with Jesus!'

"He looked at me and said, 'Hanna, you tell Michael, the Lord plowed deep in me. I finished the race. I kept the faith. I'll see him again.'

"Then he raised his hand toward heaven, his cane dropped to the floor, and the most beautiful smile came across his face. It scared me but in a good way. What do you think it means, Mr. Michael?" she asked.

"Bringing in the sheaves, Hannah. The Man of Sorrows used a man of sorrows to till some hard ground. His sickle was sharp for harvest time, which is what your grandfather prayed for. We shall come rejoicing, bringing in the sheaves," Michael said.

Michael picked up the phone to call Dr. Kurt Hopkins to tell him of Mr. Hunt's passing. Kurt had helped Michael, a fledgling evangelist at Edgefield, and held classes on the Bible.

When Kurt answered, Michael told him that Mr. Hunt had died, but Kurt didn't remember Mr. Hunt, and he didn't remember Michael.

"I know your voice but not the name. I've had a stroke and lost some memories that were all bruised anyway. I've been battered and scattered in my battles with the government. I've been rummaging around in the attics of my life trying to find yesterday. I found Jesus there. Maybe I'll find you there, too," Kurt said.

It was all suddenly too much for Michael, the dam broke, and the stabbing pain was released through his burning eyes.

"Kurt, I remember all those days at Edgefield when you drew lines on the dry-erase board from Genesis to now and said, 'We are here.' You helped me as I began to grasp the old, old story and the seamless telling of it from Genesis to Revelation. God put you in my path, and I will always be grateful," Michael said.

"Thank you, brother," Kurt said.

When Michael hung up, gratitude and regret crowded his heart, and the land of used-to-be receded again. He thought of the line from an old Dolly Parton song, "If tears were pennies, and heartaches were gold, I'd have all the money my pockets could hold."

CHAPTER FIFTY-FOUR

*"If I find in myself a desire which no experience
in this world can satisfy, the most probable explanation is
that I was made for another world."*—Mere Christianity,
C.S. Lewis

*"When you don't hear 'Yes, sir,' 'No, ma'am,' and 'Jesus'
on FM, I hope I'm in Heaven by then. If I don't wake up
tomorrow to a world I don't know, don't cry, just my time
to go."*—"Heaven by Then," Brantley Gilbert

*"It is easy to dodge our responsibilities, but we cannot
dodge the consequences of dodging our responsibilities."*
—Josiah Stamp

COVID, the Chinese Communist virus, began to ramp up just after Michael's last visit with the men at Broken Lives.

It didn't take Michael long to realize that his feeble immune system could not handle the virus that was bringing the world to its knees. He hunkered down at home, spurned the injections he felt his autoimmune system couldn't handle, turned a deaf ear to criticism born out of fear, and placed himself under the wings of the Almighty.

Sarge's daughter, Kathy, called to tell Michael that her dad had the bug from the lab in Wuhan.

"Mr. Michael, Daddy's in the hospital in Hattiesburg and not doing well at all. They won't let Mama in to see him much, and he can't move, so we brought a cellphone to him to call us when he was about to go stir crazy and those moments when he couldn't breathe, when he was afraid of dying in the hospital alone.

"I know it would mean the world to him if you could call him," she said.

So began a year-long mission to call Sarge, listen to his concerns, complaints, and sorrows and to pray without ceasing for the Lord to bring him home from the hospital.

"Michael, all I want is to come home one last time, sit on my front porch, and drink my coffee. Is that too much to pray for?" Sarge asked in a raspy, whispery voice.

"No, Sarge. We will trust in Him with all of our hearts, and He will make straight your path home," Michael said.

Whatever Sarge needed, Michael took it to the Lord in prayer, and on the other end of the phone, Sarge was sometimes only able to mumble a gravelly "Amen. Amen."

When the doctors and nurses irritated Sarge, when it stuck in his craw, Michael said, "You know, Sarge, what we need to do is get that big old cast-iron washpot you used to baptize inmates in at the Hattiesburg jail and just give those folks a good dunking."

Sarge laughed and said, "That's right, Michael. I might have to hold them under an extra second or two." They laughed and laughed, and Sarge never mentioned it again and didn't feel so helpless.

The months passed slowly, and the prayer calls continued until Sarge could read more of Michael's books his kids brought to the hospital. He began to tell Michael stories about outlaws and former sheriffs and a story about a man he arrested who wore a toupee that looked like a stuffed possum.

"He couldn't pass up the hooch, Michael. So, we called him the exorcist because spirits disappeared every time he showed up somewhere," Sarge said, laughing until he began to cough, followed by his old chuckle.

"You know, Michael, everything you wrote about in *Deputy* wasn't exactly how it happened," he said one day.

"I know, Sarge. It was the way it was, plus a pinch of how it could have been, with a dash of how it should have been," Michael said.

"Well, you're the writer. Maybe you can help me with my book when I come home," Sarge said.

"That one should be a humdinger," Michael said.

One day, after nearly a year, Michael's partner from the Lee County Sheriff's Department had his prayers answered, and he was allowed to come home.

Michael's private line rang one day, and it was Sarge.

"Hey, boy, guess what I'm doing?" he asked.

"I have a sneaking suspicion you're sitting on your front porch and drinking coffee from your favorite cup," Michael said.

"That's right! You got it, and it's mighty fine! I guess the Lord heard our prayers," he said with a hearty laugh.

"I never had any doubt," Michael said.

Sarge paused for a sip of hot brew and said, "Me neither."

Michael's birthday rolled around a few months later, and he heard Sarge was strong enough to attend the church where he was a deacon.

One day, Michael saw he had a private message on Facebook from Sarge. When he opened it, it was Sarge singing happy birthday to Michael. Sarge just didn't do such things, and it reached into Michael's chest and gripped his heart so tightly he couldn't breathe for a moment.

Then Sarge's daughter called to say that her father had been called home. She said he sat on his front porch drinking coffee, making up for lost time, and thanking the Lord for every sip, sup, and breath he was granted, after doctors said he would never leave the hospital alive.

No matter how much Michael pleaded for more time with loved ones, anchors in his life's story, time marched on to the Timekeeper's bittersweet conclusions.

***

Early one morning, when the rooster woke up the sun, news came from Memphis that there had been a homegoing at East Trigg Baptist Church, the church where a young Elvis went to listen to Dr. William Brewster preach and listen to the music of Mahalia Jackson.

Reverend Brewster had broadcast on WHBQ where George Klein was a DJ, and on WDIA where Elvis and George attended the annual Goodwill Revue with B.B. King, the night Elvis cracked the Memphis segregation laws just by his presence.

Friends said when James Walker, former bootlegger, womanizer, and old Beale Street proprietor of a virtual buffet of sin, first entered the church, the preacher stopped preaching, the choir stopped singing, and the deacons dropped their collection plates.

Asked why he was there, he said, "I met an old friend a while back and decided to see what all the fuss was about."

Church members said he came every Sunday. He came early, stayed late, and one day he said he wanted to be baptized, just like Memphis Minnie, before it was too late. The faithful at the church claimed they heard the devil scream when "Superfly" went beneath the waters, and James Walker came up smiling from ear to ear. People swore he looked like Morgan Freeman at that moment.

The following Sunday, when they were singing Reverend Brewster's most famous song, "Move Up a Little Higher," Walker slumped forward in his reserved spot on the front pew and moved up a little higher.

"I'm gonna move up a little higher. Gonna meet my loving mother. Gonna meet that Lily of the Valley. I'm gonna feast with the Rose of Sharon. Meet me there, early one morning. Meet me there, somewhere round the altar. Meet me there, oh, when the angels shall call God's roll."

Michael smiled for James Walker, then his eyes leaked for him and all those who had gone on before him. He remembered their handshakes, laughter, and twinkling mischief in their eyes.

He leaned back in his chair, weariness draped across his face. He punched up the birthday song Sarge had left for him and listened to the most beautiful flat singing he had ever heard. His voice was a bit raspy, weakened by a year-long battle with a relentless virus, but the vocals had a beauty that was otherworldly and reminded him of a man at Edgefield who sang the Psalms when life had him by the throat.

He listened to the man who once told him that he couldn't carry a tune in a bucket, and his mind returned to long walks with Susan and Judy along the seashore on Okaloosa, where nature sang in a lower key, where sobs were sometimes embedded in the rush of the waves as they collapsed on the shore.

He thought of the poignancy and perfection of the bleached shells he had found by the seaside, houses vacated by inhabitants that had shed their mortal coils. He stared down the long, cloudy table of life and thought of disappearing faces, empty chairs, and place settings quietly removed from grammar school to the present.

Michael listened over and over to Sarge's message and was suddenly surrounded by words he wished he had said and words he meant to say. He swallowed a bucketful of teardrops for too many people now beyond a phone call, too many friends and loved ones whose absence now pricked at his heart every time he said their names out loud.

"Happy birthday to you. Happy birthday to you. Happy birthday, buddy. I love you, son."

CHAPTER FIFTY-FIVE

"A time it was, and what a time it was, a time of innocence,
a time of confidences. Preserve your memories."
—"Bookends," Paul Simon

"And now the night is fading, the storm is through.
Everything You sent to shake me from my dreams, they
come to wake me in the love I find in You. And now the
morning comes and everything that really matters become
wings You send to gather me."—"Home," Rich Mullins

"The Christian shall gain that which he cannot lose,
by parting with that which he cannot keep."
—John Flavel, Puritan

On his way home from T.K. Moffet's funeral, Michael took the road less traveled and drove by a revival in progress at the Primitive Baptist church on Mud Creek Road.

General MacArthur once said, "Old soldiers never die. They just fade away." General Moffet had faded away into the long corridor behind the invisible veil, leaving a gaping hole in Michael's heart, grief crowding the corners of his eyes.

There was one less friend to remember shared memories, one less port in life's storms when advice was needed, but T.K. believed in Christ Who is the resurrection and the life and knows the way out of the grave. J.R. Miller once said the only thing that walks back from the tomb with the mourners and refuses to be buried is the character of a man, what he leaves behind. Michael thought T.K.'s character survived him and could not be buried.

There was a mist in Michael's eyes and in the hollows, and gusts of winds rustled through the trees that surrounded the house of God. A crude tornado shelter had been carved into a mud bank, and in the thickets, an abandoned clapboard house with broken windows was held upright by woody muscadine vines.

The small church sign informed parents that the annual Psalters quiz for kids was scheduled for Sunday night, the last night of Bible school.

As Michael slowly passed the chapel, the congregation sang, "Shall we gather at the river? Where bright angel feet have trod, with its crystal tide forever flowing by the throne of God. Yes, we'll gather at the river, the beautiful, beautiful river, gather with the saints at the river, that flows by the throne of God."

He had driven by the church before when it was empty, when the brick and mortar and small steeple stood in contrast to the green of the dense forest. He thought then there was a quality to the silence of small churches in Mississippi that was unique, outposts resting before glory when the breath of God would fill the sails of waiting vessels when heaven could no longer wait.

Sometimes, when he sat on his deck, and the wind was blowing just right, he imagined he could hear their hymns drifting across the lake in North Ridge with a whippoorwill providing harmony and a great horned owl singing bass. His hungry ears could almost taste the sounds of worship.

Michael's garden tools were rusting, the daffodils on the hill were blooming too early in a midwinter spring or a blackberry winter, an in-between time when both death and life are visible, and the sun seems feeble.

The forsythia showed yellow, the sap was running, the redbud trees were blushing pinky-red color, and Lent was near. Songbirds had changed their melodies to courtship, the swallows were back, and there seemed to be a turning, a permanent twilight tint to the sky, a silence louder than everyday sounds, and an astringent shift of some sort that was more than seasonal.

Diseases with funny names were nipping at Michael's heels, and he couldn't seem to outrun them in his growing lassitude. Some early morning frost was still on the rooftops, cold breath stung the lungs, and he was reluctant to give up his nights by the fireplace, his last delectation. It was where he gazed at the flickering flames, glowing embers, and the foggy rearview mirror of yesteryear as gray smoke puffed up from the chimney like smoke signals or SOS messages.

He thought of days when life took a turn down a hard road, of righting rusted wrongs and healing ancient wounds, but wearing the scars of it all as his testimony, as God's Purple Hearts and armor. He wanted to leave nothing unsaid or undone before that day when we will know fully and be fully known.

Michael's illnesses had snowballed and had, for the most part, confined him to home. The iron infusions no longer worked, and he could not shake the effects of shingles in his right eye. Multiple surgeries had failed to correct his vision problems. He was dizzy, exhausted much of the time, and felt underwater as if he had been buried at sea.

His world had become monochromatic, and he sometimes felt as if he had been put out to pasture. He needed to feel needed and undiminished by his ailments, and he was nursing a case of what a doctor called ennui, a feeling of boredom and listlessness from inactivity.

He could no longer travel, speak, or attend book signings, but he answered notes from readers and honored requests for prayers, which were not bound by the scrim of time and distance.

One such request for prayer came from a man of Aboriginal descent. He said he didn't want to be separated from God but was angry with Christians who had separated him from his family when he was a child. Michael told him man did that, not God, and his new friend began to follow Michael's posts on social media and sent a birthday greeting to Michael.

Happy birthday, sir. I certainly appreciate the anniversary of your birth. Your prayers and your life example have been of enormous personal benefit to myself. Thank you! I was going to write 'God bless you,' but I know He already has.

When Michael took radiation for cancer, he met Jimmy, a wiry 75-year-old man who wasn't saved and said he couldn't sit still to read books. Michael brought Jimmy the first book, *Deputy*, which was set in the clubs Jimmy frequented when he was young and Michael was a deputy.

"Just try this and see if it holds your interest," Michael said.

The next day Michael asked him, "Could you get into the book?"

"Get into it? I stayed up all night. I couldn't put it down. What's next?" Jimmy asked.

He read all five books, his family and friends said he was a changed man, and Michael introduced him to Christ. "Bloom where God plants you" were words for the fenced life of illness, just as they had been for the confines of prison. Two young men had passed like ships in the night in nightclubs that no longer existed, unaware they would be reunited a half-century later through illness and Jesus Christ.

The discarded years and deprivations of prison sculpted Michael's days. His adrenals were red hot, trapped in the fight-or-flight mode left over from prison. Sleeping with one eye open, dealing with corrupt officials, eating food marked not fit for human consumption, and never entering deep restorative sleep had taken its toll. His immune system had buckled.

He could hear the woo-woo or woe-woe rush of the wind at his window, and it seemed a eulogy for a stark, overcast, and sepulchral day. He looked up to admire an antique clock Judy had purchased and turned the key so it would chime on the hour.

Faithfully, each hour on the hour, the clock softly chimed the Doxology. Michael bowed his head, closed his eyes, and let it soak into him. It filled him up like the tolling of Christ's bell, and he heard the peal of his own bell in the chime.

Within his time of stasis, Michael had been lost behind the walls of introspection, and for the umpteenth time, he reread John D. MacDonald's last Travis McGee novel, *The Lonely Silver Rain*.

Michael had eagerly consumed them all when they first came out. He read the books when he was in college and on trips to Okaloosa with Susan when he visited the library in Fort Walton

Beach and dreamed of writing his own books and seeing them in the little library by the sea.

God answered his prayers. The library near Brooks Bridge had all of his books. He had spoken, interviewed, and signed books from Pensacola to Panama City and many sandy Panhandle points in between.

The Lonely Silver Rain spoke to Michael differently in his old age, as McGee wrestled with mortality. McGee was sometimes crestfallen and moody at times, and his closest friends were gone to what Shakespeare called "the land from which no one returns."

Time was sneaking up on Travis and Michael. Past, present, and future were bunching up and colliding. Travis felt his end pursuing him. His advancing years and an increasing distance from a changing world left him, like Michael, on the outside looking in, more unsure than ever if he is welcome or even relevant.

McGee resisted conformity, only to find his past catches up with him in the daughter he didn't know he had. Michael had no children to spoil, one of his greatest regrets. There would be no one left to grieve over his final goodbye.

The unraveling of McGee's life hit close to home, and like McGee, he had recognized the con artists running the con games. There were signposts aplenty but Travis and Michael didn't always see them, and blew by all of the warning signs that shouted, stop, danger, wrong way.

All the McGee books had a color in them. Black was the signal that Travis' luck had run out, but then MacDonald died. Michael thought of his last novel and felt again that he was arriving where he started. All of it seemed familiar somehow, that he had dreamed it all, chapter and verse, but one thing he and Travis agreed on. "The hard thing to do is the right thing to do."

Michael felt he was born in the wrong century. Times had changed, and the modern world was a wasteland twisting old words to make sentences that sounded too much like surrender. Michael didn't like sentences about surrender unless they had Jesus in them, and his greatest fear was that he might become a part of what he once wanted to fix. He felt something was gaining on him, that he was slow-walking through glue, his feet stuck to the ground as the footfalls drew near.

It suddenly thundered in the distance, and he heard the ping of an email hit his inbox. He opened it, and darkness suddenly crawled up out of the past and barged into his life. It was a note from Mary Ruth Robinson delivered via his website.

Hello. I hope you are well. You came to mind, and I happened upon your website. Congratulations on all your accomplishments. God bless. Mary Ruth.

It was a curious or guilty ghost speaking from atop distant hills of agony that had briefly united, then divided them. The ghost neither offered nor sought forgiveness or healing, only permission to come aboard, to wade ashore on the beach of a familiar dead sea that had drowned everything worthy to be called treasure, save faith and the eternal verities.

It was a stone that needed to be left unturned, so Michael closed and bolted the door lest darkness follow the entreaty and slip through the cracks. When all else fails, Satan recycles old sins to tempt and distract.

Michael was left with the smell of bitterweed in the garden as newsreels of yesteryear played in his mind. A thousand tiny and not-so-tiny dramas of misplaced loyalty and betrayal were spinning around and through each other, meeting and meshing, but he had lived through the penitential years of his life to see their funerals, replaced by images of Michael's pilgrim journey that flooded his memory and tethered him to the tender mercies of Christ.

Michael closed his eyes and remembered the day he spoke to students in the Delta, the fertile soil and giant floodplain some called the "most Southern place on earth." After his talk, the younger kids lined up to ask him to autograph their books, backpacks, and shirts and pose for pictures with them.

One little girl with pigtailed red hair was holding back, and it occurred to Michael that she might be autistic.

A watchful teacher said, "Don't take it personally. Betsy is autistic and very wary of strangers."

As he signed more items for her classmates, he saw Betsy edge closer and closer to the large images of his book covers mounted on easels. She stood beneath the image of *The Redeemed* and soaked it in. The character is suspended in midair in a leap of faith over the fires of hell reaching up for him as the white dove of heaven comes down to him.

Then she spoke for the first time.

"Is that you jumping over the fire?" she asked in a tentative voice of innocent inquiry and her own leap of faith.

"Yes, honey, that was me," Michael said as he bent down to hear her, choked back tears, and tried to swallow the dryness in his throat.

She grabbed Michael then in an embrace of acceptance and comfort and buried her face against his chest. It was an acknowledgment that Michael knew the God she did, that he was in the circle of life with her. She held on to him and looked at him as if they shared a secret no one else knew. She would not let him out of sight until he left later that day.

As he walked to his car, he looked back, and she was at the door watching him, waving a tiny-handed goodbye, her teacher by her side. He could see her raised freckled hand until the school was lost in the rearview mirror.

Michael felt he was leaving behind an old friend he had met for the first time. He prayed on the way home to Tupelo and asked, "Lord, what did you show her in that beautiful mind?"

More memories rushed at him, washing away the sorrow that had knocked at his door. He saw himself speaking to the Fellowship of Christian Athletes at Destin Middle School, where another young girl softly and shyly whispered something as he spoke.

Michael put his hands on his knees and leaned down to where she sat on the front row.

"Hmm?" he asked.

"I've always wanted to meet you," she said.

"Really? Well, I've always wanted to meet you, too," Michael replied.

"Thank you," she said, a tiny voice that lodged in his heart forever.

Michael was weary and began to drift and nod. He had stayed up all night, scouring the internet in deep searches, for what he wasn't sure. He happened upon what looked like a gathering point for book lovers, like an old chatroom. He clicked on the site and saw young people discussing books...his books.

"I just found *Deputy* over here for a good price," one said.

"Yeah, I got *A Ghostly Shade of Pale* there, too," another said.

"I'll go there right now. Those two would complete my set of his books in my library," a third one said.

Just as Michael was about to click in and say, "I'm that writer," the room emptied, and they were off to buy his books on some discount site they'd found.

Michael stared at the screen and thought of novels God had used. Ignace Lepp, a disgruntled communist, once happened upon a copy of *Quo Vadis* (Where are you going?). It was fiction but showed Christ and His followers in a way Lepp had never seen.

"I felt suddenly as if everything for which I had been confusedly longing ever since I was fifteen, and had vainly sought in communism, was not, at all, to be found only in some imaginary utopia. The early Christians had made it come true," Lepp wrote of his decision to follow Christ.

Michael thought about *Quo Vadis* and Peter's question as he fled Rome and met Jesus, "Where are You going, Homini?" Jesus responded, "Because you are leaving the flock I gave to your care, I am going to Rome to be crucified again." Then, against what Lepp thought of Christians, the aging fisherman returned to Rome to be crucified.

The sun suddenly showed its full face at Michael's door, and the doorbell jolted Michael from memories and musings.

Marius McKinnon, a salt-of-the-earth deputy sheriff Michael had ridden with before Michael became ill, was at the front door with a young woman with dark hair and big, nervous eyes.

"Hey, Brother Michael, we were in the neighborhood and thought we'd drop in and say hello. You remember Ashton Ellis from Saltillo High? You spoke there, and she decided that day that she wanted to work for the FBI. She's working with us while her application is processed in Washington," Marius said.

"Yes, I remember Ashton. So, you're trying to get to the FBI?" he asked.

"Yessir, if they'll have me. After I read your book, I heard you speak when you came to Saltillo High. I knew then what I wanted to do," she said, shrugging her shoulders and flashing a timid smile.

"Long ago, before you were born, before there were many women in law enforcement, I used my draft picks from the new academy class to pick two female agents. They were my secret weapons as undercover agents.

"Pray about it, and if this is the career you want to pursue, then go for it and trust the Lord to go with you. Just remember that the FBI is not what it once was. There are some good people there, but they have a ghoul convention at the top," Michael said.

"Yes, sir, I will," she said.

They made pictures in the driveway and froze the memories and smiles of that day onto digital images that would not fade like the flowers of youth. They hugged goodbye and as they were leaving, Marius came over to Michael and said, "This meant a lot to her. When I told her you lived here and we should stop by and say hello, she was very nervous," he said.

"Really?" Michael asked. Purpose and faithfulness rained down on him, and he remembered how it was to be young and meet someone you respected.

After they left, Michael returned to his desk to savor the moment when the doorbell rang again. Michael thought they had forgotten something or left something behind at the house of the hermit author.

It was not his previous visitors but an older woman standing at the door admiring the first hints of green in Michael's flower beds. She was slender with silver, crinkly hair, and her small, pinkish hands showed the shadows of old scars. A small towheaded boy was hiding behind her.

When Michael had first opened the door, he thought the silver in her hair matched a book cover image of *The Lonely Silver Rain*. Absent the cruelty of the bright light, she bore a quiet beauty and a certain elegance, likely stunning before the bloom of youth faded.

She asked, "Are you Michael, the Michael Parker who used to be in the MBN?"

"Yes, a long time ago, I'm afraid," Michael said.

The little boy looked up at Michael, his eyes wide and mouth open in awe, as if Michael were the tallest man he'd ever seen.

The woman, whose eyes he first thought were dead, began to shine, exude warmth, and release long-restrained anticipation. She said, "It's been nearly fifty years, Captain. I'm Tammy Sue Jenkins, Tammy Sue Jenkins Rogers now."

Michael thought he heard a bell toll, and Someone whisper his name again. She was not blonde and young anymore, and she spoke with a tremulous voice, a speaking vibrato. When he looked closer, he could see the beautiful young woman who had been so savagely beaten and left for dead, and she still had a way of leaning one word against another when she spoke and balanced strength with vulnerability.

"I sent you a letter when you were in prison, but I don't know if you got it," she said, her eyes glistening in the sun.

"I did, but there was no return address. It meant so much to hear from you," Michael said.

The boy tugged at the hem of her dress and then hid behind her again.

"This is my grandson," she said, patting his head.

"Say hello to Mr. Parker," she said.

Michael leaned forward and asked, "Hello, what's your name?"

"Michael," the boy said.

"Michael? Well, that's my name, too," Michael said.

"He was named after my son, who was killed in combat. You were like a father figure to me, Michael, though you weren't much older than I was. We aren't related, but after we surrendered to Christ, we have the same Blood donor. I named my son after you, Captain," Tammy Sue said.

Michael felt the sudden heaviness of the air, the rush of blood to his face. He felt the Divine touch, and inside his heart he cried out, "Lord, Lord."

"Oh, Tammy. I don't know what to say. I am unworthy," Michael said, dabbing at the wetness suddenly clotting his lashes.

Flustered and overwhelmed, Michael leaned down again to young Michael and said, "See those pretty books over there on the table? How about I sign them for you, and your grandmother will keep them for you until you are old enough to read about your grandma and me?"

"Okay," he nodded after looking at her for approval.

Michael signed the books and talked with Tammy Sue as young Michael thumbed through the books, pretending to read.

"Before you leave, I have one more thing to show him," Michael said as he went to his desk to retrieve an old but treasured possession.

"Michael, have you ever seen a big shell like this one?" he asked the boy as he handed him the shell that housed the sea and fueled the dreams of another young boy.

"No, sir," the boy said with a look of wonderment.

"The ocean is trapped in here. If you put it up to your ear and listen close, you can hear the roar of the sea," Michael said.

Little Michael put it to his ear. His eyes became blue saucers, and his mouth formed a perfect O for an extended "Ooh!"

"Isn't that pretty," Tammy Sue asked, and the boy nodded his head up and down.

fishing pole he traded to be a fisher of men. It was dark, but then came the Light, the same Light that had burned away hell in his nightmare.

Angels rolled back the firmament, and the heavenlies seemed to blush. He saw the narrow sea, like the river Jordan, the passage between the here and now and the hereafter. He turned his eyes upon Jesus, and all that was grew strangely dim, troubles melted like lemon drops, and death died and tears dried as the world and his infirmities faded away before his Beloved.

For a moment, he could have sworn he heard a conductor say, "Willoughby. Next stop, Willoughby," while behind him in the house, the ancient clock began to chime a benediction that will last until the last amen.

"Praise God from Whom all blessings flow. Praise Father, Son, and Holy Ghost."

EPILOGUE

"He saved others, yet at the last Himself He did not save. There is nothing in history like the union of contrasts which confronts us in the gospels. The mystery of Jesus is the mystery of divine personality."—James Stewart, Scottish theologian

"Choose not then to cleave to this aged world, to be unwilling to grow young in Christ, who tells you, 'The world is perishing, the world is waxing old, the world is failing, distressed by the heavy breathing of old age. But do not fear, your youth shall be renewed as the eagle's.'"—St. Augustine

"What else would you write about if you knew God Almighty?"—Rich Mullins

"The Holy Spirit waits between the pages."—Merle Temple

"I'll love thee in life, I'll love thee in death, and praise thee as long as you lendest me breath, and say when the deathdew lies cold on my brow; if I ever loved thee, my Jesus, 'tis now."—William Featherstone